« *RECEVEZ CE MIEN PETIT LABEUR* »

STUDIES IN RENAISSANCE MUSIC
IN HONOUR OF IGNACE BOSSUYT

« *RECEVEZ CE MIEN PETIT LABEUR* »

STUDIES IN RENAISSANCE MUSIC
IN HONOUR OF IGNACE BOSSUYT

Edited by
Mark Delaere & Pieter Bergé

LEUVEN UNIVERSITY PRESS

ISBN 978 90 5867 650 4
D / 2008 / 1869 / 1
NUR: 662

Layout: Friedemann Vervoort (Friedemann BVBA)
Illustration jacket: Joke Klaassen
Design jacket: Orlando di Lasso, *Miserere mei Deus*, from *The Poenitential Psalms*,
Mus. ms AI, p.172 (Bayerische Staatsbibliothek München)

CONTENTS

'UNA COSA RIUSCITA':
IGNACE BOSSUYT'S ACADEMIC CAREER

Mark Delaere & Pieter Bergé

By the end of September 1556, Orlando di Lasso had arrived at the court of the Bavarian duke Albrecht V in Munich, in order to take up a position as a tenor singer in the ducal chapel. In 1993, in his contribution to Horst Leuchtmann's Festschrift, Ignace Bossuyt presented the correspondence that he had discovered in the library of the Palacio Real in Madrid between Johann Jakob Fugger, Antoine Perrenot de Granvelle and Orlando di Lasso. These letters were written between 29 September 1556 and 28 May 1559, during the first years of Lasso's Munich appointment. Although wrapped up in the usual diplomatic terms, this correspondence nevertheless reveals that Lasso was anything but happy at the beginning of his time in Munich. Bossuyt discussed several possible grounds for Lasso's initial discontent. The composer may have been uneasy with the 'costumi strani' in Germany after having spent most of his life in Italy and in Antwerp. Also, his relationship with his patron Albrecht V turned out to be less than cordial, and the fact that Lasso's initial appointment was as a rather lowly singer surely cannot have helped. However, the most irritating thorn in Lasso's side must have been the fact that he was not allowed to publish important work cycles such as the *Sacrae Lectiones ex Propheta Job* or the *Prophetiae Sibyllarum*, since they were destined for the duke's private use only. How could he have been happy with his modest position when he was denied the chance of spreading his reputation as a composer of outstandingly original and groundbreaking works? In his letter to Lasso of 28 May 1559, Granvelle expresses his regret over the fact that he had been unable to help remedy the situation: 'mi duol bene che la cosa non sia riuscita come io haverei desiderato'. From this phrase, Bossuyt speculated that Lassus had asked for Granvelle's mediation to get a better job elsewhere, possibly as a chapel master at the royal court of Philip II of Spain. All's well that ends well: in 1562 Lasso obtained the prestigious post of chapel master at the Bavarian court, where he was to stay for the rest of his career.

Ignace Bossuyt's academic career has been anything but a 'cosa non riuscita'. On the contrary, his professorship at the University of Leuven has been so successful that he did not have to call upon a contemporary Granvelle to solve his problems or to get him a better job elsewhere. Born on 13 May 1947 in Waregem and proud ever since of his West Flanders origins, Bossuyt may well have been struck by Leuven's 'costumi strani' when he first arrived as a young student in Leuven. However, he quickly assimilated the university town's observances, and both he and his family have been perfectly at home in the city ever since. In 1967 Bossuyt earned a bachelor's degree in classical studies, and in 1969 he added bachelor degrees in art history and musicology to his academic basket. By then it was clear that music was his one and only vocation. A master's degree in musicology followed in 1971. His master's dissertation on the nineteenth century Kortrijk composer and chapel master Pieter Vanderghinste was sufficiently impressive for Bossuyt to be hired as a teaching and research assistant from that year onwards. He obtained his PhD in musicology on 29 November 1978 'summa cum laude' and with the congratulations of the examining jury with his dissertation *Alexander Utendal (ca. 1543/45-1581). Een bijdrage tot de studie van de Nederlandse polyfonie in de tweede helft van de zestiende eeuw.* It comes as no surprise that such a brilliant researcher was offered a permanent position at his home university, first as an associate professor (from 1980 onwards), then as a full professor ('hoogleraar', from 1989 onwards) and finally as 'ordinarius' ('gewoon hoogleraar', from 1993 onwards).

It is clear from this brief overview that Ignace Bossuyt's rapid climb up the academic ladder can have been as little a cause for discontent as his swift adaptation to Leuven's 'costumi strani'. With Lasso and Albrecht V, further difficulties were caused by a strained personal relationship, yet anyone even superficially acquainted with Bossuyt will be well aware that this was never a risk in his case. In addition to his research and teaching abilities, his relations with students, colleagues and the governors of the university are characterised by an enormous social intelligence. This quality was already obvious to the renaissance music specialist René Bernard Lenaerts, who founded the Leuven musicology department in 1944, and directed Bossuyt's PhD. Bossuyt's relationship with Lenaert's successor Jozef Robijns was equally harmonious. In his laudatory speech on Robijns's retirement in 1985, Bossuyt highlighted their 'perfecta consonantia', and this was hardly an exaggeration. Bossuyt's loyalty, friendship and support extend equally to his younger colleagues, even if the music they are studying is more dissonant.

Whereas Lasso was denied the opportunity to publish his most ambitious works, it is clear from Ignace Bossuyt's impressive publication list that he found no such obstacles in his academic path. In this respect too, his life as a musicologist has been a 'cosa riuscita' indeed. Four main areas of research can be distinguished in his publications, all related to the music of the second half of the sixteenth century: the music of Alexander Utendal, of Adriaan Willaert, of Jean de Castro and of Orlando di Lasso. Although Utendal was deputy chapel master at the Habsburg court of archduke Ferdinand of Tirol, his music was hardly known before Bossuyt's impressive doctoral dissertation (published by the Belgian Royal Academy in 1983) and his subsequent articles in journals such as *Archiv für Musikwissenschaft*. Further research interests in sixteenth-century music led to an exhibition focussing on Adriaan Willaert as well as the first ever monograph study of the composer. A very successful large scale research project on the music of Jean de Castro resulted in four volumes and a cd-rom of a projected *Opera omnia*, in several articles for periodicals such as *Revue de Musicologie*, in book chapters for the *Yearbook of the Alamire Foundation* and for the Albert Dunning Festschrift, in contributions to the proceedings of the Munich (1994), Münster (2001) and Utrecht (2003) conferences, and in the new Jean de Castro entry for *The New Grove*. Incidentally, the title of this Festschrift is a quotation from a Preface to one of Jean de Castro's music prints. However, it is safe to say that no other composer has stirred Ignace Bossuyt's academic imagination more than Orlando di Lasso. His lifelong admiration for the versatility and quality of Lasso's music has yielded a plethora of publications. The most important include the catalogue of the exhibition that Bossuyt organized in 1982, numerous journal articles and contributions to conference proceedings, Festschrift contributions (Horst Leuchtmann, Willem Elders), an article in *Orlando di Lasso Studies* (ed. Peter Bergquist), and his authoritative *Lassus* entry for the new edition of *Die Musik in Geschichte und Gegenwart*. In 1994 and 1996 Bossuyt published the abundantly illustrated book *Flemish Polyphony* in four languages, a major achievement crowning several decades of devoted renaissance music scholarship. In addition to his publication output, Bossuyt has also been active in the Alamire Foundation and as a supervisor of doctoral projects.

The smaller a country, the more important its foreign affairs office. Likewise, to have a successful academic career, an international orientation is a prerequisite for a musicologist from a tiny country such as Belgium. One suspects, from his keen interest in meeting new colleagues and exploring other cultures, that this was Ignace Bossuyt's favourite part of his job. His research has brought him not only to libraries, universities and conferences in most European countries and in the United States but also to exotic places such as Japan and Bolivia. Bossuyt was a welcome guest at the 'Centre d'Etudes Supérieures de la Renaissance' in Tours, and he has hardly missed a meeting of the IMS-congress. He has been a guest professor at the universities of Utrecht and Bristol and at the 'Ecole Normale Supérieure' in Paris (1991). In 2004-5, he held the 'Erasmus Lectureship' at Harvard University, a position described by the Dean of the Arts Faculty as 'one of Harvard's most prestigious visiting positions'. Together with Jean-Jacques Nattiez he was responsible for the assessment of all the musicology departments in Switzerland in 1997. Bossuyt's amicable contacts with musicologists from Holland have resulted in collaborative early music research projects between the universities of Leuven and Utrecht. He was on the editorial board of the extensive history of music in the Netherlands published by Amsterdam University Press (2001) and has been a member of the editorial board of the *Tijdschrift van de Koninklijke Vereniging voor Nederlandse Muziekgeschiedenis* for many years.

No account of Ignace Bossuyt's academic life would be complete without mention of one final aspect: his ability to relate to a broad audience of non-specialists. His infectious enthusiasm and skill as a communicator have inspired many who were previously unfamiliar with renaissance music. For Bossuyt, sharing his passion for music – not just renaissance music, but music of all kinds – is vitally important. At the same time, the outstanding quality of his research is widely admired by specialists. An academic career crowned with the Presidency of the International Musicological Society congress (Leuven, 2002), with the Erasmus Chair at Harvard University and with the authorship of an article on one of the most important composers in the history of music for *Die Musik in Geschichte und Gegenwart* is without the slightest doubt 'una cosa riuscita'.

In view of these impressive achievements, it comes as no surprise that the finest of today's renaissance music specialists enthusiastically accepted the invitation to contribute to this Festschrift. The editors have been left in no doubt, from their correspondence with the authors, that both terms in use for volumes of this kind apply: it is both a Festschrift in which specialists honour an outstanding colleague, and a Liber Amicorum compiled for a dear friend.

Leuven, October 2007

LIST OF PUBLICATIONS BY IGNACE BOSSUYT

1. Books

Alexander Utendal (ca. 1543/45-1581). Een bijdrage tot de studie van de Nederlandse polyfonie in de tweede helft van de 16de eeuw (Verhandelingen van de Koninklijke Academie voor wetenschappen, letteren en schone kunsten van België. Klasse der schone kunsten, 36; Brussels, 1983).

Adriaan Willaert (ca. 1490-1562). Leven en werk. Stijl en genres (Symbolae Facultatis litterarum et philosophiae Lovaniensis. Series B, 1; Leuven, 1985).

Antonio Vivaldi (1678-1741) en het concerto (Leuven, 1988, reprint 1989).

W.A. Mozart (1756-1791) en het pianoconcerto (Leuven, 1989).

Vergilius, Horatius en Ovidius in de muziek van de 16de eeuw (Leuven, 1990).

Heinrich Schütz (1585-1672) en de Historia (Leuven, 1991).

De Vlaamse polyfonie (Leuven, 1994).
French edition: *De Guillaume Dufay à Roland de Lassus. Les tres riches heures de la polyphonie franco-flamande* (Brussels and Paris, 1996).
English edition: *Flemish Polyphony* (Leuven, 1996).
German edition: *Die Kunst der Polyphonie. Die flämische Musik von Guillaume Dufay bis Orlando di Lasso* (Zürich and Mainz, 1996).

Beknopt overzicht van de muziekgeschiedenis (Leuven, 1995).

Georg Philipp Telemann. Johannespassie (1745) (Leuven, 1995).

Joseph Haydn. Die Tageszeiten (Leuven, 1995).

Wolfgang Amadeus Mozart. Concerti voor blazers (Leuven, 1996).

Passietijd in polyfonie (Leuven, 1997).

Georg Friedrich Händel. Delirio amoroso. Italiaanse solocantaten (Leuven, 1999).

Joseph Haydn. Symfonieën nr. 47,48 & 49 (Leuven, 2000).

De Missae breves (BWV 233-236) van Johann Sebastian Bach (Peer, 2000).

Antonio Vivaldi. Concerti con molti stromenti (Leuven, 2001).

Luigi Boccherini (1743-1805) (Leuven, 2002).

Felix Mendelssohn-Bartholdy (1809-1847) (Leuven, 2003).

Het Weihnachtsoratorium *(BWV 248) van Johann Sebastian Bach* (Leuven, 2002).
English edition: *Johann Sebastian Bach.* Christmas Oratorio *(BWV 248)* (Leuven, 2004).

Johann Sebastian Bach. Matthäuspassion *(BWV 244)* (Bruges, 2007).

2. Dissertations

Pieter Vanderghinste (1789-1860) een bio-bibliografische studie (MA Diss., K.U.Leuven, 1971).

Alexander Utendal (ca. 1543/1545-1581); een bijdrage tot de studie van Nederlandse polyfonie in de tweede helft van de zestiende eeuw; transcriptie van de volledige werken, 10 vol. (Ph.D., K.U.Leuven, 1978).

3. Editions
a. Editions of Music

Leonhard Lechner, *Septem Psalmi Poenitentiales sex vocibus compositi, 1587* (Leonhard Lechner. Werke, ed. K. Ameln, 10; Kassel and Basel, 1988).

Jean de Castro, *Opera omnia* (Leuven, 1993-96):
1. Sonets, avec une chanson... livre premier (1592). Chansons, stanses, sonets, et epigrames...livre second (1592), 1993.
2. Bicinia seu duarum vocum cantiones aliquot sacrae... (1593), 1993.
3. Il Primo libro di madrigali, canzoni e motetti a tre voci... (1593), 1994.
4. Triciniorum sacrarum... liber unus (1574), 1996.

Alexander Utendal. Motetten/Motets (Monumenta Flandriae Musica, 5; Leuven and Peer, 1999).

Jean de Castro, *Opera Omnia. Tricinia* (Leuven, 2000) (edition on cd-rom).

b. Editions of Books

Orlandus Lassus 1532-1594 (exhibition catalogue) (Leuven, 1982).

Orlando di Lasso and his Time. Colloquium Proceedings Antwerpen 24.-26.08.1994 (Yearbook of the Alamire Foundation, 1) (Peer, 1995) (co-editors Eugène Schreurs and Annelies Wauters).

Een muziekgeschiedenis der Nederlanden (Amsterdam, 2001) (general editor Louis Peter Grijp, co-editors Ignace Bossuyt, Mark Delaere, Rokus de Groot, Lutgard Mutsaers, Rudolf Rasch, Kees Vellekoop and Emile Wennekes).

Mozart 06 (Bruges, 2006) (co-editor Pieter Bergé).

4. Articles in Journals and Articles or Chapters in Edited Books

'Pieter Vanderginste (1789-1860). Kortrijks componist en kapelmeester', *De Leiegouw*, 15 (1973), 195-234.

'De Franse chansons van Philippus de Monte', in *De muziek en tijd van Philippus de Monte. Programmaboek Festival van Vlaanderen Mechelen & Brussel-Leuven 1976* (Mechelen, 1976), 54-9.

'De Acta Capituli van de Onze-Lieve-Vrouwkerk te Kortrijk als muziekhistorische bron', in G. Persoons (ed.), *Jaarboek 1977. Vereniging voor Muziekgeschiedenis* (Antwerp, 1977), 59-100 (co-author Jan De Cuyper).

'Newly-Discovered Part Books of Early Madrigal Collections of Philippus de Monte (1521-1603)', *Fontes Artis Musicae*, 26 (1979), 295-7.

'Het 'drama per musica' *Der Streit zwischen Phoebus und Pan* (BWV 210) van Johann Sebastian Bach: een 'oratio pro domo' en uiting van een muzikaal generatieconflict', *Kleio. Tijdschrift voor oude talen en antieke cultuur*, 10 (1980), 126-44.

'La chanson française polyphonique en Allemagne et en Autriche dans la seconde moitié du XVIe siècle', in Jean-Michel Vaccaro (ed.), *La chanson à la Renaissance. Actes du XXe Colloque d'Etudes humanistes du Centre d'Etudes Supérieures de la renaissance de l'Université de Tours. Juillet 1977* (Tours, 1981), 294-303.

'Die *Psalmi poenitentiales* (1570) des Alexander Utendal. Ein künstlerisches Gegenstück der Busspsalmen von O. Lassus und eine praktische Anwendung von Glareans Theorie der Zwölf Modi', *Archiv für Musikwissenschaft*, 38 (1981), 279-95.

'Benedictus Appenzeller', in *Nationaal Biografisch Woordenboek*, 9 (Brussels, 1981), 17-22.

'Alexander Utendal', in *Nationaal Biografisch Woordenboek*, 9 (Brussels, 1981), 770-80.

'Orlandus Lassus (1532-1594). Leven en werk', in I. Bossuyt (ed.), *Orlandus Lassus 1532-1594* (exhibition catalogue) (Leuven, 1982), 29-59.

'Orlandus Lassus (1532-1594)', *Onze Alma Mater* 36 (1982), 281-90.

'Alexander Utendal i jego tworczosc', *Muzyka. Polska Akademia Nauk. Institut Sztuki*, 27 (1982/3-4), 3-24.

'De componist Alexander Utendal', *Spiegel Historiae*, 18 (1983), 255-61.

'Benjamin Britten (1913-1976) en de *Six Metamorphoses after Ovid* voor hobo-solo (op. 49, 1951)', *Kleio. Tijdschrift voor oude talen en antieke cultuur*, 13 (1983), 29-40.

'Maurice Ravel (1875-1937) en het ballet *Daphnis et Chloé* (1909-1912)', *Kleio. Tijdschrift voor oude talen en antieke cultuur*, 13 (1983), 199-211.

'*Ick seg adieu* – het volkslied en onze componisten', in *Op harpen en snaren. Volksmuziek, volksdansen, volksinstrumenten in Vlaanderen* (Antwerp, 1983), 164-70.

'Orlandus Lassus', in *Nationaal Biografisch Woordenboek*, 10 (Brussels, 1983), 380-92.

'Regnart', in *Nationaal Biografisch Woordenboek*, 10 (Brussels, 1983), 526-36.

'Jacobus Vaet', in *Nationaal Biografisch Woordenboek*, 10 (Brussels, 1983), 634-9.

'Anversa' in A. Basso (ed.), *Dizionario Enciclopedico Universale della Musica e dei Musicisti. Il Lessico*, 1 (Torino, 1983), 94-6.

'Bruges', in A. Basso (ed.), *Dizionario Enciclopedico Universale della Musica e dei Musicisti. Il Lessico*, 1 (Torino, 1983), 403-5.

'Courtrai', in A. Basso (ed.), *Dizionario Enciclopedico Universale della Musica e dei Musicisti. Il Lessico*, 1 (Torino, 1983), 724-5.

'Gand', in A. Basso (ed.), *Dizionario Enciclopedico Universale della Musica e dei Musicisti. Il Lessico*, 2 (Torino, 1983), 328-30.

'Liegi', in A. Basso (ed.), *Dizionario Enciclopedico Universale della Musica e dei Musicisti. Il Lessico*, 2 (Torino, 1983), 720-2.

'Lovanio' in A. Basso (ed.), *Dizionario Enciclopedico Universale della Musica e dei Musicisti. Il Lessico*, 3 (Torino, 1984), 9-10.

'Malines', in A. Basso (ed.), *Dizionario Enciclopedico Universale della Musica e dei Musicisti. Il Lessico*, 3 (Torino, 1984), 38-9.

'Le compositeur Roland de Lassus (1532-1594)', *Septentrion* 13 (1984/1), 52-7.

'Het muziekleven te Brussel in de jaren van de opstand (1566-1610)', *Tijdschrift voor Brusselse Geschiedenis*, 1 (1984), 135-52.

'Adriaan Willaert', in *Nationaal Biografisch Woordenboek*, 11 (Brussels, 1985), 835-49.

'Andreas Pevernage (1542/43-1591), componist uit Harelbeke. Leven en werk', introduction to the facsimile edition *Andreas Pevernage 1542/43-1591. Beeldmotetten* (Harelbeke, 1985).

'De gebroeders Regnart uit Dowaai, een familie van componisten uit de tweede helft van de 16de eeuw', *De Franse Nederlanden/Les Pays-Bas Français*, 11 (1986), 124-39.

'Adriaan Willaert (ca. 1490-1562) en het ricercar. Adriaan Willaert (ca. 1490-1562) and the ricercar', introduction to the facsimile edition *M. Adriano & de altri autori Fantasie Recercari Contrapunti a tre voci, Venetia, Antonio Gardano, 1559* (Peer, 1986).

'Johannes Ockeghem (vers 1410-1497). Un compositeur flamand au service des rois de France', *Septentrion*, 15 (1986/2), 37-40.

'Josquin Desprez (vers 1440-1521), le Michel-Ange de la musique', *Septentrion,* 15 (1986/4), 44-8.

'Musik, Mensch, Religion und Weltbild in der Renaissance', in *Roczniki Teologiczno-Kanoniczne. Muzykologia. Musicae Sacrae Ars et Scientia. Ksiega ku czci Prof. Karola Mrowca* (Lublin, 1987), 307-14.

'Verdwenen unica-drukken uit de zestiende eeuw opnieuw opgedoken', *Musica Antiqua*, 4 (1987), 89-90.

'Johannes de Cleve', in A. Basso (ed.), *Dizionario Enciclopedico Universale della Musica e dei Musicisti. Le biografie*, 2 (Torino, 1987), 275-6.

'Over de wortels van de westerse muziek in het Griekse denken', in J. Boonen, C. de Vocht and V. D'Huys (eds.), *Gisteren en morgen voorbij. Tweemaal vier opstellen over de oudheid* (Leuven, 1987), 30-44.

'Clemens non Papa en de Souterliedekens', *Musica Antiqua*, 5 (1988), 140-3. In English as 'Introduction' to the facsimile edition *Clemens non Papa. Het sevenste musyck boexken (Souterliedekens IIII), Antwerpen, Tielman Susato, 1557* (Peer, 1987).

'De battaglia en de villotta. Hermann Matthias Werrecore', *Musica Antiqua*, 5 (1988), 40-4.
In English as 'Introduction' to the facsimile edition *Matthias Werrecore. La Bataglia Taliana, Venetia, Antonio Gardane, 1549* (Peer, 1987).

'Andreas Pevernage', in *Nationaal Biografisch Woordenboek*, 12 (Brussels, 1987), 595-9.

'Le compositeur Guillaume Dufay (vers 1400-1474)', *Septentrion* 16 (1987/2), 46-53.

'De kathedraal van Kamerijk als muzikaal centrum tijdens de Renaissance', *De Franse Nederlanden/Les Pays-Bas Français*, 13 (1988), 49-63.

'Ovidius in musica. Ovidius als inspiratiebron in de muziek van de vijftiende tot de achttiende eeuw', *Lampas*, 21 (1988), 400-18.

'De Sayve', in A. Basso (ed.), *Dizionario Universale della Musica e dei Musicisti. Le Biografie*, 6 (Torino, 1988), 598.

'Jean de Castro: *Chansons, odes et sonnets de Pierre Ronsard (1576)*', *Revue de Musicologie*, 74 (1988), 173-87.

'Jacobus de Kerle' in A. Basso (ed.), *Dizionario Enciclopedico Universale della Musica e dei Musicisti. Le biografie*, 4 (Torino, 1989), 99-100.

'Petrus Maessens', in A. Basso (ed.), *Dizionario Enciclopedico Universale della Musica e dei Musicisti. Le biografie*, 4 (Torino, 1989), 567-8.

'Orlandus Lassus en het contrafact', *De zeventiende eeuw*, 5 (1989), 190-7.

'Bernardus van Clairvaux en de hervorming van de liturgische zang', in M. Sabbe, M. Lamberigts and F. Gistelinck (eds.), *Bernardus en de Cisterziënzerfamilie in België 1090-1990* (Leuven, 1990), 115-25.

'Mozart in de ban van de nieuwe klaviermuziek', in F. de Haas and I. Smets (eds.), *Mozart in België. Een wonderkind op reis door de Zuidelijke Nederlanden. 1763-1766* (Antwerp, 1990), 154-61.

'Allein! Weh, ganz allein!: *Elektra* bij Hugo von Hofmannsthal (1903) en Richard Strauss (1906-08)', *Kleio. Tijdschrift voor oude talen en antieke cultuur,* 20 (1990-91), 39-58.

'De Vlaamse polyfonie en de Portugese muziek', in J. Everaert and E. Stols (eds.), *Vlaanderen en Portugal* (Antwerp, 1991), 213-29.

'Franciscus Galletius en de Contrareformatie in Dowaai in de tweede helft van de 16ᵈᵉ eeuw', *De Franse Nederlanden/Les Pays-Bas Français*, 16 (1991), 145-60.

'Wolfgang Amadeus Mozart (1756-1791) en de klassieke wereld', *Hermeneus. Tijdschrift voor antieke cultuur,* 63 (1991), 298-307.

'Het zevenstemmig madrigaal *Occhi piangete* van Adriaan Willaert', *Muziek & Wetenschap*, 2 (1992), 3-23.

'Georg Friedrich Haendel (1685-1759). Componist van muzikale drama's', *Onze Alma Mater*, 46 (1992), 318-29.

'De muziek in België', in *Expo Sevilla. België 1492-1992* (Antwerp, 1992), 113-6.
Editions in Dutch, French, English and Spanish.

'Lassos erste Jahre in München (1556-1559): eine "Cosa non riuscita"? Neue Materialen aufgrund unveröffentlicher Briefe von Johann Jakob Fugger, Antoine Perrenot de Granvelle und Orlando Lasso', in Stephan Hörner and Bernhold Schmid (eds.), *Festschrift Horst Leuchtmann zum 65. Geburtstag* (Tutzing, 1993), p. 55-67.

'Adriaan Willaert (ca. 1490-1562)', in *Apollo en de python. Muziekprogramma Antwerpen 93. Culturele hoofdstad van Europa* (Antwerp, 1993), 39-42.

'Orlandus Lassus (1532-1594)' in *Apollo en de python. Muziekprogramma Antwerpen 93. Culturele hoofdstad van Europa* (Antwerp, 1993), 43-6.

'Orlandus Lassus, "le plus que divin Orlande": Europees componist', in *Programmaboek Festival van Vlaanderen Antwerpen 1994* (Antwerp, 1994), 11-7.

'Het muziekleven in Kamerijk, Dowaai en Rijsel tijdens het Ancien Regime', *Jaarboek De Franse Nederlanden/Annales Les Pays-Bas Français*, 20 (1995), 91-116 (co-authors Eugène Schreurs and Bruno Bouckaert).

'The Art of Give and Take, Musical Relations between England and Flanders from the 15th to the 17th Centuries', *The Low Countries. Arts and Society in Flanders and the Netherlands. A Yearbook*, (1993-94), 39-50.

'Orlandus Lassus en Antwerpen', in *Orlandus Lassus en Antwerpen 1554-1556* (exhibition catalogue, Museum Vleeshuis) (Antwerp, 1994), 7-9.

'Orlandus Lassus (1532-1594), Europees componist', in *Orlandus Lassus en Antwerpen 1554-1556* (exhibition catalogue, Museum Vleeshuis) (Antwerp, 1994), 11-19.

'Orlandus Lassus en Perrenot de Granvelle', in: *Orlandus Lassus en Antwerpen 1554-1556* (exhibition catalogue, Museum Vleeshuis) (Antwerp, 1994), 59-64.

'Jean Pollet and the Theft in 1563 of Lassus' 'Secret Poenitential Psalms'', in A. Clement and E. Jas (eds.), *From Ciconia to Sweelinck. Donum Natalicium Willem Elders* (Amsterdam and Atlanta, 1994), 261-7.

'Brügge', in L. Finscher (ed.), *Die Musik in Geschichte und Gegenwart*, 2nd. ed., Sachteil, 2 (Kassel and Basel, 1995), 178-82.

'Orlando di Lasso and his Time. Some Reflections', in Ignace Bossuyt, Eugène Schreurs and Annelies Wouters (eds.), *Orlando di Lasso and his Time. Colloquium Proceedings Antwerpen 24.-26.08.1994* (Yearbook of the Alamire Foundation, 1) (Peer, 1995), 11-20.

'Vlaamse polyfonisten in Rome', *Kunst en Cultuur*, 28 (1995/3), 19-21.

'Heroverwegingen. Bewerken, herwerken, arrangeren, citeren, ontlenen: basisprocédé's voor het componeren in Middeleeuwen en Renaissance', in *November Music. Programma 1995* (Ghent, 1995), 71-5.

'Pierre de Ronsard: onuitputtelijke inspiratiebron voor het Franse chanson in de tweede helft van de 16de eeuw', in *Programmaboek Festival van Vlaanderen Vlaams-Brabant 1995* (Leuven, 1995), 16-7.

'De briljante madrigaalkunst van Giaches de Wert als schakel tussen Cipriano de Rore en Claudio Monteverdi', in *Programmaboek Festival van Vlaanderen Vlaams-Brabant 1995* (Leuven, 1995), 30-1.

'De collega's van Josquin: voorgangers, generatiegenoten en navolgers, een duurzaam hoogtepunt in de Renaissancepolyfonie', in *Programmaboek Festival van Vlaanderen Vlaams-Brabant 1995* (Leuven, 1995), 44-6.

'Löwen', in L. Finscher (ed.), *Die Musik in Geschichte und Gegenwart*, 2nd. ed., Sachteil, 5 (Kassel and Basel, 1996), 1493-5.

'La polyphonie flamande et la musique portugaise 15e-17e siècle', in A. Vandewalle (ed.), *Internationaal Historisch Colloquium Vlaanderen-Portugal 15de-18de eeuw, Handelingen; Colloque Historique International Flandre-Portugal 15e-18e siècle, Actes; International Historical Symposium Flanders-Portugal 15th-18th Century, Proceedings* (Bruges, 1996), 125-9.

'Jean de Castro and his Three-Part Chansons Modelled on Four- and Five-Part Chansons by Orlando di Lasso. A Comparison', in Bernhold Schmid (ed.), *Orlando di Lasso in der Musikgeschichte. Bericht über das Symposium der Bayerischen Akademie der Wissenschaften. München, 4.-6. Juli 1994* (München, 1996), 25-67.

'The Counter-Reformation and Music in Douai', in *Actas del XV Congreso de la Sociedad Internacional de Musicologia 'Culturas musicales del Mediterraneo y sus ramificaciones', Madrid, 3-10/IV/1992*, 5 (Madrid, 1997), 2783-2800.

'Lassos Motette *Praesidium Sara*. Ein Epithalamium für seinen Kopisten Jean Pollet?', *Musik in Bayern*, 54 (1997), 107-12.

'De gedrevenheid van een getourmenteerde ziel. Carlo Gesualdo en het experimentele madrigaal', *Tijdschrift voor Oude Muziek*, 12 (1997/3), 23-5.

'De *aurea vox* van Johannes Ockeghem', in *Programmaboek Festival van Vlaanderen Vlaams-Brabant 1997* (Leuven, 1997), 15-9.
Also in *Programmaboek Festival van Vlaanderen Antwerpen 1997* (Antwerp, 1997), 11-7.

'Twaalf maal *Fors seulement* of evenzovele her-interpretaties van een Frans chanson: van Johannes Ockeghem tot Nicolaas Gombert', in *Programmaboek Festival van Vlaanderen Vlaams-Brabant 1997* (Leuven, 1997), 36-8.

'De *Missa Caput*: Ockeghem aan het hoofd van traditie en vernieuwing', in *Programmaboek Festival van Vlaanderen Vlaams-Brabant 1997* (Leuven, 1997), 42-4.

'Bel *accueil*: uitnodiging tot een verkenning van een 15de-eeuws muziekmanuscript', in *Programmaboek Festival van Vlaanderen Vlaams-Brabant 1997* (Leuven, 1997), 50-3.

'Jean de Castro's *Il Primo Libro di Madrigali, Canzoni e Motetti*. De Castro's Tricinia of 1569' in Eugène Schreurs and Henri Vanhulst (eds.), *Music Fragments and Manuscripts form the Low Countries. Alta Capella. Music Printing in Antwerp and Europe in the 16th Century. Colloquium Proceedings Alden Biezen. 1995* (Yearbook of the Alamire Foundation, 2) (Leuven-Peer, 1997), 341-51.

'*O socii durate*. A Musical Correspondence from the Time of Philip II', *Early Music*, 26 (1998), 433-43.

'De Vlaamse polyfonie en haar Europese uitstraling. Flemish Polyphony and its appeal in Europe', in *Culturele Ambassadeurs van Vlaanderen 1998. Cultural Ambassadors of Flanders* (Brussels, 1998), 13-7.

'Het romantisch klavierlied: onschatbaar en onderschat', in *Programmaboek Festival van Vlaanderen Vlaams-Brabant 1998* (Leuven, 1998), 56-8.

'Bachs muziek voor traverso en klavecimbel: een meesterlijke demonstratie van abstract muzikaal denken en affectieve geladenheid', in *Programmaboek Festival van Vlaanderen Vlaams-Brabant 1998* (Leuven, 1998), 72-4.

'Viola da gamba en klavecimbel verenigd in een spel vol Franse gratie, Duitse ernst en Italiaanse musiceervreugde', in *Programmaboek Festival van Vlaanderen Vlaams-Brabant 1998* (Leuven, 1998), 80-2.

'Arrangement en virtuositeit. Een andere kijk op Orlandus Lassus en zijn tijd', in *Programmaboek Abdijconcerten Leuven. Twee eeuwen muziek van Vlaamse polyfonisten en hun Europese tijdgenoten* (Leuven, 1998), 20-1.

'Antoine Brumel en Alexander Agricola, grootmeesters van de virtuoze polyfonie omstreeks 1500', in *Programmaboek Abdijconcerten Leuven. Twee eeuwen muziek van Vlaamse polyfonisten en hun Europese tijdgenoten* (Leuven, 1998), 26-8.

'Orlando di Lasso as a model for composition as seen in the three-voice motets of Jean de Castro', in Peter Bergquist (ed.), *Orlando di Lasso Studies* (Cambridge, 1999), 158-82.

'Karel V: Een levensverhaal in muziek. Chronologisch overzicht van Karels politieke loopbaan via de muziek', in Francis Maes (ed.), *De Klanken van de Keizer. Karel V en de Polyfonie* (Leuven, 1999), 85-164.
English edition: 'Charles V: A Life Story in Music. Chronological Outline of Charles' Political Career through Music', in Francis Maes (ed.), *The Empire Resounds. Music in the Days of Charles V* (Leuven, 1999), 83-160.

'De polyfonie rond 1500', in Eugène Schreurs (ed.), *De schatkamer van Alamire. Muziek en miniaturen uit keizer Karels tijd (1500-1535)* (Leuven, 1999), 13-25.

'Petrus Alamire en de polyfonie omstreeks 1500', in *Programmaboek Festival van Vlaanderen Vlaams-Brabant 1999* (Leuven 1999), 16-24.

'De *ars perfecta* van Pierre de la Rue, toonaangever in mis en motet', in *Programmaboek Festival van Vlaanderen Vlaams-Brabant 1999* (Leuven 1999), 28-31.

'*Piae memoriae:* de dood in de polyfonie omstreeks 1500', in *Programmaboek Festival van Vlaanderen Vlaams-Brabant 1999* (Leuven 1999), 56-7.

'Bachs raadselachtig geschenk voor de eeuwigheid: *Das musikalisches Opfer'*, in *Programmaboek Festival van Vlaanderen Vlaams-Brabant 1999* (Leuven 1999), 96-7.
Also in *Programmaboek Festival van Vlaanderen Gent & historische steden 2004* (Ghent, 2004), 148-50.

'Antoon van Dyck en de muziek van zijn tijd', in *Programmaboek Festival van Vlaanderen Antwerpen 1999* (Antwerp, 1999), 11-8.
Also in *Tijdschrift voor Oude Muziek,* 14 (1999/3), 20-23.

'*O socii durate*: Antoine Perrenot de Granvelle en de Vlaamse polyfonist Adriaan Willaert (ca. 1490-1562). Nieuwe gegevens op basis van de in Madrid bewaarde correspondentie van Granvelle', in Krista De Jonge en Gustaaf Janssens (eds.), *Les Granvelle et les anciens Pays-Bas* (Leuven, 2000), 321-40.

'*The Orpheus of Amsterdam*. The Life and Work of Jan Pieterszoon Sweelinck', *The Low Countries. Arts and Society in Flanders and the Netherlands*, 8 (2000), 259-62.

'Jean de Castro', in Stanley Sadie (ed.), *The New Grove Dictionary of Music and Musicians*, 2nd. ed., 5 (London, 2001), 270-2 (co-authors Saskia Willaert and Katrien Derde).

'Karel V en de muziek van zijn tijd', in *Holland Festival Oude Muziek Utrecht. Programmaboek 2000* (Utrecht, 2000), 17-9.
Also in English as 'The Empire resounds: a bird's eye view. Charles V and the music of his time', *ibid.*, 21-23.

'Karl V. – Ein Reich, in dem die Musik nie verklingt', in Barbara Schwendowius (ed.), *Tage alter Musik in Herne 2000. Das Reich, in dem die Sonne nicht untergeht. Musik aus der Welt Karls V. und seiner Nachfolger. Programmheft* (Herne, 2000), 30-3.

'Het beklijvende van het klassieke repertoire: de universaliteit van de symfonieën en concerti van Mozart en Haydn', in *Programmaboek Festival van Vlaanderen Vlaams-Brabant 2000* (Leuven, 2000), 62-3.

'Nicolas Payen, el aun desconocido maestro de capilla de Carlos V y Felipe II', in Juan José Carreras and Bernardo José Garcia Garcia (eds.), *La Capilla Real de los Austrias. Musica y ritual de corte en laz Europa moderna* (Madrid, 2001), 175-91.
Also in English: 'Nicolas Payen, an unknown chapelmaster of Charles V and Philip II', in Tess Knighton (ed.), *The Royal Chapel in the Time of the Habsburgs. Music and Ceremony in the Early Modern European Court* (Woodbridge, 2005), 121-32.

'Muziek en mecenaat ten tijde van Granvelle', in Louis Peter Grijp (ed.), *Een muziekgeschiedenis der Nederlanden* (Amsterdam, 2001), 160-7.

'De muziek in de veertiende eeuw: een kwestie van (noten)waarden', in *Programmaboek Festival van Vlaanderen Vlaams-Brabant 2001* (Leuven, 2001), 40-2.

'Francesco Landini (†1397), de Verdwaalde Valk van het Florentijnse Trecento', in *Programmaboek Festival van Vlaanderen Vlaams-Brabant 2001* (Leuven, 2001), 16-24.

'*Simplicitas* en *subtilitas* – of de veelzijdigheid van de polyfonie tussen 1200 en 1400', in *Programmaboek Festival van Vlaanderen Vlaams-Brabant 2001* (Leuven, 2001), 62-4.

'Music and Context: The Secular Motets of Jean de Castro (ca. 1540/45- ca. 1600)', in Giacomo Fornari (ed.), *Album Amicorum Albert Dunning in occasione del suo LXV compleanno* (Turnhout, 2002), 3-19.

'Venetiaanse kerkmuziek', in *Programmaboek Festival van Vlaanderen Gent & historische steden 2002* (Ghent, 2002), 267-70.

'Nicolaas Gombert and Parody', *Tijdschrift voor Muziektheorie,* 8 (2003), 112-22.

'Solo e pensoso: alleen en van geen mens gestoord. Intieme madrigaalkunst op teksten van Petrarca', in *Programmaboek Festival van Vlaanderen Vlaams-Brabant 2003* (Leuven, 2003), 24-6.

'*Affetti* en *effetti*. Het virtuoze madrigaal in Ferrara', in *Programmaboek Festival van Vlaanderen Vlaams-Brabant 2003* (Leuven, 2003), 44-5.

'De muziek en het muziekleven aan de Habsburgse hoven in Oostenrijk in de tweede helft van de 16de eeuw', in *Programmaboek Festival van Vlaanderen Antwerpen* (Antwerpen, 2003), 15-25.

'Johann Sebastian Bach: de ultieme synthese', in *Programmaboek Festival van Vlaanderen Gent & historische steden 2003* (Ghent, 2003), 108-16.

'Lassus, Familie (Orlande, Ferdinand, Rudolph)', in Ludwig Finscher (ed.), *Die Musik in Geschichte und Gegenwart*, 2nd. ed., *Personenteil*, 10 (Kassel and Basel, 2003), 1244-1310 (co-author Bernhold Schmid).

'Blaest de cornetten, steckt de trompetten. Kerstmis in de muziek der Nederlanden', in Sijbold Noorda and Christien Oele (eds.), *Er is een kindeke… De geboorte van Jezus in de Nederlandse en Vlaamse cultuur* (Amsterdam, 2004), 107-22.

'Johann Sebastian Bach en de cantate: een perfecte symbiose tussen componist en muzikaal genre', in *Programmaboek Festival van Vlaanderen Gent & historische steden 2004* (Ghent, 2004), 139-43.

'Johann Sebastian Bach en het aftasten van de grenzen: de kamermuziek', in *Programmaboek Festival van Vlaanderen Gent & historische steden 2004* (Ghent, 2004), 144-7.

'Orlandus Lassus', in *Programmaboek Festival van Vlaanderen Gent & historische steden 2004* (Ghent, 2004), 209-14.

'Jean de Castro (ca. 1540/45-ca. 1600) und seine driestimmigen Bearbeitungen italienischer Madrigale', in Michael Zywietz, Volker Honemann and Christian Bettels (eds.), *Gattungen und Formen des europäischen Liedes vom 14. bis zum 16. Jahrhundert. Internationale Tagung vom 9. bis 12. Dezember 2001 in Münster* (Studien und Texte zum Mittelalter und zur frühen Neuzeit, 8) (New York and Berlin, 2005), 31-9.

'Clemens non Papa and Thomas Crequillon as Models for Latin Tricinia by Gerard van Turnhout and Jean de Castro', in Eric Jas (ed.), *Beyond Contemporary Fame. Reassessing the Art of Clemens non Papa and Thomas Crequillon. Colloquium Proceedings Utrecht, April 24-26, 2003* (Turnhout, 2005), 141-52.

'De muziekdruk in het 16de-eeuwse Europa', in Nele Gabriëls and Eugène Schreurs (eds.), *Petrus Phalesius en het stedelijk muziekleven in de Vlaamse Renaissancestad Leuven*, (Leuven, 2005), 39-42.

'Joseph Haydns oratorium *Die Schöpfung* (1798): een 'neue Welt' – voor kinderen van alle leeftijden', in *Programmaboek Festival van Vlaanderen Vlaams-Brabant 2005* (Leuven, 2005), 57-9.

'*La Lucrezia*, Wraak en zelfdoding van de gekwetste vrouw in een dramatische cantate van Georg Friedrich Händel', *Hermeneus*, 78 (2006), 277-85.

'*Idomeneo, rè di Creta*, een klassiek 'dramma per musica' van Wolfgang Amadeus Mozart', *Kleio. Tijdschrift voor oude talen en antieke cultuur*, 36 (2006), 22-38.

'Mozarts biografie', in Pieter Bergé and Ignace Bossuyt (eds.), *Mozart 06* (Bruges, 2006), 18-33.

'Mozart & het concerto', in Pieter Bergé and Ignace Bossuyt (eds.), *Mozart 06* (Bruges, 2006), 50-71.

In addition, Ignace Bossuyt has written numerous short contributions in cultural periodicals (such as *Vlaanderen*, *Kultuurleven*, *Ons Erfdeel* and *Muziek en Woord*), liner notes for CD-recordings (for labels including *Eufoda*, *Harmonia Mundi* and *Claves*) and concert introductions (for the Concertgebouw Bruges, among others).

HUMOR IN THE MOTETS OF ORLANDO DI LASSO[1]

Peter Bergquist

A brief definition of the motet in the sixteenth century would usually say that it is a composition that sets a sacred Latin text in a more or less polyphonic style for a vocal ensemble. A more extended definition would add that many composers in this period set secular Latin texts, commemorative, celebratory, or classicistic, in a similar manner, and that these compositions are also considered to be motets. None of these definitions speak to the possibility that a motet might contain humorous elements, and indeed humor is probably not something one would expect to find in such a work. Nonetheless, it can be encountered from time to time, and nowhere more frequently than in the motets of Orlando di Lasso. Lasso clearly had a lively sense of humor, as is evident in his letters with their constant joking and word play in several different languages. Humor emerges clearly in many of his settings of vernacular texts, as Annie Cœurdevey observes in the section of her study of Lasso that is titled 'L'invention de l'humour en musique'.[2] She also includes some examples from the motets in her discussion. James Haar's article on Lasso in *New Grove* has a subsection on 'Humorous Motets' that cites a few other examples.[3] The present study takes a more comprehensive look at humor in Lasso's motets, following the lead of these and other writers.

Lasso composed some sixty-five motets that can be considered to have secular texts. Most of the examples of humor can be found among them, but there are at least a few instances of humor in his settings of sacred texts. Among them are four of his five settings of the Marian antiphon *Ave Regina caelorum*.[4] When the word 'Salve' first occurs in each of these motets, Lasso sets it with the *la-sol-la-re* motive that begins the standard chant for another Marian antiphon, *Salve Regina*. In every instance the 'Salve' motive sounds clearly in long notes against more rapid motion in other voices. Whether Lasso intended this musical

---

[1] In this paper Lasso's compositions are identified by the numbers assigned to them in the Lasso-Verzeichnis (= LV; Horst Leuchtmann and Bernhold Schmid, *Orlando di Lasso: Seine Werke in Zeitgenössischen Drucken, 1555-1687*, 3 vol., Kassel, 2001). Their location in *Orlando di Lasso: The Complete Motets* (CM), *Recent Researches in the Music of the Renaissance*, ed. Peter Bergquist et al., 21 vol. and supplement, Madison, 1995-2007, is shown by volume and page reference. Many of the discussions of individual pieces in this paper are drawn from the introductions to *CM*. References to Lasso, *Sämtliche Werke* (Leipzig, 1894-1927) are not given, since many of the motets discussed here were published in that edition with contrafacted texts.

[2] Annie Cœurdevey, *Roland de Lassus* (Paris, 2003), 516-22.

[3] James Haar, 'Orlande de Lassus' in *New Grove* and *New Grove II*.

[4] LV 554 a3, CM 11:61; LV 717 a6, CM 13:12; LV 1078 a4, CM 19:19; LV 1093, CM 21:57.

pun to be humorous could be debated, but one can imagine it drawing smiles to the faces of the performers and perhaps some listeners.

Humor is manifested in a number of ways in the secular motets. In some cases the humor may reside more in the text itself than in the music. The word play in *Quid facies facies* is similar to what one finds in Lasso's letters, with its repetitions of the same word with two different meanings ('Quid facies facies Veneris cum veneris ante?' [What will you do when you come before the faces of Venus?]).[5] The lively musical setting, however, does not appear to respond to this aspect of the text. Word play of another sort is seen in *Bestia curvafia*, one of a number of sixteenth-century settings of poems about the flea.[6] In it every word of the poem except 'bestia curvafia' begins with the letter 'p'. Lasso was possibly taken with this aspect of the poem as well as with its inherent humor. However, humor in the musical setting is confined mainly to its exact reproduction of the metric quantities of the poem's elegiac couplets. Lasso set many poems in elegiacs, both sacred and secular, but in no other is that meter duplicated so completely in the music. In another motet it is the treatment rather than the content of the text that is humorous. In 'S, U, su, P, E, R, per' Psalm 136:1a is deconstructed and rebuilt letter by letter and syllable by syllable so that it almost sounds like gibberish.[7] For example, one line reads, 'B, I, bi, babi, na babi, mina babi, flumina babi, per flumina babi, super flumina babi'. Lasso's setting, almost entirely note against note using mostly semibreves and minims, lets all the foolishness be heard very clearly, punctuating with clear cadences at the end of each phrase. Rebecca Oettinger suggests that this treatment of the text may derive from methods of teaching children to read and write that were practiced in Lasso's time.[8]

Specifically musical responses to humor in the texts are quite varied. One possibility is a solmization pun, seizing on a segment of the text that contains a succession of Guidonian solmization syllables and setting them to appropriate pitches. This is hardly confined to Lasso's music, but he made it his own in a way by using the syllables 'la-sol' as a signature, not only in Latin settings but also in vernacular texts. Perhaps his most elaborate solmization pun is found in one of the motets from the Four-Language Print of 1573, *Quid estis pusillanimes*.[9] Its text includes the following passage: 'an nescitis justitiae ut sol fami relaxatas...', and at that point all four voices join in a chorus of *ut-sol-fa-mi-re-la*'s at various pitch levels.

[5]   LV 695, CM 19:116.
[6]   LV 588, CM 18:77.
[7]   LV 325, CM 17:130.
[8]   CM Supplement, 14.
[9]   LV 473, CM 10:5.

Example 1. Lasso, *Quid estis pusillanimes*, bb. 21-6, CM 10:6

Solmization is the source of humor in another way in *Ut queant laxis*, the hymn to St. John that is the source of the Guidonian syllables.[10] Here Tenor 1 intones only the first syllable of each line of the poem, which the other four voices then complete in a strictly note-against-note style. Oettinger speculates that this little motet might also have had a pedagogical purpose, and she notes its position at the end of a motet book in its first edition, suggesting that '*Ut queant laxis* is the dessert, the reward for the 'good ear' introduced in the first motet [*Auris bona est*] that has diligently worked through the motets in this collection [RISM 1582d]'.[11]

Example 2. Lasso, *Ut queant laxis*, bb. 1-2, CM 12:98

A text that refers directly or by implication to music readily provokes a musical response, sometimes a humorous one. *In hora ultima* and *Laudent Deum cithara* include musical references to music making and dancing that inevitably call up smiles from a listener, even though the message of *In hora ultima* is fundamentally serious: 'All this shall pass away'.[12] In this motet the words 'cithara', 'tuba', and 'cantus' are directly imitated in their settings, as are 'jocus', 'risus', and 'saltus'. The obvious pleasure with which Lasso seized

---

[10] LV 715, CM 12:98.
[11] CM 12, p. xix.
[12] LV 1088 and 1120, CM 21:51 and 169.

on these images seems to negate the admonition with which the motet begins. Perhaps the motet is really saying, 'Carpe diem!'

In two other motets humor arises from an association with animals. *Hispanum ad cenam* sets a humorous text in elegiacs that Ignace Bossuyt has suggested may have been performed in a theatrical production at the festivities associated with the wedding in 1568 of Wilhelm of Bavaria and Renata of Lorraine.[13] The text ends with the Belgian host berating his churlish Spanish guest, saying that the Spaniard is drinking the same water that his own donkey is drinking: '... bibit hoc voster asellus idem'. The mocking repetitions of 'bibit hoc' might almost suggest the braying of the donkey.

Example 3. Lasso, *Hispanum ad cenam*, bb. 86-95, CM 7:53

13   LV 360, CM 7:47. For Bossuyt's suggestion see CM 7, p. xvi.

The animal imitation in another motet is unmistakable. *Dulci sub umbra* is a pastoral idyll based on classical models.[14] As David Crook observes, several images in the poem evoke musical imitations. Most of them are typical madrigalisms, but at the end of the motet Lasso goes beyond the typical and brings in a chorus of bleating sheep on the words, 'me meae'.[15] The poem and music are attractive throughout, but the final measures enter the realm of comedy. A performance of the piece sung one on a part could no doubt convey this most effectively.

Example 4. Lasso, *Dulci sub umbra*, bb. 25-33, CM 20:78

Nine Latin drinking songs comprise a large subgroup within the Lasso motets that display humor in some aspect. Such pieces had been a staple of university

---

[14] LV 1047, CM 20:78. For David Crook's discussion of the motet, see CM 20, p. xx.
[15] Coeurdevey, *Roland de Lassus*, 521-2, discusses this passage and includes a musical example.

life for years before Lasso's time, probably also of monastic life. In both of these venues parodies of Latin hymns were very popular, and Lasso's motets include settings of three of them. The sequence *Verbum bonum et suave* gave rise to a whole family of parodies, one of which is the text of Lasso's *Vinum bonum et suave*.[16] In this text the content of the original is the subject of parody rather than its structure, since the stanzas in the original sequence have four lines, while the parody's have three. Lasso's playful approach to the text is especially obvious in the enthusiastic repetitions of 'fiat' at the end of the motet and the shouts of 'porrigat' by Altus 2 in measures 64-6 and 82-4. Was he perhaps imitating the shouts of the drinkers in the tavern? Another parody of *Verbum bonum et suave* is *Ave color vini clari*, which is the third stanza of one of the 'Vinum bonum' poems.[17] Lasso's lively setting contains no specifically musical humor, unless the setting of the words 'beata viscera' in measures 77-88 includes a chant cantus firmus in long notes. However, at present I have been unable to identify such a chant. 'Jam lucis orto sidere' is the opening line of a hymn that in the Editio Vaticana is appointed for Sundays at Prime.[18] Lasso's motet with this title, however, sets a parody of the hymn that turns it into a drinking song.[19] Lasso's animated setting for eight-voice divided chorus is similar in style to his *Vinum bonum et suave*, with its rapid fire exchanges between the two choirs. Its humor resides mainly in the irreverent text, with no specifically musical responses to its words or ideas.

None of the other drinking songs are explicitly parodies, though that aspect is not far from the surface in any of them. *Nunc gaudere licet* goes so far as to include a quotation from Catullus.[20] Its scandalous suggestion that a woman was the leader of the revels and the numerous attempts to emend the text have been explored thoroughly by Bernhold Schmid.[21] Much of the text is delivered in a fairly straightforward note-against-note style, but Schmid notes two instances of musical humor. The first occurs in measures 7-12 when the four-syllable phrase 'bibendum est' is repeatedly set in triple meter. At the end of the motet, the words 'gaudeamus omnes' provoke an unmistakable quotation in the Bassus, measures 38-42, of the opening of the introit that begins with those words.[22]

---

[16] LV 389, CM 7:206. This group of parodies is discussed in Paul Lehman, *Die Parodie im Mittelalter*, 2nd ed. (Stuttgart, 1963), 123-50.

[17] Lehman, *Die Parodie*. Lasso's setting is LV 347, CM 6:184.

[18] See e.g. *The Liber Usualis, with Introduction and Rubrics in English* (Tournai, 1938), 224.

[19] Lehman, *Die Parodie*, 127-8, published two versions of the parody that correspond closely to the poem Lasso set. Lehman suggests that the poem is of Italian origin.

[20] LV 339, CM 6:87.

[21] Bernhold Schmid, 'Lassos "Nunc gaudere licet" – Zur Geschichte einer Kontrafaktur', in *Compositionswissenschaft: Festschrift für Reinhold Schlötterer und Roswitha Schlötterer* (Augsburg, 1997), 47-56.

[22] *Liber usualis*, 437.

A similar quotation is found in *Fertur in conviviis*, a text which originated in the Archpoet's poem in *Carmina Burana*, no. 191.[23] Like *Nunc gaudere licet*, much of the text of *Fertur in conviviis* is set in a lively note-against-note style. At the end of the motet where the poem reads: '...sanctos angelos...cantantes pro ebriis, "Requiem aeternam"', the standard 'Requiem' chant is intoned, first by the Bassus alone, then continued in the Tenor as the other voices join in. Both of these pieces have more in common with the chanson than the motet; indeed, they were more often published in chanson books than in collections of motets. The same is true of *Deus qui bonum vinum creasti*.[24] This text parodies the structure of a prayer or collect in which the drinker asks for the good sense at least for the company to find their beds.[25] Specifically musical humor occurs at the end of the piece, where the Bassus almost literally sinks into bed in three stepwise descents.

Example 5. Lasso, *Deus qui bonum vinum creasti*, Bassus, bb. 34-43, CM 17:96

The drinking songs mentioned thus far all date from 1570 or earlier. Lasso returned to the genre a few times thereafter. His *Si bene perpendi*, a short, silly text that offers five reasons for drinking, was first published in 1579.[26] The lively musical setting does not appear to contain humorous responses to the text, except perhaps for the phrase 'propter pulices', where for a moment the fleas seem to crawl around more rapidly.

Lasso included two more songs about wine in his last motet book.[27] *Ad primum morsum* is a drinking song pure and simple.[28] David Crook's discussion of the motet notes that it surely would have been included in a list of motets banned

[23] LV 229, CM 17:71. Bernhold Schmid, 'Lasso's "Fertur in conviviis": on the History of its Text and Transmission', in Peter Bergquist (ed.), *Orlando di Lasso Studies* (Cambridge, 1999), 116-31, is the source for much of this discussion.

[24] LV 229, CM 17:94.

[25] See CM 17, p. xx, for a detailed discussion of this aspect of the motet.

[26] LV 642, CM 18:279.

[27] *Cantiones sacrae sex vocum* (Graz, 1594).

[28] LV 990, CM 16:133.

because of their texts and music drawn up at the Jesuit College in Munich in 1591-92, had it been available at that time.[29] Crook also notes the piece's secular musical style and its frequent madrigalisms. It appears that even in his last years Lasso was ready to celebrate the pleasures of drink. One other motet in the 1594 book has wine as its subject, *Luxuriosa res vinum*.[30] It is not a celebration of wine, however, but a brief admonition against it from the book of Proverbs. Lasso nonetheless responds to details in the text; Crook notes that 'on the pivotal word "ebrietas", note values suddenly lengthen in all parts as the Bassus falls into a drunken stupor on the low *D* below the staff'.[31] The motet includes much contrast of rhythm and register, to the extent that one might be excused for thinking that Lasso ended by celebrating wine rather than warning against it, perhaps subverting the presumed meaning of the text in the same way he seems to have done in *In hora ultima*.

What conclusions may be drawn from this brief survey? As was remarked at the outset, Lasso clearly had a lively sense of humor that included playfulness, mockery, and joking of all sorts. In his music it probably is most apparent in his settings of vernacular texts, but he hardly put it aside altogether when he set a Latin text. The character of the text clearly governs the amount of humor that a musical setting might exhibit. Secular texts are obviously the most likely venue for such a display, and when those texts come to resemble the texts for chansons, madrigals, and lieder, the likelihood of humor in music seems to be greatest.

[29] CM 16, pp. xxi-xxii.
[30] LV 984, CM 16:88.
[31] CM 16, p. xxi.

A NEW SOURCE, AND NEW COMPOSITIONS, FOR PHILIPPE DE MONTE

Stanley Boorman

A recently-discovered collection of manuscript and printed part-books, given to New York University by anonymous donors specifically for research by members of the Department of Music, contains two small fascicles devoted to music by Philippe de Monte.[1] The collection was acquired from a European dealer, and has every appearance of originating in Prague or a related area, in the years around 1600. No set of part-books is complete, though the fascicles to be discussed here are present in four books, of a set of at least six. Only Discantus, Altus, Tenor and Sextus are extant.

These two fascicles are part of a konvolut binding of six different manuscripts.[2] With one minor exception, each fascicle now comprises a single gathering in each part-book, and each was evidently planned to contain a pre-determined repertoire.[3] The two fascicles are interesting for being in the same hand, clearly that of a professional scribe, preparing unified collections of music, apparently for performance (See Plates 1 and 2.) The scribe has a very clear and fluent musical hand: he apparently proof-read his text before sending the manuscripts on, for there are corrections evidently made in the same hand. Equally significantly, he was scrupulous about underlay and accidentals. Both are carefully and consistently noted, even to excess.[4] While de Monte's style

---

[1]   A detailed study of these books by the present author is shortly to appear.

[2]   Other fascicles include music by Lassus, by other composers from the Imperial circle, and by some of the more popular Italian composers: all the music is sacred, much of it liturgical.

[3]   Full details of the structure and copying of these manuscripts will appear in the study cited in note 1. The first of the fascicles discussed here is actually the second in the manuscript, and survives as three part-books, Cantus, Altus and Tenor. Each may have been intended to be a single gathering of twelve folios. The Cantus now lacks one, and the Tenor two of those folios. The second fascicle, the fifth in the konvolut, adds a Sextus part. Again each part-book has only one fascicle, with the exception of the Altus, where the music is divided among two. One of the watermarks in this fascicle carries the name AVSSIG, indicating the paper-making town in Bohemia that was closely associated with the court at Prague. At one time the mill there was owned by Antonio Scandello, the Imperial chapel-master. See Charles Marie Briquet, *Les Fili-granes. Dictionnaire historique des marques du papier dès leur apparition vers 1282 jusqu'en 1600* (Geneva, 1907; reprinted many times, most importantly as *The New Briquet*, Amsterdam, 1968), 85, 1938-39, and Georg Eineder, *The Ancient Paper-Mills of the Former Austro-Hungarian Empire and their Watermarks*, Monumenta Chartæ Papyraceæ Historiam Illustrantia, viii (Hilversum, 1960), 113.

[4]   Some accidentals seem to be later additions, though not necessarily in a different hand. They have the same appearance, written with a very similar pen and in an identical ink. They may be the result of the careful reading and correction of the music, which is apparent from other evidence.

allows for some repetitions of text, the scribe invariably marked them in, often with a distinctive sign: there is almost no opportunity for adding further repetitions. Although the scribe also added decorative flourishes to the text entered beneath the lowest stave on each page, both fascicles seem to have been intended for use by performers, perhaps a group of singers not fully experienced in singing polyphony as an ensemble.[5]

Plate 1. Philippe de Monte, *Exsultavit spiritus meus*, Tenor, 96r

[5] This sort of evidently speculative statement can be bolstered by two observations: the first is that the great majority of manuscripts of polyphony were from the beginning intended for specific institutions or performance situations (and this fascicle clearly belongs with that majority); the second is my belief that many variations between treatment of detail in different manuscripts (when intended for different institutions) reflect performing advice for singers with a different set of performing experiences.

Plate 2. Philippe de Monte, *Lamentationes* à 6, Tenor, 152r

Both fascicles are in landscape quarto, and both appear to have been intended to be self-contained, prepared exclusively for a pre-selected repertoire, for each contains blank folios at the end. Although the two fascicles were bound into the same collection, it is not evident that they were intended for the same users. One, shown on Plate 1, contains a red caption in all parts, and a number of initials colored in red or green. The other, for which see Plate 2, uses no colour, but stylish calligraphic initials in ink are present throughout.

The first of these fascicles is headed similarly in all extant parts, as 'Ph: de M: à 4 per octo Tonos', and contains a set of ten Magnificats. The first eight of these are indeed the cycle of Magnificats attributed to de Monte, found elsewhere in the Stadt- und Staatsbibliothek in Augsburg, and also in the Universitätsbibliothek at Graz.[6] The scribe of the new manuscript started to number these works consecutively, but abandoned the process after the numeral 4. Similarly, the decorative coloured initials do not continue throughout the set of Magnificats. The scribe apparently intended them to be present, for he omitted the initial capital of a number of movements, including the opening '[E]t exultavit', throughout, thereby leaving room for the later addition of coloured initials.

The Magnificats are all simple, largely chordal, with sections that are actually homophonic: some verses have brief imitative openings, often reflecting chant melodic figures.[7] The first of the set, for example, exploits reflections of the contour of the first mode, with incipits rising from f to a', which serves as a reciting tone or as a central pitch around which the melody of the Discantus is constructed. There is a fair amount of text repetition, occasionally extending verses to some twenty breves in length. Rhythms in all voices show a continual concern with the accentuation of the text, and this allows for some cross-rhythms as one voice is set off against the others. This simple style, with little textural variety, contrasts markedly with de Monte's large-scale motets, and no doubt reflects the institution for which the works were composed, as much as the liturgical occasion.

At the end of this fascicle are two further Magnificats, entered as if they were also by de Monte. They appear to have been part of the same consistent copying process, and are treated in an identical manner to that for the first eight works: in other words, an unsuspecting user might believe that here were two otherwise-unknown Magnificats by de Monte. In fact, they are both by Lassus, being that on the chanson *Si par souhait*, in the first mode, and a second-mode parody of the chanson *Il est jour.*[8] At some time in their early history, both works

---

[6]   In Augsburg they appear in Ms. Tonk.Schl.20, copied in 1602 for S. Ulrich and Afra. This is a large manuscript, containing cycles of Magnificats by Morales, Palestrina, de Monte, Cavaccio, Gastoldi and Lechner, as well as single settings by Asola and Tudino. See Clytus Gottwald, *Die Musikhandschriften der Staats- und Stadtbibliothek Augsburg. Handschriftenkataloge der Staats- und Stadtbibliothek Augsburg* (Wiesbaden, 1974), 116-20. The manuscript in the Universitätsbibliothek in Graz (Ms.Mus.12) is earlier, for it has inscribed dates from 1586-1591: it was copied for the Jesuit College in Graz, and contains music by a number of composers, including Herner, Padovano and Gatto, Animuccia and Ruffo, as well as six Magnificats by Lassus, one of which is the second of the two preserved in the new source, and mentioned above.

[7]   De Monte's cycle has been edited in *Philippe de Monte: Opera*, ed. Charles van den Boren and Georges van Doorslaer (Bruges, 1927-39), xii.

[8]   These have been given numbers 37 and 38 respectively in Wolfgang Boetticher, *Orlando di Lasso und seine Zeit 1532-1594* (Wilhelmshaven, 1998), ii, 119-20.

underwent minor revisions, detailed in the modern edition.[9] In each case, one version (which James Erb regards as the earlier)[10] survives only in a source from the Munich court: in each, the new source followed the more widely circulated (and presumably revised) versions. The minor variants in the new source argue, not very convincingly, that it was copied from the versions in the Magnificat volume of Lassus's *Patrocinium Musices*, published in 1587.[11]

The other fascicle is, as I say, in the same hand, for both music and text. The only details of presentation that mark it off from the first are i) the absence of any colour, which is replaced by decorative initial letters, and ii) the style of caption at the beginning of each part. As this caption states, the fascicle contains a set of nine nocturns for the Lamentations of Holy Week, set for six voices by Philippe de Monte. Again only four part-books survive, containing, in addition to the Discantus, Altus and Tenor books carrying the Magnificat section, a Sextus part. Once again the Bassus is missing, as is a Quintus part. The attribution to de Monte, on the first page of each part, uses the abbreviated form of his name also found in the fascicle containing his Magnificats. The appearance of these attributions (see Plate 2, which shows the Tenor voice), seems to suggest that the composer's name was not entered when the music was copied, and when the title of 'Lamentations' and the initials were added. However, it is in the same hand as that of the text underlay, and was probably entered at that time. The underlay is again exceptionally clear, and when taken with the occasional ligatures, allows for virtually no freedom on the part of the singer: when compared with the Magnificat section, repeated phrases of text are more frequently copied out, rather than indicated by the simple repetition sign.

The setting reflects what was by then the conventional textual sequence for a setting of Lamentations, as laid down by the Council of Trent, though in a shortened version. Although all nine nocturnes are present, they often have only three verses from Jeremiah's book, followed by 'Jerusalem convertere'. The sections which have more than three verses still retain a quadripartite division to the polyphony, the sole exception being the addition of the 'Incipit' phrase to

---

[9] Both Magnificats are edited in the *Sämtliche Werke, Neue Reihe*, ed. James Erb, xiv (Kassel, 1986), 126-40. The commentary lists the variants, which are given in appendices to the volume, on pp. 292-4.

[10] See his commentary, cited in the preceding note.

[11] This edition (RISM L974) was published by Adam Berg in Munich. The two Magnificats in the new source are the first two works in Berg's edition.

the first Nocturn. The cycle as set by de Monte contains the following texts:[12]

I   Incipit lamentatio Hieremiæ; Aleph. Quomodo sedet; Beth. Plorans
     ploravit;
     Gimel. Migravit Juda; Hierusalem convertere [Lamentations, i, 1-3]
     Vau. Et egressus; Zain. Recordata est; Heth. Peccatum peccavit;
     Hierusalem convertere [Lamentations, i, 6-8]
     Jod. Manum suum; Caph. Omnis populus ejus; Lamed. O vos omnes;
     Hierusalem convertere [Lamentations, i, 10-12]
II   Heth. Cogitavit Domino; Theth. Defixæ sunt in terra; Caph. Defecerunt;
     Hierusalem convertere [Lamentations, ii, 8-9, 11]
     Lamed. Matribus suis; Mem. Cui comparabo te; Samech. Plauserunt
     super te;
     Hierusalem convertere [Lamentations, ii, 12-13, 15]
     Aleph. Ego vir videns - Aleph. Me minavit - Aleph. Tantum in me; Beth.
     Vetustam fecit - Beth. Aedificavit - Beth. In tenebrosis; Beth. Aedificavit
     in gyro meo;
     Hierusalem convertere [Lamentations, iii, 1-6]
III Heth. Misericordiæ domini - Heth. Nova diluculo - Heth. Pars mea;
     Theth. Bonus est Domius - Theth. Bonum est prestolari - Theth. Bonum
     est viro; Jod. Sedebit solitarius - Jod. Ponet in pulvere - Jod. Dabit
     percutienti;
     Hierusalem convertere [Lamentations, iii, 22-30]
     Aleph. Quomodo obscuratum; Beth. Filli Sion; Gimel. Sed et lamiæ;
     Hierusalem convertere [Lamentations, iv, 1-3]
     Incipit oratio Hieremiæ; Recordare Domino; Pupilli facti sumus;
     Hierusalem convertere [Lamentations, v, 1-7]

It is notable that the Handl setting of Lamentations, scored for four voices,
follows a very different division of the text,[13] and surely represents an earlier
freedom in selecting and ordering the verses of the scriptural text.

---

[12] There are some slight deviations from the text of the Vulgate: in *Beth. Plorans*, the phrase
'spreverunt illam' reads 'spreverunt eam', and the following 'facti sunt ei inimici' omits the
'ei'; in *Vau. Et egressus*, 'non invenientes pascuam' reads 'non invenientes requiem' in the Altus and Tenor parts only; in *Caph. Omnis populus*, 'Vide Domine considera' has an interpolated
'et'; in *Mem. Cui comparabo*, the phrase 'Magna enim velut mare' starts 'Magna est enim'; in
Samech. Plauserunt, the text reads 'Sibilaverunt et moverunt capita', rather than 'caput'; and
in *Pupilli facti sumus*, 'cervicibus minabamur' reads 'cervicibus nostris minabamur'.
[13] This was originally published as the first music in volume 3 of Gallus' *Opus Musicum* (Prague,
1587). Modern editions can be found in *Denkmäler der Tonkunst in Österreich*, 15 (1959),
1-30, and in *Monumenta artis musicae Sloveniae*, 8.

There is virtually no evidence of the chant normally used in polyphonic settings in the later sixteenth century, the 'tonus lamentationum' prescribed by the Council of Trent. Not only is de Monte's cycle not in the 'correct' mode, none of the voices shows more than the most casual occasional reference to chant-like figurations: the sets for Thursday and Friday both cadence on *D* and are effectively in Dorian: Saturday's cycle, however, is strongly focussed on *A*, with a cadence on *E* at the end of the first Nocturne and the other two ending on *A*. It is true that some of the settings of 'Jerusalem convertere' show more use of *B flats* than does the rest of the music, but this is more a result of the harmonic thinking than it is of either the use of chant or the presence of imitation.

The ranges of the extant parts are indicated clearly by the pattern of clefs: the grouping of C_1, C_1, C_3, C_4 clefs is maintained for the nocturns for Thursday and Saturday, while the Friday series of three nocturns has the high clef pattern of G_2, G_2, C_2, C_3. In both combinations, the Sextus was effectively a top voice, overlapping with the Discantus: indeed, it often cadences above it. The missing Quintus was probably a second Altus, lying above the Tenor and the missing Bass part.[14]

A strong indicator for the range of the two missing parts, apart from the texture of the surviving parts, lies in the manner in which the style and tessitura of the music imitates that to be found in the six-voiced works of de Monte's second book of *Madrigali spirituali*, of 1589.[15] These have the same layout of voices (Cantus, Sextus, Altus, Quintus, Tenor and Bassus, in order) and a similar clef combination, regularly $C_1, C_1, C_3, C_3, C_4, F_4$. The top two voices interchange roles: the fourth voice, here the Quintus, has almost the same range as the Altus (occasionally falling a pitch or two lower at the top of the range) and frequently overlapping with it. This voice is therefore pitched higher than the Second Tenor frequently found in madrigalian writing, even though it often serves a similar function. In terms of range and the interlocking of the parts, the four surviving voices of the Lamentations behave in almost exactly the manner of the same voices in the *Madrigali Spirituali*: in addition, they often leave room for a fifth voice overlapping Altus and Tenor. Example 1 gives the first notes of the cycle, with conjectural Quintus and Bassus parts.

---

[14] See for example, the attempted reconstruction of the opening 'Incipit'.
[15] Published by Angelo Gardano in 1589 (RISM M3322): and see Richard Agee, *The Gardano music printing firms, 1569-1611* (Rochester, 1998). A modern edition has been published as *Il Secondo Libro de Madrigali Spirituali a Sei e Sette Voci*, ed. by Piet Nuten (Brussels, 1958).

Example 1. Philippe de Monte, *Incipit Lamentatio Hieremiae* (First Nocturn), opening

This pattern of ranges is only one of a combination of features arguing that the cycle was composed during the 1580s. These are the years in which, as Brian Mann has said, de Monte passed through a 'Crisis in Style' during 1580-1584, and resolved the crisis in the following years.[16] Mann draws attention to de Monte's adoption early in the decade of a high-voiced scoring in six-voiced textures, involving two Discantus parts, and he shows how central was the practice of various reduced scorings reflecting the textual structure. However, Mann suggests that the later years of the decade show an increasing use of small note-values, especially semiminims, reflecting a strong influence of Italian canzonetta style, regardless of the quality of the text.

Not all these features are found in de Monte's liturgical music of the time, no doubt partly because of the music's function within the church's ritual. But, significantly, these new Lamentation settings fit well into Mann's description of music from the mid-1580s. They have many features in common with the *Madrigali Spirituali*: both tend to use fewer seminims, keeping them for short melismas or cadential decoration; both have only occasional moments of imitation, more often opting for a largely chordal structure over a functional bass part;[17] finally, both show a desire to vary the texture very frequently, often after very short subsidiary clauses. The result is a number of different reduced scorings. Among these, the madrigals favour the four-voiced combination of Cantus, Sextus, Altus and Tenor, or the slightly higher one of Cantus, Sextus, Altus and Quintus, alongside the expected grouping of the four lowest voices. All three of these combinations are also used freely in the Lamentation settings: fortunately the first of these combinations survives intact, as in Example 2.

(This example also shows the extent to which de Monte was concerned with the accentuation of the text, as well as the importance of harmonic movement by thirds in the more homophonic sections.)

---

[16] Brian Mann, *The Secular Madrigals of Filippo di Monte, 1521-1603* (Studies in Musicology, 64; Ann Arbor, 1983). The phraseology used here comes from his captions to chapters 4 and 5. The following remarks reflect his analyses in those chapters. Thorsten Hindrichs makes a similar point in his *Philipp de Monte (1521-1603): Komponist, Kapellmeister, Korrespondent* (Göttingen, 2002), where he refers to 'Der *nuovo stile* der 1580er und die 1590er Jahre' (a section of chapter 3), and in his discussion of the seven-voice *Già fu chi m'hebbe cara* in the 11th Book of 5-part madrigals of 1586. See also Robert Lindell, *Studien zu den sechs- und siebenstimmigen Madrigalen von Filippo di Monte* (Ann Arbor, 1980).

[17] The bass line for the *Madrigali Spirituali* survives: in full textures, it is often more linear in its progression from chord to chord, than the functional bass in reduced scorings.

Example 2. Philippe de Monte, *Facti sunt principes* (Thursday, Second Nocturne),
bb. 14-21

In almost all cases, the change of scoring reflects a grammatical structure in the text – de Monte sets off sequences of phrases by scoring them for different combinations of voices, stressing different vocal ranges, the top four contrasted, for example, with a following phrase for the lower four voices (with two singing in both groups). Some sections were certainly scored for only three voices, for only the Tenor survives, to have been joined by the Quintus and Bassus, and other sections seem to be self-sufficient with only the Cantus, Sextus and Altus – another combination popular in the composer's *Madrigali Spirituali*. Example 3 is from the Second Nocturn for Saturday.

Example 3. Philippe de Monte, *Filii Sion* (Saturday, Second Nocturne), bb. 34-40

These reduced sections are used as part of the larger structure, placed to provide a lively sequence of sonorities, and to allow for final tutti sections, in all the nocturnes, and even within the majority of verses. They do not normally seem to reflect the emotional or significative content of the text in any way. There are, it is true, one or two exceptions: after a four-voiced 'Migravit Juda propter afflictionem', all six voices apparently sing 'et multitudinem servi tuis'; after the words 'Matribus suis dixerunt', there is a change of scoring for the reported speech; and the only section in triple metre carries the words 'gaudium universae terrae' – the only moment of rejoicing in the whole text. But these are exceptional: more frequently, the possibilities of 'everyone' or 'multitude' are ignored: and there are no instances of 'musica ficta' used for truly expressive purposes. Although there is some text repetition, it is used less for emphasis than to accommodate a change in scoring.

In this respect, this setting can be distinguished from much writing by northern European composers, with their liking for denser textures: it reflects the newer taste of the Emperor's circles, following the influence of Graz, in lying closer to de Monte's madrigalian writing, especially in the extent to which it was influenced by prevailing madrigalian styles in and reflecting Italy. Like the Magnificats, it is largely syllabic, and harmonically conceived. The Hebrew

Example 4. Philippe de Monte, *Aleph, aleph* (Saturday, Second Nocturne), bb. 1-7

letters provide the principal opportunities for short melismas, often for all the voices; Example 4 shows the surviving voices for the opening of the Second Nocturn for Holy Saturday.

The settings of the verses, however, are largely chordal and even homophonic, although often one or two voices will adopt a slightly different rhythm, and occasionally there is some slight imitation. But harmonic, rather than contrapuntal thinking prevails throughout. In many places, the lowest-sounding voice must have provided the bass or third of a chord, before moving on to serve the same function in the next tactus. This is most obvious in those cases where the four extant parts seem to be self-sufficient. In other cases, this sort of bass movement seems to be the only acceptable solution. The settings are tonally adventurous, in keeping with a possible compositional date of the mid-1580s: accidentals are entered freely, and there are examples of rapid chromatic inflections of pitches, from sharp to natural or vice-versa, alongside juxtapositions such as between *C sharp* and *B flat*.[18] These reflect a pattern in which the underlying harmony moves from one pitch to another a third away, by means of some intervening chord or chords. This pattern is evident in those reduced-scoring sections that have survived intact, and can be extended to other sections, where the missing Bassus would certainly have had to fulfill the same function.

The rhythmic treatment of the text is very supple and advanced, the accentuation is precise, resulting in frequent syncopations and sections with three-minim accentuation. There is no doubt that the text was heard as accentual, with duration acting as the indicator of stress more often than harmonic movement could.

Some of this reconstruction of the texture must be conjectural, since two voice-parts have not survived. But, fortunately, the style of the surviving parts, and in particular the free use of accidentals, allows us to reconstruct at least the harmonic content of these two missing voices and the speed of movement (both verbal and musical) although we can seldom be sure of the actual part-writing.

This newly-discovered Lamentation cycle fills an important gap in de Monte's output. It relates closely to his madrigalian style of the time, with its syllabic setting, its fast declamation of the text, and its fragmented textures. In the same

---

[18] These juxtapositions are only occasionally found in a single vocal line, rather being the result of the chordal movement. They rarely have a dramatic or expressive function.

way, the text-treatment and the harmonic world can be related to his Magnificat settings, although they are for only four voices. At the same time, the cycle is important as a bridge between the cycle by Jacob Handl and the later setting by Karl Luython.[19] That setting has a different series of texts, for only the first and the last lessons have the bulk of their texts in common. Luython's setting is more expansive than the one by de Monte, with longer melismatic initials, followed by conventionally expansive points of imitation. While there are again sections in reduced scoring, the total effect is grander and more spacious than in de Monte's setting.

Philippe de Monte's new set of Lamentations, on the other hand, seems more to belong to that phase of music at the court of Rudolf II, when taste encouraged a lighter style and simpler devices for contrast and 'varietas' – to the time when de Monte himself resolved the stylistic dilemma which that taste imposed on him as a court composer.

---

[19] The setting was published in Luython's *Opus Musicum* (Prague: Nigrinus, 1604: RISM L3118). See Klaus Wolfgang Niemöller, 'Studien zu Carl Luythons *Lamentationes* (Prag 1604)', in *Kirchenmusik in Geschichte und Gegenwart: Festschrift Hans Schmidt zum 65. Geburtstag* (Köln, 1998), 185-196 (including a listing of the verses set on p.191).

HEINRICH ISAAC AND HIS RECENTLY DISCOVERED
MISSA PRESULEM EPHEBEATUM

David J. Burn

INTRODUCTION

The discovery of a major new source is always exciting, especially when it contains previously unknown music, and still more so when that music is attributed to a recognized composer of the first rank. Among the most significant such recent finds for sixteenth-century music was the Czech National Library's acquisition, in 1994, of a large paper choirbook from private hands.[1] The source contains eight four-voice mass-cycles, as well as choral settings of the responses during mass: 1. [Anon., *Missa Domenicalis*]; 2. *MISSA Hercules Dux Ferrarie Josquin*; 3. *Josquin Ave maris stella*; 4. *H: Isac Presulē Ephebeatū*; 5. *Isac Missa Carminum*; 6. *Briml'* [Brumel, *Missa A l'ombre d'ung buissonet*]; 7. [Responses]; 8. [Isaac, *Missa Salva nos*]; 9. [Anon., *Missa Vulnerasti cor meum*]. Important as the new concordances are for five already-known masses, the addition of three entirely new ordinary cycles (Nos. 1, 4, and 9) is spectacular.[2] Two of the new cycles are unattributed: a chant-based cycle that may be determined to be a *Missa Dominicalis*;[3] and a mass in imitation of the motet *Vulnerasti cor meum*, published anonymously in Petrucci's *Motetti della corona* of 1514, but attributed elsewhere (probably incorrectly) to Conrad Rein.[4] The third new mass is identified in the source as the work of Heinrich Isaac. Its model is also identified, as *Presulem ephebeatum*, a rotulum in honour of St. Martin by Petrus Wilhelmi de Grudencz. This potential new addition to Isaac's work-list inevitably also brings questions. Can the testimony of the source be taken at face value? If it can, what are its implications? An edition of the *Missa Presulem ephebeatum* was published by Martin Horyna in 2002 (see footnote 2). This edition includes an admirable introductory study of the source

[1] Praha, Národní knihovna České Republiky, hudební oddělení, MS 59 R 5117 (abbreviated to Pn in what follows).
[2] The concordance for Isaac's *Missa Salva nos* was identified independently by Martin Horyna (Heinrich Isaac, *Missa Presulem ephebeatum*, ed. Martin Horyna (Fontes musicae, 1; Prague, 2002), p. xiii) and Birgit Lodes (reported in Jürgen Heidrich, 'Heinrich Isaacs (?) *Missa Carminum*. Überlieferung – Werkgestalt – Gattungskontext', *Ständige Konferenz Mitteldeutsche Barockmusik,* Jahrbuch 2001, 126 n. 17).
[3] Isaac, *Missa Presulem ephebeatum*, p. xi.
[4] The identification of this model was made independently by Horyna (Isaac, *Missa Presulem ephebeatum*, p. xiii) and Joshua Rifkin (reported in Heidrich, 'Heinrich Isaacs (?) *Missa Carminum*', 126 n. 17). On the motet attribution, see Friedhelm Brusniak, *Conrad Rein (ca. 1475-1522) – Schulmeister und Komponist* (Wiesbaden, 1980), 162-3.

– the only significant discussion of the manuscript to date. The exact dating and provenance of the manuscript are as yet undetermined. From its watermarks, Horyna places it between 1506 and mid-century.[5] The binding is obviously sixteenth-century, but may post-date the copying of the pages themselves, perhaps by several decades.[6] The music is copied by two easily separable scribes.[7] Horyna limits the place of production only to 'an undoubtedly Catholic milieu', but shows that, by the mid-century, the manuscript was in the possession of a literary brotherhood or perhaps a school choir in Ústí nad Labem, near the Bohemian-Saxon border, where it appears to have remained until the early twentieth century.[8] Its eventual resting place may suggest that it was originally made somewhere in that vicinity, perhaps in adjacent Saxony. Horyna's edition includes a short discussion of the *Missa Presulem ephebeatum* itself. Apart from this, the mass has attracted surprisingly little further attention. Nonetheless, doubts over its authenticity have already been expressed by at least one of the edition's reviewers.[9] The present essay aims to offer the first detailed assessment of the work, its attribution, and the context in which the mass may have been produced and used.

THE *MISSA PRESULEM EPHEBEATUM*: MANUSCRIPT CONTEXT

There is not, *a priori*, any reason to distrust Pn on the circumstantial grounds of chronology, geography, and isolation alone. Other undoubtedly authentic pieces, both by other composers of Isaac's generation, and by Isaac himself, survive under similar circumstances. For example, Isaac's motet *Quid retribuam tibi, Leo* survives only in Georg Rhau's 1542 print *Tricinia tum veterum tum recentiorum in arte musica symphonistarum.*[10] Yet more strikingly, at least 40% of the nearly 400 mass-proper pieces published in the *Choralis Constantinus* (1550-55) have no source prior to the print, and many remain *unica* thereafter.[11]

---

[5] Isaac, *Missa Presulem ephebeatum*, p. ix. Pn is mentioned briefly in Lewis Lockwood, 'Petrucci's Edition of Josquin's *Missa Hercules dux Ferrariae*', in Giulio Cattin and Patrizia Dalla Vecchia (eds.), *Venezia 1501: Petrucci e la stampa musicale. Atti del convegno internazionale di studi, Venezia, 10-13 ottobre 2001* (Venice, 2005), 391-5. Lockwood suggests a dating of *c*.1530.

[6] Isaac, *Missa Presulem ephebeatum*, p. vii, ix.

[7] Isaac, *Missa Presulem ephebeatum*, p. vii, xx-xxi.

[8] Isaac, *Missa Presulem ephebeatum*, p. ix, xi. Lockwood, 'Petrucci's Edition', proposes an origin in southern Germany or Austria.

[9] Ryszard J. Wieczorek, in *Muzyka*, 49 (2004), 111-4.

[10] Martin Staehelin, 'Eine musikalische Danksagung von Heinrich Isaac. Zur Diskussion einer Echtheitsfrage', in Peter Niedermüller, Cristina Urchueguía, and Oliver Wiener (eds.), *Quellenstudien und musikalische Analyse. Festschrift Martin Just zum 70. Geburtstag* (Würzberg, 2001), 23-32.

[11] See, most recently, David J. Burn, *The Mass-Proper Cycles of Henricus Isaac: Genesis, Transmission, and Authenticity*, 2 vols. (D.Phil. thesis, University of Oxford, 2002).

An examination of the trustworthiness of Pn should begin with an examination of the source in its own terms.

Wherever precisely the manuscript was produced, the concordance for the *Missa Salva nos* shows that it was in a region where authentic music by Isaac continued to circulate. Nonetheless, closer consideration of Pn's attributions looks somewhat unpromising: three of the masses are unattributed, including one by Isaac, and, of those that are attributed, the *Missa Carminum*, again said to be Isaac's, could well be wrong.[12] This suggests no privileged knowledge of Isaac's work. However, a logic does emerge when the choirbook's physical structure and scribal division are taken into account. Structurally, the source can be divided into four units:[13] i) The *Missa Dominicalis*, occupying its own set of gatherings, and separated from the masses that follow by blank leaves; ii) The next five masses (and the Responses), copied as a unit, with no intervening blank pages; iii) *Salva nos*, occupying its own set of gatherings; and iv) *Vulnerasti cor meum*, again occupying its own set of gatherings. Units (i) and (ii) were copied by one scribe, and units (iii) and (iv) were copied by a different scribe. As mentioned above, although the binding is clearly original, it may not necessarily be exactly contemporary with the copying of the fascicles themselves. Accordingly, it is open to question not only whether the four units were ever intended to form a coherent choirbook, but also whether the two scribes worked at the same time, or in the same place. All of the manuscript's attributions are found in its second unit, and, what is more, every mass in this second unit is attributed. The impression of comprehensivity, and also of accuracy, is supported not only by the undoubtedly correct Josquin and Brumel attributions, but also, paradoxically, by that for the *Missa Carminum*. Isaac's name was attached to this piece from its earliest surviving source.[14] Although the *Missa Carminum* as a whole is probably not by Isaac, some of the mass-sections are by him, and the attribution is thus not entirely wrong, nor was it made arbitrarily. That it appears in Pn can be seen to reflect faithful transmission from the exemplar from which Pn was copied.[15] In this light, it seems safe to claim that the *Missa Presulem* attribution too represents an accurate transmission, at least as far as the Pn scribe was concerned. This still leaves open the question of whether Isaac's name was mistakenly attached to the piece at some earlier stage. The absence of other sources makes this undeterminable

---

[12] Heidrich, 'Heinrich Isaacs (?) *Missa Carminum*'.
[13] Isaac, *Missa Presulem ephebeatum*, p. xx.
[14] Heidrich, 'Heinrich Isaacs (?) *Missa Carminum*', 125.
[15] Heidrich, 'Heinrich Isaacs (?) *Missa Carminum*', 125-6, admits that the place of Pn in the stemma of the *Missa Carminum* is very unclear, but suggests (unconvincingly) that it may be dependent on Georg Rhau's 1541 *Opus decem missarum*.

on transmissional grounds, and there is as yet no further external evidence that can be brought to bear on the issue. No other mass-setting of *Presulem* is otherwise documented either anonymously or attributed to anyone else. Nor can the *Missa Presulem ephebeatum* be matched to any of Isaac's known lost masses.[16] The only remaining choice is to examine the mass itself.

The *Missa Presulem ephebeatum*: structure and style

A logical place to begin examining the mass is through its relationship with the pre-existent material on which it is modelled. Wilhelmi's piece exists in three formats: i) A single melodic line, to be sung as a four-part round; ii) A polytextual motet in four separate voice-parts; iii) As format (ii), with the contrafact text Pangat nostra/Dulcisona/Sanctissimi/Chorus noster.[17] The title of the mass in Pn shows that the model was either format (i) or (ii). The mass does not draw on the model polyphonically, but uses only the first section of the format (i) melody, up to the entry of the second voice.[18] This melody, and its distribution through the mass, are set out in Ex. 1 and Table 1.

Example 1. Petrus Wilhelmi de Grudencz, *Presulem ephebeatum*, first section

---

[16] Martin Picker, *Heinrich Isaac: A Guide to Research* (New York, 1991), 42-3; Martin Staehelin, *Die Messen Heinrich Isaacs*, 3 vols. (Bern and Stuttgart, 1977), i, 44-7.

[17] Petrus Wilhelmi de Grudencz, Magister Cracoviensis, *Opera Musica*, ed. Jaromír Černy (Kraków, 1993), 35-6, 73-8, 119-20, 138-9.

[18] Alternatively, it uses the entirety of the voice always notated first in format (ii).

Immediately striking is the almost constant presence of the cantus firmus throughout the mass. Not only is no section cantus-firmus free, but also, within each section, there are very few moments when it is not sounding in one or several of the vocal lines. Such dominance is rare among mass-compositions as a whole among Isaac's generation. However, it is a feature of two undisputed Isaac masses, both also settings of non-chant-derived, but monophonically treated, cantus firmi. In the *Missa Comment peut avoir joye*, the elaboration is freely decorative. In the *Missa Une musque de Biscaye*, the cantus firmus is altered little, and keeps an invariant presence in the uppermost voice.[19] Two further restrictions are also striking, yet have parallels in Isaac's masses. First, the mass is scored almost exclusively in four voices. Only one section differs from this norm: in the second Agnus Dei, the Tenor is silent. Isaac's *Missa Misericordias Domini* is still more extreme, in applying a full four-voiced texture throughout its entirety. Second, the mass is mensurally restricted entirely to *tempus imperfectum diminutum*. This is found also in the *Missa Comment*

Section	Model Unit and Place in mass
Kyrie I (bb. 1-7)	**1**: B. (1-4) → T. (4-7)
Christe (bb. 8-15)	**2**: B. (8-12) → T. (11-5)
Kyrie II (bb. 16-25)	**3**: B. (16-8) → T. (17-9); B. (20-2) → T. (22-5)
Et in terra pax (bb. 1-39)	**4**: B. (1-4) → T. (3-6); **5**: B. (8-11) → T. (11-4); **6=3**: B. (15-8) → T. (17-20); **4**: B. (20-4) → T. (23-7); **5**: B. (28-31) → T. (31-4); **6**: B. (34-7) → T. (36-9)
Qui tollis (bb. 40-85)	**7**: B. (41-4) → T. (44-9); **8**: B. (47-51) → T. (51-5); **9**: B. (56-9) → T. (58-61); **10**: B. (62-5) → T. (65-8); **11+12**: B. (69-74) → T. (72-6); **12**: D. (76-8, 79-81, 82, 83-4)
Patrem (bb. 1-73)	**1**: D. (1-6) → T. (5-9); **2**: A. (9-13) [→ B. (10-2)] → T. (12-6) → B. (13-6); **3**: D. (16-9) → T. (17-20); **4**: D. (20-4) → T. (24-8); **5**: D. (27-30) → T. (30-3); **6**: D. (33-6) → T. (36-9); **7**: A. (39-42) → T. (41-4); **8**: D. (45-8) → T. (46-8); **9**: T. (49-52) → D. (52-5); **10**: T. (56-60) → D. (59-63); **11+12**: T. (63-9) → D. (64-9); **10=9=3**: T. (69-73)
Et resurrexit (bb. 74-105)	**4**: T. (74-8) → D. (78-82); **5**: T. (81-4) → D. (84-6); **6**: T. (87-90) → D. (90-3); **5**: T. (93-8); **6**: B. (97-9) → T. (98-101) → D. (100-3)
Qui cum patre (bb. 106-45)	**7**: A. (106-8) → T. (108-12); **8**: T. (114-7); **9**: B. (119-22) → T. (120-3); **10**: T. (124-8); **11+12**: B. (128-33) → T. (131-5)
Sanctus (bb. 1-36)	**1**: B. (1-4) → T. (4-8); **2**: B. (8-12) → T. (13-7); **3**: B. (17-9) → T. (19-23); **4**: T. (23-8); **5**: T. (29-32); **6=5=1**: T. (33-6)
Pleni-Osanna (bb. 37-67)	**1**: B. (37-41); **3=9**: B. (43-7) [→ A. (47-9)] → T. (48-52); **10**: D. (54-58); **11+12**: T. (58-63) → D. (59-67)
Benedictus (bb. 68-102)	**4**: T. (70-5); **5**: T. (85-8) → D. (85-9); **9**: T. (88-92); **10**: T. (95-8)
Osanna (II) (bb. 103-24)	**10**: B. (103-7) → T. (105-10); **11+12**: B. (110-5) → T. (113-7)
Agnus Dei I (bb. 1-19)	**1**: B. (1-4) → T. (4-7); **2**:D. (7-12) → T. (8-14); **3=6**: B. (15-7) → T. (17-19)
Agnus Dei II (bb. 20-51)	**7**: A. (20-3) → D. (24-7); **9**: A. (28-31) → D. (30-3); **9=3**: A. (33-5); **5**: D. (36-41); **9**: A (42-6) → D. (43-6) → B. (45-8) → A. (47-51) → D. (48-51)

Table 1. Cantus firmus distribution in the *Missa Presulem ephebeatum*

---

[19] For model distributions in Isaac's masses, see Staehelin, *Die Messen*, iii, 23-106.

peut avoir joye, the *Missa 't Meiskin was jonck*, and the *Missa Une musque de Biscaye*. The cantus firmus is primarily carried in the Tenor, though imitative or second statements of cantus firmus units are very frequent. At the start of the mass, this is rigorously methodical. Every phrase is heard first in the Bass, and then in the Tenor. The pattern is only broken at the end of the Gloria, where the material migrates to the Discantus, and is subject to fourfold re-iteration. The divergence from the preceding norm can be heard as a signal of imminent closure, the gesture reinforced by a syllabic, homophonic texture unlike anything previously heard. The Credo is less systematic in its distribution of material, though, like the previous movements, it almost invariably states each cantus firmus unit twice, except in its last section. The end of the movement is again clearly signalled, by a rare absolute departure from the model, and by the saturation of the texture for the final ten bars by a small motivic cell that appears at least ten times. Similar patterns remain observable in subsequent movements. Dialogic treatment is a typical structural device of Isaac's, as is the breaking of previously established patterns for closure, not only in mass-ordinaries, but also in other genres (see e.g. *Choralis Constantinus* III/3, Introit 5, *Sapientiam sanctorum*).[20] Occasionally, the cantus firmus material is heard simultaneously in a proportional relationship in another voice. The opening of Kyrie II, the opening of the second Osanna, and Agnus Dei I (b. 15) each simultaneously sound the cantus firmus in halved values against its main statement. This was a favourite device of Isaac's, for which many parallel examples could be cited.[21] Whether cantus firmus-derived, or free, all the voices of the *Missa Presulem* show a strong motivic consistency. While the typical free-voice patterns are largely common property that cannot be said to be distinctive of any single individual, they do pin the work down to Isaac's generation, and their appearance within Isaac's own works further bolsters the plausibility of his authorship. The opening passages of the two sections that do not begin immediately with the cantus firmus can suffice as examples. A figure similar to that which opens the 'Qui tollis' can be found at the beginning of the 'Et incarnatus' of the *Missa Quant j'ay au cueur*. An exact match for the two upper voices that begin the Benedictus can be found at the start of the Benedictus of the *Missa 't Meiskin was jonck*.

---

[20] Heinrich Isaac, *Choralis Constantinus III*, ed. Louise Cuyler (Ann Arbor, 1950), 103-6.
[21] E.g. the openings of the final three sections of the sequence for Epiphany; see Heinrich Isaac, *Choralis Constantinus II*, ed. Anton von Webern (Denkmäler der Tonkunst in Österreich, 16/i; Vienna, 1909), 22-3.

The *Missa Presulem* is conceived on a very compact scale. This is offset at the beginning by using the model to bind the Kyrie and the Gloria together into a larger unit: the two are heard in immediate succession in the liturgy, and continuity is created by distributing the first complete presentation of the cantus firmus across both movements. This novel idea is not found in any other Isaac mass. When the succession of individual units does not simply follow the model, the cantus firmus distribution is nonetheless not arbitrary. Rather, the appearance of recurrent material in the model is fascinatingly exploited to allow the separate units to be reordered in logical, but surprising ways. The first departure from the straightforward ordering of the model occurs in the 'Et in terra pax': Unit 4 follows Unit 6 because of the latter's near-identity with Unit 3. The succession for the rest of the movement is as expected. However, that Units 3 and 6 share their near-identity also with Unit 9 is highlighted, on the appearance of the latter, by a repetition of the entire contrapuntal fabric of the ambiguous Unit 6/3 moment (bb. 15/2-20 = bb. 56/2-61). That this is not laziness or economy, but a deliberate strategy to draw attention to the relationship is evident from the almost total lack of plain repetition elsewhere in the mass. The end of the 'Patrem omnipotentem' is similar, though more complex: Unit 12 becomes the first three notes of Unit 10, the end of which is then treated as the beginning of Unit 9. The latter unit closes the section. That this is not an over-interpretation of a generic cadential procedure is confirmed by another rare example of plain contrapuntal repetition at the explicit appearance of Unit 9 later in the Credo (bb. 70-3 = bb. 120-3). The continuation with the 'Et resurrexit' adds a final complication. In beginning with Unit 4, the same equivalence between Units 9 and 3 to which attention was drawn in the 'Et in terra pax' is once again exploited. Similar procedures explain the succession of model units in and between all of the remaining sections of the mass. The process behind them all may have been inspired by the potentially endlessly circling form of the model.[22] Although in that sense, the *Missa Presulem* is sui generis, such an interest in drawing attention to the motivic relationships within borrowed material is widespread throughout Isaac's music. It is a central ingredient in his compositional thinking.[23]

---

[22] This applies to all formats: the motet versions cue a return to the beginning at the end of each voice-part.

[23] A simple, but typical example is given in Burn, 'Heinrich Isaac, *Choralis Constantinus*: Introit for Mary Magdalen', in Jos Leussink and Jan Nuchelmans (eds.), *Handboek van de Koormuziek* (in press).

One last indicator of Isaac's authorship can be found in the treatment of dissonance. The manuscript offers a largely faultless redaction of the mass.[24] Only two moments cause concern. The first, in the Credo, b. 40, suggests a miswritten pitch in the source. The obvious emendation would be to replace the Discantus *f'* with an *e'*. The second occurs in the Sanctus, b. 90/2, where the Altus arrives on a sixth over the Bass, while the Tenor simultaneously arrives on a fifth. The simplest emendation here would be to alter the Tenor rhythm, dotting the *bb* and halving the *c'*. These questionable moments aside, the dissonance practice of the *Missa Presulem* shows a feature isolated by Martin Staehelin as particularly distinctive of Isaac in comparison to his contemporaries. In this pattern, the cadential tenor-clausula is a three-note form, rising and falling by a second, its initial pitch creating a suspended dissonance and resolution in one of the other voices.[25] This pattern is found numerous times throughout the *Missa Presulem* (e.g. Kyrie, bb. 14-5; Credo, bb. 144-5; Sanctus, bb. 3-4, 6-7, 35-6, 83-4, 122-4). Despite its compact scale, the *Missa Presulem* is clearly the work of a skilled composer. Its musical language fits squarely into Isaac's generation of composers. Although the precise constellation of features is found in no other single work of Isaac, most, including those that are very rare, can be paralleled individually. Thus, the *Missa Presulem* also fits plausibly within his output. Given that the attribution is credible in terms of manuscript transmission and in stylistic terms, it follows to ask where it may be placed within Isaac's career, and why it might have been written.

Context

Isaac's career can be split into three sections: an early (and undocumented) part, from his birth to *c.*1484, in his homeland in the Low Countries; employment in Florence from *c.*1485 to 1493; and employment as 'Hofkomponist' by Emperor Maximilian I from *c.*1496 until his death in 1517.[26] The appearance of the *Missa Presulem ephebeatum* in a central-European source has no implications for where or for whom Isaac may have originally composed it, as is shown by the Pn concordance for the *Missa Salva nos*, which Isaac had

---

[24] Errors listed in Isaac, *Missa Presulem ephebatum*, p. xix. The Credo, Altus, b. 115/1, does not read *e*, but *d'* (correctly); the Altus, b. 117/1, reads *d*, which Horyna has tacitly corrected to *e*. The wrong pitch in the Agnus Dei, b. 34/3, is in the Bassus. An unsignalled correction is made in the Sanctus, Altus, b. 120: the original note-values are semibreve-minim-semibreve.

[25] *Die Messen*, iii, 173.

[26] Comprehensive documentary overview in Staehelin, *Die Messen*, ii, 10-88. For new documents placing Isaac in Florence – perhaps continually – from 1502-1505, see Giovanni Zanovello, *Heinrich Isaac, the Mass* Misericordias Domini, *and Music in Late-Fifteenth-Century Florence* (Ph.D. thesis, Princeton University, 2005), 50ff.

composed in Florence by *c.*1492.[27] However, the choice of a composition by Petrus Wilhelmi as a model is sufficient to rule out the possibility that Isaac composed the mass for an Italian patron or an Italian institution. *Presulem*, composed perhaps in the 1430s, survives in numerous sources up to the mid-sixteenth century, testifying to its continued popularity throughout Isaac's lifetime.[28] All sources, however, are regionally confined, to Bohemia, Saxony, and Austria. Furthermore, new documentary evidence, naming Wilhelmi as 'cappellanus' to Maximilian's father Emperor Frederick III in 1452, proves his direct connection to the Imperial court.[29] Isaac could thus have become acquainted with *Presulem* as a piece by a distinguished predecessor at the same institution at which he was also employed post-1496.

Despite the fact that Isaac's mass-output outstrips that of any of his contemporaries in quantity, this limitation of the *Missa Presulem* to an Imperial context, however broad, lends the mass an unusual significance among his ordinary settings. Although the chronology of Isaac's masses is uncertain in its details, the masses that Isaac is thought to have produced after entering the service of Emperor Maximilian in 1496 are almost exclusively of an 'alternatim' type, based on chant.[30] Of Isaac's nearly twenty through-composed mass-settings, only a few may be reckoned to post-date 1496: *'t Meiskin was jonck*, *Misericordias Domini*, *La mi la sol* (*O praeclara*), *Wohlauff, gut Gsell* (*Comment peut avoir joye*) à6, and *Virgo prudentissima*.[31] Of these, the dating of *'t Meiskin* is unclear. Staehelin places it in the 1490s before Isaac joined Imperial service, but Reinhard Strohm proposed that it may possibly date

---

[27] Staehelin, *Die Messen*, iii, 28-33.

[28] Wilhelmi, *Opera Musica*, 32 (dating), 36-7 and 138-9 (sources). For a further, fragmentary source, see Joachim Lüdke, *Kleinüberlieferung mehrstimmiger Musik vor 1550 im deutschen Sprachgebiet VI: Fragmente und versprengte Überlieferung des 15. und 16. Jahrhunderts im nördlichen und westlichen Deutschland*, Nachrichten der Akademie der Wissenschaften zu Göttingen I. Philologisch-historische Klasse (2002/4), 9-17.

[29] Martin Staehelin, *Kleinüberlieferung mehrstimmiger Musik vor 1550 im deutschen Sprachgebiet III: Neues zu Werk und Leben von Petrus Wilhelmi. Fragmente des mittleren 15. Jahrhunderts mit Mensuralmusik im Nachlaß von Friedrich Ludwig*, Nachrichten der Akademie der Wissenschaften in Göttingen, I. Philologisch-historische Klasse (2001/2); Martin Staehelin, 'Uwagi o wzajemnych związkach biografii, twórczości i dokumentacji dzieł Piotra Wilhelmiego z Grudziądza' ['Petrus Wilhelmi de Grudencz: Notes on the Coherence of his Biography, his Work, and its Transmission'], *Muzyka*, 49 (2004), 9-19.

[30] See Staehelin, *Die Messen*, iii, 107-51. Almost all can be assumed to have been composed expressly for the Imperial chapel. However, on the likelihood that the music commissioned from Isaac by the authorities at Constance cathedral in 1508 included 'alternatim' ordinary settings along with propers, see Burn, 'What did Isaac Write for Constance?', *Journal of Musicology*, 20 (2003), 45-72.

[31] Strictly speaking, the four-voice *Missa Ferialis*, certainly composed for Imperial usage, is also through-composed in that it does not require 'alternatim' performance.

from the beginning of the sixteenth century.[32] *Misericordias domini* and *La mi la sol* both appear to be post-1496, but nonetheless stem from an Italian context. The former, possibly based on a lauda-contrafactum of the frottola *In focho in focho*, may have been intended for the Florentine confraternity of St. Barbara, while the latter, derived from a piece that Isaac composed in competition for a job at Ferrara in 1502, is unlikely, for that reason, to have subsequently been offered to Maximilian.[33] *Wohlauff, gut Gsell* is a six-voice reworking of the much earlier four-voice *Missa Comment peut avoir joye*.[34] This leaves *Virgo prudentissima* as the only surviving through-composed mass that may be reckoned with any certainty to have been composed for usage in Imperial lands. Following a proposal of Staehelin, this mass is commonly supposed to have been the 'messe...de l'assomption' that Antoine de Lalaing reports as performed at the meeting between Maximilian and his son Philip the Fair in Innsbruck in September 1503.[35] A hint, to place alongside that given by the *Missa Presulem*, that the full extent of Isaac's Imperial mass-compositional activities may have been broader than the current picture suggests, can be found in the fragmentary source Budapest, Országos Széchényi Könyvtár, MS Bártfa 20, a set of partbooks for which only the Discantus and Tenor survive. This set contains an otherwise unknown 'officium H. Isaac', based on an as-yet unidentified cantus firmus that is probably a German song.[36] The source is late – estimates vary as to its precise dating, but none places it earlier than the second half of the sixteenth century – and for that reason, along with the difficulty of a full assessment from what survives, this mass is currently classed amongst Isaac's doubtful works. Nonetheless, Isaac's authorship seems entirely plausible in stylistic terms, in so far as they may be determined.[37]

The linking of the composers of both the *Missa Presulem* and its model to the Imperial court need not imply that the mass itself was composed for that institution. Nonetheless, it is the most obvious possibility, and there is no compelling evidence against it. However, the mass's differences from the other cycles that Isaac is known to have written for that institution suggest that if this was so, then the mass was not composed for the routine chapel liturgy. The mass is modelled on a piece in honour of St. Martin, but this does not mean

---

[32] Staehelin, *Die Messen*, iii, 103; Reinhard Strohm and Emma Kempson, 'Isaac, Henricus', *New Grove II*, §2(i).

[33] Zanovello, *Heinrich Isaac, the Mass* Misericordias Domini, *and Music in Late-Fifteenth-Century Florence*, 146-8; Staehelin, *Die Messen*, iii, 63-7.

[34] Staehelin, *Die Messen*, iii, 45-54; Thomas Noblitt, '*Contrafacta* in Isaac's Missae *Wohlauf, Gesell, von Hinnen*', *Acta Musicologica*, 46 (1974), 208-16.

[35] Staehelin, *Die Messen*, ii, 59-60.

[36] Staehelin, *Die Messen*, iii, 181-2.

[37] Staehelin, *Die Messen*, iii, 182.

that the mass was composed for the celebration of his feast-day (November 13th). Though it could have been used on that occasion, within the Imperial court chapel repertory, the comprehensive set of 'alternatim' ordinaries would have satisfactorily covered this requirement: the feast would have needed ordinaries 'de confessoribus', and appropriate four- and five-voice settings by Isaac survive. Nor, given the mass's scale, would it seem to be an appropriate composition for lavish events of state such as may have provided the setting for *Virgo prudentissima*. Rather, the mass and its model suggest that its most likely context was votive: a by-no-means uncommon situation with St. Martin, as one of the most popular saints of the late Middle Ages. Such a votive mass may have taken place within the Imperial court, though other venues must also be considered.

Two further dealings between Isaac and patrons in the Empire seem unlikely to have provided the trigger for the composition of the *Missa Presulem*. First, between 1497 and 1499 Isaac had connections with Elector Frederick the Wise of Saxony.[38] Documents show a gift of three ells of cloth, as well as the receipt of clothes, though the nature of the services Isaac provided remains unstated. They could have included performing, training, and copying existing music, but new composition does not seem to have played a role. Frederick's chapel choirbooks do not survive in their entirety.[39] However, none of Isaac's known music in those that do survive seems to have been composed specifically for him. Second, the *Missa Presulem* would not have been an appropriate part of the music that Isaac was commissioned to compose by Constance cathedral in 1508. This is not because it is an ordinary, but because it is votive. Two remaining musical and institutional contacts are more promising. From 1506 (or later), Isaac became a member of the lay-brotherhood at the Augustinian abbey of Neustift (Novacella) in Brixen. Beyond a single citation in a membership list, nothing further is known of Isaac's involvement.[40] The possibility that it could have included musical activities, as may have been the case with the Florentine confraternity of St. Barbara in Florence, is entirely plausible. It is particularly tempting to try to associate the *Missa Presulem* with a lay-brotherhood such as this because the sources of the *Presulem* original frequently stem from a similar context. Another indication of the less official circumstances under which Isaac

---

[38] Staehelin, *Die Messen*, ii, 48-50; Jürgen Heidrich, *Die deutschen Chorbücher aus der Hofkapelle Friedrichs des Weisen. Ein Beitrag zur mitteldeutschen geistlichen Musikpraxis um 1500* (Baden-Baden, 1993).

[39] There are obvious gaps, for example, in the mass-propers; see Kathryn Duffy, *The Jena Choirbooks: Music and Liturgy at the Castle Church in Wittenberg under Frederick the Wise, Elector of Saxony*, 5 vols (Ph.D. diss, University of Chicago, 1995), i, 5-6.

[40] Staehelin, *Die Messen*, ii, 63-4.

produced music is revealed by the heading attached to an intabulation of his motet *Sub tuum praesidium* in the Fridolin Sicher Organ Tablature: 'Hainricus Isaac. Ex petit[i]one Magistri Martini Vogelmayer Organistae tunc temporis Constancie'.[41] Could Isaac have composed the *Missa Presulem* at the request of a friend or (musician) colleague with particular attachment either to St. Martin, or to the *Presulem* melody? Or even for Vogelmaier himself, who shares a name with the saint that *Presulem* honours? The possibility is as tantalising as it is elusive.

CONCLUSION

Despite some singular features, there seems to be no compelling reason to doubt the authenticity of the *Missa Presulem ephebeatum* as a work of Isaac's, either on source grounds, or in stylistic terms. If that is accepted, the mass is valuable not only as an attractive addition to Isaac's output. It contributes also to expanding his stylistic profile, his treatment of borrowed material, and his range of musical reference. More far-reachingly, as a witness to Isaac's through-composed mass style in the first (or second?) decade of the sixteenth century, the *Missa Presulem* may provide a welcome landmark in re-assessing the chronology of the remainder of his masses. Only hypotheses can currently be offered about the precise context in which this mass was composed. However, it is a new and valuable challenge in itself to consider these contexts among Isaac's working relationships in Imperial territories in conjunction with an actual piece of music.

[41] Staehelin, *Die Messen*, ii, 61.

Josquin in the Sources of Spain.
An Evaluation of Two Unique Attributions

Willem Elders

Since Josquin des Prez spent a large part of his life in France – supposedly, he was born in the county of Vermandois (Picardy) – and, as far as we know, never set foot on Spanish or German soil, one would expect to find his musical legacy better represented in his homeland than in these two neighbouring countries.[1] The recension of his works and their sources that has been undertaken in the context of the new edition of his complete works (NJE), shows that fate has decided otherwise. Since however in Spain, unlike France, Germany, and Italy, no printed editions of music in mensural notation with works by Josquin have been issued, this contribution can pay attention to the printed Spanish tablature books only.

As for the amount of the manuscript sources in itself, the numbers that can be given for France and Spain respectively are telling. For France, the count is not more than three manuscripts that are kept in Cambrai, and eight in Paris. Leaving apart works that are considered to be spurious, the manuscript sources together transmit five Mass settings and one Mass movement, ten motets, and nine secular works, some of them doubtful or incomplete. Should we suppose a loss of sources in France because of wars and fire? Or has the anti-clerical movement during the French Revolution sealed the fate of church and monastic libraries in which musical books were kept? In any event, even in the case of printed editions of which usually some hundreds of copies were produced, almost nothing has come down to us. For example, of the most famous French edition of the composer's works, Le Roy & Ballard's *Josquini Pratensis, musici praestantissimi, moduli* [motets] ... *et in 4, 5, et 6 voces distincti. Liber primus*, published at Paris in 1555 in four individual partbooks, only one partbook is preserved in France.[2]

---

[1] The question of Josquin's nationality is discussed by Paul A. Merkley and Lora L.M. Merkley in *Music and Patronage in the Sforza Court* (Turnhout, 1999), 462: 'The territory that included Condé was referred to as part of Picardy in some records and part of Hainaut in others at roughly the same time. As for Josquin, his name was French and it seems that he spoke that language. His early court service was most probably as a singer in the court of René of Anjou'.

[2] No complete copies of this edition are known. An Altus partbook is owned by the Bibliothèque Nationale, copies of the Altus and Bassus partbooks by the Chapter Library at Saragossa in Spain.

As is shown in Table 1, the picture in Spain is rather different. Of the listed works, only the following are preserved in one or two of the French manuscripts as well: 6.2, 6.3, 11.2, 14.6, 19.13, 20.7, 23.13, and *28.18. Preserved in France and not in Spain are 18.4 (*Misericordias domini*), 21.8 (*O bone et dulcis domine*), and 23.2 (*Alma redemptoris mater / Ave regina*), all in ParisBNN 1817.

Titles are preceded by their NJE number; works with a number marked by an asterisk may not be by Josquin. Manuscripts are identified by their call numbers as found in the *Census-Catalogue of Manuscript Sources of Polyphonic Music 1400-1550*, 5 vols. (American Institute of Musicology, 1979-1988). The sigla given below refer to the following cities and libraries:

BarcBC	Barcelona, Biblioteca Central
BarcOC	Barcelona, Biblioteca de L'Orfeó Català
SaraP	Saragossa, Iglesie Metropolitana de la Virgen del Pilar
SegC	Segovia, Archivo Capitular de la Catedral
SevBC	Seville, Catedral Metropolitana, Biblioteca del Core
TarazC	Tarazona, Archivo Capitular de la Catedral
ToleBC	Toledo, Biblioteca Capitular de la Catedral Metropolitana
ToleF	Toledo, Catedral, Obra y Fabrica
VallaC	Valladolid, Catedral Metropolitana

3.1	Missa Ave maris stella	ToleBC 9
3.3	Missa De beata virgine	BarcBC 454; ToleBC 16; ToleF 23
4.2	Missa Gaudeamus	ToleBC 27
4.3	Missa Pange lingua	ToleBC 16
6.2	Missa L'homme armé sexti toni	SegC s.s.; VatC 234
6.3	Missa L'homme armé super voces musicales	BarcOC 5; ToleBC 9; ToleBC 21
8.1	Missa Faysant regretz	ToleBC 9
8.2	Missa Fortuna desperata	BarcOC 5
9.1	Missa Malheur me bat	ToleBC 9
11.1	Missa Hercules Dux Ferrarie	BarcBC 681; ToleBC 27
11.2	Missa La sol fa re mi	ToleBC 19
12.2	Missa Sine nomine	ToleBC 9
14.6	Ecce tu pulchra es	SevBC 1
16.10	Domine, non secundum peccata	BarcOC 5
17.4	In exitu Israel de Egypto	ToleF 23
18.7	Qui habitat in adjutorio altissimi	ToleF 23
19.5	In illo tempore assumpsit Jesus	ToleBC 13
19.8	In principio erat Verbum	ToleBC 17; ToleF 23
19.13	Liber generationis Jesu Christi	ToleF 23

*20.2	Magnificat tertii toni (Verses 1-8)	SegC s.s.
20.7	Missus est Gabriel angelus	ToleBC 10
20.9	Pater noster - Ave Maria	ToleBC 18; ToleF 23; VallaC 15
	Ave Maria only	SaraP 17; SevBC 1; VallaC 5
23.6	Ave Maria	BarcBC 454; BarcOC 5; SegC s.s
23.11	Ave nobilissima creatura	ToleBC 13
23.13	Benedicta es, celorum regina	SevBC 1; TarazC 8; ToleBC 18; ToleF 23; VallaC 17
24.4	Inviolata, integra et casta es	BarcBC 681; SevBC 1; ToleBC 10
24.11	Preter rerum seriem	SevBC 1; TarazC 8; ToleF 23
25.5	Salve regina	BarcBC 681; BarcOC 7; SaraP 17; SevBC 1
25.9	Stabat mater	ToleBC 10; VallaC 16; VallaC 17
25.14	Vultum tuum deprecabuntur	BarcBC 454; SegC s.s.
26.1	Absolve, quesumus, domine	ToleBC 21
*27.11	Fortuna desperata	SegC s.s.
*27.13	Helas madame	SevC 5-I-43
*27.24	Madame helas	SevC 5-I-43
*27.29	O Venus bant	SevC 5-I-43
27.33	Que vous madame	SegC s.s.
*28.18	In te, domine, speravi	MadP 1335

Table 1. Works attributed to Josquin, preserved in manuscripts in Spain

On the basis of the data presented in Table 1, the following preliminary conclusions can be drawn:

a) With ten large choirbooks, Toledo appears to have by far the greatest importance for the preservation of Josquin's music in Spain, followed by Barcelona and Valladolid, each having four manuscripts.

b) The compositions based on texts of the Ordinary of the Mass and other liturgical or paraliturgical texts are more numerous than settings based on a secular text. Among Josquin's motets, those in honour of the Holy Virgin were more widely spread than the other ones.[3]

c) Josquin's music was performed not only in the context of the celebration of the liturgy, but made part of the more intimate home life as well. This is not only indicated by the manuscripts SegS s.s. and SevBC 5-I-43, but also by the arrangements for plucked and keyboard instruments of numerous works, printed in Spanish tablature books.[4]

---

[3] For example, three of the six sources for *Pater noster - Ave Maria*, transmit the *secunda pars* only.
[4] For the sources see Table 2.

Narvaez	*Los seys libros del Delphin de musica ... para tañer vihuela* (Valladolid: D. H. De Cordova, 1538)
Vaena	*Libro de musica de vihuela ... Arte nouamente inuentada pera aprender a tanger* (Lisbon: G. Galharde, 1540)
Mudarra	*Tres libros de musica en cifras para vihuela ...* (Seville: J. de Leon, 1546)
Valderrábano	*Libro de musica de vihuela, intitulado Silva de sirenas ...* (Valladolid: F. Fernandez de Cordova, 1547)
Pisador	*Libro de musica de vihuela ...* (Salamanca: D. Pisador, 1552)
Fuenllana	*Libro de musica para vihuela, intitulado Orphenica lyra* (Seville: M. de Montesdoca, 1554)
Venegas	*Libro de cifra nueva para tecla, harpa, y vihuela* (Alcala: J. de Brocar, 1557)
Cabeçon	*Obras de musica para tecla arpa y vihuela* (Madrid: F. Sanchez, 1578)

Table 2. Spanish tablature books containing works attributed to Josquin

However, even though Josquin, as Robert Stevenson rightly has observed, 'completely captivated Spain (...) from the moment Petrucci's prints first began circulating abroad',[5] it should be obvious that the socio-historical value of the Spanish sources needs not to be on par with their musico-textual value, that is, with their reliability vis-à-vis the reconstruction of the hypothetical archetype of Josquin's individual works. The aim of the present contribution is therefore to give, on the basis of the new critical edition of his works, more insight into the quality of the Spanish manuscripts.

Four out of the nineteen motets that, in addition to the sources from other countries, are transmitted in one or two of the above listed Spanish manuscripts, present a version that has been chosen as the basis for their edition in the NJE: *In exitu Israel de Egypto* (NJE 17.4), *Qui habitat in adjutorio altissimi* (NJE 18.7), *In illo tempore assumpsit Jesus* (NJE 19.5), and *In principio erat Verbum* (NJE 19.8). The first two of these motets will be edited after ToleF 23 (1520-35), a manuscript probably copied in the Low Countries, but that

---

[5]   Robert Stevenson, 'Josquin in the Music of Spain and Portugal', in Edward Lowinsky in collaboration with Bonnie Blackburn (eds.), *Josquin des Prez, Proceedings of the International Josquin Festival-Conference New York 1971* (London, 1976), 217-46, at 217. In this essay, Stevenson offers a brilliant outline of the influence Josquin has exerted on musical and literary life in the Iberian peninsula during the whole of the sixteenth century.

nevertheless is included because it seems to have come to Spain soon after its production was completed. With no less than eight works firmly attributed to Josquin, among which such a famous composition as his *Missa De beata virgine*, and the motets *Benedicta es*, *Preter rerum seriem* and *Pater noster*, this source stands out both for its beautiful decoration and for its generally reliable readings. In the case of NJE 19.5, the choice of ToleBC 13 (1553-1554) is 'faute de mieux', since of the two other sources, one consists of the Bassus partbook only (BerGS 7), and the other is badly damaged and virtually illegible (VatS 38). However, because ToleBC 13 is also in bad shape, the gap in its Altus has been supplied from the Vatican manuscript. The other gospel motet (NJE 19.8), which is preserved in many more sources, takes its reading again from ToleF 23. With the transmission of the *Magnificat tertii toni* (NJE *20.2) and *Absolve, quesumus, domine* (NJE 26.1), the situation is different in that SegS s.s. and ToleBC 21 are their unique sources. The first of these pieces is only fragmentarily preserved (Verses 1-8), and the text underlay is limited to the incipits of the individual verses. All this makes the question whether or not the piece is correctly ascribed to Josquin not easy to answer. The source for *Absolve*, on the other hand, offers a complete piece. Yet, several musicologists have expressed their doubts about the attribution to Josquin, among them and still recently Ludwig Finscher.[6] I therefore shall go into more detail regarding the authorship question, later in this text.

TRANSMISSION

ToleBC 21 belongs to a group of choirbooks (9, 10, 13, 16, 17, 18, and 19) that were all copied in Toledo for use by the cathedral choir, about *c*.1550. These manuscripts comprise nine Masses (one incomplete) and seven motets, all attributed to Josquin and all considered authentic. There are two more motets ascribed to Josquin: *Absolve* in Ms. 21 (dated 1549) and the six-voice *Victime paschali laudes* (NJE **22.7) in Ms. 10 – in RomeV 35-40 also attributed to Josquin, but almost certainly by Brunet.[7] Furthermore, in ToleBC 19, Josquin is, erroneously, credited with the *Missa Da pacem*. However, this can easily be explained by the fact that the Mass was copied from the German edition Grapheus 1539[2], where it appears under Josquin's name.[8] From all this may be concluded that the Toledo choirbooks are actually rather trustworthy in their

---

[6] See *MGG*[2], Personenteil, vol. 9, col. 1227. Another scholar having doubted the attribution is Martin Just (see his review of vol. 49 of *Werken van Josquin des Prés* in *Die Musikforschung*, 18 (1965), 110).

[7] The mistaken ascription may have its origin in confusion with Josquin's four-voice setting of the same text.

[8] See Edgar H. Sparks, *The Music of Noel Bauldeweyn* (American Musicological Society, 1972), 73.

Josquin attributions. Moreover, what other motif could the scribe of ToleBC 21 have considered *Absolve* to be by Josquin unless it was attributed to him in the source from which he copied the piece? Since the source transmits the motet free of errors, the model was probably likewise. That it was not the scribe's desire to credit Josquin with music from another composer is shown by the motet *Sancta mater istud agas*. While this work bears the name of Josquin in BarcBC 454 (*c*.1500), it appears in ToleBC 21 under the name of Peñalosa, an attribution supported by two other Spanish sources.

Reasons for which the authenticity of *Absolve* has been doubted are, first, that its sole source is late, and second, that the manuscript should be peripheral. However, though it is admitted that ToleBC 21 is rather late, it is not a peripheral source. Because of the political contacts between the Netherlands and Spain, and because of the presence of Flemish musicians on the Iberian peninsula, Spanish sources of Franco-Netherlandish polyphony generally inspire more confidence regarding their Josquin ascriptions than do the German sources from the same period.

STYLISTIC EVIDENCE

The density of the texture of *Absolve* is thick, and therefore deviates from Josquin's motet style in general, which shows more transparency. But if we compare the motet with Josquin's five-part *Nymphes des bois* – his famous lament for Ockeghem – it becomes apparent that, as far as its texture is concerned, *Absolve* is in excellent company: the music of *Nymphes des bois* is even less transparent. Moreover, while both works are based on the introit from the Gregorian Requiem Mass, the elaboration of the chant is, as one would expect with Josquin, entirely different, as is the chordal setting of the prayer 'Requiescat in pace' at the end. Finally, *Nymphes des bois* as well as *Absolve* have in the ultimate chord the falling third. Used at this place, this interval can rightfully be called Josquin's fingerprint.[9]

---

[9] For other examples, see the Gloria and Credo from *Missa Pange lingua*, the Sanctus from *Missa Mater patris* (NJE 10.1), the five-part *De profundis clamavi* (NJE 15.13), *Liber generationis Jesu Christi* (NJE 19.8), *Pater noster - Ave Maria* (NJE 20.9), *Preter rerum seriem* (NJE 24.11), etc.

CIRCUMSTANTIAL EVIDENCE

There are two apparent references to Obrecht: the opening motif drawn from the Credo of Obrecht's *Missa Fortuna desperata*, and the number of ninety-seven notes – in gematria the equivalent of Jacob Obrecht – in the closing section at the words 'Requiescat in pace'.[10] Because Obrecht, after he had succeeded Josquin as Ercole d'Este's chapelmaster, died from the plague in Ferrara, Josquin had indeed good reasons to mourn the loss of his former colleague. But Josquin's authorship is also supported by other evidence. Martin Picker discovered in an incomplete set of partbooks in the archives of the Cathedral at Piacenza an anonymous setting of the same prayer, in which at the place of the letter 'N' the name 'Josquini' is written.[11] Picker mentions that, though the music of this work is totally different from the Toledo *Absolve*, the motets share the introit 'Requiem eternam' as 'cantus prius factus', which is moreover treated in the same way, i.e. as a canon at the fifth. Now, if the motet in ToleBC 21 was not a work by Josquin, why should the anonymous composer have chosen the text 'Absolve' as a prayer for him, modelling his composition after the earlier setting of the text? That the presence of direct musical references is indeed common practice in works written to the memory of a deceased composer, is shown in my study *Sign and Symbol in Music for the Dead*.[12]

THE PRINTED TABLATURE BOOKS

Table 2 presents the titles of the Spanish tablature books, which together contain a large number of arrangements of works by Josquin for plucked and keyboard instruments. How important these books are for our knowledge of Josquin is demonstrated by the fact that two of them ascribe a work to him that is not known from any other source. The first piece is a duo *Fecit potentiam* of 75 bars, found in Fuenllana's *Orphenica lyra* (1554). According to Martin Just, this is an excerpt from a lost *Magnificat quarti toni*. It has been published as a dubious work (NJE *20.4).[13] The second piece, *Obsecro te, domina*, appears in Valderrábano's *Silva de sirenas* (1547).[14] This is a work of larger scope, set for two instruments (vihuela menor and vihuela mayor), which are tuned a

---

[10] See Willem Elders, 'Josquin's *Absolve, quesumus, domine*: A Tribute to Obrecht?, *TVNM* 37 (1987), 14-24.

[11] See the Proceedings of New York 1971 (fn. 5), 247-260.

[12] See Willem Elders, *Symbolic Scores. Studies in the Music of the Renaissance* (Leiden - New York - Cologne, 1994), 121-149.

[13] See the Critical Commentary to NJE 20, p.41.

[14] For modern editions, see Victor Coelho, *La musique de tous les passetemps le plus beau: Hommage à Jean-Michel Vaccaro* (Paris, 1998), 62-5, and the transcription by Anthony Fiumara in NJE 24, Critical Commentary, 116-21.

fifth apart (in *B* and *E*). The table of contents lists *Obsecro te* as 'a cinco', and the performance direction tells us that the text, printed underneath the vihuela mayor part, is to be sung to the notes that in the tablature are marked with a dot. Consisting of twenty words, the fifty-six syllables are distributed, sometimes at large distances from one another, over the 235 staff squares of the tablature. The notes produce a cantus firmus which is otherwise unknown (Ex. 1).

Example 1. The cantus firmus in *Obescro te* according to its notation in the tablature

However, the following details in the chant make certain discrepancies between the cantus firmi in the intabulation and the original motet version of *Obsecro te* likely: first, the leap of the seventh between the note *g* of 'orphanorum' and the first *f* of 'quam filius ...' would seem unacceptable in a pre-existing chant; and second, the text 'quam filius tuus unigenitus' requires an additional verb. While the question whether or not the cantus firmus in Valderrábano's arrangement is an exact copy of that of his model cannot be answered, we only can assume that the original version at this place may have been sligthly manipulated. On the other hand, the insertion of the verb 'coronavit' after 'quam filius tuus unigenitus' leaves the instrumental arrangement intact. It meets the popular representation of the Virgin enthroned, and at the same time appropriately introduces the final plea, in which Mary is called 'honorificentia' (most honourable).

The text of the cantus firmus is a free paraphrase on the incipit of a favourite, lengthy medieval prayer to the Holy Virgin about the fear of sudden death:

> Obsecro te, domina sancta Maria, mater dei, mater gloriosissima,
> mater orphanorum, quam filius tuus unigenitus [coronavit],
> salva me honorificentia populi mei.

> [I implore you, mistress Holy Mary, mother of God,
> most glorious mother, mother of the orphans, who has been [crowned]
> by your only-begotten son, save me, most honourable of my people.]

No further setting of this text has so far been recorded.

Valderrábano's setting leaves also the question open whether or not the motet's main text has been a section from the prayer *Obsecro te, domina*. This notwithstanding, in the reconstruction the cantus firmus text can easily be transferred to the other voices as well, and hypothetically completed with some phrases from the prayer as found in *The Book of Hours* of Mary of Burgundy. In the text following below, these phrases are printed in italics:

> Obsecro te, domina sancta Maria, mater dei, *pietate plenissima, summi regis filia,* mater [dei] gloriosissima, mater orphanorum, *consolatio desolatorum,* quam filius tuus unigenitus [coronavit], salva me honorificentia populi mei.

> [I implore you, mistress Holy Mary, mother of God, most full of piety, daughter of the most Highest King, most glorious mother [of God], mother of the orphans, consolation of the desolate, who has been [crowned] by your only-begotten son, save me, most honourable of my people.]

The Authorship Question

Though the tablature notation of *Obsecro te* leaves us in the dark regarding the actual duration of the notes of the cantus firmus (which, as we saw above, are marked with a dot), it is likely that the melody was quoted continuously throughout the original piece. That this is customary in the period is testified by Josquin's *Stabat mater* (NJE 25.9), *Ave nobilissima creatura* (NJE 23.11) and *Huc me sydereo* (NJE 21.5), to name but a few examples. The long note values, then, stand out in sharp contrast to the surrounding voices. The opening motif of the piece, consisting of a triadic figure beginning with the third, is similar to that of the opening of the *secunda pars* of Josquin's *Domine, ne in furore tuo* (NJE 16.6), and resembles, because of the repeated use of the minor third, the first bars of Josquin's *O virgo prudentissima* (NJE 24.9). As in the latter motet, low and higher voices may alternate, as for example in bb. 64-77. The distribution of the highest, climactic notes is perfectly balanced (see bb. 36-37, 60-61, and 83-84). Constructivist devices, characteristic for Josquin, are the stepwise descending paired melodic lines in bb. 32-39 and 46-52 and the repeated fifth in the Altus bb. 40-46.[15] The exceptional series of statements of the same melodic motif at 'coronavit' (bb. 84-91) recalls bb. 36-43 in the *tertia pars* of Josquin's *Miserere mei, deus*, where the words 'non delectaberis' are sung five times in succession. Such bold cumulations of the same musical material are very Josquinian indeed. Finally, Valderrábano's *Silva de sirenas* contains eleven arrangements of sections from seven Masses by Josquin,[16] as well as a part of three of his most renowned motets.[17] Since all these works are attributed in the book to Josquin, it seems allowed to conclude that the intabulator was well informed, and that there seems thus to be no reason to not accept the motet as a possibly newly discovered motet of his hand. It is published as an 'opus dubium' in vol. 24 of the NJE under no. 24.8, in a hypothetical reconstruction of the vocal version by Willem Mook.

[15] For descending lines in works by Josquin see, for example, *Huc me sydereo* (NJE 21.5), bb. 19-35; *Stabat mater*, bb. 48-52; and *Miserere mei, deus*, final bars. For the fifths see *Ave maris stella* (NJE 23.8), bb. 1-9; *Virgo prudentissima* (NJE 25.12), bb. 65-73 in the Critical Commentary to NJE vol. 23, pp. 116-117; and *Preter rerum seriem* (NJE 24.11), bb. 27-29.

[16] These are: *Missa Ave maris stella* (NJE 3.1), *Missa de beata virgine* (NJE 3.3), *Missa Gaudeamus* (NJE 4.2), *Missa Pange lingua* (NJE 4.3), *Missa L'homme armé super voces musicales*, *Missa Faysant regretz* (NJE 8.1), and *Missa Ad fugam*.

[17] *Ave Maria* [= Pars II of *Pater noster*] (NJE 20.9), *Benedicta es, celorum regina* [Pars II] (NJE 23.13), and *Inviolata, integra et casta es* [Pars I and Pars III].

OLD TESTAMENT MOTETS
FOR THE WAR OF CYPRUS (1570-71)

Iain Fenlon

Writers since Voltaire have contributed to an almost unanimous ironic chorus describing the victory of the forces of the Holy League over the Turkish armada at Lepanto, off Corfu, in October 1571, as an empty achievement, a great spectacle that led nowhere.[1] Yet whatever the judgements of history, the authentic period voice should be heard. For most contemporaries, the victory marked a decisive turning point in the fortunes of Christendom, a critical moment of enormous psychological importance in an historic struggle that, in recent years, the Christian west had seemed destined to lose. No matter what occurred in the following years, as the Venetians reached a separately-negotiated peace treaty with the Turks, to the disgust of Spain and the Papacy, compared with what had gone before, the victory at Lepanto marked the end of a genuine crisis of confidence that had only intensified with the loss of Cyprus in the previous year. For most Europeans the victory seemed to mark the beginning of the end of an era of Ottoman supremacy, after a period of some three hundred years in which the Turks had risen from obscure origins to become the terror of the Christian world.

It was the sheer enormity of the achievement of Lepanto, as it was perceived at the time, together with its great symbolic importance, that helps to explain the extraordinary round of celebrations that greeted the news of the victory throughout Europe. Perhaps nowhere was the sense of relief and achievement felt more keenly than among the Venetians, for whom the Siege of Malta and the loss of Cyprus were still very fresh in the memory. The apogee of Turkish sea power in the Mediterranean had been reached in 1560 when the stronghold on the island of Djerba was taken, and the victorious Turkish fleet returned home by way of Gozo, Sicily, and the Abruzzi, where villages were plundered and torched.[2] The Christian world, unaware of the fundamental concept of a holy war conducted to defend the faith and extend the boundaries of Islam, regarded such incidents as isolated if worrying indications of Turkish power. In practice, the Ottoman state was in a permanent condition of war with Christian Europe from the fall of Constantinople in 1453 until the Treaty of Zsitva-

---

[1] For a revisionist assessment see Fernand Braudel, *The Mediterranean and the Mediterranean World in the Age of Philip II,* trans. Sian Reynolds, 2 vols. (Berkeley, 1979), ii, 661-9.
[2] Braudel, *The Mediterranean,* ii, 973-87.

Torok in 1606.[3] Within this arc of two-and-a-half centuries, the final years of
Suleiman I (1520-66) and the first ones of his successor, Selim II, mark the
moment when territorial ambition extended the limits of the Ottoman empire
to their greatest. From the siege of Malta in 1565, until the separate Venetian
peace treaty of 1573, the Turks dominated the external politics of the Republic,
the Papacy and, though to a lesser extent, the Empire. During these years the
general climate of apprehension grew in intensity as each spring posed afresh
the question of whether or not the Ottoman fleet would re-appear in the Adriatic.
In Venice, Turkish adventures of this kind had never been regarded as a serious
threat to the treaty of Constantinople, which had brought to an end the war
between the Holy League and the Ottoman empire in 1540. The intervening
years of peace had brought some stability, and a certain degree of prosperity to
the Republic's affairs, justifying the position of those Venetians who pressed
for accommodation with the Turk at all costs. Many never doubted that
peaceful co-existence, beneficial to both sides, was seriously at risk, not even
after the spring of 1565 when Turkish troops had landed on Malta, fiercely and
successfully defended by the combined forces of the Knights and a contingent
of Spanish soldiers.[4]

In a society which had assiduously cultivated the image of its special relationship
with the Almighty, religious and devotional practices naturally formed the
most important element of the official Venetian celebrations of Lepanto itself.[5]
As an immediate response the doge and signoria led the way by voting alms
to monasteries, convents, and charitable foundations in the city.[6] On the first
Sunday after news of the victory had arrived in Venice, High Mass was sung in
San Marco by the Spanish ambassador in the presence of the doge and signoria,
festally dressed for the occasion. This was accompanied by music, described
by Rocco Benedetti as 'concerti divinissimi', in which the two organs of
the Basilica played together with voices and instruments, an unambiguous

[3] John Francis Guilmartin, 'Ideology and Conflict: The Wars of the Ottoman Empire, 1453-
     1606', *Journal of Interdisciplinary History*, 18 (1988), especially 727-37.
[4] Braudel, *The Mediterranean*, ii, 1014-20.
[5] For a general account see Iain Fenlon, 'Lepanto: The Arts of Celebration in Renaissance Ven-
     ice', *Proceedings of the British Academy*, 73 (1987), 201-35.
[6] Venice, Biblioteca Nazionale Marciana, MS. It. VII. 73 (8265), f. 394v; Rocco Benedetti, *Rag-
     guaglio delle allegrezze, solennita, e feste fatte in Venetia per la felice vittoria* (Venice, 1571),
     f. A4.

reference to the Venetian tradition of music for *cori spezzati*.[7] Although the 'concerti' which he describes cannot be identified with certainty, a number of pieces by Andrea Gabrieli with texts appropriate for the occasion have survived in the Venetian repertory. A number of these, such as *O salutaris hostia* and *Isti sunt triumphatores*, are fully liturgical and are generally appropriate for the sentiments of the moment; it is impossible to say whether they were specially composed in honour of the victory or not.[8]

As these two musical examples demonstrate, the prime emphasis in the official Venetian celebrations of Lepanto was upon the confirmation of the victory as Christ's victory, and the same is true of many of the more permanent memorials to the victory which began to appear in the months following the battle. As early as the Consistory of May 1571, which had ratified the articles of the League, Pius had attributed the successful conclusion of the discussions between Spain, Venice, and the Papacy, to the power of Divine protection, and in consequence had projected the League's military campaign as a divinely-ordained Christian crusade on historical lines, pursued through the agency of Papal guidance. This was common rhetoric. According to one Friulian writer, the military preparations that were undertaken on a grand scale in the area at the beginning of 1571, were 'not just to preserve our state, but for the health of all Christendom and particularly for the glory of God'.[9] Contemporary codes of chivalry required the nobility to fight crusades as and when they were asked to do so. This, an important part of Pius V's conception, was taken up by writers and commentators everywhere. Orazio Toscanella argued that it was a Christian duty to reclaim the Holy Land, the birthplace of Adam and Christ, from the Turks. The spread of Islam was a great danger. The Holy League should overcome their differences, and sustained by their common love of Christ, should take up arms and drive the Turks back to their own lands, just as Alexander the Great had done with Darius, Xerxes with the Athenians,

---

[7] Benedetti: *Ragguaglio*, f. A4: 'si fecero concerti divinissimi, perché sonandosi quando l'uno, e quando l'altro organo con ogni sorte di stromenti, e di voci, conspiranno ambi a un tempo in un tuono, che veramente pareva, che s'aprissero le cattarate dell' harmonia celeste, & ella diluviasse da i chori angelici'. See also the report of the Papal nuncio given in Franco Gaeta et al, *Nunziature di Venezia (secoli XVI-XVIII)* (Rome, 1958-), 10, 118-120. Benedetti's account is confirmed by the description of the Mantuan Paolo Moro, who notes that the 'voci rissonanti' are accompanied by 'varii et molti instrumenti di mano et da fiato' (Moro's letter, Venice 22 October 1571, is in Mantua, Archivio di Stato, Archivio Gonzaga 1503).

[8] David Bryant, *Liturgy, Ceremonial and Sacred Music in Venice at the Time of the Counter-Reformation*, 2 vols. (Ph. D. diss, University of London, 1981), i, 44-54, summarised in the same author's 'Andrea Gabrieli e la "musica di stato" veneziana', in *Andrea Gabrieli 1585-1985* [=42 Festival Internazionale di Musica Contemporanea] (Venice, 1985), 29-45.

[9] Udine, Biblioteca Civica, MS 58 (Annales 1571-74).

and Hannibal with the Romans. The alternative was bloodshed, misery, and death.[10]

In these circumstances it was inevitable that victory, when it came, was universally regarded as a manifestation of Divine providence. Pietro Buccio's oration, one of a number that were delivered publicly, attributed even the mechanics of the battle to God's intervention. The ships of the League had triumphed, he wrote, because the wind changed in their favour at the crucial juncture, a sure sign of Divine Justice, while the fact that the Turks had clearly underestimated the size of the opposing fleet could only be attributed to Divine Goodness.[11] A sense of amazement at the unexpected reversal in Turkish military fortunes and of its significance was common. Lepanto was surely the greatest victory in history, greater than anything that had been achieved by the Greeks or the Romans, declaimed Buccio. All this had happened because God had finally opened his ears to the prayers of the faithful.[12] The topos of Christ's Victory, expressed in the title of Celio Magno's play *Il Trionfo di Christo*, is a major component of Lepanto celebratory art in Venice and throughout the Veneto. When official representatives from Verona presented themselves to the Doge to offer the congratulations of the city for the victory, and to confirm an annual subsidy for the continuation of the war, they referred explicitly to the idea that the hand of God had been responsible for defeating the enemy, destroying its fleet, and flooding the sea with pagan blood. The general familiarity of this theme is neatly illustrated by the title-page of an anonymous pamphlet of poetic paraphrases of the psalms, 'accomodate,' according to the title-page, 'per render gratie a Dio della vittoria donata al Christianesimo contra Turchi'. Here, within a central decorative frame, the Lion of St. Mark is shown being guided by the hand of God. Every conceivable ingenuity was deployed by Venetian poets and printers to exploit the Christian theme. In one commentary on the *Pater Noster* 'in lingua rustica', the prayer itself is intertwined with celebratory observations on the victory, and paraphrases of the psalms and other well-known prayers are common in the Lepanto literature.[13]

In addition to the theme of the victory as Divinely ordained, there is a second common topos to be found in the literature that appeared in the bookshops and squares of Venice after Lepanto, namely that of the Venetians as the Chosen

---

[10] Orazio Toscanella, *Essortatione ai Cristiani contra il Turco* (Venice, 1572).

[11] Pietro Buccio, *Oratione al serenissimo Prencipe, et illustrissima Signoria di Venetia sopra la vittoria christiana contra Turchi ottenuta l'anno felicissimo MDLXXI* (Venice, 1571), fos. 4v-5.

[12] Buccio, *Oratione*, ibid.

[13] *Discorso sopra il Pater Noster in lingua rustica, per la vittoria dei Christiani contra Turchi* (n.p., n.d.).

People.[14] Comparisons between the Israelites and the citizens of the Republic also appear in a number of texts set to music by composers working in Venice and the Veneto. One of Andrea Gabrieli's large-scale polychoral compositions, *Benedictus Dominus Deus Saboath*, is a composite text whose explicit references to battle, and use of Old Testament themes, preceded by the opening words of the *Santus-Benedictus* section of the Ordinary of the Mass, seems to constitute an explicit reference to both the battle and to the special status of the Venetians. It too might well have been written in celebration of Lepanto:

> 'Benedictus Deus Deus Saboath. Benedicti qui pugnant in nomine
> Domini. Manus enim fortis et terribilis pugnat pro eis. Manus Domini
> protegit illos. Pugnavit Samson, pugnavit Gedeon, vicit Samson, vicit
> Gedeon. Pugnaverunt nostri in nomine Domini. Pugnavit Dominus
> pro nobis et vicit Dominus inimicos eius. Laetamini et exultate et
> psallite'.[15]

> [Blessed be the Lord of Hosts. Blessed be those who fight in the
> name of the Lord. His powerful and inexorable hand fights for them.
> The hand of the Lord defends them. Samson has fought, Gideon has
> fought. Samson has won, Gideon has won. Our armies have fought in
> the name of the Lord. God has sustained us in battle and won over His
> enemies. Let us exult and rejoice and sing his praise].

The twin references to Samson and Gideon, both of whom are portrayed in the Book of Judges as hero-liberators who protected the Israelites from extinction at the hands of the Philistines, places Gabrieli's piece among a number of late sixteenth-century motets on Old Testament texts written by composers associated with San Marco. The notion that the Venetian constitution was based on Judaic law was frequently asserted by writers and public orators who claimed that the Venetians were a 'chosen people', and that the doge, whose wisdom was comparable to that of Moses and Solomon, was divinely

---

[14] Among many examples, see Bartolomeo Meduna della Motta, *Dialogo sopra la miracolosa vittoria ottenuta dall'armata della Santissima Lega Christiana, contra la Turchesca nel quale si dimostra essa vittoria esser venuta dalla sola mano di Dio. Et si discorre a pieno l'ordine del conflitto* (Venice, 1572), fo. [A2]v.

[15] Andrea and Giovanni Gabrieli, *Concerti...continenti musica di chiesa, madrigali, a6.7.8.10.12 & 16...libro primo e secondo* (Venice, 1587); Bryant, *Liturgy, Ceremonial and Sacred Music*, i, 49.

sanctioned.[16] The city itself was often extolled as a New Jerusalem, and as a Promised Land.

Another work in this group of Old Testament motets, Giovanni Croce's setting of *Benedictus Deus Deus Saboath*, perhaps influenced by Gabrieli's example, was published in his book of double-choir motets of 1594. There it appears alongside Croce's eight-voice motet *Percussit Saul*, whose text is taken from the words of the Israelite women following David's killing of Goliath:

> 'Percussit Saul mille & David decem millia quia manus Domini erat cum illo. Percussit Philistaeum & abstulit approbrium. Nonno iste David de quo canebat in choro dicentes. Percussit Saul mille & David decem millia quia manus Domini erat cum illo'.[17]

> [Saul has slain his thousands, and David his ten thousands, because the hand of the Lord was with him. He killed the Philistine and removed disgrace from Israel. Is this not David, the one they made songs about in their dances, saying, Saul has slain his thousands and David his ten thousands?].

There was already a history of association between this text and the War of Cyprus by the time that Croce wrote his piece. A medal by Federico Cocciola showing Jean de la Vallette, Grand Master of the Order of Malta, makes a reference on its obverse to the defence of Malta in 1565. This shows David, holding a sabre in both hands, standing over a recumbent Goliath, against the background of the sea with galleys. The legend around the border reads VNVS X. MILLIA (one [has slain] ten thousand), a clear adaptation of the phrase 'David decem millia'.[18] Croce went on to make his own composition text the basis for his *Missa Percussit Saul*, the first of three masses published in 1596 with a dedication to Lorenzo Priuli, where it is immediately followed by a *Missa sopra la battaglia*.[19] Croce rose to prominence at San Marco during the 1590s,

---

[16] See, for example, Giuliano Scarpa in Francesco Sansovino, *Delle orationi recitate a Principi di Venetia nella loro creatione da gli Ambasciadori di diverse citta libro primo* (Venice, 1562), 66v; Luigi Groto, *Le orationi volgari...dall'autore istesso ricorrette...e tutte insieme...raccolte in un sol volume* (Venice, 1586), 37, 108, 111; Francesco Sansovino, *Venetia citta nobilissima...descritta...nella quale si contengonotutte le guerre passate, con l'attioni illustri de molti senatori, le vite de I Principi & gli scrittori veneti del tempo loro* (Venice, 1581), 137.

[17] Giovanni Croce, *Motetti a otto* (Venice, 1596). For the Old Testament text see I Samuel 18:7, repeated by the servant of Achish 21:11, and Deuteronomy 32:30.

[18] Philip Attwood, *Italian Medals c.1530-1600 in British Public Collections*, 2 vols. (London, 2003), no. 970.

[19] Giovanni Croce, *Messe a otto voci*, Vanice, 1596.

becoming vice-master of the chapel under Donato,[20] and these grandiloquent works (the title-page specifies performance by both instruments and voices), reflect the resources now at his disposal. Equivalents in sound to the large-scale battle-pieces painted by Tintoretto and others, they also perhaps evoke the troubled nature of the post-Lepanto world as well as commemorations of the victory itself. They could be thought of as equivalents in sound to the engravings which continued to evoke the spirit of Lepanto during the same decade (Figure 1).

Figure 1. The Battle of Lepanto. Engraving, 1571 (Museo Correr, Venice)

Old Testament analogies also make an appearance in a motet by Pietro Vinci, *Intret super eos formido et pavor*, whose existence is linked to the heroic actions of Astorre Baglione, one of the officers of the Venetian garrison which

[20] *Dizionario Biografico degli Italiani*, 31, 210; *New Grove*, 700-711.

bravely defended Famagosta for eleven months before it fell to the enemy in the summer of 1571.[21] Together with the commander, Marc'Antonio Bragadin, Baglione was determined to hold out until Famagosta could be relieved by a counter-offensive led by the Venetian fleet and its allies, but with the passing of the months these reasonable if ill-founded hopes gradually faded. The Turks, who had camped around the city since September of the previous year, kept up a continuous attack, aimed at slowly demoralising the Venetians as their supplies dwindled and their defensive walls began to give way. Hardly a day passed without some minor offensive action of some kind until June, when a large enemy mine exploded under the walls and the Turks were able to make their first general assault. A week later there followed a second. In the face of the inevitable, the Bishop of Limassol appealed to Bragadin to accept defeat rather than risk the massacre of the inhabitants. Sustained by a firm sense of duty and family pride, allied to a strong belief in the mission of a Christian crusade, Bragadin continued to resist throughout July until, with supplies of food and munitions virtually exhausted, the garrison was effectively reduced to a few hundred. With the walls of the city now seriously breached, he was finally forced to accept the advice of Baglione and other officers, and agreed to capitulate. A treaty signed the next day allowed for the safe conduct of all the defending forces and civilians to Crete.

The fate of Bragadin and his officers was to be different. Seizing a pretext to break the terms of the agreement, the Turkish commander, Mustafà Pascià, proceeded to exact vengeance on those who, for almost a year, had inflicted considerable losses on the Turkish forces holed up under the city walls. After being forced to witness the summary execution of his officers, including Baglione, Bragadin was briefly imprisoned before his own long torture and execution began. Already seriously wounded (the Turks had cut off his ears and infection had followed), he was now forced to carry two heavy baskets of earth along the enemy trenches to the jeers and shouts of the enemy soldiers. Following this he was lashed to the mast of one of the galleys anchored in the harbour, and was then left for some time suspended above the deck. Finally dragged to the main square of the city and tied to a column, he was now subjected to the final torture. It is recorded that the skin had been stripped from both his chest and arms before Bragadin, who had never stopped reciting the 'Miserere' and calling upon Christ for aid, expired.[22] His body was then quartered and his skin, stuffed with straw and cotton, and dressed in his uniform, paraded

---

[21] Kenneth Setton, *The Papacy and the Levant*, 4 vols. (Philadelphia, 1976-84), iv, 1027-44. For a contemporary account see Cristoforo Brenzone, *Vita e fatti del valorossismo capitan Astorre Baglione da Perugia* (Verona, 1591).

[22] Brenzone, *Vita et fatti*, 92-3.

around the streets of Famagosta before being taken to Constantinople, together with the heads of the other Venetian officers, as a war trophy.[23] Witnessed by Nestore Martinengo, a Venetian captain who managed to escape execution, the grim details of Bragadin's fate were reported to a shocked public in a short pamphlet that went through at least three editions.[24]

Vinci's motet was published in his *Secondo libro de mottetti* of 1572, where it is headed in all the partbooks 'In destructione Turcharum'. A Sicilian who had then been working as 'maestro di cappella' at Santa Maria Maggiore in Bergamo for three years, Vinci gathered together a number of occasional pieces for this second motet collection. Dedicated to the governors of the Misericordia in the city, it includes one piece (*Calliope colles sibi legit Apollo*) in honour of Bergamo, and two (*Urbs gladijs* and *Plange urbs Bergomea*) lamenting Baglione's heroic sacrifice. Born in Perugia, Baglione had pursued an extremely successful military and administrative career, initially in the service of the Papacy and the Farnese, latterly in that of the Republic.[25] As a skilled military he oversaw the fortifications at Udine, Padua, and Bergamo; overseas he served as governor of Corfu and Nicosia. At Bergamo in particular, his efforts were much admired, so much so that in 1560 he was given the honorary title of 'Capo dei Priori'.[26] In addition to his military exploits and valour in the face of the enemy, Baglione was also a man of considerable social stature, having been born into one of the most prominent noble families in Perugia, and having taken as his wife Ginevra Salviati, whose father was the nephew of two Medici popes, Leo X and Clement VII. Some sense of Baglione's contemporary importance is conveyed in Girolamo Ruscelli's *Le imprese illustri*, where his device [Figure 2] is illustrated together with an elaborate analysis of its meaning interwoven with fragments of his biography.[27]

---

[23] Giovanni Pietro Contarini, *Historia delle cose succese dal principio della guerra mossa da Selim ottomano a Venetiani fino al di della gran giornata vittoriosa contra Turchi* (Venice, 1572), fos. 23v-31; Paolo Paruta, *Della guerra di Cipro*, (Venice, 1605), 183, 194-7; Venice, Biblioteca Nazionale Marciana, MSS. It. VII. 519 (8434), f. 331v, It. VII. 553, 26-9; Vatican City, Biblioteca Apostolica Vaticana, MS. Patetta 969, fos. 105v-108. Modern accounts in *Dizionario Biografico degli Italiani*, 13, 686-89 (Ventura); Setton, *The Papacy and the Levant*, iv, 1039-42.

[24] Nestore Martinengo, *Relatione di tutto il successo di Famagosta* (Venice, 1572).

[25] *Dizionario Biografico degli Italiani* 5, 197-99 (De Capo).

[26] Id.

[27] Girolamo Ruscelli, *Le imprese illustri. Aggiontovi nuovamente il quarto libro da Vincenzo Ruscelli da Viterbo* (Venice, 1584), 61-74.

Figure 2. Device of Astorre Baglione. From Girolamo Ruscelli, *Delle imprese illustri*
(Venice, 1584)

Certainly his heroic death was marked in Bergamo where, in 1572, elaborate
obsequies were organized for him in Santa Maria Maggiore; it was in this church
that had been founded the Compagnia of the Gonfalone of S. Giuseppe.[28] In
the centre of the church a sepulchre, mounted upon an obelisk, was draped
with cloth-of-gold and surrounded by more than a hundred torches to create
the traditional 'cappella ardente'. More than one hundred priests were present,
half chanting, the rest incensing the sepulchre. At some point during the
proceedings, some of Vinci's music was performed.

With its text, based on the account in Deuteronomy of the Israelites crossing
the Red Sea, *Intret super eos formido et pavor* is one of the clearest examples
in the Venetian musical repertory of a specially-composed motet text woven
out of the theme of the Venetians as the Chosen Race:

[28] *Le suntuossime esequie celebrata nella magnifica citta di Bergamo in morte dello illustrissimo
signore A. B. con alcuni leggiadri componimenti latini e volgari* (Venice, 1572), with a dedication (to Ginevra Salviati).

'Intret super eos formido et pavor. In magnitudine Brachij tui
Domine disperde illos et fiant immobiles donec transeat populus
tuus quem possedisti'.[29]

[Let terror and dread descend upon them. In the greatness of your
arm disband them and let them become motionless until your people,
Lord, whom you have chosen, pass by].

These post-Lepanto commemorations are the latest in a long process, in which
the Venetians had celebrated the virtues and deeds of the heroes of the War of
Cyprus. The fall of Nicosia, where the Turks had behaved with great brutality,[30]
had already prompted Antonio Molino to publish, under his pseudyonym Manoli
Blessi, a long barzelletta written in 'lingua stradiotesca' (Venetian dialect
mixed with Greek, Istrian and Dalmatian elements), analyzing the reasons why
the city had been taken by the Turks. On the one hand, according to Molino,
the Venetians had not been adequately supported by the Cypriots, and on the
other the failure of the Spanish fleet to arrive had been decisive. Following
these general considerations Molino goes on to speak of the Turkish atrocities
in Nicosia, and in particular of the execution of Nicolo Dandolo, whose head
had been sent to Bragadin as a warning of the consequences of intransigence.[31]
With his account of the loss of Nicosia, Molino was one of the first poets to
be stirred to publication by the war. Following the fall of Famagosta he was
followed by many others, inspired not only by the garrison's resolute defence
of the city, but more particularly by the heroic deaths of Baglione and Bragadin.
Together with the dozens of poems, broadsheets, and engravings [Figure 3]
that were printed in Venice to celebrate the victory of the Holy League through
the military achievements of Marc' Antonio Colonna, Don John of Austria,
and Sebastiano Venier, or the wisdom of Pius V, this corpus forms part of an
extensive cultural phenomenon to which composers also contributed.[32]

---

[29] Pietro Vinci, *Il secondo libro dei motetti a cinque voci* (Venice, 1572).

[30] Gaeta et al (eds.), *Nunziature di Venezia*, ix, 403 (Venice, 6 December, 1570).

[31] Manoli Blessi [Antonio Molino], *Il vero successo della presa di Nicosia in Cipro* (Venice, 1572). For further information on his poetry for the War of Cyprus see Antonio Medin, *Storia della repubblica di Venezia nella poesia* (Milan, 1904), 233-40.

[32] For Venetian literary reactions see Medin, *La storia della Repubblica*, and Carlo Dionisotti, 'Lepanto nella cultura italiana del tempo', in Gino Benzoni (ed.), *Il Mediterraneo nella seconda meta del '500 alla luce di Lepanto* (Florence, 1974), 127-51. Dialect poetry is treated in Manlio Cortelazzo's article 'Pluriliguismo celebrativo' in the same volume. See also Iain Fenlon, '*In destructione Turcharum*': The Victory of Lepanto in Sixteenth-Century Music and Letters', in Francesco Degrada (ed.), *Andrea Gabrieli e il suo tempo: Atti del convegno internazionale (Venezia 16-18 settembre 1985)* (Florence, 1987), 293-317, and the same author's 'Lepanto: Music, Ceremony, and Celebration in Counter-Reformation Rome' in Iain Fenlon, *Music and Culture in Late Renaissance Italy* (Oxford, 2002), 139-61.

Figure 3. Title-page of Bartolomeo Malombra, *Nuova canzone nella felicissima vittoria contra infideli* (Venice, 1571)

CARON AND FLORENCE: A NEW ASCRIPTION AND THE COPYING OF THE *PIXÉRÉCOURT CHANSONNIER*

Sean Gallagher

Biographical information on Firminus Caron is entirely lacking, but there is ample evidence that contemporaries recognized him as one of the major composers of the second half of the fifteenth century. Johannes Tinctoris, writing in the 1470s, consistently names him among the five musicians 'most outstanding in composition of all those I have heard' (the others being Ockeghem, Busnoys, Regis, and Faugues), and musical sources indicate that his chansons enjoyed wide circulation.[1] Indeed it seems likely his reputation stemmed mainly from his chansons, some of which number among the most popular of the period. When Tinctoris twice mentions specific works by Caron, in both instances he selects chansons, rather than one of the composer's five masses (no motets by him are known).[2] Similarly, the text of Loyset Compère's singers' motet *Omnium bonorum plena* (composed before 1474, possibly for the 1472 dedication of Cambrai Cathedral), refers to Caron, Busnoys and Johannes du Sart as 'magistri cantilenarum'.

Most of the musicians cited in Compère's motet are known to have had ties to Cambrai Cathedral, the French royal court, or the court of Burgundy under Charles the Bold. Thus far no trace of a Firminus Caron has been discovered in the records of any of these institutions, and attempts to identify the composer with a Philippe Caron have been predicated on the assumption that Tinctoris got Caron's first name wrong (twice), something for which there really is no justification.[3] In the absence of documents the biographical problems remain intractable. It is possible nevertheless to make a few inferences on the basis of the musical sources.

---

[1] For recent brief overviews of Caron and his works, see Sean Gallagher, 'Caron, Firminus', *MGG²*, Personenteil, vol. 4; David Fallows, *A Catalogue of Polyphonic Songs, 1415-1480* (Oxford, 1999), 684-5.

[2] Tinctoris criticizes Caron's handling of dissonance in the song *Helas que pourra devenir*, but chooses another of his songs, *La tridaine* (now lost), as one of six works that exemplify the compositional/aesthetic ideal of 'varietas' (*Liber de arte contrapuncti*, Bk. III, Ch. 8).

[3] See Barbara Haggh, 'Busnoys and 'Caron' in Documents from Brussels', in Paula Higgins (ed.), *Antoine Busnoys. Method, Meaning, and Context in Late Medieval Music* (Oxford, 1999), 295-315. Beyond this reference in Compère's motet, the possibility that Caron had connections to Cambrai Cathedral in the early 1470s is suggested by the copying of an unnamed Mass by him at the Cathedral in 1472-73.

Wherever Caron was in the early 1470s, he had already been composing for at least a decade. The index of Escorial B, a manuscript of Italian (possibly Milanese) origin, shows that it once contained his rondeau *Accueilly m'a la belle*, copied in a layer dating probably from the early 1460s.[4] The earliest surviving copies of any of his music are a mass and two chansons in the manuscript Trent 89, on paper reliably dated to between 1460 and 1463. It is in the same layers of Escorial B and Trent 89 that we also find some of the earliest known sources for Busnoys's music.[5] The two composers were probably close in age, and the broader circulation of their chansons evidently began around the same time. It is significant, then, that Caron's songs, unlike Busnoys's, are so poorly represented in the five *Loire Valley* chansonniers. These are major sources for Busnoys, thirty-one of whose securely attributed chansons appear in one or more of them (equalling roughly half his known songs). By contrast, Caron does not appear at all in two of the five chansonniers, and the remaining three together contain just four of his approximately twenty songs. In general the *Loire Valley* manuscripts are weighted toward composers active in central France (as Busnoys is known to have been in the early to mid 1460s), while those associated with the Burgundian court are largely neglected. From this one can infer that Caron was almost certainly not working in France in these years. Whether he was active in Burgundian circles remains an open question, but a period of service there in the 1470s as a colleague of Busnoys would go some way toward explaining why the two composers' chansons show up in so many of the same sources, in some cases with conflicting attributions.

It is in certain Florentine manuscripts of the 1480s and early 90s that one first finds songs of Caron and Busnoys appearing together in large numbers. Particularly striking in this respect is the *Pixérécourt Chansonnier* (Paris, Bibl. nat., fonds fr. MS 15123; hereafter Pix), a large collection from the 1480s in which Caron and Busnoys are by a wide margin the most heavily represented composers, complete with numerous ascriptions. During a recent examination of the manuscript I noted two intriguing scribal details. One of these involves a previously unrecognized ascription to Caron, while the other affects our understanding of the copying of the collection as a whole, as well as the Florentine reception of both Caron's and Busnoys's songs.

---

[4]   Fallows, *Catalogue of Polyphonic Songs*, 684.
[5]   Respectively, the three- and four-voice versions of his rondeau *Quant ce viendra*.

Pix contains more works by Caron than any other source, with eighteen of the twenty-one surviving chansons attributed to him, including one *unicum*.[6] Together these constitute more than a tenth of the entire collection. His works also appear in the other six Florentine chansonniers copied between *c*.1480 and the mid-1490s, prominently so in some cases. An indication of Florentine collectors' interest in Caron's songs is the fact that even if Pix did not survive we would still possess at least one other Florentine source for all of his works found in it (excepting the *unicum* of course). Perhaps inevitably, the strong presence of Caron's music in these and other Italian sources has led to speculation that he spent part of his career on the peninsula. Here, too, we find a parallel with Busnoys, for whom an Italian sojourn has also been proposed (and for much the same reasons). But for neither composer is there any documentation at all to support this theory. Indeed, in the case of Busnoys, Joshua Rifkin has recently demonstrated that what would appear to be the strongest evidence for the 'Italian hypothesis' – the existence of two Italian-texted songs attributed to him – does not withstand closer scrutiny (one of the works is certainly not by Busnoys, but rather an Italian composer, while the other song's Italian text is spurious, a replacement for what must have been a French original).[7] The same holds true for Caron, one of whose songs survives – in the same source as the Busnoys – with an Italian text that is surely not original. On balance, then, there is no reason to assume that the concentration of Caron's music in Italian sources was the result of his having worked there.

What is clear, however, is that by the time Pix was copied (probably in the early to mid-1480s), some of Caron's songs had already been circulating in Florence for several years. Nine of his chansons appear in two slightly earlier Florentine manuscripts (Florence 176 and Riccardiana 2356, both probably copied *c*. 1480).[8] Six of these nine are also in Pix, with the difference that the Pix scribe provided ascriptions for most of these. In part, this difference

---

[6] Of these twenty-one, five are attributed in at least one musical or theoretical source to another composer, though the only of these for which Caron's authorship is perhaps questionable is *Rose plaisante*, not for any stylistic reasons, but because the other composers to whom it is ascribed – 'Dusart' (in Rome, Bibl. Casanatense, Ms. 2856) and 'Philipon' (presumably Basiron, in Petrucci's *Canti C* [1504]) – are less well known figures in the period and (it is usually argued) thus less likely to have had works incorrectly attributed to them. But here this line of reasoning breaks down, since of course in this case at least one of them *has* had the song incorrectly attributed to him. In my view, Caron's authorship should remain an open question for now; accordingly I include it whenever referring here to the number of songs attributed to Caron.

[7] Joshua Rifkin, 'Busnoys and Italy: The Evidence of Two Songs', in Higgins (ed.), *Antoine Busnoys*, 505-71.

[8] Florence, Bibl. Nazionale, MS Magl. xix.176; Florence, Bibl. Riccardiana, MS 2356 ('Second' Riccardiana Chansonnier).

may simply reflect the much larger number of ascriptions in Pix compared to the earlier manuscripts.[9] Of the 171 works in Pix, at least forty-seven carry ascriptions. There might well have been many more originally: six of the forty-seven are heavily trimmed, some to the point of illegibility. Almost certainly some were removed entirely. But the continuity of transmission within this complex of Florentine sources helps account for the Pix scribe's apparent confidence in explicitly ascribing nine songs to Caron. Here it is worth noting that although four chansons ascribed to Caron in at least one source bear a conflicting attribution elsewhere, none of the nine with ascriptions in Pix appear elsewhere under another composer's name.

Two of the heavily trimmed ascriptions have already been deciphered. Enough survives of the name above the ballade *Resjois toi terre de France / Rex pacificus* to reveal that it matches the other ascriptions to Busnoys found in the manuscript.[10] Visible above another song, *Seulette suis sans ami*, is the bottom of a majuscule 'C', which (as David Fallows rightly observes) 'can really only be Caron'.[11] The shape of this initial is the same as in all the other Caron ascriptions. The only other composers with attributions in the manuscript whose names begin with 'C' are Cornago and Compère (though in fact the only instance of the latter's name is given as 'L. compere'). Both can be dismissed as possible candidates: a comparably trimmed example of either of these would have left a visible descender.[12]

To these two songs one can now add a third. The rondeau *Depuis le congé que pris* (fol. 75v-76) has a trimmed ascription that has not been previously noted. Moreover, what remains of it is essentially identical to the one found above *Seulette suis sans ami*: the same bottom hook of an initial 'C', even placed in approximately the same spot in relation to the left margin. Visible on microfilm, this trimmed letter is unmistakable in the original. There are no

[9] That said, in relative terms Florence 176 has a slightly greater number of ascriptions than Pix, with twenty-eight works ascribed out of a total of eighty-six.

[10] Pix, fols. 43v-45; see Andrea Lindmayr-Brandl, 'Resjois toi terre de France / Rex pacificus: An Ockeghem Work Reattributed to Busnoys', in Higgins (ed.), *Antoine Busnoys*, 277-94. The work also survives, without ascription, in Montecassino, Bibl. dell'Abbazia, MS 871, 375.

[11] Pix, fols. 23v-24; see Fallows, *Catalogue of Polyphonic Songs*, 369, where he notes also that the song's *secunda pars* begins with a melodic gesture found in many of Caron's works. The chanson is also in Florence, Bibl. Nazionale, MS Magl. xix.178 (without ascription) and thus must have been circulating in Florence prior to the copying of Pix. This trimmed 'C' was first noted in Edward Pease, *Music from the Pixérécourt Manuscript* (Ann Arbor, 1960), 89 (with an edition of the song on p. 29).

[12] The same holds true for 'Petrus Congiet', the otherwise unknown name attached to two songs in the later Florentine chansonnier Florence, Bibl. Nazionale, Banco Rari 229. One of these works, *Trays amoureulx*, appears in Pix as well, though without any trace of an ascription.

vestiges of descenders, and so like *Seulette suis*, this is the remnant of what must have been an ascription to Caron.

A transcription of the song is given as Example 1. Quite apart from the fact that it survives in the manuscript with the largest number of Caron songs, it is easy to accept *Depuis le congé* as his on stylistic grounds alone. All but one of its five phrases begin with brief passages of uncluttered imitation involving Tenor and Cantus, of a sort characteristic of a number of his songs (in the final phrase, beginning at bar 43, the Contratenor joins in as well). There are clear similarities between *Depuis le congé* and three of his works (all of them in Pix), *Le despourveu*, *Mort ou mercy*, and *Se doulx penser*. A small but telling detail in *Depuis le congé* is the counterpoint in bar 17, where Tenor and Contratenor move directly from unison to octave, a curiously naked progression that appears also in *Mort ou mercy* and his *C'est temps perdu*, a song found not in Pix but in both earlier and later Florentine sources (Riccardiana 2356 and Florence 229).[13]

However it is another of Caron's songs, *Du tout ainsy*, that *Depuis le congé* most closely resembles. Beyond similarities in their melodic contours and use of imitation, they share a rhythmic style simpler than that found in many of his other works. In turn, these features may be an indication that both songs come from relatively early in his career. His point of departure in composing *Du tout ainsy* was almost certainly Du Fay's late rondeau *Puis que vous estes campieur*. The two songs begin with much the same music and both consistently employ imitation (Du Fay is the stricter of the two, with one voice derived canonically, while Caron simply begins each phrase with short imitative passages initiated by either the Tenor or the Cantus). *Du tout ainsy* is an attractive and perfectly competent song, but its relative simplicity and straightforward use of Du Fay as a model suggest a less experienced composer. If true, we might then take the many similarities with *Depuis le congé* to mean that both songs were written during the same, possibly early, phase of his career. At all events, the stylistic details of *Depuis le congé* give every reason to accept the trimmed ascription in Pix and to add this to the list of securely attributed songs of Caron. This addition brings to twenty-two the number of songs ascribed to him in at least one source.

---

[13] On the use of this progression in Caron's songs, see David Fallows, *Robert Morton's Songs: A Study of Styles in the Mid-Fifteenth Century* (Ph.D., University of California, Berkeley, 1978), 442.

Example 1. Caron, *Depuis le conge que je pris*, Pix., fols. 75v-76r

The second scribal detail in Pix to be discussed here involves not ascriptions but voice designations. Part of the visual appeal of this manuscript is its consistency and apparent completeness, with 171 pieces filling twenty gatherings, all of them copied by a single scribe, and decorated initials done in a similar manner on every opening. Amidst this kind of near uniformity, even small discrepancies stand out. In this case the inconsistency is very small indeed – the scribe's way of writing the letter *r* in the voice designation 'Tenor' – but turns out to be unexpectedly revealing. The shape of this *r* changes abruptly at the final opening of Gathering 12 (fol. 117v). Whereas up through fol. 116v (Gatherings 1-12) the scribe consistently writes 'Tenor' using one type of *r* (Type-1), from fol. 117v to the end of the manuscript (i.e., Gatherings 13 to 20) he uses a clearly different form (Type-2). Judging from other aspects of the scribe's work, there is no reason to suspect a significant break in copying at this point. To the contrary, the four exceptional occurrences of Type-1 after fol. 116v are all found within the subsequent gathering (Gathering 13). This kind of mixing of types within the space of a few openings is just what one would expect from a scribe who had continued copying after having made a change (consciously or otherwise) in his way of writing a particular word, especially a word that appeared on every opening of the manuscript.[14]

The potential significance of this minor change in the scribe's practice became clear only as I began to notice a pattern in the concordances between Pix and other manuscripts. (For clarity's sake I will refer here to Gatherings 1-12 as Pix1, and Gatherings 13-20 as Pix2.) The pattern that emerged is chronological in orientation. In manuscripts copied earlier than Pix, the concordances cluster in Pix1, with few or none in Pix2. This holds true even for Riccardiana 2356, a manuscript copied in Florence perhaps just a few years earlier: of the thirty-nine pieces it shares with Pix, thirty are in Pix1. Conversely, manuscripts copied in the mid to late 1480s or later have concordances mostly with Pix2. Another Florentine manuscript illustrates the point: Florence 229, a large collection securely dated to *c.*1492 and decorated by the same artists who worked on Pix, has forty-one works in common with it.[15] Thirty-one of these concordances are

---

[14] The four occurrences of the Type-1 *r* after fol. 116v are on fols. 121v, 123v (the middle opening of Gathering 13), 125v, and 128v. Everywhere else in this gathering one finds the Type-2 *r*. The only exceptional appearance of this Type-2 before fol. 117v is on fol. 15v (the middle opening of Gathering 2 and, as it happens, a Caron song, the combinative chanson *Corps contre corps*). The song is copied over two openings, on the second of which one finds the expected Type-1 *r*. The likeliest explanation for this apparent anomaly is that the voice designation on fol. 15v was inadvertently omitted during initial copying and then added at some later point, after the scribe had switched to the Type-2 *r*.

[15] On the decoration of Pix and Florence 229, see Howard Mayer Brown (ed.), *A Florentine Chansonnier from the Time of Lorenzo the Magnificent: Florence, Biblioteca Nazionale Centrale MS Banco Rari 229*, MRM 7, Text Volume (Chicago and London, 1983), 9-15.

in Pix2, constituting nearly half of all the music in this part of Pix. By contrast, Pix1, which contains one hundred works, shares just ten songs with Florence 229. As one can see in Table 1, the pattern is consistent not only for Florentine sources, but also those copied elsewhere in Italy and in France.

Pix1= Gatherings 1-12, 100 works total
Pix2= Gatherings 13-20, 71 works total

	Pix1	Pix2
Northern MSS from 1460s and 70s		
Laborde (Layer 1)	14	1
Wolfenbüttel	14	2
Nivelle	7	1
Dijon	15	5
Italian or Savoyard MSS from 1450s to ca.1480		
Porto	5	0
Escorial B (main corpus, through f. 120)	17	1
Berlin	14	0
Cordiforme	13	2
Mellon 1 (later repertory)	6	8
Mellon 2 (earlier repertory)	5	0
Montecassino	15	6
Florence 176	21	9
Riccardiana 2356	30	9
Italian MSS from mid-to-late 1480s to early 1490s		
Bologna Q16	14	17
Casanatense	11	13
Verona 757	3	5
Florence 229	10	31

Table 1. A selection of manuscripts copied between the 1450s and 1490s and the number of their concordances with the two repertorial layers of the *Pixérécourt Chansonnier*

These different concordance patterns for Pix1 and Pix2 recall in some ways the two distinct repertorial layers of the *Mellon Chansonnier*, first noted by Leeman Perkins.[16] But whereas in Mellon one of the layers consists of obviously older

---

[16] Leeman L. Perkins and Howard Garey (eds.), *The Mellon Chansonnier: Volume 2, Commentary* (New Haven, 1979), 3-5.

music than the other, in Pix the chronological distinction between Pix1 and Pix2 involves when these pieces began circulating in Florence. Elsewhere I have noted the uneven distribution of Busnoys's songs in Pix (just 4 songs in Pix1, but 18 in Pix2), which when taken in conjunction with other factors (including a re-dating of the *Berlin Chansonnier* to no earlier than 1472) strongly suggests that the first substantial appearance of his chansons in Florence occurred not in the 1470s, but rather around the time the scribe was finishing Pix1, probably in the mid 1480s.[17]

In the case of Caron, the distribution is more balanced: eleven songs in Pix1, eight in Pix2. This confirms what could be inferred from the larger number of songs by him found already in the slightly earlier Florence 176 and Riccardiana 2356; namely, that his songs began circulating in Florence some years before Busnoys's. Even here, though, recognition of these two layers in Pix can tell us something further about when certain of Caron's songs appeared in Florence. Of his eleven songs in Pix1, two are *unica* (here I include *Depuis le congé*). Of the remaining nine songs, six appear already in Florence 176 and Riccardiana 2356, but none of these are included in Florence 229 in the early 1490s. Interestingly, the three songs from the eleven in Pix1 that are *not* in either Florence 176 or Riccardiana 2356 are all in Florence 229, which suggests these three became available in Florence only around the time of Pix1. What is puzzling here is that two of these three, *Helas que pourra devenir* and *Cent mille escus*, are his most widely copied songs; moreover they appear already in some of the earlier sources of his music (including the *Laborde* and *Wolfenbüttel Chansonniers*, copied probably in the mid to late 1460s). So they were around, but apparently not in Florence. The eight Caron songs found in both Pix2 and Florence 229 tell much the same story. Most of these were probably not circulating in Florence before the mid 1480s, since they do not appear in earlier Florentine sources. Here again, though, at least two of these works (*Le despourveu* and *Mort ou mercy*) had already existed for a number of years by *c*.1480. All of which is to say that the existence of a chanson that had been composed in France or at the Burgundian court – even perhaps as much as a decade or two earlier – should be taken as no guarantee that it was circulating in Italy, even in as active a center of song collecting as Florence evidently was in these years. The copying and compilation of Pix sketched here can help clarify when particular songs actually became available in Florence, thereby sharpening our understanding of the Florentine reception of chansons by Caron, Busnoys, and their contemporaries.

---

[17] Sean Gallagher, 'The Berlin Chansonnier and French Song in Florence, 1450-1490: A New Dating and its Implications', in *Journal of Musicology* 24 (2007), 339-64.

THE *OFFICIUM* OF THE *RECOLLECTIO FESTORUM BEATE MARIE VIRGINIS* BY GILLES CARLIER AND GUILLAUME DU FAY: ITS CELEBRATION AND REFORM IN LEUVEN

Barbara Haggh

In 1457, Michael de Beringhen, a canon at Cambrai Cathedral, requested that a new Marian feast be added to the Cathedral's liturgical calendar. Its purpose was to recall or recollect the six Marian feasts then celebrated there – her Conception, Nativity, Annunciation, Visitation, Purification, and Assumption – within one feast. He commissioned the texts and music for this new office, the *Recollectio festorum beate Marie virginis*, from two distinguished canons of the Cathedral, its dean, Gilles Carlier (c.1390-1472), who had left his mark at the Council of Basel, which had deputed him to Bohemia to resolve the Church's disputes with the Hussites, and Guillaume Du Fay (1397?-1474), a leading composer of the fifteenth century, whose career had taken him to Bologna, Florence, Rome, and the two Councils at defining moments in history. Thus, it should not surprise that the *Officium* of the *Recollectio* composed by these two eminent men inspired others to establish it in churches and convents outside of Cambrai with their foundations.[1]

One man, Walter Henry, founded the *Recollectio* in more establishments than any other individual.[2] In this essay, we will consider the foundations he made in the university town of Leuven, the diffusion of the *Officium* in manuscripts and prints in Leuven, its later reform, and its survival into the twentieth century. As we shall see, Leuven played a central role in the history of the celebration of the *Recollectio.*

---

[1] The attribution of the *Recollectio* texts and chant to Du Fay was announced in Barbara Haggh, 'The Celebration of the *Recollectio festorum beatae Mariae virginis*, 1457-1987', in Angelo Pompilio and others (eds.), *Atti del XIV congresso della Società internazionale di musicologia. Trasmissione e recezione delle forme di cultura musicale*, (Turin, 1990), vol.3, 559-71. The *Officium* is edited and discussed in Barbara Haggh, *Gilles Carlier and Guillaume Du Fay, 'Recollectio festorum beate Marie virginis': A History, Analysis, Edition and Commentary* (Turnhout, forthcoming). Gilbert Huybens recognized the interest of the *Recollectio* in 'Guillaume Dufay en zijn tijd', *Voorlichtingsblad van het Belgisch muziekleven*, 13/5 (1974), 5, but did not know that chant for the celebration survived.

[2] Here I use the name given in his will. Elsewhere I have used the name 'Henrici', which is found in the 'acta capituli' of St. Goedele. Biographical information is published in Micheline Soenen, 'Un amateur de musique à Bruxelles à la fin du XVe siècle. Gautier Henri, chanoine et écolâtre de Sainte-Gudule', in Hilda Coppejans-Desmedt (ed.), *Album Carlos Wyffels* (Brussels, 1987), 423-36, and in Barbara Haggh, *Music, Liturgy, and Ceremony in Brussels, 1350-1500* (Ph.D. diss., University of Illinois at Urbana-Champaign, 1988), 605-7. A table of the foundations made by Henry is in Haggh, *The Celebration*, 563-5.

Wautier Henry de Thymon, as he is named in his will, no doubt came to be interested in the university town of Leuven, because of his training and career as an educator. In the 1430s he received instruction in music as a choirboy at Cambrai Cathedral under Nicolas Grenon, who was then Guillaume Du Fay's neighbor.[3] Henry subsequently served in the 'chappelle' of Duke Philip the Good as fourth 'sommelier' in 1445 and third 'clerc' by 1456. In 1457, he was a 'clerc' in the 'chappelle' of Charles, Count of Charolais; in 1461 he left Philip's 'chappelle'; then, he was listed in Charles's 'chappelle' in 1462 and intermittently until 1476. In 1470, he became first 'sommelier' of the oratory, replacing the departing Jean Caron.[4] Henry also served as the councillor of the Duke, who made him Dean of Christianity for the bishop of Cambrai in Brussels and Mechelen, a post of some importance, since his proximity to the bishop may have given him the authority to promote the new Marian feast as he did.[5]

While still at the court, Henry began to accumulate benefices. On 23 May 1465, already holding the position of scholaster at the collegiate church of St. Goedele in Brussels, Henry came into possession of a major canonicate at this church, with the tenth prebend.[6] The position of 'scholasticus' in Brussels required its holder to take responsibility for all local schools.[7] As elsewhere, highly-educated canons held this position, such as, at Cambrai Cathedral,

---

[3] David Fallows, *Dufay* (London, 1987), 60.

[4] Soenen traces his career at court in *Un amateur*, 425-6. The 'escroes' (lists of persons present to receive daily distributions) of the courts of Philip the Good and Charles the Bold are transcribed and discussed in Jeannine Douillez, *De muziek aan het bourgondische-habsburgse hof in de tweede helft der XVde eeuw* (Ph.D. diss., Universiteit Gent, 1967); David Fiala, *Mécénat musical des ducs de Bourgogne et des princes de la maison de Habsbourg (1467-1506)* (Ph. D. Diss., University of Tours 2002; Turnhout, in press); Barbara Haggh, *The Status of the Musician at the Burgundian Habsburg Courts, 1467-1506* (MA thesis, University of Illinois at Urbana-Champaign, 1980); Jeanne Marix, *Histoire de la musique et des musiciens de la Cour de Bourgogne sous le règne de Philippe le Bon (1420-1457)* (Strasbourg, 1939; repr. Baden-Baden, 1974).

[5] See Josse Ange Rombaut, *Bruxelles illustrée, ou déscription chronologique et historique de cette ville* (Brussels, 1779), vol. 2, 82.

[6] See his biography in Soenen, *Un amateur*, 428-9, and in Haggh, *Music*, 605. On 23 May 1465, Walter Henry received the canonicate and prebend at St. Goedele of Magister Nicolas Calculi with letters of collation from the Duke of Burgundy (Brussels, Algemeen Rijksarchief, ASG 910, f. 105r). Henry also possessed chaplaincies in Brussels, that at the chapel of the Virgin Mary in the Zavelkerk in Brussels, received 9 April 1461 (ibid., f. 98v [not 11 April as in Soenen]), and that at the altar of the Holy Spirit and Cross in the church of St. Nicholas in Brussels, received 9 November 1478 (ibid., f. 115v; a later possessor of the chaplaincy was the composer Antoine Busnoys, see Barbara Haggh, 'Busnoys and 'Caron' in Documents from Brussels', in Paula Higgins (ed.), *Antoine Busnoys: Method, Meaning and Context in Late Medieval Music* (New York, 1999), 295-315.

[7] See Paul De Ridder, *Inventaris van het oud archief van de kapittelkerk van Sint-Michiel en Sint-Goedele te Brussel* (Brussels, 1987), vol. 1, 25-8; and Haggh, *Music*, 149-54.

Guillaume Du Fay's acquaintance, Robert Auclou, who, like Henry, was well-known at the Court of Burgundy.[8] Although we have no information about Henry's education after he left Cambrai, his library, which is described in his will, and the three 'clavicordia' and songbooks he owned at his death, attest to his intellectual interests and musical training.[9] He also donated to Cambrai Cathedral a collection of polyphonic masses and another of music theory treatises.[10]

Further evidence that he considered himself a musician is the request for his epitaph at St. Goedele. Henry died in Brussels on 5 December 1494.[11] He was buried in the western side of the church where the bell-tower was, with a funeral 'sine pompa'. In his will, he had asked that his epitaph resemble that of the singer-composer, Richard de Bellengues dit Cardot (1380-1471) in its size and in its inclusion of an image of the Annunciation, a devotion Henry promoted with foundations at Cambrai Cathedral and at St. Goedele:[12]

> Brussels, Algemeen Rijksarchief, Kerkarchief van Brabant (hereafter ARB) 11673, 14 September 1486, f. 3r: 'Item soe verre Ic sterve binnen der stadt van Bruessel en dat Ic gecoren hadde mijn sepulture binnen der kerken van sinte Goedelen, Ic wille begraven worden voir de capelle dair Ic mijn fondatie gemaect hebbe en wille dair hebben een epythaphie van cooperen als wijlen her Cardoet epythaf gemaect is, dair inne gegraven sal worden Onser Vrouwen Bootscap gelijc zij staet inde gelasen venstre my dair voire kniesende, en sullen dair onder gescreven worden deese woerden, 'Cy devant gist maistre Gautier Henry, jadis chanonne et escolastre de ceste eglise serviteur dommesticque et chr. es chapelles et oratoires des ducs Philippe et Charles de Valois, ducs de Bourgognes, de Brabant etc. Conte de etc.', welc voirs. epytaphie gestels sal worden tusschen de twee cleyne

---

[8] On Auclou, see Barbara Haggh, 'Guillaume Du Fay's *Missa Sancti Jacobi*: A Mass for his Friend, Robert Auclou?', in Martin Czernin (ed.), *Gedenkschrift für Walter Pass* (Tutzing, 2002), 307-19.

[9] Brussels, ARB 11673, f. 5r-v: "Item Ic ordineere den voirs. heer Janne Henricx [...] Item alle mij boeken die men vinden sal dat Ic dair af niet gedisponeert en sal hebben lat Ic hem om die te gebruykene en die te bewaren den tijt van twee jairen behoudelijc dat hij zeker setten sal die over te leveren en dat de prior en procurator vanden Chartroysen te Loven dair op dooge hebben tentgetal dair af in gescrifte om die ten eynde van desen twee jairen in huer cloester geloet te wordene niet hier inne begrepen de sancboeken die heer Jan behouden sal." Also see Brussels, Algemeen Rijksarchief, Archief Sint-Goedele (hereafter ASG) 276, f. 212r.

[10] Soenen, *Un amateur*, 436.

[11] The very next day, 6 December 1494, Philip the Fair placed Magister Sixtus Scharffenegker in the canonicate vacated by Henry's death (Brussels, ASG 139).

[12] See Eugeen Schreurs, 'Cardot, Richard', *MGG* 4 (2000), cols. 194-5.

pylairkens tusschen de beelden van sinte Ligier en sinte Dominicus vander Lingden van Cardots epytaphe en voorder meeste breyden dat moegelyc sal zijn tusschen de voirs. twee pylaerkens.'[13]

Henry was a generous benefactor even by fifteenth-century standards. He founded two celebrations in fourteen churches throughout the Low Countries, the first the new Marian feast from Cambrai known as the *Recollectio festorum beate Mariae virginis* and the second, a yearly obit for himself, as well as religious establishments and other services. It may be significant that most of his foundations date from after Carolus Soillot replaced him as scholaster at St. Goedele on 28 May 1479.[14] He would have had the time then to supervise the initiation of his foundations. Henry's own collection of ten original charters of foundation of the *Recollectio* survives, and testify to the personal meaning those foundations had for him. He kept the charters carefully until his death, asking in his will that they be stored at the Charterhouse convent of Our Lady of Grace in Brussels. The charters remained together until today, and, along with many other documents, they give evidence that the *Recollectio* and obit endowed by Henry were celebrated into the eighteenth century in many establishments, further evidence of the significance of the Henry foundations in their time.[15] We do not know how Henry learned of the *Recollectio*, but the court of Burgundy visited Cambrai in 1468, and Henry was among the chaplains present. If he did not know of the *Recollectio* before, he might have heard of it then.[16]

One of Henry's many foundations for the *Recollectio* was made at the collegiate church of St. Pieter in Leuven on 16 January 1476.[17] Henry had become canon of this church by 1450, but had left this canonicate by 1476.[18] A note in a fifteenth-

---

[13] The copy of this entry in French is Brussels, ASG 266, f. 39v: "Item se Je moroye en la ville de brousselles et que Jeslisse ma sepulture en leglie[se] sy[n]te goule, Je voel estre ensevely devant le capelle ou Jay fait ma fondacon et voul avoir ung epithase de guenre a la samblance de Richart de belenges dit Cardot jadis chanonne deladite eglise, ouquel y sera gravet lannon-ciation nostre damme alasamblance de le verriere deladite capelle, et moy dessoubz, ou y ara en escript, "Cy deuant gist maistre gautier henrj, jadis chanoine et escolastre de ceste eglise, seruiteur dommesticque et clericus es chapelles et oratoires des ducs ph[i]l[ipp]e et charles de valois, ducs de bourgogne, de brabant, etc., conte de flandre et de haynnau, et natif de la ville de terlon, item conte de haynnau, qui trespassa en lan etc." Lequel epithase sera mis entre deux petis pilers entre st ligier et st dominicque, de le longheur comme celuy dud[it] cardot, et ossy large qui porra estre entre les desd[is] petis pilers."

[14] Brussels, ASG 910, f. 116r.

[15] Brussels, ARB 11587bis, nos. 1049-1062. The charters do not correspond entirely to the four-teen different foundations of the *Recollectio*, some of which are documented in separate char-ters. On the foundations, see Soenen, *Un amateur*, 434-6 and Haggh, *The Celebration*, 563-5.

[16] Marix, *Histoire*, 151.

[17] Brussels, ARB 1281, nos. 1205-1206; Soenen, *Un amateur*, 435.

[18] Soenen, *Un amateur*, 428.

century breviary of St. Pieter without musical notation (Brussels, Koninklijke Bibliotheek, Ms. ll788) indicates that the *Recollectio* was first celebrated on the first Sunday in September 1477,[19] which was also the day after the 'kermes' or town fair and included a procession:[20]

> 'NOTA: Istud festum solempnitatum omnium festorum beate Mariae virginis fuit primitus celebratum, in ecclesia Sancti Petri Lovaniensis, prima dominica septembris anno septuagesimo septimo, que tunc fuit septima dies mensis septembris. Et deinceps semper celebrabitur prima dominica septembris, quia tunc est processio Lovaniensis.'[21]

The texts in the breviary are those that were in use at Cambrai Cathedral.[22] Some years later, in a will dated 14 September 1486, Henry established the *Recollectio* at the Augustinian convent in Leuven. The new feast should be celebrated at some time between the feast of the Assumption and the Nativity of Mary. The date was eventually fixed as 1 September:

> Brussels, ARB 11673, f. 3r: 'Item Ic ordineere den Vrouwenbroeders van Bruessel 3 L. Artoys erffelike renten, te wetenen deen L. voir mijn jairgetide en dander twee anderen om gecelebreert te wordenen de feeste vander Collectien van alle den feesten van Onser Vrouwen op eenen dach tusschen der octaven van Onser Vrouwen Opvaert en van huere geboirte. Ende insgelijcx soe selen de Minderbroederen te Bruessel. Ende soe vele oic den Augustijnen van Loevene voer gelijke officie en jairgetijde, dair af zij brieven mijnen executeuren geven sullen om die diensten eeuwelijc wel en loffelijc te doenen, dwelc zij aenveert hebben en geaccordeert. Ende zoe verre dese renten afgequeten worden datmen die wederom leggen sal aen gelijke goede renten sullen oic dese renten bekeert worden tot twee pytantien voir de twee dagen datmen den voirs. dienst doen sal. Ende dat huer brieven die zij geven sullen inhouden selen, dat zij dese renten niet en selen

---

[19] The full *officium* by Carlier and Du Fay is found on ff. 238r-244r, with an addition on f. 245v made in the script of the main text of the book, but clearly added, since it is in lighter ink. On the manuscript, see Joseph Van den Gheyn, *Catalogue des manuscrits de la Bibliotheque Royale de Belgique* (Brussels, 1901), i, 342-3, no. 543. Incipits of the texts are published in Placide Lefèvre, *Les Ordinaires des collégiales Saint-Pierre a Louvain et Saints-Pierre-et-Paul a Anderlecht d'après les manuscrits du XIVe siècle* (Leuven, 1960), xv, xvi, 278, 280, 282, 284, 286.

[20] The *Recollectio* was also celebrated with a major procession at the church of Onze Lieve Vrouw in Antwerp. See Haggh, *Gilles Carlier and Guillaume Du Fay*, chapter six.

[21] Lefèvre, *Les Ordinaires*, 284.

[22] See A.P. Frutaz, 'La 'Recollectio festorum B. Mariae Virginis'. Testi liturgici in uso nella diocesi di Aosta dal sec. XV al sec. XIX', *Ephemerides liturgicae* 70/1 (1956), 24.

moege verklere. Ende in gevalle dat zij den voers. dienst niet en daden sullen de Chartroysen van Loven den rente de Augustinen van Loeven gemaect hebben en distribueren in twee pytantien. Ende aengaene den Minderbroeders en Vrouwenbroeders van Bruessel zelen dair af doege hebben die Chartroysen van Onser Vrouwen van Gracien, welke twee cloesteren van Chartroysen Ic late tghelt om de voirs. renten gecocht te wordenen en dat zij vanden Chartroysen die renten betalen sullen.'[23]

Brussels, ASG 266 [1493], f. 57r: 'Item betaelt inden handen vanden priore van Onser Vrouwen van Gracien en vander nuwen cloestere vanden Chartroysen te Loven om te funderene metten penninck 20 alsvore de feesten vander Recollectien van Onser Vrouwen feesten inden cloesteren van Onser Vrouwenbruederen en Minderbruederen te Bruessel ende vander Augustijnen te Loven met 3 gemeynen guldene erflic telker plaetsen hondert en 40 R. gulden in goude dair inne begrepen worden 9 gemeyne Rinsgulden die men betalen sal voer dierste jaer die maken - 47 L. 5 s.g.'

Henry's foundations of the *Recollectio* at monastic houses in Brussels were to be supervised by a Charterhouse dedicated to Notre Dame de Grâce, which had been founded in the 1450s with generous donations from the Court of Burgundy.[24] Henry may have wished to recreate a similar situation in Leuven, because on 26 September 1491, he founded a Charterhouse convent in Leuven, with the support of Margaret of York, the widow of Charles the Bold.[25] Henry's books were willed to the Leuven Charterhouse,[26] and he also stipulated in his will that bread, wine, and ornaments for the divine service should be donated to the community.

Brussels, ASG 266, f. 41r: 'Et 4 florins a Chartroix de Louvain pour employer a leur luminaire, pain, vin a celebrer, et a leurs livres et ornemens deleur couvent.'; f. 61r: 'Item den prioer en convente vanden Chartroysen te Loven om aldus geleert te worddene alle zijn boeken.'

The Charterhouse was incorporated into the University of Leuven in 1521, by which time its community included twenty-seven clerics and six lay brothers.[27]

---

[23] Brussels, Algemeen Rijksarchief, Kerkarchief van Brabant, Ms. 11673.
[24] Haggh, *Music*, 74-5.
[25] Soenen, *Un amateur*, 435. Also see Brussels, ARB 14956, the charter of foundation of 1491.
[26] See note 9 above.
[27] Alfons d'Hoop, *Inventaire des archives ecclésiastiques de Brabant* (Brussels, 1914), vol. 4, 280, note 2.

(The clergy lived in small individual cells when they were not worshipping in the church.) This community, like that in Brussels, was not expected to sing the *Recollectio*, only to oversee Henry's foundations of it at other monastic houses.

Presumably the *Recollectio* continued to be celebrated in Leuven at St. Pieter's (the records of the Augustinian convent have not yet been studied), because in the sixteenth century, the office of this collegiate church was reformed. The reforms are described in a booklet printed in Leuven in 1614, which includes only the *Recollectio*. The title page reads: *Officium Recollectionis Gaudiorum et Festorum Beatae Mariae Virginis, iuxta ritum Romani Breviarij concinnatum ad usum Collegiatae Ecclesiae D. Petri Lovaniensis* (Lovanii: Ex Officina Ioannis Masii, sub viridi Cruce, 1614).[28] On the verso of the title page, the reform of the office is described:

> 'Hoc Recollectionis officium, Romae visum et probatum, ex decreto Capituli collegiatae D. Petri Ecclesiae Louaniensis collectum et concinnatum, ego subscriptus imprimi feci. Actum Louanij 16 Augusti, Anno 1594. H. Cuyckius, Decanus D. Petri Louanij, Vicarius et Officialis Curiae Mechliniensis Louanij constitutae, et Pontificius ac Regius librorum Censor.'

The reformed *Recollectio* was surely inspired by the reforms of the Council of Trent.[29] After the end of the Council in 1563, a bull of Pope Pius V of 1568 prescribed the use of the new Roman breviary. Just before this time, bulls of 1559 and 1561 had established new dioceses in the Low Countries; the first synods held by the new bishops discussed the implementation of the reforms. Yet iconoclasm, other religious disputes, and war prevented much from being accomplished before the end of the century, though progress was made surreptitiously in some cases. It is telling that the earliest source for the reformed office is a manuscript antiphoner completed in 1583 with a note on the inside cover explaining how two canons copied the book for the church of St. Germain in Mons during their exile from Brussels, a city that they had been

---

[28] Brussels, Bollandist Library, Impr. B 373.
[29] The sources for the Post-Tridentine *Recollectio* as well as its diffusion in the Low Countries are discussed in Barbara Haggh, 'The Medium Transforms the Message? Conflicting Evidence from the Printed Sources of the *Officium Recollectionis festorum beate Mariae Virginis*', in Giulio Cattin and others (eds.), *Il canto piano nell'era della stampa*, (Trent, 1999), 73-80.

forced to leave because of the Calvinist heresy.[30] Indeed, on 6 June 1579 and 22 April 1581 the collegiate church of St. Goedele in Brussels was pillaged, whereafter it was closed until 22 March 1585. The Calvinist magistrates of Brussels sold the raided items.[31]

How the scribe of the Mons manuscript learned of the office is not known, but Brussels is not far from Leuven, and there is much evidence to suggest that the reformed office was created in Leuven. It was first printed there in three separate editions, in 1594, 1599, and 1614, and the notice in the 1614 edition, cited above, states that the new office had been seen and approved in Rome (which the office by Carlier and Du Fay never was), and collected and assembled following the Roman rite — by decree of the chapter of the collegiate church of St. Pieter in Leuven. The dean of St. Pieter in Leuven in 1594 was Henricus Cuyckius, then vicar and official of the new archdiocese of Mechelen, and papal and royal censor of books. He was thus in a position to obtain the necessary permissions for the celebration of the office.

If Cuyckius did not assemble the revised *Recollectio* himself for the chapter of St. Pieter, then he was surely responsible for delegating the task, possibly to colleagues at the University in Leuven. After brilliant studies in philosophy and theology there, Cuyckius taught at the University and served as rector in the 1570s and 1580s; by 1592 he was a canon and dean of the church of St. Pieter and no less than chancellor of the University.[32]

In 1596, Cuyckius became bishop of Roermond, where he supervised the reform of that diocesan ritual and ordered an entire series of reformed service books to be printed. He may have introduced the new *Recollectio officium* to his diocese as well. The most convincing evidence for this is the name given to the feast in Roermond. It varied considerably from church to church, and of the books dating from before 1600, only those from Leuven or for the diocese of Roermond use the word 'gaudiorum' in the title: in Leuven the feast was called the *Recollectio gaudiorum et festorum beate Marie virginis*; in Roermond it

---

[30] Mons, Treasury of St. Waudru, Ms. s.s., ff. 115v-124v. The inside front cover has this note: 'En ces temps ou l'hérésie (calviniste) ne permit aux fidèles du pape et du roi de vivre sur le sol patrial, Francois Daens et Antoine Bergheim (coeurs unis liés par la foi) expulsés de Bruxelles et forcés de gagner les murs de Mons, ont travaillé ensemble à ce livre. Celui-ci écrit la notation à l'aide d'une plume longue; celui-la a écrit de sa main le texte sacre. Ce livre a été écrit aux frais du Chapitre de Saint-Germain [the male chapter belonging with the canonnesses of St Waudru] sous le Procureur Maître Jean Erconius, chanoine du même chapitre collégiale. L'an 1583."

[31] See Placide Lefèvre, 'Documents relatifs aux vitraux de Sainte-Gudule à Bruxelles du XVIe et du XVIIe siècle', *Revue belge d'archéologie et d'histoire de l'art*, 15 (1945), 130.

[32] This and the next paragraph summarize arguments presented in Haggh, *Gilles Carlier and Guillaume Du Fay*, chapter nine.

was known as the feast of the *Gaudiorum beate Marie virginis*. And since the reformed office was printed first in Roermond and Leuven, while Cuyckius was bishop and dean of the church of St. Pieter, it seems unlikely that anyone else could have introduced the feast. The archives of the Roermond churches have many lacunae, but they show no trace of the *Recollectio* before the time of Cuyckius, nor are there any documents recording individual foundations of the feast while he was bishop or afterwards. Further evidence that Cuyckius was indeed responsible for the reformed office is the fact that only the name given to the feast in Leuven appears in most of the 'officiae propriae' and 'missae propriae' after 1600 that included the *Recollectio*. These were for churches in Mons, Condé, Douai, and several Praemonstratensian abbeys, as well as for Leuven and Roermond.

One manuscript and three printed booklets containing the *Recollectio* texts of Leuven are known to survive:

> Brussels, Algemeen Rijksarchief, Kerkarchief van Brabant, Ms. 1406: *Officium Recollectionis Gaudiorum et Festorum Beatae Mariae Virginis juxta ritum Romani Breviarii concinnatum ad usum collegiatae ecclesiae Divi Petri Lovaniensis*, undated, written in the late sixteenth or early seventeenth century; probably copied from the print of 1594. Edited by Leon Van der Essen in *Notre Dame de St-Pierre (Louvain) "Siège de la Sagesse" (1129-1927)* (Leuven, 1927), 85-91, with the mass at 89-90.

> *Officium Recollectionis Gaudiorum et Festorum Beatae Mariae Virginis, iuxta ritum Romani Breuiarij concinnatum: ad vsum Collegiatae Ecclesiae D. Petri Louvanensis*. Lovanii, ex officina Ioannis Masij, sub viridi Cruce, 1599, [12 unnumbered fols.]. Brussels, Koninklijke Bibliotheek Albert I, Kostbare Boeken, Impr. II.73.171 A.

> *Festa et Officia Peculiaria: In insigni Collegiata Ecclesia D. Petri Lovaniensi servari consueta.* Lovanii: Typis Ioannis Masii, sub Viridi Cruce, 1616, 109-118. Brussels, Bollandist Library, Impr. B 373.

> *Officia Peculiaria Sanctorum in insigni Ecclesia Collegiata Divi Petri Lovaniensi servari solita. In quibus omnia suis locis extense posita sunt, pro majori recitantium commoditate.* Lovanii, Typis Petri Sasseni, 1663, 43-59. Personal collection of Gilbert Huybens of Leuven.

The comparison of the pre- and post-Tridentine *Recollectio officia* is revealing.[33] The original texts and chant for the *Recollectio* by Carlier and Du Fay constitute a highly organized meditation on those events in Mary's life that were celebrated on her six feast days: the Conception, Nativity, Annunciation, Visitation, Purification, and Assumption. Many of the texts are original poetry, but some were borrowed. These include only a few apocryphal texts: some of the chapters for the Lesser Hours are from *Ecclesiastes* and the *Book of Wisdom*; and the texts of the Gradual and Communion of the Mass are from the apocryphal book of *Tobit*. The non-Biblical poetry on the Immaculate Conception, a topic of fifteenth-century controversy, may have seemed inappropriate in the post-Tridentine environment.

Several kinds of organization are evident in the original *Recollectio*, and these bear mention, because they contrast so markedly with the reformed office.[34] In the original, successive texts for both Vespers, Matins and Lauds summarize the content of the six Marian feasts in order: the first antiphon tells of the Conception, the second of the Nativity, and so on. The successive texts are set to the modes in ascending numerical order. General praises of Mary or reflections on her attributes appear, but they never interrupt the flow of these short histories of her life, except in the Mass. There, proper texts drawing on themes from Mary's Visitation and Assumption are combined with praises of Mary, and only the sequence recalls the entire life of the Virgin. In the original office, the antiphons borrow words and themes from the psalms they accompany; similarly, the responsory texts reflect the lessons preceding them. The relationship of music to text is also evident within individual chants. For example, most of the antiphons of first Vespers have many notes or especially high pitches grouped to emphasize Mary's name, which appears only once in each chant.

The reformed office, dating from around 1580, is sober and utilitarian by comparison. Non-biblical texts in the original office were replaced by biblical texts, most from the *Song of Songs* and many taken from well-established Marian chant (see below).[35] The result was a change in emphasis from that on Mary's life to that on her role as 'mediatrix', and from all of her feasts to only one, her Assumption, the feast that the *Recollectio* followed in the calendar. Yet

---

[33] Ibid.

[34] Ibid., chapters three and four.

[35] Some of the antiphons of the reformed *Recollectio* can be traced back to those sung at Cluny for the Assumption, such as the Magnificat antiphon *Tota pulchra es*. See Ruth Steiner, 'Marian Antiphons at Cluny and Lewes', in Susan Rankin and David Hiley (eds.), *Music in the Medieval English Liturgy* (Oxford, 1993), 175-204.

some texts from the old office were retained: those for the chapter and collect of first Vespers and the (borrowed) introit of the Mass, *Gaudeamus*.

My analysis of the office that was adopted by Cuyckius for the *Recollectio* led me to identify a possible model. Cuyckius's office borrows a series of five antiphons for first and second Vespers from an earlier Annunciation office, which survives in the original, twelfth-century layer of the antiphoner of the church of St. Mary's of Utrecht now at Utrecht, Bibliotheek der Rijksuniversiteit as Ms. 406.[36] This Annunciation office differs from that in use at the churches of St. Pieter in Leuven and St. Goedele in Brussels, which only share the first antiphon of first Vespers with the *Recollectio*, and not the rest.[37]

> The *Recollectio* Compiled by Cuyckius
> (CAO=René-Jean Hesbert, *Corpus antiphonalium officii*, 6 vols.,
> Rome: Herder, 1963-79)
>
> First Vespers
> A1 Hortus conclusus (CAO 3137, BEHRDFS)
> A2 Quam pulchra es (CAO 4434, BEHR)
> A3 Dilecte mi (CAO 2224, CHR)
> A4 Adjuro vos filie (CAO 1277, CVDS)
> A5 Sicut malus (CAO 4940, BEVHRDS)
> A Magnificat Tota pulchra es (CAO 5162 BRS) (not in the Utrecht
> antiphoner)
>
> Lauds (here Second Vespers)
> A1 Vulnerasti cor meum (CAO 5511 EHR)
> A2 Surge Aquilo (CAO 5070 CBEHRDFL)
> A3 Descendi in hortum nucum (CAO 2155 BRS)
> A4 Anima mea liquefacta es (CAO 1418 BS)
> A5 Tota pulchra es (CAO 5162 as above)
> A Benedictus Nigra sum sed formosa (CAO 3878 CBE VHRDFL)

---

[36] Ruth Steiner (ed.), *Utrecht, Bibliotheek der Rijksuniversiteit, Ms. 406 (3.J.7)*, Publications of Mediaeval Musical Manuscripts, 21 [facsimile], with an introduction by Ike de Loos and index by Charles Downey (Ottawa: Institute of Mediaeval Music, 1997), f. 159r-v (first vespers) and f. 161r-v (second vespers).

[37] See Lefèvre, *Les Ordinaires*, 232 and 234 (the Leuven manuscript only prescribes the first antiphon of first vespers, but no other prescribed chants correspond to those of Cuyckius's *Recollectio*). Also see the Breviary of 1516 of St. Goedele, where first vespers begins with the antiphon *Hortus conclusus*, but then varies from the Cuyckius office. The two antiphoners from Cambrai Cathedral, Cambrai, Médiathèque Municipale, Ms. 38 and Impr. XVI C 4, contain an entirely different Assumption office.

> not in the Utrecht antiphoner
> A Magnificat Quam pulchra es (CAO 4434 BEHR) (not in the
> Utrecht antiphoner)

As we can see from the presence of this chant in the earliest antiphoners, in the Cuyckius office melodies from the oldest layer of Gregorian chant replaced the new plainchant melodies composed by Du Fay.[38] Some of the older melodies were adjusted to fit the text more closely or by filling in disturbing intervals, but there is no evidence of any recomposition to match the accents of the text. Indeed, any characteristics of the music that could draw attention away from the text, or bring undue attention to it, were removed. Moreover, since texts from the Bible replaced the original poetry, there were no patterns of rhyme and meter in the new ritual to distract the listener. Finally, the subtle allusions and cross-references between the chants and readings within the original office were lost.

The Abbey of Park in Heverlee near Leuven in Belgium, a Praemonstratensian abbey dedicated to the Virgin Mary,[39] still celebrates the *Recollectio* today as a proper feast at triplex minus rank, to be held on the first Sunday in September.[40] Numerous manuscripts and printed books in the Abbey's library attest to the celebration of the *Recollectio* in the Abbey from after the Council of Trent until Vatican II. Although we do not know who founded the feast there initially, the Abbey had ties to the Court of Burgundy, and it may have celebrated Carlier and Du Fay's office before adopting the reformed office.[41] When I visited the Abbey

---

[38] There are no sources from Leuven with the music for the Post-Tridentine *Recollectio*, but the Mons antiphoner sharing the texts from Leuven transmits the music. See note 30 above.

[39] Edmond Speelman, *Belgium Marianum* (Paris, 1859), 42.

[40] Frutaz, *La 'Recollectio'*, 24.

[41] Oxford, Bodleian Library, Ms. Douce 200 (21774), a late fifteenth-century festive Epistle book from the Low Countries is the earliest Praemonstratensian source for the pre-Tridentine *Recollectio*, but its place of origin has not been determined. The Dedication of the Church falls between Easter and the Ascension (f. 26v); the rubric for the *Recollectio*, "In festo recollectionis omnium festivitatum beate Marie virginis," is on f. 49r. The material for the *Recollectio* follows that for the Nativity of the Virgin and precedes that for All Saints' Day, evidence of the solemnity accorded to the *Recollectio* in this manuscript. On the covers of the book are the erased arms of an abbot or bishop. The book has 'trompe l'œil' illuminations. On the manuscript see the notes of Van Dijk in the Bodleian Library and the earlier catalogue by Walter Howard Frere, *Bibliotheca musico-liturgica*, vol. I.1.2 (London, 1894, repr. Hildesheim 1967), no. 247, 87. Frere considers the manuscript to be Italian, but Van Dijk correctly argues that it is not. The documentary evidence from Park is inconclusive. A parchment 'necrologium', Park Abbey, Library, Ms. R VII 87, at 25 August has the entry, 'Walteri Henrici, Alberti et Walteri Fratrum ad succurrendum Ermengardis Conversae', which reappears in Raphael Van Waefelghem's edition, *Le Nécrologe de l'Abbaye du Park*. The journal by Libert de Pape, Abbot of Park from 1648 until 1682, published by Paul Lenaerts (Leuven, 1914), follows the order of the calendar, but nowhere mentions the *Recollectio*.

in 1993, the *Recollectio* was still in its calendar. The prior of the Abbey, canon Swarte, admitted to me that the celebration of the feast was often neglected, in part because the Latin texts had not yet been translated into Flemish. Two chants for the *Recollectio* were composed at Park, but I was unable to gain more information about these. I gave canon Swarte transcriptions of the two Du Fay hymns for the *Recollectio*.

The last printed book known to include notated chant for the *Recollectio*, the *Supplementum Antiphonarii pro Ecclesia Parcensi* (Paris, Tournai, Rome: Desclee, 1934) includes the *Recollectio* on pp. 6-8. When it is compared to the much earlier Cuyckius office, it proves to have identical chant for first and second Vespers and first Compline. Matins and Lauds are omitted, and only a hymn, antiphon, and 'responsorium breve' are given under the rubric 'Ad horas'. A responsory, *Christi mater*, is part of second Vespers – it was borrowed from a collection of Marian chant in the antiphoner preceding the supplement.

From this brief study, we learn that the history of the *Recollectio* in Leuven as elsewhere was marked by the decisions of prominent, highly educated individuals. Walter Henry received his wealth and authority from his association with the Court of Burgundy, Henricus Cuyckius from his position as a high-ranking servant of the Church and of the University. The decisions of men such as Cuyckius are described in the prefaces of the Post-Tridentine printed books containing the *Recollectio,* and although bishop Cuyckius's contribution was emphasized here, he was not alone: several Praemonstratensian abbots reformed the proper offices of their Order, which included the *Recollectio,* and other bishops corrected and emended the legacy of Cuyckius. Cuyckius was surely the most influential, however. It seems especially appropriate that the *Recollectio* remains in only one calendar today, that of the abbey of Park near Leuven, the city where the reformed *Recollectio Gaudiorum et Festorum beate Marie virginis* was first printed.[42]

[42] I wish to thank the Univerity of Maryland for the GRB Semester Research Award which made the completion of this article possible.

'EXCELLENT FOR THE HAND':
WRITING ON JOHN BULL'S KEYBOARD MUSIC IN ENGLAND

John Irving

Without a doubt, keyboard music was one of England's most glorious achievements during the period *c.*1550-1630. Among the composers found in contemporary manuscript anthologies of this repertoire such as the famous Fitzwilliam Virginal Book[1], two names stand out above all the others: William Byrd (*c.*1540-1623) and John Bull (1562-1628). Whereas Byrd's keyboard music has generally been regarded as rather 'intellectual' in quality, Bull's has typically been noted for its virtuosity. Moreover, it is frequently assumed that these two qualities comprise a hierarchy of value in which virtuosity is the inferior partner and that Byrd's achievement is the greater precisely because it rises above the merely virtuosic (which by implication, Bull's does not). Thus, Oliver Neighbour's groundbreaking survey of Byrd's keyboard works[2] presumes the composer's complete technical command of his craft, its excellence grounded in counterpoint, harmony, phrasing, design, and offering both an assurance of its canonical acceptance and a benchmark against which everything by his lesser colleagues (including Bull) must be measured. Shortly after Neighbour's study appeared Walker Cunningham's book on Bull's keyboard works, an account clearly influenced by Neighbour's in key methodological respects.[3] Fundamentally, Cunningham sought to retrieve some status for Bull in the wake of Neighbour's magisterial account of Byrd, and in particular to demonstrate that Bull's keyboard music is not all virtuosic showmanship, but that there is much 'intellectual' achievement to admire too, thus nuancing the received wisdom. In adopting canonical benchmarking as a methodology for their analytical enquiries and judgements, Neighbour and Cunningham implicitly signal their membership of a tradition of writing regulated by respect for compositional mastery that generates masterworks and a consequent hierarchisation of composers, forms, styles and genres. Canonicity as a validating tool for music is a historiographical practice dating back at least to institutional traditions that arose in the nineteenth century: examples include Mendelssohn's resurrection of Bach's *St. Matthew Passion*; the attempts at collected editions of composers such as Mozart; Fétis's 'concerts historiques'; the foundation across Europe of

---

[1] Cambridge, Fitzwilliam Museum, Mu. MS 168. Possibly copied by Francis Tregian between *c.*1609 and 1619, the Fitzwilliam Virginal Book is the most extensive and certainly the most famous of manuscript sources of virginal music.
[2] Oliver Neighbour, *The Consort and Keyboard Music of William Byrd* (London, 1978).
[3] Walker E. Cunningham, *The Keyboard Music of John Bull* (Ann Arbor, 1984).

music conservatoires and university musicology faculties offering a particular syllabus of instruction; and musical textbooks (dictionaries and histories). But such a tradition of canonically-based judgements of value – establishing the relative merits of 'intellectual' composition and virtuosity, for instance – and likewise the bases upon which such judgements are made, cannot and must not escape the test of authority. They are not *a priori*, but operate *historically* – that is, as social products, reflecting concerns or agendas particular to the time and place of writing. Thus, the story of our reception of Bull's keyboard music is not just about the construction of a composer of virtuoso passagework lacking in intellectual depth (or, indeed, the sufficiency of such a claim), but equally a tale about musicologists, their habits, prejudices and changing estimations of musical value *en route*. That duality is explored in the following (necessarily selective) account of English scholarly writing about Bull's keyboard music.[4]

The earliest recorded distinction between these two qualities of intellect and virtuosity in the keyboard music of Byrd and Bull is found in a manuscript copied by Thomas Tomkins (1572-1656) and containing keyboard music by himself as well as works by Byrd and Bull which he evidently admired.[5] On p. [iii] of the manuscript, Tomkins notes that Byrd's so-called *'Quadran' Pavan and Galliard*[6] are 'Excellent For matter' (meaning musical substance, or material construction). On the same page, he describes a setting of the *Quadran Pavan* by Bull[7] as 'Excellent For the Hand' (meaning that it was good for developing the technical aspects of keyboard playing). With the same distinction in mind, Tomkins lists more works by these two composers at this point in his manuscript: 'doct. Bulls Ut.re.my.fa.sol.la. For the Hand' and 'Mr Byrd's ut.Re.my.Fa.sol.la & ut. My.re: Bothe For Substance'.[8] It is a neat distinction which, according to Neighbour, captures 'the difference between Byrd and Bull [...] in a nutshell'.[9] Neighbour's application of this 'difference' is revealing. Comparing Byrd's pavans with those of Bull, he praises Bull's *Lord Lumley Pavan*[10] as 'a fine work, showing Bull's use of virtuoso keyboard

---

[4]　This is not intended as an exhaustive survey. For a sense of the scope of the literature on Bull, see the Bibliography to 'Bull, John' in *New Grove II*.

[5]　Paris, Bibliothèque Nationale, Fonds du Conservatoire, Ms. Rés. 1122. A facsimile reproduction is available: *Pièces pour Virginal 1646-1654. Fac-similé du manuscrit de la Bibliothèque Nationale, Paris, Rés. 1122*, introduction de François Lesure (Geneva, 1982).

[6]　*William Byrd: Keyboard Music II*, ed. Alan Brown (Musica Britannica, 28; rev. 2nd. edn., London, 1976), no. 70. (Musica Britannica is henceforth abbreviated to MB.)

[7]　*John Bull: Keyboard Music II*, ed. Thurston Dart (MB, 19; rev. 2nd. edn., London, 1970), either no. 127a or c.

[8]　*John Bull: Keyboard Music I*, ed. Thurston Dart (MB, 14; rev. 2nd edn., London, 1970), no. 18; Byrd: MB, 28, nos. 64 and 65.

[9]　Neighbour, *Consort and Keyboard Music*, 143.

[10]　MB, 19, no. 129a; Neighbour, *Consort and Keyboard*, 210-4 *passim*.

style at its most imaginative', but goes on to rubbish Bull's competence in matters of 'substance', singling-out his 'rather haphazard consonances and suspensions' and poor phraseology (a galliard printed in *Parthenia*[11] has, towards the beginning, 'a 4-bar phrase with an unwanted extra half bar for the sake of appearances'):

> 'Bull usually has two strands of quavers going at once; imitation, if present, is incidental, and the intention, apart from fuller keyboard sonority, is to give a semblance of harmonic activity where the basic pulse is slow and perhaps not very purposeful [...]. For Byrd [...] it is the melodic progress within imitation, with its expressive nuances and power of structural control, that counts'.

Bull's pavans emerge as structurally featureless pieces, relying wholly on imaginative keyboard figuration, or else 'seek[ing] contrast in striking harmonic progressions' though even these 'cause stylistic inconsistency'. Byrd, by contrast, has a sure eye for structure: 'His object was not to avoid problems which in any case did not normally arise in his music, but to solve them'.[12]

But is Tomkins's distinction between music 'For Substance' and music 'For the Hand' also a judgement of relative value? It is arguable that Tomkins might have had a higher regard for Byrd than for Bull, since Byrd had evidently been his teacher[13] and Bull had in any case left England to pursue a career on the continent before Tomkins himself became at all established as a composer. Moreover, his own keyboard works[14] are conservative rather than exploratory, grounded firmly in the 'intellectual' style of Byrd. Regardless of genre, Tomkins's keyboard pieces are founded on a solid basis of musical craftsmanship. Generally, he seems to have modelled his keyboard style on that of Byrd, especially regarding the contrapuntal approach to the composition of pavans and galliards, and the tendency towards thematic interrelationships between successive strains. Sometimes, Byrd's keyboard works served Tomkins as actual models, as in the plainsong setting *Clarifica me Pater*, a hexachord fantasia based on the rather strange pattern *Ut, mi, re*, and variations on the song *Fortune my foe*.[15] Nevertheless, Tomkins also copied works by Bull into his manuscript and there are fairly clear resemblances between his settings

---

[11] London, 1612/13. MB, 19, no. 131b.

[12] Neighbour, *Consort and Keyboard Music*, 214.

[13] Tomkins dedicated his 5-part madrigal *Too much I once Lamented* to 'My ancient & much reverenced master, William Byrd'; Thomas Tomkins, *Songs of 3. 4. 5. & 6. Parts* (London, 1622).

[14] *Thomas Tomkins Keyboard Music*, ed. Stephen D. Tuttle and Thurston Dart (MB, 5; rev. 2nd. edn., London, 1964).

[15] MB, 5, nos. 4, 38 and 61.

of the *In nomine* plainsong and those of Bull,[16] showing that Tomkins could devise challenging passagework when it suited him, though he rarely mimiced Bull's more extravagant effects. The issue is really one of degree; Tomkins was not necessarily ranking Byrd's 'Substance' over Bull's virtuosic writing 'For the Hand'; he may simply have been pointing to Byrd as a model to follow in one respect and Bull in another.

Bull's keyboard works were much discussed in the two most impressive English music histories of the eighteenth century, *A General History of the Science and Practice of Music* by the magistrate and musical dilettante Sir John Hawkins (1719-89)[17] and *A General History of Music from the Earliest Ages to the Present* by Charles Burney (1726-1814).[18] Both works appeared in 1776 and from the start were rival publications betraying conflicting ideologies. Hawkins's five-volume study appeared complete in 1776, and while the first of Burney's four volumes had appeared earlier that year his *History* was not finished until 1789. Their respective attitudes, especially towards music of Bull's era, should be placed in the broader context of music historiography in the English Enlightenment. In particular, there was a tension between the desire to study original source materials carefully and methodically, documenting and interpreting earlier musical styles (rather than simply 'glossing' past traditions of written scholarship), and the desire to act out this knowledge as a creative practice enriching the music of the present. In this respect, Hawkins and Burney were in opposing camps. Burney and his associates ridiculed Hawkins's *History* as a piece of pedantic antiquarianism, possibly because Hawkins expressed an adverse opinion about modern Italian opera of the kind Handel had established in London, extolling, on the other hand, the virtues of earlier English masters such as Byrd and Bull. This was anathema to Burney, a champion of Handel and of Italian style, whose great strength as a musical commentator and historian was his sense of contemporaneity derived from first-hand contact with composers and performers established during lengthy European tours during the 1760s and 1770s. Regrettably, Burney allowed his distaste for what he saw as Hawkins's preference for older over modern music, to inflect some of his own opinions of earlier English music in volume 3 of his own *History* (1789).

---

[16] See John Irving, 'Keyboard Plainsong Settings by Thomas Tomkins', *Soundings*, 13 (1985), 22-40.

[17] Sir John Hawkins, *A General History of the Science and Practice of Music* (5 vols; London, 1776).

[18] Charles Burney, *A General History of Music from the Earliest Ages to the Present* (4 vols; London, 1776-89).

To be fair, Hawkins's antiquarian cast of mind occasionally clouds his judgement too. Thus, he acknowledges that Bull was 'equally excellent in vocal and instrumental harmony'[19] but, referring to his appointment to the Gresham Readership in Music in 1597, observes (disapprovingly, one feels) a special concession allowing him to deliver his lectures in English rather than Latin which he did not speak: '[and] it may be presumed that he was unable to read it; and if so, he must have been ignorant of the very principles of the science, and consequently but indifferently qualified to lecture on it, even in English'.[20] Nevertheless, there were striking compensations:

> 'By some of the [keyboard] lessons in the *Parthenia* it seems that he was possessed of a power of execution on the harpsichord far beyond what is generally conceived of the masters of that time. As to his lessons, they were, in the estimation of Dr Pepusch,[21] not only for the harmony and contrivance, but for air and modulation, so excellent, that he scrupled not to prefer them to those of Couperin, Scarlatti and others of the modern composers for the harpsichord'.[22]

Note that, for the evaluative part of his essay, Hawkins invokes the authority of Pepusch's professional judgement on Bull's musical qualities. Perhaps in order to reinforce that link, he remarks that Pepusch's wife, the opera singer Margarita de L'Pine 'who had a very fine hand on the harpsichord' practised Bull's pieces in the Fitzwilliam Virginal Book diligently:

> 'In which she succeeded so well, as to excite the curiosity of numbers to resort to [Pepusch's] house […] to hear her […]. [The book] in some parts of it is so discoloured by continual use, as to distinguish with the utmost degree of certainty the very lessons with which she was most delighted. One of them took up twenty minutes to go through it'.[23]

---

[19] Hawkins, *History*, i, 480. (All page references are to the new Novello edition, London, 1875.)

[20] Hawkins, *History*, 481. His point (which censures Bull's likely competence as a lecturer, rather than as a composer) is presumably that most music theory up to *c*.1600 was in Latin, though one detects too a certain social snobbery.

[21] Johann Christoph Pepusch (1667-1752), German-born composer, conductor, organist, editor and theorist who settled in London about 1704 and became a prominent figure in London theatre music, especially in popular musical theatre in Drury Lane and Lincoln's Inn.

[22] Hawkins, *History*, 481. Pepusch was referring to works by Bull copied into the Fitzwilliam Virginal Book, then in Pepusch's possession. In a footnote (‡) on page 481 Hawkins comments that this manuscript 'contained many lessons of Bull, so very difficult, that hardly any master of the Doctor's [ie. Pepusch] time was able to play them'.

[23] Hawkins, *History*, 481. The long piece to which Hawkins refers is undoubtedly Bull's thirty variations on the popular tune *Walsingham* (MB, 19, no. 85), a work of extraordinary difficulty for its time, involving an impressive array of technical devices including parallel scales in thirds and sixths, rapid repeated notes, crossing of the hands, contrary motion arpeggios and the like.

Burney was not so appreciative of Bull's output, almost certainly because Hawkins had deferred to the opinion of Pepusch, whom Burney despised for promoting the composition and production of popular 'ballad opera' in England (notably *The Beggar's Opera*, 1728), a genre that provided stiff competition to Handel's Italian operas. Ridiculing Pepusch's reported preference for Bull's keyboard works over those of Couperin, Scarlatti and the like, Burney dismisses that opinion as 'an assertion which rather proves that the Doctor's [Pepusch's] taste was *bad*, than Bull's *music* good'.[24] Sadly, this prejudice colours the whole of Burney's account of Bull's keyboard works:

> 'Though I should greatly admire the hand, as well as the patience, of any one capable of playing his compositions; yet, *as music*, they would afford me no kind of pleasure: *Ce sont des notes & rien que des notes*: there is nothing in them which excites rapture. [...] it may with truth be said, that the loss, to refined ears would not be very great, if they should for ever remain unplayed and undeciphered.[...] the crowded harmony and multiplied notes with which they are loaded, have not rendered them more pleasing. Indeed, the [...] bestowing [of] such time and labour on them as may be necessary to subdue the difficulties of execution they contain would be a corruption of taste, and a neglect of more useful studies.... Bull [...] seems in his riper years, to have made the invention of new difficulties of every kind, which could impede or dismay a performer, his [w]hole study'.[25]

Not content with parodying Bull's apparently aimless virtuosity (underpinned by 'crowded harmony'), Burney next criticises *Dr Bull's Jewel*[26] as 'a violation of *all present rules and sensations* [author's italics] as seems rude and barbarous. Indeed, Bull seems to have had a bad taste in modulation, and to have been as harsh and strained in this particular as Bird [sic] was natural and pleasing'.[27] Note in the formulation 'all present rules and sensations' the trace of Burney's historiographical stance: the business of historical study is to validate the present, which is a creative continuation and, ultimately, improvement of a stylistic past whose function it is to be documented and classified by historical process. Historical enquiry into the past is but a tool for the justification of a greater present. Not for Burney the abstract opinions of Pepusch musing among his ancient manuscripts, or the painstaking labours of

---

[24] Burney, *History*, iii, 109.
[25] Burney, *History*, iii, 109-11 *passim*.
[26] MB, 19, no. 142.
[27] Burney, *History*, iii, 113. Incidentally, his critical judgements on harmony and modulation are diametrically opposed to Pepusch's.

Hawkins in the British Museum or various private libraries in which the research for his *History* was undertaken. History must enrich the creative present, but equally subordinate the documented past to the march of progress. Note also the critical terms of reference here: 'harsh', 'strained', *versus* 'natural' and 'pleasing'. The unstated benchmark here is the *style galante*. Not only is Bull damned against these modern criteria, but the preferable Byrd (despite the era from which he came) is made to be preferable precisely by being constructed by Burney within exactly those same stylistic terms. At the same time, Burney lays bare his own historiographical identity. Neither the description of Bull's music nor the comparison with Byrd is impartial, but constructed; and in this case – disappointingly – constructed in the context of a ridiculous squabble with a rival historian in which Bull becomes merely a vehicle for the venting of petty jealousy.[28]

Writing on the English virginalist repertoire is scarce in the decades following Hawkins and Burney. No qualitative or comparative assessment of Bull's keyboard music is attempted in John Sainsbury's *A Dictionary of Musicians*[29] whose entry for the composer is straightforwardly biographical (though Bull is described as 'the first [i.e. foremost] performer in the world'). Interestingly, in Sainsbury's entry for 'Bird' there is disparaging mention of keyboard virtuosity:

> 'It has been imagined that the rage for variations, that is, multiplying notes, and disguising the melody of an easy and generally well-known air, by every means that a *note-splitter* sees possible, was the contagion of the present century; but it appears from the [Fitzwilliam] *virginal book*, that this species of influenza or *corruption of air* was more excessive in the sixteenth century than at any other period of musical history'.[30]

---

[28] One forward-looking aspect of Burney's account (Burney, *History*, iii, 115-17) is its inclusion of musical examples ('Specimens of Dr Bull's difficult Passages from Queen Elizabeth's Virginal Book'). These are extracted from the *Ut, re, mi, fa, sol, la*, MB, 14, no. 18, the first of the three settings of the plainsong *Miserere*, MB, 14, no. 34, and *Dr Bull's Jewel*, MB, 19, no. 142.

[29] John Sainsbury, *A Dictionary of Musicians* (London, 1824) i, 116. Sainsbury's is the only English music dictionary of its kind in the first half of the nineteenth century.

[30] Sainsbury, *Dictionary*, i, 92. Sainsbury's account is perhaps the earliest to make a specific association between technically challenging virginal music and the then-ascendant school of piano virtuosity. It is interesting that Bull is not singled-out as a precursor.

Besides occasional published comment on virginal music, there is evidence of a healthy antiquarian interest in its manuscript sources throughout the eighteenth and nineteenth centuries. For instance, the Tomkins keyboard manuscript, referred to earlier and containing some of Bull's pieces, was owned in 1780 by one Thomas Bever, Fellow of All Souls, Oxford. Bever bequeathed his extensive collection of sixteenth- and seventeenth-century manuscripts to John Hindle, lay-vicar of Westminster Abbey in 1791. Following Hindle's death in 1798, Bever's collection was sold; by 1801 Tomkins's manuscript was in the possession of J. Finley Foster junior, and circumstantial evidence suggests that it was subsequently purchased in 1825 at a Sotheby's sale by Aristide and Louise Farrenc, editors of the series *La Trésor des Pianistes*, ultimately published in 20 instalments in Paris between 1861 and 1872.[31]

After several generations of relative neglect in English musical writing, interest in Bull's keyboard music was rejuvenated during the last quarter of the nineteenth century and the first quarter of the twentieth within a broad context of rediscovery of the country's Elizabethan musical heritage. That rediscovery manifested itself in several ways. One was the establishment of small-scale madrigal societies which sprang up in several major cities outside London (the Bristol Madrigal Society, for instance, dates from 1837), exploring the Elizabethan repertoire alongside newly-composed works for similar forces (by the Bristol composer, Robert Lucas Pearsall (1795-1856), for example). By 1899 Godfrey Arkwright had begun publishing a series entitled the *Old English Edition*, promoting sixteenth- and seventeenth-century sacred vocal works, while keyboard music was championed by John Fuller Maitland and William Barclay Squire who published the first complete edition of the *Fitzwilliam Virginal Book*.[32] Interestingly, none of these pioneers were professional musicologists, though each had intimate contact with Elizabethan and Jacobean keyboard repertoire: Arkwright compiled a catalogue of the music manuscripts of Christ Church, Oxford (including several important virginalist manuscripts); Fuller Maitland was a harpsichordist, his brother-in-law Barclay Squire was Music Librarian at the British Museum, curator of the King's Music Library (donated to the museum on permanent loan in 1911), and author of several catalogues of the British Museum's holdings.

---

[31] In the Preface to volume 6 of *La Trésor*, Aristide Farrenc notes that he had previously bought several collections of early keyboard music in London sales.

[32] *The Fitzwilliam Virginal Book*, ed. J. Fuller Maitland and W. Barclay Squire (2 vols; London and Leipzig, 1894-99).

Scholarly interest in the virginalist repertoire had meanwhile found a voice in the first edition of Sir George Grove's groundbreaking *Dictionary of Music and Musicians*.[33] The entry for Bull, by Edward Rimbault[34] is merely biographical in nature, referring to the Fitzwilliam Virginal Book as a source for Bull's keyboard works but avoiding any commentary on the music itself. Rimbault's entry was considerably expanded by William Barclay Squire in the second edition of *Grove* (1904). Barclay Squire had a detailed grasp of the principal source materials for Bull's keyboard music as then known, and, having been educated partially in Leipzig, a knowledge of and respect for modern traditions of German musical scholarship which infuse his account; indeed, for an impression of Bull's 'merits as a composer', he refers the reader to Willibald Nagel's *Geschichte der Musik in England*[35] and Max Seiffert's *Geschichte der Klaviermusik*.[36] Barclay Squire's own view was that '[Bull's] music is very unequal, and generally is more ingenious than beautiful. The most striking examples of his innovations, both rhythmic and harmonic, are to be found in an 'Ut, re, mi'[37]. But as an executant he occupied a place in the first rank. He has been aptly termed 'the Liszt of his age', and he belongs to the group of composers who did much to develop harpsichord music'.[38] Bull's 'innovative' hexachord fantasia had previously caught the eye of Sir Hubert Parry in his account of Bull's keyboard works written for *The Oxford History of Music*

---

[33] Sir George Grove (ed.), *A Dictionary of Music and Musicians* (4 vols; London, 1877-90).

[34] Rimbault (1816-76) was another important figure in the English antiquarian movement; he was instrumental in founding the Musical Antiquarian Society in 1840 and from that time was extremely active in collecting, editing and lecturing on early music. Much of his large collection of musical manuscripts (including the Mulliner Book – London, British Library, Add. MS 30513 – perhaps the most significant document of liturgical keyboard plainsong settings in sixteenth-century England) was ultimately sold (1877) to the British Museum.

[35] Willibald Nagel, *Geschichte der Musik in England* (Strasbourg, 1894), 155-60. Nagel's uncomplimentary account of Bull's keyboard music appears at 158-60. He condemns Bull's impoverished musical invention, lack of harmonic beauty and rhythmic interest (though, as in Barclay Squire's article, the chromatic *Ut, re, mi*, MB, 14, no. 17 is mentioned favourably) and undeveloped relationship between form and content. Moreover, Nagel notes that Bull's passagework is not novel, as claimed by, for instance, Henry Davey, *History of English Music* (Brighton, 1895), 214, but directly descended from the keyboard works of his teacher, Blitheman among others. Nevertheless, Nagel places Bull's passagework into an appropriate context and acknowledges its significance in the broader development of idiomatic keyboard technique.

[36] Max Seiffert, *Geschichte der Klaviermusik* (Leipzig, 1899), 54-72 (a general account of virginal music in England, with passing reference to some of Bull's remarkable keyboard figurations, illustrated from the variations on *Walshingham*, MB, 19, no. 85).

[37] MB, 14, no. 17.

[38] Barclay Squire notes that Bull's 'connection with Sweelinck is of interest'. He does not claim that Bull's keyboard style was directly influential on Sweelinck – and by extension on a whole later tradition of continental keyboard music – though this point is considered in Seiffert, *Geschichte der Klaviermusik*, 86-8. It lies beyond the scope of this chapter however, except to remark that it is never raised as a relevant context for Bull's keyboard music by any English writers up to World War II.

(1902).[39] Parry, who had contributed to the original Grove's *Dictionary* in 1877 and succeeded Grove as Director of the Royal College of Music in 1894 (a post he held concurrently with that of Professor of Music at Oxford University from 1900-1908), wrote volume three of this ambitious *History*. His view of Bull's hexachord piece is rather more subtly nuanced than Squire's: 'As a piece of speculation the whole composition is carried out with remarkable ingenuity and the idea of setting the balance right by reiterating the [hexachord] formula in the principal key at the end is a striking instance of early instinct for tonality, and the justness at that particular moment of John Bull's judgement.'[40] Note the constructed value-judgement in which the success of Bull's piece is attributed to a conception of tonal 'balance' in which resolution of extraneous harmonic features within an overall controlling tonal frame is the dominant structural factor (as indeed it was in Parry's own compositions and those of many of his English contemporaries). Parry's high estimation of Bull hangs on the identification of a blend of 'modern' instrumental virtuosity, bordering on 'genius', and the ability to achieve a satisfying structure by exercising long-range tonal control over complex harmonic materials.[41]

For one school of thought, then, Bull passes the test of acceptability by satisfying a modern benchmark. A different construction of Bull's historical placement is offered in Jeffrey Pulver's *A Biographical Dictionary of Old English Music and Musicians*.[42] According to Pulver, Bull was

> 'perhaps the most celebrated virginalist, organist, and writer of music destined for these instruments that this country has ever produced. His influence upon the development of the music for the keyboard was very great. [...] judging by the esteem in which he was held by his contemporaries, John Bull must have been a performer of amazing ability [...]. As a composer his one aim [...] seems to have been at brilliant virtuosity. There can be no doubt that his knowledge was very profound; but he did not hesitate to make musical beauty step into the background in favour of the technicalities of his instrument when the latter required them to do so [...]. At an age when the majority of the

---

[39] *The Oxford History of Music*, iii 'The Music of the Seventeenth Century', ed. C. H. H. Parry (2nd. rev. ed. E .J. Dent; London, New York and Toronto, 1938), 87-93 *passim* on Bull.

[40] Nagel, *Geschichte der Musik in England*, 159 also regards the composer's harmonic understanding as tonal ('Im grossen und ganzen ist in seinen Arbeiten die moderne Tonalität schon recht scharf ausgeprägt.').

[41] Compare Pepusch's opinion, reported by Hawkins (above, footnote 22, referring to harmony and modulation). The principle is similar, though Parry gives it a different slant.

[42] Jeffrey Pulver, *A Biographical Dictionary of Old English Music and Musicians* (London and New York, 1927). Bull is assessed at 73-9.

great musicians were devoting almost the whole of their energies to the service of the church, Bull came as a welcome force that helped to preserve the balance between the two classes of composition'.

Bull's compositional maturity is once again characterized by its judicious balance of musical intellect and technical virtuosity, each of which, by implication, have their place and compete as equals within the expressive discourse either of a musical style in general or of a particular piece. But Pulver gives this by now familiar interpretation a subtle twist. Over and above the observation of stylistic detail he defines a historical level on which Bull's music signifies. Whereas his contemporaries composed preponderantly sacred vocal works, Bull specialized by choice in secular keyboard music. And that choice had a further consequence: whereas the *status quo* had foregrounded 'musical beauty' over 'technicalities', Bull took an alternative view, responding to an expressive impulse to celebrate virtuosity. Such a claim positions Bull out of the mainstream, as something of a free spirit – an individual who rejoiced in a direct relationship with the materials of music (patterns, for instance, and their replication and variation), treating those materials as an expressive end in themselves, rather than as foundations for a beautiful but functional adjunct to liturgy. That is a novel context for appreciating his extraordinary achievement. Pulver simply refuses to consider Bull's virtuosity as evidence of a limitation. Whereas Parry hypothesizes an anachronistic, quasi-symphonic context of tonal propriety mediating the virtuoso element ('bordering on 'genius'…the ability to exercise structural control over complex harmonic materials'), Pulver takes that virtuosity for what it is: a compositional preference in favour of expressivity. And in order to empower it, he evokes a broad historical context in which Bull's exciting keyboard works open up the possibility of a legitimate instrumental art. Perhaps that evocation asks Bull's keyboard pieces to bear rather a heavy historical load, but it is a brave strategy nevertheless, and one that side-steps both the depressing comparison of intellectual merit *versus* shallow virtuosity, and the anachronistic habit (of which Barclay Squire is guilty, for instance) of explaining Bull's idiosyncratic keyboard writing in terms of a tradition of nineteenth-century concert pianism.[43]

Tomkins's contrasting definitions of Byrd's keyboard music ('For Substance'), and of Bull's ('For the Hand') appear to offer us a valid and valuable typological tool. But his distinction should be treated cautiously. To apply it as a *qualitative comparison* leading to a value judgement can deceive us into mistaking what are

---

[43] Pulver's exemplary scholarship, notable for its close inspection of primary sources, was published in more than 170 books and papers between 1913 and 1939.

in fact historically-situated constructions for what we might wish to be essential qualities residing within the music. As we have seen, such constructions have persisted in a variety of forms across the centuries, reflecting changing sets of values brought to music and musical understanding by the socially-situated practice of musicology. That Bull's music – wherever its essence lies – survives the experience is surely a measure of its enduring quality.

JOSQUIN, WILLAERT AND *DOULEUR ME BAT*

Eric Jas

It is remarkable to see how little attention has been paid to Willaert's chansons in the musicological literature of the past twenty years. The 1980's witnessed a promising start with Lawrence Bernstein's edition of *La Couronne et fleur des chansons*, containing almost all of Willaert's three-voice chansons.[1] Whereas Bernstein's edition, and especially his thorough historical commentary, should have become an excellent point of departure for further in-depth research, it has remained, to this date, an isolated example of the kind of research that Willaert's chansons deserve.[2]

Of course such a lacuna cannot be remedied with a short contribution to a Festschrift. This article, therefore, is meant to offer merely a glimpse of the richness that lies hidden in the study of Willaert's parody chansons. The work I have singled out for analysis is Willaert's six-voice setting of *Douleur me bat*. As a relationship with Josquin's setting of the same text has already been suggested – but not yet demonstrated – it may be useful to start with a description of Josquin's chanson.

Among the late chansons of Josquin, *Douleur me bat* stands out as one of his finest contributions to the genre.[3] The text of the chanson is remarkably doleful and the music makes every attempt to follow, suit and paint the agony of the desperate lover:[4]

---

[1] Lawrence F. Bernstein (ed.), *La Couronne et fleur des chansons a troys* (Masters and Monuments of the Renaissance 3, 2 vols.; New York, 1984).

[2] A minor, but positive exception is Jacques Barbier's '*Faulte d'argent*. Modèles polyphoniques et parodies au XVIe siècle', *Revue de musicologie,* 73 (1987), 171-202. Barbier discusses three chansons by Willaert: *Faulte d'argent* (6vv), *Je l'ay aymée* (5vv), and *Qui a beau ne* (6vv), at 184-85, 190-93.

[3] Despite the quality of the work, *Douleur me bat* has come down to us in but three sources (VienNB Mus. 18746, Susato 1545[15], and Attaingnant 1549 [J681]). A modern edition was published by Albert Smijers in *Werken van Josquin des Prés, Wereldlijke Werken*, Bundel II, Afl. 5 (Amsterdam and Leipzig, 1924; repr. 1971), No. 18, 45-46. For the present article I prepared a new transcription (based on VienNB Mus. 18746) with voice designations deviating from those in Smijers's edition (Smijers: Superius, Quinta Pars, Contratenor, Tenor, Bassus *versus* Superius, Altus, Tenor, Quinta vox, Bassus).

[4] Translation by Paul Rans and Nell Race (CD *De Vlaamse Polyfonie. Adriaan Willaert en Italië*. Capella Sancti Michaelis, Currende Consort conducted by Erik van Nevel, Eufoda, 1993).

'Douleur me bat et tristesse m'afolle
Amour me nuyt et malheur me consolle
Vouloir me suit mais aider ne me peult
Jouyr ne puis d'ung grant bien qu'on me veult
De vivre'ainsi pour dieu qu'on me decolle'.

[Sorrow beats me, sadness maddens me
Love hurts me, misfortune is my solace
Longing pursues me but cannot help
I cannot relish the great joy that is wished upon me
God, take me away from such an existence!]

Like most of Josquin's other five- and six-voice chansons, *Douleur me bat* is constructed around a canon. The canonic voices present an unadorned version of the melody, with the *comes* imitating the *dux* after two breves at the fifth. As Lawrence Bernstein already remarked, it seems highly improbable that this melody was pre-existent. A monophonic version of the tune has not surfaced and the text is not cited in the French secular theatrical tradition. Furthermore, there are no rival settings that are suggestive of a circulating monophonic melody.[5]

An analysis of the melody seems to confirm that it originated with the composer himself. Verses 1 and 2 of the text are sung to the same musical phrase, as are verses 3 and 4. The fifth verse has a phrase of its own, which is repeated too, and which is followed by a short codetta.[6] When all repeats and the tiny coda at the end are removed, the nucleus of the melody remains: the three concise melodic lines that are given in Example 1. These lines are neatly tailored to the French poetic text. They all divide into two halves, thus reflecting the bipartite structure of each of the verses, and all end on *E*, thus clearly suggesting the Phrygian mode, a choice of tonality that was no doubt inspired by the gloomy text.

---

[5] Lawrence F. Bernstein, 'A Canonic Chanson in a German Manuscript. *Faulte d'argent* and Josquin's Approach to the Chanson for Five Voices', in Frank Heidlberger, Wolfgang Osthoff, and Reinhard Wiesend (eds.), *Von Isaac bis Bach: Studien zur älteren deutschen Musikgeschichte. Festschrift Martin Just zum 60. Geburtstag* (Kassel etc., 1991), 53-71, at 71.

[6] This amounts to the AABBCC-coda structure that is also found in other late five- and six-voice chansons by Josquin (cf. Helmuth Osthoff, *Josquin Desprez* (Tutzing, 1962-65), ii, 211ff.; Bernstein, 'A Canonic Chanson', 66). The codetta slightly elaborates the final melodic gesture of the third phrase of the melody.

The three musical lines are connected by several motivic relationships. The first line is built around the (minor) second *E-F* (labelled 'a' in Ex. 1) which occurs both at its beginning and at its end. The interval that is heard in between – *A-G-A* – also stresses the second, but now a major one, the direction of which is inverted. The first phrase of the second line opens with a fresh interval stressing new pitches (*G* and *D*), but quickly returns – in its second half – to the minor second *E-F* from the first line. The third line again starts on *G* and introduces a *B-flat*, a clear and dramatic departure from the Phrygian mode of expression in the chanson melody thus far. Although this phrase gives the impression of a new melodic direction, it is actually a transposition of the notes that were first heard in the second phrase of the second line. Interestingly enough, the second phrase of the final line is also borrowed from material that was introduced earlier, in this case the melodic curve in the second phrase of the first line. In all the melody seems to betray the hand of a skilful composer, who diligently moulded his melodic material.

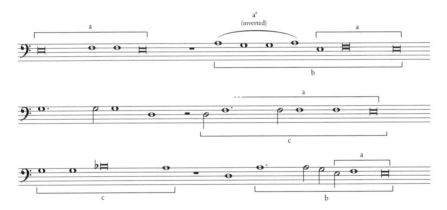

Example 1. Josquin, *Douleur me bat*: analysis of the *dux*

The canonic melody is placed, as is the case in most other late chansons by Josquin, in the inner voices (Quinta vox and Altus), and the introduction of the *B-flat* in the third line of the melody ensures an exact imitation at the upper fifth.[7] The remaining, free voices share most of their basic material with the Quinta vox and the Altus, thus hiding the canonic structure in overall pervading imitation.

---

[7] Cf. Peter Whitney Urquhart, *Canon, Partial Signatures, and 'Musica Ficta' in Works by Josquin DesPrez and his Contemporaries* (Ph.D. diss., Harvard University, 1988), 181-4.

The musical repeats in the canonic melody (see above) are all mirrored by the other voices, amounting to three restatements of complete blocks of polyphony:[8]

	Verse 1	Verse 2	Verse 3	Verse 4	Verse 5 (1st)	Verse 5 (2nd)
S	4-11	= 13-20	22-28	= 29-35$_1$	36$_5$-45$_1$	= 44$_3$-53$_1$
A	7-14	16-23	25-30	32-37	39-46	47-54
T	5-11$_1$	14-20$_1$	22$_2$-30	29$_2$-37	36$_2$-43$_3$	44$_3$-51
Qv	5-12	14-21	23-28	30-35	37-44	45-52
B	6-12	15-21$_3$	23-30	30-37$_1$	37-45$_1$	45-53

If one ignores these repeats, one is left with the scaffolding of the chanson: a structure that is designed with a minimum of melodic material and a high motivic density. A clear example of this method of working is found in the setting of verses 3 and 4. Nearly all of the melodic motifs are drawn from the canonic melody; departures from this material are slight.[9] The most striking bit of non-canonic material is introduced by the Superius in bb. 35 ff. and pulls the composition into the next phrase, setting verse 5, with a very poignant *B-flat* in bb. 38-46 (see Ex. 2). This moment asks for special attention, as it resolutely leads us away from the Phrygian mode of expression at the beginning of the chanson. On closer examination, the cadences and sonorities that predominate in *Douleur me bat* are far removed from the unambiguous tonal structure of the canonic melody itself. The music focuses on sonorities on G-major (bb. 23-30), G-major/minor (bb. 37-8/45-6), D-minor (bb. 39-47), and C-major (bb. 43-51), before the chanson comes to an end with a strong plagal cadence.[10]

---

[8] An interesting aspect of these restatements is the clever way in which Josquin announces the repeats by re-using bits of non-canonic material (compare, for example, T bb. 22-23 with 29-30, and S bb. 36^5-39^1 with S 44^3-47).

[9] See Smijers's edition. It should be noticed that some of the apparently new material in these bars was actually introduced earlier in the chanson (compare, for example, the short ascending motif in T bb. 229-30 with S b. 3).

[10] This aspect, too, can be found in other late chansons by Josquin; cf. Bernstein, 'A Canonic Chanson', 67. Elsewhere, Bernstein adds that this approach to the Phrygian mode is characteristic for Josquin and that comparable examples can be found in the Masses *La sol fa re mi*, *Malheur me bat, Pange lingua*, and *Sine nomine* and in some eighteen motets – not all of them authentic – assigned by Cristle Collins Judd to modes III or IV (cf. Bernstein, '*Ma bouche rit et mon cueur pleure*: A Chanson *a 5* Attributed to Josquin des Prez', *The Journal of Musicology*, 12 (1994), 253-286, at 282).

Example 2. Josquin, *Douleur me bat*, bb. 32-9

In comparing Willaert's setting of *Douleur me bat* with Josquin's work, the first thing to attract one's attention is that Willaert's setting is for six voices and that it, too, is based on a canonic scaffolding.[11] On closer examination, Willaert's composition turns out to be a very clever and intriguing parody setting of Josquin's chanson. Willaert did not content himself by simply paraphrasing Josquin's points of imitation, but cunningly remodelled the canonic scaffolding of his model.

[11] Willaert's chanson has been published twice: Charles Jacobs (ed.), *LeRoy & Ballard's 1572 'Mellange de Chansons'* (Pennsylvania State University Press, University Park and London, 1982); Jane A. Bernstein (ed.), *Adrian Willaert: The Complete Five and Six-Voice Chansons* (The Sixteenth-Century Chanson 23; New York and London, 1992). Unfortunately, neither of these editions was available to me. For the present contribution, I transcribed the chanson from Susato's 1544 edition (cf. note 18).

Example 3. Comparison of Josquin's and Willaert's *dux*

On the whole, Willaert follows Josquin's melody faithfully. A comparison of Willaert's and Josquin's *dux* is illustrated in Example 3. Departures from the original involve the shortening of one or more notes in each phrase[12] and two melodic adjustments in bb. 43 (Josquin b. 40) and 64 (Josquin b. 53).[13] A more telling intervention is found at bb. 49-51, where Willaert has inserted a varied repeat of the concluding material of the third phrase (see below). The most radical interference, however, affects the canonic scaffolding itself. Josquin's canon 'ad longum' in the upper fifth is turned into a canon in the lower fifth, with the *comes* following the *dux* after three breves.[14] Changing the interval of imitation to a descending fifth necessitated transposing the *dux* up an octave.

[12] Willaert's shortening of notes in phrases 2 and 3 (see Ex. 3) may possibly be regarded as modernisations of Josquin's rather neutral declamation of the French text.

[13] Willaert furthermore changed the number of rests separating the three phrases (not shown in the example), which explains the differences in bar numbers for Willaert's and Josquin's setting.

[14] In his reworking of Josquin's *Faulte d'argent*, Willaert also changed the time interval between *dux* and *comes* (but not the interval of imitation); see Barbier, '*Faulte d'argent*. Modèles polyphoniques', 184.

The repercussions are, of course, far-reaching. First, whereas Josquin's canonic scaffolding is buried in the five-voice texture, the *dux* in Willaert's chanson competes with the second, freely composed, Superius for the highest position. Second, and more importantly, Willaert's *comes* starts not on *B* but on *A* and is thus, in view of the mode of the composition, forced to render a diatonic imitation of the *dux*.[15] This diatonic reading of the melody on *A* without *B-flat*, is a clear step away from Josquin's chanson, where the melody loses its characteristic Phrygian flavour in neither of the voices. An intriguing aspect of Willaert's remodelling of the canonic scaffolding is that, despite these major interventions, in the first phrase the sonorities resulting from *dux* and *comes* are very much like those in Josquin's chanson (see Ex. 4).

Example 4. Intervals resulting from *dux* and *comes* in Josquin's and Willaert's canon

This intellectual conversion of Josquin's canon is clear evidence that Willaert's chanson must be considered a parody setting of Josquin's original. For those who, in spite of the close connection between Willaert's and Josquin's canonic structure, might still want to entertain the possibility that the two composers both set a pre-existing monophonic melody, the opening measures of Willaert's piece should be of particular interest. The chanson opens with, in its second Superius part, a suspension formula that, as Bernstein puts it, 'is strangely devoid of a dissonant relationship with any other part' (Ex. 5).[16] Remarkably enough, the formula with its accompanying non-dissonant counterpoint is repeated in both the Contratenor (bb. 4-5) and the Tenor (bb. 6-7). This bewildering course of events is finally resolved in bb. 7-9, when the motif is heard again, but this time with appropriate counterpoint forming a Phrygian cadence on *E* (Ex. 6). There can be little doubt that this formula was copied from Josquin's chanson, where it emphatically and repeatedly functions as counterpoint against the opening phrase of the *Douleur me bat* melody.

---

[15] There can be no doubt regarding exact or diatonic imitation here: already in b. 9, at the third note of the *comes*, Willaert's second Superius voice sounds an unequivocal *B* (which is reached from the lower fifth *E*), thus preventing the *comes* from delivering an exact imitation of the *dux* (cf. Ex. 6).

[16] Bernstein, 'A Canonic Chanson', 71.

Example 5. Willaert, *Douleur me bat*, suspension formula bb. 1-3

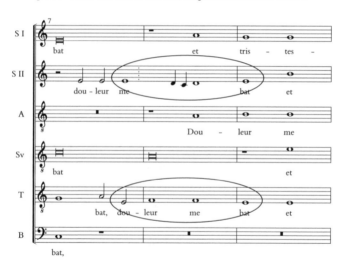

Example 6. Willaert, *Douleur me bat*, suspension formula bb. 7-9

One further quotation from Josquin's chanson is found in bb. 47-9 (see Ex. 7).[17] This passage calls for specific attention, as Willaert seems carefully to have avoided copying polyphonic blocks from his model elsewhere in his setting. The quotation is built on the second half of the third phrase of the canonic melody. Willaert's Tenor quotes the melodic phrase as it occurs in Josquin's Quinta vox, while his second Superius doubles the melody a third higher, as does Josquin's Superius. Five notes from Josquin's Tenor are divided over Willaert's Altus

---

[17] The passage is literally repeated in bb. 61-4.

and Sexta vox, whereas Willaert's Bassus takes only two notes from the model. The quotation is short, but unmistakably clear, as this is the only moment in Willaert's chanson where the second half of the third phrase of the *Douleur me bat* melody is used with its original ascending fifth *D-A*. All other occurrences of the phrase sound Willaert's remodelled version of it (cf. Ex. 3).

Example 7. Willaert, *Douleur me bat*, bb. 47-51; Josquin, *Douleur me bat*, bb. 40-5

The comparison of Josquin's with Willaert's *dux* illustrated that Willaert inserted a varied repeat of the concluding material of the third phrase of the melody in his canon at bb. 49-51. Remarkably enough, this deviation from Josquin's canonic structure is created with melodic material taken from the model (cf. Josquin's Superius, bb. 43-5/51-3). In Josquin's chanson this material, which starts on *G*, arises by doubling the *comes* at the upper third and sounds, just like in Willaert's setting, concurrently with the final part of the melody in the *comes*.

As mentioned earlier, Josquin's setting is ambiguous from a modal point of view. Willaert's response seems to be one of enlarging this aspect of the chanson. In Josquin's chanson there are only two clear cadences both occurring on A-minor (bb. 13, 56-7). Willaert introduced more cadences with a feeling of closure, placed on D-minor (bb. 15-6), G-major (bb. 23-4, 54, 68-9), C-major (bb. 26-7) and A-minor (bb. 51-2, 66, 73-4). Tallying the sonorities that most frequently occur in Josquin's *Douleur me bat* reveals the following picture: roughly 30% of Josquin's chord formations centres around *D*, some 20% around *E*, about 18% on *A* and about the same percentage on *G*. Willaert, too, prefers chord formations on *D* (some 30%), but his second choice is clearly *A* (24%), while *E* brings up the rear with a modest 11%, and comes even after *G* and *C* (both approximately 15%).

That it may indeed have been Willaert's intention to give a (harmonically) more colorful rendering of the chanson text, is also shown by the presence of a remarkable sharp in the *dux*. This sharp occurs only in the repeat of the first phrase of the melody and turns the E-minor sonority of b. 9 into an ardent E-major sonority in b. 19 (see Ex. 8). No doubt, the sharp was also meant to affect the *comes* (thus turning the A-minor sonority of b. 12 into an A-major sonority in b. 22). However, when the second Superius imitates the *dux* at the unison in bb. 23ff, the sharp is cancelled! This remarkable course of events probably explains why the sharp, which is clearly present in Susato's edition of the chanson, is suppressed in the other sources.[18]

---

[18] According to David M. Kidger, Willaert's chanson is transmitted in the following sources: Kriesstein 1540[7], Susato 1544[13], Roy & Ballard 1560b, Roy & Ballard 1572[2], HamSU (IV) (now lost), and ParisBNC 851 (cf. *Adrian Willaert. A Guide to Research* (New York and London, 2005), 264). A quick analysis of the variants in the transmission of the chanson makes it abundantly clear that the Paris transmission was slavishly copied from Le Roy & Ballard and that Kriesstein's and Susato's edition both belong to another branch of a possible stemma. Unfortunately I had no access to the Le Roy & Ballard edition of 1560. Based on the descriptions of the editions in the Le Roy & Ballard bibliography, it seems reasonable to expect that the 1560 and 1572 editions both contain the same reading; cf. François Lesure and Geneviève Thibault, *Bibliographie des Éditions d'Adrian Le Roy et Robert Ballard (1551-1598)* (Paris, 1955), 91-4, 156-9, and also: Kate Van Orden, 'Imitation and "La musique des anciens". Le Roy & Ballard's 1572 *Mellange de chansons*', *Revue de musicologie*, 80 (1994), 1-37.

Example 8. Willaert, *Douleur me bat*, bb. 18-27

Interestingly enough, the sources also disagree on the flat in the third phrase
of the canonic melody. Kriesstein's edition is the only one to prescribe it in bb.
41 and 56. In view of Willaert's dependence on Josquin's chanson, it seems
sensible to assume that the flat was intended by Willaert. It is not difficult to
imagine that an editor who did not know Josquin's setting by heart could have
considered the introduction of the flat far too radical to be acceptable here.
Performing Willaert's chanson without the flat – which can be, and has been,
done[19] – robs the piece of a purposely colorful moment.

[19] Cf. the CD *De Vlaamse Polyfonie. Adriaan Willaert en Italië.*

Willaert's handling of the repetitions in Josquin's setting, too, seems to underline his desire for both imitation and variation. Whereas Josquin's large-scale structure is dominated by the literal repeats of three blocks of polyphony, Willaert uses three different kinds of repetition. When the first phrase of the canonic melody is repeated (bb. 15-27), it is accompanied by a good deal of counterpoint that was already heard during its exposition.[20] The restatement of the second phrase of the melody (bb. 32-9), however, is placed in a new contrapuntal context. It is only in the third phrase that Willaert follows Josquin's example and uses a literal repeat in all voices (bb. 40-54 = 55-69). This allows him to make much work of the line 'pour dieu qu'on me decolle', including the literal (polyphonic) quote from Josquin's chanson.[21]

In all, it may be concluded that Willaert was extremely successful in turning Josquin's highly expressive *Douleur me bat* into a new, breathtaking work. The parody technique he used is sophisticated and enabled him to follow his model closely and introduce radical changes at the same time. No doubt Willaert followed this procedure to unite ideals that were considered of paramount importance in parody compositions: homage, stylistic appropriation and emulation.

---

[20] Compare especially bb. 15-24 with 5-14.

[21] The melodic material of this line returns in the final phrase of the chanson. Interestingly enough, Willaert changes here Josquin's first note (*G*) to *E* (see Ex. 3). This may have been done for contrapuntal reasons (see the imitation starting in bb. 47-9; retention of Josquin's *G* would have either caused undesirable note doublings or have prevented the scheme of imitations used here).

GARDANO'S *MOTTETTI DEL FRUTTO* OF 1538-39
AND THE PROMOTION OF A NEW STYLE

Mary S. Lewis

Patterns of patronage, travels of musicians, and the impact of influential teachers were among the many factors that contributed to changes in musical styles during the sixteenth century. The advent of music printing and the cheaper single-impression printing process accelerated those changes and their dissemination. In exploring the role of printing in the spread of musical styles, the tastes and personal musical preferences of the music printers themselves warrant more attention from scholars than they have heretofore received. This paper will show how the musical preferences of one printer, Antonio Gardano, had an important impact on the dispersion of a particular compositional style to a wider musical public, beyond the few courtly chapels and patrician circles in which it first flourished.[1] The style in question is pervading or syntactic imitation, a style that represented a pronounced shift from the practices of previous generations. It is best known to us today in the music of Nicholas Gombert, but was adopted by other composers as well, including Gardano himself. Pervading or syntactic imitation first began to appear in a few works shortly after 1520, and as I shall show, appeared sporadically through the 1520s and 1530s, primarily in manuscripts. In this study I will demonstrate Gardano's own determination to propagate the style of pervading imitation in some of his earliest publications, the three volumes of the *Mottetti del Frutto*. I will also speculate on how Gardano might have obtained the compositions using this procedure for inclusion in the *Frutto* volumes. After a survey of the three volumes, I will concentrate on the first to be published, that for five voices.

Gardano first issued the series of three anthologies entitled *Mottetti del Frutto* in 1538 and 1539, at the very beginning of his career (Table 1).[2]

---

[1] While Gardano originally used the French spelling of his name, in the mid 1550s he began employing the Italian form; it was that form his sons also adopted. For that reason, and to prevent confusion, I have chosen to use the Italian spelling when discussing the father as well.

[2] Complete descriptions may be found in Mary S. Lewis, *Antonio Gardano, Venetian Music Printer 1538-1569. Vol. 1 1538-1549.* (New York, 1988), 173-77, 225-30, 242-46.

> *Primus liber cum quinque vocibus. Mottetti del Frutto.* [colophon] *In Venetia ne la stampa d'Antonio Gardane, ne l'anno del Signore, M. D. XXXVIII. del mese di Settembre. Con gratia et privilegio.* (RISM 1538[4])
>
> *Primus liber cum sex vocibus. Cum gratia et privilegio. Mottetti del Frutto a sei voci.* (colophon) *In Venetia nella stampa d'Antonio Gardane ne l'anno del signore. M. D. XXXIX nel mese di Mazo con privilegio ...* (RISM 1539[3])
>
> *Primus liber cum quatuor vocibus cum gratia et privilegio Motetti del Frutto a quatro in Venetia per Antonio Gardane.* (Colophon) *In Venetia nella stampa d'Antonio Gardane Nellanno del Signore M. D. XXXIX con gratia et privilegio.* (RISM 1539[13])

Table 1. Full titles of Gardano's *Mottetti del Frutto* anthologies

Visually, the first *Frutto* partbooks represented a radical departure from the initial product of Gardano's press, the *Venticinque Canzone Francese* of the same year. The earlier print, the only other surviving edition of Gardano's from 1538, is a small octavo, with a simple title page graced, in the tenor book, by a calligraphic initial as the only ornament.[3] For the first volume of the *Mottetti del Frutto*, however, Gardano adopted the oblong quarto format characteristic of most of his subsequent publications.[4] Moreover, the title pages were adorned with a particularly fine woodcut still life of fruit[5] and in the colophons, Gardano used his famous lion-and-bear printer's mark that Thomas Bridges has argued must have first appeared in the lost Arcadelt volume as well.[6] Thus, the first volume of the *Mottetti del Frutto* and the Arcadelt madrigals represent a kind of coming of age for Gardano as a printer, and the launching of two categories of music that were to play a central role in his publishing career.

The *Mottetti del Frutto* volumes continue a tradition of publishing motets in anthologies that goes back to the beginning of the sixteenth century. The

---

[3] RISM 1538[19] *Venticinque canzone francese a quatro di clement iannequin e di altri excel-lentissimi authori novamente racolte e reviste per antonio Gardane musico e poste ne la sua stampa. Stampate in vinegia et in realto per antonio gardane In calle de la scimia al'insegna de la Phenice. Tenor. Libro Primo* (Venice, 1538). See Lewis, *Antonio Gardano I*, 178-81 and Pl. 10 for a full description of the print and a facsimile of the title page.

[4] His first edition of Arcadelt's first book of madrigals, also published in 1538 and now lost, probably was also in oblong quarto format. See Thomas Bridges, *The Printing of Arcadelt's First Book of Madrigals* (Ph.D, Harvard University, 1982), 71-2.

[5] Lewis, *Antonio Gardano I*, Pl. 12.

[6] *Ibid.*, Pl. 17.

tradition began with the motet collections of Petrucci – most notably the *Motetti de la corona* – as well as those of Andrea Antico in Venice, of Moderne and Attaingnant in France, and the 1520 *Liber selectarum* of Grimm and Wyrsung of Augsburg.[7] From the early 1530s the motet had established itself as a small but important part of the publications of most music-printing centers. Motet anthologies formed a publishing phenomenon separate from the many motet books devoted to the works of a single composer. Single-composer prints relied on the name of the composer to promote sales, or were financed by patrons or the composers themselves. Anthologies were usually dependent for their market on interest in a genre, and on the appeal of their contents to the tastes of the musical public.[8] The title of Gardano's series was probably chosen to complement that of the *Motteti del Fiore*, a group of motet volumes published earlier by Jacques Moderne of Lyons.[9] In fact, concurrently with the 1539 books of his *Frutto* series, Gardano openly drew on Moderne's volumes for another set of his own entitled *Fior de Mottetti*.[10] A list of composers appearing in both series can be seen in Table 2.

Arcadelt (8, 1)	Lasson (1, 1)	*Numbers in parentheses represent the*
Claudin (2, 1)	Lheritier (8, 4)	*number of the composer's works in each*
du Billon (2, 1)	Lupi (7, 4)	*series, with those in Moderne's series*
Gardane (2, 2)	Maistre Jan (2, 2)	*given first.*
Gombert (23, 17)	Pieton (5, 3)	
Gosse (2, 1)	Verdelot (7, 2)	
Jachet (7, 10)		

Table 2. Composers included in both the *Mottetti del Frutto* and the *Motteti del Fiore* series

---

[7] See, for instance, RISM 1502[1] *Motetti A. numero trentatre* (Venice, 1502); 15191 *Motetti de la corona libro secondo* (Venice, 1519); 1520[1] *Motetti novi libro secondo* (Venice, 1520); 1520[4] *Liber selecctarum cantionum quas vulgo Mutetas appellant* (Augsburg, 1520); 1529[1] *XII. Motetz musicaulx a quatre et cinq voix* (Paris, 1529); 1532[10] *Primus liber cum quatuor vocibus. Motteti del fiore* (Lyons, 1532).

[8] The first two books of the *Frutto* series are unusual in that their dedicatory letters appear to be a response to some sort of patronage. Gardano was, at this stage of his career, just beginning to establish his business, so we should not be surprised that someone may have underwritten at least some of the cost of printing. The third *Frutto* book and many of his subsequent anthologies lacked evidence of outside financial support.

[9] RISM 1532[9], *Secundus liber cum quinque vocibus* (Lyons, 1538); 1532[10], *Primus liber cum quatuor vocibus. Motteti del fiore* (Lyons, 1532); 1532[11] *Secundus liber cum quatuor vocibus. Motteti del fiore* (Lyons, 1532).

[10] RISM 1539[6] *Secundus liber cum quinque vocibus. Fior de mottetti tratti dalli Mottetti del fiore.* (Venice: Gardano, 1539); and 1539[12] *Primus liber cum quatuor vocibus. Fior de mottetti tratti dalli mottetti del fiore. Primus liber cum quatuor vocibus* (Venice, 1539).

While many of the composers' names are the same, only two pieces from Moderne's *Fiori* volumes appear in Gardano's *Frutto* books.[11] In Gardano's eyes then, the two series of anthologies represented two distinct publishing and musical entities. Gardano may well have envisioned an even grander set of editions in his *Frutto* series, for each of the books is designated *Primus liber*, thus suggesting more books for four, five, or six voices would follow. As far as we know, however, such a plan was never realized. In Table 3 I have listed the contents of each of the three books of the *Mottetti del Frutto*.

Primus Liber cum Quinque vocibus. Mottetti del Frutto (RISM 1538[4])

Iachet	In die tribulationes mee
Iachet	Repleatur os meum
Finot	Pater peccavi in celum / Quanti mercenarii
Iachet	Locutus est dominus / Stetit moyses
Gombert	Hic est discipulus ille / Et vox clara intonuit
Lupi	Adoremus regem magnum / O quanta est exultatio
Lupi	Stirps Iesse virgam / Virgo dei genetrix
Iachet	Salvum me fac domine / Veni in altitudinem
Finot	Spiritus meus attenuabitur / Si sustinuero in fernus
Finot	Ne derelinquas me
Finot	Exurge quare
Lupi	Sancta dei genetrix / Hoc est regina virginum
Gombert	Respice domine in testamentum / Respice domine
Iachet	Nunquam super terram
Gombert	Tribulatio cordis mei
Gombert	Sancta et immaculata / Que est ista que processit
Gardane	Dum complerentur / Facta autem hac

Primus Liber cum Sex Vocibus . . . (RISM 1539[3])

Gombert	In illo tempore loquente Iesu
Iachet	Surge petre et indue / Si diligis me simon petre
Berchem	Qualis es dilecta mea
Gombert	Descendi in ortum meum
Gombert	Ego sum qui sum / Tulerunt dominum meum
Gombert	O rex glorie / Omnis pulchritudo domini
Gombert	O crux splendidior / O crux gloriosa
Gombert	Media vita in morte sumus
Pionnier	Quem dicunt homines
Pieton	Verbum bonum et suave / Ave solem genuisti
Pieton	Benedicta es celorum regina / Per illud ave prolatum
Pionnier	Exultent et letentur in te

[11] They are du Billon's *Nativitas tua dei genetrix* and Lheritier's *Beata es virgo Maria*, both in the four-voice *Frutto* volume, RISM 1539[13].

Iachet	Descendit in ortum meum
Gombert	Duo rogavi te domine
Gombert	Oculi omnium in te sperantium / Qui edunt me
Gombert	Si bona suscepimus
Gombert	Sancta Maria succurre miseris
Gombert	Ave salus mundi
Gombert	O domine Iesu Christe adoro te / O domine Iesu Christe
Iachet	Murus tuus dilecta nostra / Ego murus sum

Primus Liber cum Quatuor Vocibus (RISM 1539[13])

Iachet	In illo tempore dixit Iesus / Dicebant ergo
Gombert	Qui seminant in lachrimis / Que parce seminant
Lheritier	Alma redemptoris mater / Tu que genuisti natura
Mestre Ihan	Thomas unus de duodecim / Et post dies octo
du Pont	Cenantibus illis accepit Iesus / Dixerunt viri
Alart	Dum transisset sabbatum / Et valde mane
Mestre Ihan	Cerne meos ero gemitus
Lupi	Benedictus dominus deus israel / Honor virtus
Verdelot	In te domine speravi / Quoniam fortitudo mea
Lasson	Congratulamini mihi omnes / Recedentibus
Arcadelt	Domine exaltentur manus tua / Possederunt nos
du Billon	Nativitas tua dei genetrix
Gardane	Maria virgo virginum
Gose	Non turbetur cor vestrum / Ego rogabo patrem
Verdelot	Sancta Maria succurre miseris
Leretier	Beata es virgo Maria
Guarnier	Lectio actuum apostolorum / Surrexerunt autem
Pieton	Que est ista que progreditur
Finot	Virga Iesse floruit
Certon	Sub tuum presidium / Sed a periculis
Claudin	Congratulamini mihi omnes
Leretier	Ave virgo gloriosa
Leretier	Ascendens christus in altum / Ascendo ad patrem
Iaquet	Spem in alium

Table 3. Contents of the *Mottetti del Frutto* volumes

Two composers – Gombert and Jachet of Mantua – clearly dominate the collections. A survey of concordances of these motets will show whether Gardano, by 1538, obtained a cache of new motets by these two composers, or if was he drawing on earlier anthologies. Furthermore, if the emphasis on Gombert and Jachet was the result of choice on Gardano's part, the question of the reasons for his selection arises. Table 4 shows that both new and previously circulating works appeared in the *Mottetti del Frutto*.

(The first number indicates the number of motets in the *Mottetti del Frutto* by that composer without earlier concordances. The second number indicates the total number of works by that composer in the series.)

Gombert – 12/17	Pieton – 1/3
Jachet – 2/10	Gardane – 2/2
Phinot – 5/5	Pionnier – 2/2
Lupi – 4/4	M. Jan – 2/2

Berchem, Alart, Lasson, Arcadelt, Gosse, Guarnier, Certon, Claudin – 1/1

Table 4. *Mottetti del Frutto*, works without earlier concordances, listed by composer

In the case of Gombert, twelve of his seventeen *Frutto* motets had not, as far as we know, been previously printed, and they do not appear in any pre-1539 manuscripts surviving today. However, only two of Jachet's ten *Frutto* motets make their debut here: the others had already shown up in a variety of manuscript and printed sources.[12] On the other hand, all of the motets by Phinot, Lupi, Pionnier, M. Jan, Arcadelt, and a small group of French composers appear for the first time in the *Mottetti del frutto*. Apparently, Gardano had one or more sources for acquiring new music in the latest manner. While we may not be able to identify a particular source, we can inquire into particular locations from which sources may have originated.

In Table 5 I have summarized the contents of the *Mottetti del Frutto*.

---

[12] For concordances for the *Frutto* motets, see Lewis, *Gardano I*, 174-6, 226-8, 242-6.

Dates and Locations of Composers, Listed by Number of Motets in the Series			
Composer	**Motets**	**Dates**	**Location in 1530s**
Gombert	17	ca. 1495–ca. 1560	Imperial Chapel, Tournai, Bologna 1530 (?)
Jachet	10	1483-1559	Mantua
Phinot	5	ca. 1510–ca. 1555	Urbino, Lyons (?)
Lheritier	4	ca. 1480–after 1552	Rome, Ferrara, Verona
Lupi	4	ca. 1506–1539	Cambrai
Pieton	4	fl. ca. 1530-45	Italy (?), Lyons (?)
M. Jan	2	ca. 1485-ca. 1545	Ferrara
Gardane	2	1500-1569	France (?), Venice
Pionnier	2	d. 1573	Loreto
Verdelot	2	ca. 1480-85–bef. 1552	Florence (?)
du Pont	1	bef. ca. 1500–after 1564	Rome
Alart	1	ca. 1515–after 1592	Leuven (?)
Lasson	1	ca. 1500-1553	Nancy
Berchem	1	ca. 1505–bef. 1567	Venice
Arcadelt	1	1507 (?)–1568	Florence, Rome
du Billon	1	fl. 1534-56	France (?)
Gosse	1	fl. 1520-65	France (?)
Guarnier	1	fl. 1538-42	France (?)
Certon	1	d. 1572	Paris
Claudin	1	ca. 1490-1562	Paris

Table 5. Contents of *Mottetti del Frutto*

Most of the information in this table is based on the composers' biographies in *New Grove*. Geographically, the composers of the *Mottetti del Frutto* were scattered in the 1530s. However, it is clear above all else that while the *Frutto* motets were printed in Venice, they are not a Venetian repertory. The chapel of Charles V, Mantua, Urbino, Rome, Ferrara, Florence, other northern Italian cities, and to a lesser extent, France, were the areas from which this music sprang. The composers represented, like Gardano himself, are all members of the generation born between about 1480 and 1510, with Verdelot, Jachet, and Lheritier being the oldest, and Phinot the youngest. Thus, Gardano included in his *Frutto* collection no retrospective material, and nothing from the Josquin generation. Apparently, the oldest piece in the series is Verdelot's *Sancta Maria succurre miseris*, which was copied into the manuscript Padua A17 in 1522. Most of the motets appear to be from at least a decade later.

Table 6 lists the *Frutto* motets that appear in earlier manuscripts or printed sources – twenty-one motets from a total of sixty-one in the three books.

Mottetti del Frutto 5 vv (1538[4])
  Jachet—In die tribulationes. RomePM 23-24; RomeV S35; VatCG XII,4
  Jachet—Repleatur os meum. RomeV S35, VatCG XII,4
  Jachet—Salvum me fac. 1538[2] (Moderne)
  Gombert—Sancta et immaculata. VatCG XII,4

Mottetti del Frutto 6 vv (1539[3])
  Jachet—Surge petre et indue. FlorBN 125[bis]; RomePM 23-4; RomeV S35; VatCG XII,4; 1535[5] (Attaingnant); 1538[3] (Grapheus)
  Jachet—Descendi in ortum. FlorBN 125[bis]; RomePM 23-4; RomV S35; 1534[10] (Attaingnant)
  Gombert—Media vita in morte. FlorBN 125[bis]
  Gombert—Oculi omnium in te sperantium. FlorBN 125[bis]
  Gombert—In illo tempore loquente Jesus. 1538[3] (Grapheus)
  Pieton—Verbum bonum. FlorBN 125[bis]
  Pieton—Benedicta es. FlorBN 125[bis]; RomePM 23-4; VatCG XII,4

Mottetti del Frutto 4 vv (1539[13])
  Jachet—In illo tempore dixit / Dicebant. CasN
  Jachet—Spem in alium. J9-1539 (Scotto)
  Gombert—Qui seminant in lachrimis. Ulm 237
  du Pont—Cenantibus illis. VatCG XII,4
  Verdelot—Sancta Maria succurre miseris. Pad A17; 1529[1] (Attaignant); 1534[4] (Attaingnant); 1538[3] (Grapheus)
  Lheritier—Beata es virgo Maria. BolP A45; Ver 760; 1534[3] (Attaingnant); 1539[10] (Moderne)
  Lheritier—Ave virgo gloriosa. RomePM 23-4; VatCG XII,4
  Lheritier—Ascendens christus in altum. ChiN 91
  Lheritier—Alma redemptoris mater. 1534[4] (Attaingnant)
  du Billon—Nativitas tua. 1539[10] (Moderne)

Dates and Provenance of the Manuscripts Cited[13*]
  BolP A45—Bologna 1527-41; CasN—Casale Monferrato, 1538-ca. 1545; ChiN 91—Florence, 1527-29; FlorBN 125[bis]—Florence, 1530-34; Pad A17—Padua, 1522; RomePM 23-24—Rome, ca. 1532-34; RomeV S35—Florence, ca. 1530; Ulm 237—Central Germany, ca. 1530-40; VatCG XII,4—Vatican, 1536; Ver 760—Verona, ca. 1530

Manuscripts Cited
  US Cn 91   Chicago, Newberry Library, Case MS.-VM 1578 N91
  I Fn 125[bis]   Florence, Biblioteca Nazionale Centrale, MS Magl. XIX.125[bis]

---

[13] *For manuscript details, see the *Census-Catalogue of Manuscript Sources of Polyphonic Music 1400-1559* compiled by the University of Illinois Musicological Archives for Renaissance Manuscript Studies (Neuhausen-Stuttgart: American Institute of Musicology, 1979-88).

I Pc A17	Padua, Biblioteca Capitolare, MS A17
I Rv S35	Rome, Biblioteca Vallicelliana, MS S[1] 35-40
I Rmassimo	Rome, Palazzo Massimo, Cod. VI.C.6 23-24
D Usch	Ulm, Von Schermar'sche Familienstiftung, Bibliothek, MS 237a-d
I Rvat CG XII,4	Vatican, Biblioteca Apostolica Vaticana, Cappella Giulia MS XII, 4
I Rvat CS 57	Vatican, Biblioteca Apostolica Vaticana, Cappella Sistina MS 57
I VEcap	Verona, Biblioteca Capitolare, MS DCCLXIX

Table 6. *Frutto* motets according to their earliest concordances

Of these, four only began to circulate in 1538-39. Evidently then, more than two-thirds of the *Frutto* repertory was new. We also see that fewer than half the *Frutto* composers are represented by works with earlier concordances. They are Jachet, Gombert, Lheritier, Pieton, Verdelot, du Billon, and du Pont, the latter two each represented by one work, Pieton and Verdelot each only by two. While the composers of the *Frutto* motets worked in centers as widely separated as Rome and Cambrai during the 1530s, we can see that most of the early concordances – twenty-four to be exact – appear in a group of manuscripts from Rome and Florence – Cappella Giulia XII/4, the early layers of Cappella Sistina 57, the Massimo and Vallicelliana partbooks, Florence 125[bis], and ChicagoN 91, suggesting that wherever Gardano may have obtained the music for the *Motteti del Frutto*, it is representative of the tastes of some Florentine and Roman musicians and collectors in the 1520s and 1530s. Pre-1538 concordances appear in only three other manuscripts (Padua, Verona and Ulm), each having just one work in common with the *Frutto* series. All of the earlier printed concordances are from Attaingnant's publications, and they involve only three composers – Verdelot, Lheritier, and Jachet. Parallel printed concordances – those appearing in 1538-39 – include one from Moderne's press, and several published by Grapheus of Nuremberg.[14] Other concordances are with Scotto's edition of Jachet's four-voice motets from 1539.[15] Thus, while the earlier manuscript transmission is Italian, the previous published transmission is primarily French, and extremely limited. The appearance of such a large number of manuscript concordances from the Roman/Florentine orbit suggests that Gardano may have received many of the *Frutto* motets from Florentine exiles like the Strozzi who were living in Venice. The Florentines were most likely also the source of the music that Gardano published as Arcadelt's first

---

[14] They are in Moderne's *Tertius liber mottetorum* (1538[4]), and Grapheus's *Secundus tomus novi operis musici* (1538[3]).

[15] RISM J9 *Celeberrimi maximeque delectabilis musici Iachet, chori Sancti Petri urbis Mantuae magistri: Motecta quatuor vocum . . . liber primus quatuor vocum* (Venice, 1539).

book of madrigals around the same time.[16] Certainly, we can see from Ex. 6 that in the case of ten of the *Frutto* motets, whatever their place of origin, they passed through the Florentine/Roman musical orbit before reaching Gardano's press. As for the *Frutto* works found in earlier printed collections, especially those published by Attaingnant, Gardano, who had recently moved to Italy from France, could well have owned or had access to some of the Parisian printer's series of motet prints.

The question of transmission of Gombert's motets is more complex. As the leading composer in the *Frutto* series with seventeen motets, Gombert clearly set the stylistic tone for the books. However, aside from three motets in the Florentine/Roman complex and one in the 1538 Grapheus print, Gombert's motets in the *Frutto* books have no earlier concordances. No manuscripts or prints earlier than 1538 contain the other thirteen pieces by Gombert. As far as we know, Gombert probably only visited Italy once, in 1530, for the coronation of Charles V in Bologna.[17] The only hint we have of how his music made its way to Italy consists of a letter the composer wrote from Tournai to Ferrante Gonzaga in 1547, evidently with a motet enclosed.[18] Ferrante, who was in the service of Charles V, was related to Ercole Cardinal Gonzaga, employer of Jachet of Mantua. One could speculate that it was through the Gonzagas that at least some of Gombert's music entered Italy. We do know that by the time of the *Mottetti del Frutto*, Jachet's motet writing had undergone a stylistic change, from the older approach of Mouton and his French contemporaries to the Gombertian compositional procedures of syntactic imitation. All Jachet's motets in the *Frutto* books are in his later style. Perhaps Jachet's later motets were influenced by contact with Gombert's works. Moreover, could Gardano have acquired some of Gombert's music through someone at Mantua? We may never know, but he evidently had a unique source for the works by Gombert that he published.[19]

I would like to turn now to Gardano's stylistic criteria for his selection of the *Frutto* motets, and to a consideration of what traits they may hold in common.

[16] The madrigals in the 1539 edition of Gardano's first book by Arcadelt are all anonymous in the body of the work, as they are in the Florentine manuscripts that contain many of them (e.g. I Fn 99-102 and I Fc 2495). A comparison of readings between the print and the manuscripts could prove useful in tracing the transmission. Gardano later supplied attributions for most of the madrigals, not all of which are by Arcadelt.

[17] George Nugent and Eric Jas, 'Gombert, Nicholas,' in Laura Macy (ed.), *Grove Music Online* (accessed 11 May 2007, http://www.grovemusic.com).

[18] New York, Pierpont Morgan Library. Mary Flagler Cary Music Collection. MFC G632. G642.

[19] None of the Gombert motets in the *Frutto* books appeared in Scotto's collections of Gombert's motets from 1539 and 1541.

Here I will concentrate on the volume for five voices. However, my examination of the four- and six-voice volumes suggests that much that is true of the five-voice book can be applied to them as well. In presenting the five-voice collection as his first offering of motets to the Italian public, Gardano was publishing a genre and style that had not previously appeared in Venetian prints – the five-voice motet with pervading imitation, devoid of structural canons or *cantus firmi*. The fifth voice is fully integrated into the overall texture of the work. As mentioned earlier, this style had appeared only sporadically in Italian and French sources starting in the late 1520s. Five-voice motets in general were rare in previous Venetian anthologies. Petrucci printed a volume in 1508 devoted to five-voice motets,[20] and included a few five-voice works in the third and fourth volumes of the *Motteti de la Corona*.[21] Antico printed four five-voice pieces in his *Motteti novi* of 1520.[22] From that point, the publication of five-voice motets passed over to the French printers, first Attaingnant and then Moderne, and by 1537 to the Germans. All but one of these anthologies, however – Moderne's of 1532[23] – contained five-voice motets as part of a wider assortment of settings for anywhere from three to eight voices. Bonnie Blackburn has pointed out that in the early sixteenth century composers experienced great difficulty in moving from a four-voice to a five-voice texture in the motet, especially when they attempted to eliminate the structural voice or voices and write in five equally-participating, imitative parts.[24] In an unpublished paper, Lois Rosow has traced the emergence of the integrated five-voice motet as a preferred genre, showing that it held minority status in the manuscripts of the 1520s, and only began to predominate in those from the end of that decade onwards.[25] She found, for instance, that whereas the Medici Codex of 1518 (I Fl 666) contained only one five-voice motet without a canon, cantus firmus, or ostinato,[26] a decade later half of the thirteen five-voice motets in the Newberry Partbooks (US Cn 91) contain no disparate voice, and the percentage rises still farther in the Vallicelliana manuscript (I Rv S35) of a few years later. There, twenty-seven of the forty-four five-voice motets are composed without a disparate voice.[27] Thus, even in the private manuscript anthologies, the integrated five-voice motet only came to

[20]   RISM 1508[1] *Motetti a cinque libro primo* (Venice, 1508).

[21]   RISM 1519[2] *Motetti de la corona. Libro tertio* and 1519[3] *Motetti de la corona. Libro quarto* (Venice, 1519).

[22]   RISM 1520[2] *Motetti novi libro tertio* (Venice, 1520).

[23]   RISM 1532[9] *Secundus liber cum quinque vocibus* (Lyons, 1532).

[24]   Bonnie Blackburn, *The Lupus Problem* (Ph.D, University of Chicago, 1970), 156, 227.

[25]   Lois Rosow, 'The Early Development of the Imitative Five-Voice Motet' (unpublished type-script, 1976).

[26]   Richafort's *Veni sponsa Christi*. Florence, Biblioteca medceo-laurenziana, MS Aquisti e doni 666.

[27]   Chicago, Newberry Library, Case MS VM 1578.M91, second series; Rome, Biblioteca Val-licelliana, MS Inc. 107 BIS (*olim* S. Borr. E.11.55-60), first series.

predominate around 1530. As for the printed anthologies, virtually all the five-voice motets published by Petrucci and Antico between 1508 and 1521 were built on a cantus firmus, canon, or ostinato. The overall style is the familiar one of the Josquin generation. The cantus firmus is often presented in long notes and duos; reduced texture appears frequently. Cadences are clearly audible, and sections are often marked by textural or metrical changes. Homophonic sections provide contrast to the polyphonic ones, with the latter employing imitation on occasion, but not in a systematic fashion.

Five-voice pieces played almost no role in Pierre Attaingnant's Parisian motet collections before 1534. It was Jacques Moderne of Lyons who published the first anthology devoted solely to five-voice motets since Petrucci's of 1508. Moderne's anthology was the above-mentioned *Secundus liber cum quinque vocibus* of 1532; he did not publish another collection containing five-voice motets until 1538.[28] The indication *Secundus liber* on the 1532 title page suggests that Moderne may have published an even earlier five-voice collection, but no trace of it survives. The five-voice motets of Moderne's 1532 collection present a more varied picture than those printed by Petrucci and Antico. While long-note canons and cantus firmi still appear, in some cases a structural voice is not employed, and a partially imitative free counterpoint is adopted. In general, these works still tend to provide sections of textural contrast along with clear cadential breaks, though they are disinclined to use duos except in the opening point of imitation, and passages of reduced texture are brief. Points of imitation occur, but not systematically or consistently. A few of the motets in Moderne's 1532 volume, such as those by Gombert, are full-fledged examples of consistent pervading imitation, but they are far from the majority. In contrast to his pre-1535 publications, five-voice works play a substantial role in Attaingnant's motet collections of 1534 and 1535.[29] Many of the motets first printed in Moderne's 1532 collection found their way into Attaingnant's anthologies, but numerous others were published for the first time by the Parisian printer. Here again we find a mixture of styles. Canons are frequent; some involve a long-note cantus firmus, while others are rhythmically integrated within the overall texture. For example, in Ex. 1, from Mouton's *Peccantem me quotidie,* the canonic Superius and Altus stand somewhere in between the long-note canon and the rhythmically integrated style. The canon's points of imitation correspond rhythmically to those of the other voices, but as phrases progress, the free voices move in livelier rhythms than the canonic ones.

---

[28] RISM 1538[2] *Tertius liber mottetorum ad quinque et sex voces* (Lyons, 1538).

[29] For a modern edition of Attaingnant's series, see A. Smijers and T. Merritt (eds.), *Treize livres de motets parus chez Pierre Attaingnant en 1534 et 1535*, 13 vols. (Paris, 1934-63).

Example 1. Johannes Mouton, *Peccantem me quotidie*, bb. 1-25

Both canonic pieces and those with a cantus firmus in Attaingnant's volumes vary in the amount of imitation found in the free voices. Occasional passages in reduced texture, particularly for duos, occur, as do brief homophonic passages. Other five-voice pieces in Attaingnant's series dispense with canon or cantus firmus, and employ some degree of imitative structure. Frequently a piece will open imitatively, and maintain several points of imitation based on text phrases before the imitation breaks down and free polyphony or homophony take over. At other times, only two, three, or four of the five voices will participate in a point of imitation. But, as in Moderne's collection, a few of Attaingnant's five-voice motets employ consistent, pervading imitation throughout, without a disparate structural voice, and without major textural contrast or reduced forces. These motets overlap phrases and seldom allow a clear break from one section to another. Still, motets in pervading imitation make up only a small portion of the contents of Attaingnant's thirteen motet books of 1534-35. Significantly, when Gardano chose motets to publish from Attaingnant's great series, he extracted only those in the imitative style.

In sharp contrast to the collections of Moderne and Attaingnant, Gardano's entire five-voice volume is devoted to motets employing pervading imitation. All but one of the motets is constructed without canon, cantus firmus, or ostinato. The single exception, Jachet's *Repleatur os meum*, employs a canon, this one between the Soprano and Alto, but it is a canon so constructed that it is totally integrated stylistically and rhythmically within the motet's fabric of pervading imitation. The seventeen motets in Gardano's five-voice collection all subscribe to the same aesthetic, and all present similar stylistic features. The points of imitation can be strict or varied, but they almost always involve all five voices. Fresh motives introduced with each text phrase are frequently repeated and varied luxuriantly within the course of working out the point of imitation. Evaded cadences abound, and every attempt is made to cover up the joints and seams of the phrases by overlapping endings and beginnings. In many of these motets, there is an occasional cadence where all voices end together, but a new section begins immediately and the seamless texture then continues. Texture is dense throughout, with individual voices usually dropping out for only a measure or two at a time. The only exception occurs at the opening of a piece or its *secunda pars*, when the two initial voices may form an imitative duo for four to six measures before the other three voices enter to complete the point of imitation. Homorhythmic passages are rare, as are shifts to triple meter, for these works avoided almost anything that implied a contrasting section that breaks the long line of the counterpoint. Phrases are generally syllabic at the beginning and melismatic toward the end. Text declamation is workable but sometimes rough. The careful text setting and accentuation of Willaert and his followers is not of primary concern to these composers.

In the five-voice volume, Gardano's own motet, *Dum complerentur dies* (Ex. 2), reflects these same stylistic features.[30] It consists almost entirely of continuous points of imitation on each new phrase of text, without canon or cantus firmus. Often the imitation is free rather than strict, but the principle is there. In a few places the imitation is limited to just four voices, but the general intent seems to be to include all five. The texture is dense, and there is only one passage of four and a half measures in which the Bass drops out and leaves a four-voice texture. Gardano utilized several long melismas, as well as the usual brief ones at the ends of phrases. Syllabic and melismatic passages alternate, and the text is declaimed carefully.

[30] For a complete transcription of this motet, see Mary S. Lewis (ed.), *The Gardane Motet Anthologies* (The Sixteenth-Century Motet, ed. Richard Sherr, 13) (New York, 1993), 203-7.

Example 2. Gardano, *Dum complerentur dies*, bb. 1-26

Gardano's motet differs from its companions primarily in its lack of multiple text repetitions and motivic variation within each point of imitation, features that characterize most of the five-voice motets in the *Mottetti del Frutto*. This lack is probably due less to the printer/composer's taste than to his lack of compositional skill. We can see, nonetheless, that Gardano was publishing here a collection of motets wholly sympathetic to his own compositional procedures. He was, in effect, introducing the style he himself favored to the larger Italian public. His was undoubtedly the hand that chose the contents of the volume according to his own criteria. He probably felt considerable satisfaction in obtaining, assembling, and introducing motets making use of this new way of writing. The stylistic unity of the *Mottetti del Frutto* contrasts with many of Gardano's other motet anthologies, which often contain works that depart in some aspects from the procedures described here. The five-voice *Mottetti del Frutto* thus emerges as a personal collection, a repertory based on a preferred style, new fruits to be tasted by Italian musicians and music lovers. In publishing this anthology, he was the first to make available to a relatively wide public a style that had previously been known almost exclusively in manuscript to a few Italian connoisseurs and in a few northern publications. Certainly he appears to be the first to devote a whole volume to the texturally integrated, continuously imitative five-voice motet. Thus, his first motet anthologies were bound to have a considerable impact on musical tastes in Italy and beyond.

In the second book of the *Frutto* series, that for six voices, Gardano continued to devote himself to the style of pervading imitation. Moreover, by printing an entire book of motets in six voices, he was offering a genre that had had only spotty representation in earlier prints by Petrucci, Grimm/Wyrsung, Attaingnant, Grapheus, and Moderne.[31] In all these prints, six-voice works made up only a small portion of the motets in the collections, which were for four to six or even eight voices. It would appear, then, that Gardano's six-voice *Mottetti del Frutto* was the first anthology devoted solely to six-voice motets. As might be expected, the collection is dominated by the music of Gombert, who masterfully applied his well-honed skills in pervading imitation to such multi-voiced works. The other composers in the volume are Jachet of Mantua, Jachet Berchem, Pionnier, and Pieton.[32] Their motets adhere to the imitative style, and except for Jachet of Mantua, not always with the same finesse in handling this new and difficult undertaking as exhibited by Gombert. Gardano rounded out his exposition of the imitative style in the *Frutto* volume for four voices. He may not have considered the writing of four-voice imitative motets to be as challenging and worthy of note as that for five or six voices, for this edition carries no dedication. However, its inclusion in the series demonstrates again Gardano's devotion to this manner of writing. To put his personal stamp on the collection, he included a new motet of his own, *Maria virgo virginum*.[33]

Within a few years, Venetian publications were filled with music in pervading imitation and related styles. Moreover, later concordances with the *Frutto* pieces appear in manuscripts from such varied locations as Italy, Austria, Central and Southern Germany, Denmark, and Scotland, and in printed editions published in Venice, Nuremberg, Leuven, Paris, Augsburg, and Mainz. A clear understanding of the transmission and dissemination of the *Frutto* repertory can only be gained by detailed readings and studies that are beyond the scope of this paper. However, continuing interest in its music a decade after its first publication is attested by the fact that in 1549 both Gardano and Scotto issued new editions of all three books.

---

[31] See RISM 1519[2] (Petrucci), 1520[4] (Grimm/Wyrsung), [1528][2] and 1534[5] (Attaingnant), 1537[1] and 1538[3] (Grapheus), and 1538[2] (Moderne).

[32] Modern editions of the six-voice motets not published elsewhere may be found in Lewis, *The Gardane Motet Anthologies*, 214-87.

[33] Lewis, *The Gardane Motet Anthologies*, 81-5.

If any further proof is needed of Gardano's deliberate promotion of a new style, the well-known story of the *Moteti de la Simia* and Gardano's reaction to it provides delightful evidence.[34] In short, in 1539 the Ferrarese music printer Johannes Buglhat and his associates published a book of motets, the *Moteti de la Simia*[35] that mocked Gardano's *Frutto* title and his address, the Calle della Simia. Not only had the Ferrarese printed their *Simia* collection using the new single-impression process that Gardano had introduced to Venice, but the repertory in their anthology was by many of the same composers as the works in the five-voice *Frutto* volume.[36] Even more importantly, a glance through the *Simia* motets shows that they too are in the same new, syntactically imitative style as the *Frutto* motets. Gardano responded in his next publication with a woodcut showing a lion and bear attacking a monkey surrounded by pilfered fruit, along with an indignant dedicatory letter protesting the theft of his fruits by the thieving monkey. I believe that Buglhat and his colleagues essentially stole the *Simia* repertory from under Gardano's nose, and published a collection of motets that he had intended as part of his series introducing the new motet style. This, more than the use of the new printing process, would have enraged the printer who sought the honor of being the first to promulgate the most modern and learned style within a new repertory in Venice.

The compositional style that Gardano promoted in his early publications came to dominate motet and madrigal writing in Italy through the mid-sixteenth century. It was taken up by Willaert and his disciples, and spread farther through the motets of Gombert. In the north, as well, it flourished in the works of Netherlandish composers in France, the Low Countries, Germany, and Austria. Many factors must have contributed to such a radical stylistic shift. Certainly Gardano's promotion of such works in some of the very earliest single-impression prints, whose low cost contributed to their wide dissemination, must have been one of the most important of those factors.

---

[34] For details of the story, see Lewis, *Antonio Gardano I*, 31-2.

[35] RISM 1539[7] *Moteti de la Simia (Liber primus vocum quinque)* (Ferrara, 1539).

[36] Nine of the motets are published in Mary S. Lewis (ed.), *The Buglhat Motet Anthologies* (The Sixteenth-Century Motet, ed. Richard Sherr, 14; New York and London, 1995), 123-266.

LA FROTTOLA ANTICA E LA CACCIA.
INDIZI DI UN RECUPERO FORMALE E STILISTICO NELLA PRIMA METÀ DEL CINQUECENTO

Francesco Luisi

Nell'ambito della musica italiana fiorita nell'ultimo Quattrocento e assunta agli onori della stampa da Ottaviano Petrucci tra il 1504 e il 1514 con i suoi undici libri di frottole, non si trova mai dichiarato il ricorso alla trecentesca forma della caccia. A ben vedere, tuttavia, non si trova alcun cenno anche alle altre forme dell'ars nova italiana, e cioè al madrigale e alla ballata. I titoli delle sillogi di Petrucci propongono una terminologia formale di sintesi che assume la denominazione 'frottola'. A tale termine, utilizzato in guisa di compendio per un genere assai diffuso sul quale si concentra un intento stilistico comune, l'editore fa seguire l'ordine progressivo delle edizioni, così da ottenere la sequenza degli 'opera' dal *Frottole libro primo* (1504) al *Frottole libro undecimo* (1514). In due casi, tuttavia, Petrucci si preoccupa di fornire titoli o sottotitoli con dichiarazione dell'articolazione delle varie forme poetico-musicali presentate nelle antologie: accade per l'opera quarta uscita nel 1505 con l'epigrafe *Strambotti, Ode, Frottole, Sonetti. Et modo de cantar versi latini et capituli*, e per il *Frottole libro sexto* stampato il 5 febbraio 1505 ('more veneto', ma 1506) con il sottotitolo *Frottole Sonetti Stramboti Ode. Justiniane numero sesanta sie*. In ambedue i casi si riscontra una ragione plausibile che possa aver suggerito la necessità di superare o integrare il titolo generico 'frottole': il quarto libro presenta per la prima volta un repertorio massiccio di strambotti (assenti del tutto nei primi tre libri) e il sesto contiene come novità assoluta un gruppo di giustiniane, composizioni di alto valore vocalistico legate alla cultura veneziana di cui Petrucci rende qualche modello esemplare.[1]

Tuttavia, nonostante i detti due casi di chiarimento assunto nelle epigrafi petrucciane, nessun accenno è fatto alle antiche forme della ballata, della caccia e del madrigale, ma anche nessun riferimento alla barzelletta, forma poetico-musicale coeva molto presente nelle sillogi stesse e emblematica della cultura mantovana. Si dovrà ancora attendere la fine del decennio successivo e guardare all'editoria non petrucciana. A partire dal 1510 si attua infatti una forma di concorrenza editoriale, dapprima con Andrea Antico a Roma

---

[1] L'argomento è approfondito in Francesco Luisi, 'Scrittura e riscrittura del repertorio profano italiano nelle edizioni petrucciane', in Giulio Cattin e Patrizia Dalla Vecchia (ed.), *Venezia 1501: Petrucci e la stampa musicale* (Venezia, 2005), 177-214 e 190-193.

(variamente sostenuto da Giacomo Giunta, Nicolò De Giudici, Giacomo Mazochio e altri) e poi estesa a Siena con Pietro Sambonetto e a Napoli con Giovanni Antonio De Caneto. Il decennio compreso tra il 1510 e il 1520 vede uscire antologie frottolistiche con il titolo articolato di *Canzoni Sonetti Strambotti et Frottole* (Antico dal 1513 al 1518 e Sambonetto nel 1515) e finalmente una selezione antologica fornita di una epigrafe significativa che introduce la distinzione fra frottola e barzelletta, dovuta all'officina editoriale di De Caneto (Napoli 1519), che recita: *Fioretti di Frottole Barzelette Capitoli Strambotti e Sonetti, Libro secondo*.[2]

Vero è che ancora non compaiono nei titoli le tipiche forme arsnovistiche italiane, ma l'introduzione di una declamatoria a sostegno della varietà formale ha ormai innescato un procedimento che darà qualche frutto. A partire dal decennio successivo, infatti, qualcosa si muoverà in favore della definizione di forme poetico-musicali vecchie e nuove: così negli anni Venti inoltrati apparirà timidamente nelle sillogi musicali il nuovo termine 'villota' e di lì a poco, negli anni Trenta, sarà felicemente recuperato il termine 'madrigale' per apparire poi in modo massiccio e totalizzante nei frontespizi di tutto il Cinquecento e oltre. Ma in tale scia non saranno contemplate le forme della ballata e della caccia.

In realtà la poesia trecentesca era stata fatta oggetto di grande interesse nella discussione sulla poetica in lingua del Cinquecento che aveva coinvolto soprattutto Pietro Bembo e Giangiorgio Trissino,[3] ma ciò aveva portato ad accreditare in particolar modo il madrigale, forma sulla quale si era aperto anche un dibattito etimologico inteso a delinearne la genesi. Sotto quest'ultimo aspetto la discussione portò ad acquisire l'idea che i madrigali fossero stati in origine componimenti in cui "era solito cantarsi cose ben d'amore, ma rurestri e pastorali, e quasi convenevoli a mandre" (Trissino), ovvero versi senza disciplina poetica sui quali "dapprima cose materiali e grosse si cantassero in quella maniera di rime sciolta e materiale altresì" (Bembo).[4] La visione arcaicizzante in cui veniva a collocarsi il madrigale era debitrice al trattato trecentesco sui ritmi volgari di Antonio Da Tempo; ma

---

[2] Per aggiornamenti, precisazioni e analisi delle stampe non petrucciane del secondo decennio del Cinquecento si veda Francesco Luisi, 'Dal frontespizio al contenuto. Esercizi di ermeneutica e bibliografia a proposito della ritrovata silloge del Sambonetto (Siena, 1515)', *Studi musicali*, 28 (1999), 65-115.

[3] Cf. Francesco Luisi, 'Considerazioni sul ruolo della struttura e sul peso della retorica nella musica profana italiana del Cinquecento', in Marco Gozzi (ed.), *Struttura e retorica nella musica nella musica profana del Cinquecento* (Roma, 1990), 13-35.

[4] Cf. Francesco Luisi, *Del cantar a libro ... o sulla viola La musica vocale nel Rinascimento* (Torino, 1977), 463-4 e più dettagliatamente: Francesco Luisi, *Considerazioni*, 13 ss.

tale collocazione aveva altresì forti punti di contatto con quella denunciata
dallo stesso metricologo a proposito della degenerazione del 'motto
confetto' verso la frottola, laddove si assisteva all'abbandono della sentenza
gnomica eloquente per acquisire il linguaggio proverbiale popolaresco
veicolato dai 'verba rusticorum' (Da Tempo).[5] In quanto alla ballata essa
riviveva specialmente in varie forme attualizzate con ripresa e stanze: nella
versificazione in ottonari piani utilizzati dalla barzelletta o nella canzone a
ballo a cadenza giambica spesso con quinari e doppi quinari o ancora nella
tradizionale forma con endecasillabi e settenari, magari d'autore (si veda
ad esempio il ripetuto ricorso alla ballata *Amor quando fioria* di Petrarca).
La ballata, dunque, fu solo taciuta nella terminologia originale ma molto
utilizzata in forme mediate, al punto da adattare la propria individualità
poetica ed essere presente come status formale assoggettato sia allo stile
frottolistico, sia a quello successivo di marca madrigalistica.

Le forme poetico-musicali arsnovistiche di riferimento, dunque, furono
compendiate dapprima nella frottola, che finì con l'indicare lo stile
frottolistico, e più tardi nel madrigale, che a sua volta fu assunto per
identificare lo stile madrigalistico. Avendo tuttavia ambedue le forme
– a detta degli esegeti – una comune origine rusticale, prima di assurgere
definitivamente al loro ruolo di riferimento stilistico dotto e convenzionale,
furono sottoposte a una sperimentazione compositiva che ammiccava ad
approcci linguistici di derivazione popolare a scopi puramente rievocativi
e di ricostruzione. Specialmente in ambiente patavino, veneziano e padano
in generale, si coltivarono perciò forme di frottola rusticale e di madrigale
rusticale che, se non costituirono vere e proprie categorie formali, furono
molto vicine alla definizione di un atteggiamento stilistico alternativo e
propositivo. Furono designate con nomi diversi e omologhi del tipo 'Canzone
alla pavana', 'Madrigale alla pavana', 'Madrigale alla pavana in villanesco'
e simili, tutti appartenenti alle performance attoriali e musicali di Ruzzante e
compagni che un osservatore attento, già nel 1512, registra come 'vestiti a la
villota' e nel 1525 impegnati nella recita di una commedia 'a la villota'.[6] Fra
tante, quest'ultima definizione sopravvisse per il carattere di sintesi che la

---

[5] Cf. Francesco Luisi, '"Moti confecti, zoè frotole". Dal genere letterario alla codificazione
    musicale: esegesi, trasmissione e recezione', in Patrizia Dalla Vecchia e Donatella Restani,
    Trent'anni di ricerche musicologiche. Studi in onore di F. Alberto Gallo (Roma, 1996), 143-
    159.
[6] Cf. Marin Sabudo, *Diarii*, XIII, col. 483 (15 febbraio 1512) e XXXVII, col. 572 (13 febbraio
    1525; riferimento a *I Diarii di Marino Sanuto* (MCCCCXCVI-MDXXXIII) *dall'autogra-
    fo marciano Cl. VII, codd. CDXIX-CDLXXVII*, ed. Rinaldo Fulin, Federico Stefani, Nicolò
    Barozzi, Guglielmo Berchet e Marco Allegri, Venezia, 1879-1903 (Ristampa Bologna, Forni
    1969-70).

distingueva, e finì con il designare una forma poetico-musicale specifica che ebbe qualche fortuna nei frontespizi a partire dagli anni Quaranta. Quando tuttavia il termine villotta sarà codificato, indicherà un comportamento stilistico e avrà perduto, come era già accaduto alla frottola e al madrigale, il suo significato propulsivo originale che qui si cercherà di rilevare.

In origine, già la frottola trecentesca mortificata dal giudizio di Antonio Da Tempo aveva accettato nel suo contesto metrico irregolare e nella sua disponibilità linguistica aperta al popolaresco situazioni di movimentazione, di richiamo, di grida e di onomatopee che presero il sopravvento sulla forma. In altri termini la caccia, che si era insinuata come composizione di genere, ebbe un carattere stilistico talmente preponderante da essere identificata come forma a sé stante, annullando il contesto strutturale della frottola di cui era stata diretta filiazione. Quando nel secolo seguente, specialmente in ambienti veronesi e patavini ove si recuperava la tradizione metricologica tempiana, sorse un dibattito sulla frottola che sfociò in una sistemazione formale di tipo strofico sostenuta da Francesco Baratella, il modello originario con o senza elementi di 'caccia' fu comunque utilizzato da compositori attenti che non si rassegnarono a una perdita definitiva della tradizione.[7] Ne fu araldo il veronese Michele Pesenti di cui Petrucci accolse ben tre significativi esempi di frottola antica già a partire dal *Frottole libro primo* (1504). Il primo, *Dal lecto me levava*, intona 'durchkomponiert' a quattro voci in stile imitativo una forma metrica che conduce all'antica caccia.

> Dal lecto me levava
> per servir el signor,
> alhor quando arivava
> la grua suo servidor,
> gru gru gru gru gru gru.
> Gentil ambasciador,
> che disse: non levè,
> tornè a dormir.
>
> Dal lecto me levava
> per servir el signor,
> alhor quando arivava
> la grua suo servidor,
> gru gru gru gru gru gru.

---

[7] Se ne discute ampiamente, offrendo una articolata scelta di esempi testuali in Appendice, in Francesco Luisi, *Scrittura e riscrittura*, 190-214.

Ognun dica: gru gru
gru gru gru gru gru gru
tornè a dormir.

Anche l'altro esempio di frottola dello stesso Pesenti 'Cantus et verba' è 'durchkomponiert' sulla prima strofa:

O Dio, che la brunetta mia
e l'è, e l'è fora,
né vòl tornar anchora.
Oymè, ch'ella m'acora,
ché meco non dimora
almen una sol hora.
O, Dio, che la brunetta mia
è cagion ch'io mora.

Oymè, che non pò più aspectare
el cor, el cor mio
poi ch'ella andò con Dio.
Sempre in affanno rio,
io vissi con desio;
veder la mia brunetta
o, Dio, ch'è là.

La terza frottola tempiana stampata da Petrucci nel 1504, sempre con intonazione di Pesenti, è invece un esempio di struttura strofica con 'enjambement' :

Passando per una rezolla
de questa terra,
lì passa lo mio amore.

Lì passa lo mio amore.
Non mi favella.
Favellami un pocho amore.

Favellami un pocho amore,
non suspirare.
Suspira la rocha e'l fuso.

Suspira la rocha e'l fuso,
la Catarina,
d'un'arte che io so fare.

D'un'arte che io so fare
lassar la voglio.
Di quella che non so fare.

Di quella che non so fare
imparar la voglio.
D'una barchetta in mare.

D'una barchetta in mare
comprar la voglio.
D'andare a pescare in mezo.

D'andare a pescare in mezo
malenconia.
Ch'havea sol una manza.

Ch'havea sol una manza,
la m'è stà tolta.
Colui che me l'ha tolta.

Colui che me l'ha tolta
fuss'el cortese,
ch'el me la ritornasse.

Ch'el me la ritornasse,
la manza mia,
ch'el me la ritornasse.

A Pesenti si deve anche un noto esempio di frottola-caccia con refrain a ballo (*Quando lo pomo vien dalo pomaro*) e di frottola-caccia in forma di ballata (*Che faralla, che diralla*), ambedue pubblicate da Petrucci nel *Frottole libro undecimo* del 1514. Ciò che tuttavia meraviglia non è la mancanza di segnalazione della forma della caccia da parte di Petrucci, quanto il riscontro in altra sede (comunque cronistica e critica) dell'appellativo 'villotta' assegnato a questo tipo di repertorio. Difatti, come è noto,[8] nella seconda edizione del *Baldus* di Teofilo Folengo (1521) troviamo un significativo accenno all'esecuzione di 'vilottas' da parte di Cingar, di cui si annotano gli incipit:

Cingar cantabat, lingua frifolante, vilottas,
quas toties nostros sensi cantare bretaros:
Gambettam, Broccam, Passandoque per na rigiolam.

L'ultima delle villotte citate è appunto il testo musicato da Pesenti di cui sopra, il quale, evidentemente, circolava con intonazioni monodiche e popolari che l'autore dichiara di avere già sentito cantare dai berrettai.

L'apparizione della testimonianza di Folengo nel 1521 è foriera dell'affermazione del termine 'villotta' come forma musicale in sede ufficiale: sono note le 12 composizioni tramandate come 'vilote' nei Mss. It. Cl. IV, 1795-98 (= 10653-10656) della Biblioteca Nazionale Marciana di Venezia[9] e i nove brani elencati come 'villote' nella Tavola del *Libro primo de la Fortuna* (Roma, Nicolò De Giudici, 1526?= RISM 1530[1]) di cui si conserva la sola parte di Altus, segnatura R 141/4, nel Civico Museo Bibliografico Musicale di Bologna.[10] Tuttavia, come per le villotte cantate da Cingar e presenti nel repertorio a stampa già dagli inizi del Cinquecento senza altro appellativo che quello di frottola, anche per i brani contenuti nei quattro codici marciani o nell'Altus di Bologna si possono individuare i caratteri che legano il sedicente nuovo genere all'antica caccia, ovvero alla frottola tempiana che quella caccia accoglie. La situazione non cambia nemmeno allorché il genere della villotta sarà dichiarato esplicitamente sui frontespizi, e cioè a partire dagli anni Quaranta quando Alvise Castellino pubblica *Il primo libro delle Villotte* dedicato al duca di Ferrara (1541) o quando Antonio Gardano pubblica nel 1549 la *Battaglia taliana composta da*

---

[8] Cf. Giulio Cattin, 'Canti, canzoni a ballo e danze nelle Maccheronee di Teofilo Folengo', in *Rivista Italiana di Musicologia*, 10 (1975), 190 e 203-5. Si riprende l'argomento in Marco Brusa, 'Presenze villottistiche nei libri delle frottole', in Giulio Cattin e Patrizia Dalla Vecchia (ed.), *Venezia 1501*, 309-10.

[9] Cf. edizione moderna in Francesco Luisi, *Apografo miscellaneo marciano. Frottole, canzoni e madrigali con alcuni alla pavana in villanesco* (Venezia, 1979).

[10] La datazione 1526 e la probabile appartenenza all'editore romano De Giudici sono proposte, con verosimili argomentazioni, in Knud Jespen, *La Frottola (I), Bemerkungen zur Bibliographie der ältesten weltlichen Notendrucke in Italien* (København, 1968), 74-5.

M. Mathias Fiamengo ... con alcune Villotte piacevole novamente con ogni diligentia stampate et corrette.[11]

Ebbene, negli anni Quaranta la villotta designa ormai un genere musicale che somma in sé un insieme di caratteri compositivi che da una parte veicolano gli aspetti peculiari del testo letterario e dall'altra quelli dello stile musicale. La forma si colloca tra la semantica della frottola e la sapienza della scrittura contrappuntistica che avrà esiti eccellenti nel madrigale. Sul piano della comunicazione ha una fortissima incidenza sullo stimolo della memoria, da cui parte per recuperare antichi modelli a cui attribuisce una forte connotazione nella sfera dell'appartenenza culturale linguistica. Per tali motivi spesso la villotta fa uso di citazioni sintagmatiche – riprodotte intatte nel loro valore letterario e musicale e inserite a mosaico nel contesto polifonico – che rappresentano una emersione del ricordo, l'evocazione di sentimenti, il ricorso al piacere uditivo depositato nella memoria. Le villotte anonime stampate da Gardano nel 1549 sono in realtà forme che si ricollegano allo spirito della frottola tempiana: in due casi organizzano una sintassi centonizzata con un procedere irregolare dei metri e delle rime e uniscono motti nuovi e citazioni di repertorio con apparente non-senso. Il ricorso ad antichi motivi frammentari talora è stimolato da una esortazione ("Horsù, horsù compagni, state attenti ad ascoltare li canti nostri varij che vi faran 'legrare tutti quanti ..."), tal altra dal ricordo di una performance ("Una leggiadr'et bella et vaga pastorella ... cantav'in sua favella: La via de la fiumana voglio fare ..."): in questi casi è possibile ottenere una composizione sintagmatica che ricorre a quante più citazioni possibili.

Diverso è invece il caso della seconda villotta aggiunta alla *Battaglia taliana* da Gardano, che comincia *Andand'a spasso*: qui siamo di fronte a un caso di frottola-caccia ispirata alla migliore tradizione del genere, che tuttavia non rinuncia alla citazione, a cui ricorre tuttavia nel merito della tematica.[12] In altri termini, essendo oggetto della caccia un uccellino, non viene a mancare l'evocazione della canzonetta *Uccellin, bell'uccellino, come sai tu ben cantare*. La citazione, come si riscontra in molti casi del

---

[11] L'edizione è disponibile in facsimile nella serie curata da Alamire, con una introduzione di Ignace Bossuyt (ed.), *Mathias Werrecore. La Bataglia italiana. Venetia, Antonio Gardane, 1549* (Peer, 1987).

[12] Le considerazioni molto puntuali, rese da Ignace Bossuyt nella sua introduzione alla edizione in facsimile citata alla nota precedente, mi hanno suggerito di offrirgli questo saggio in segno di ammirazione, di stima e di profonda amicizia; a proposito del brano che qui si esamina egli dichiara infatti, con acuta intuizione critica: "Another theme from the caccia, bird catching, is the subject of the single-section *Andand'a spasso* – in addition an excellent subjet for sexual insinuations". (Bossuyt (ed.), *Mathias Werrecore*, 10).

repertorio frottolistico ispirato all'uso di sintagmi popolari,[13] va ben oltre il ricorso testuale e ne riproduce anche l'intonazione originale, inserendola con adattamenti nel nuovo assetto polifonico, ma riportandola in due diverse lezioni: la prima con variante testuale e impostazione ritmica ternaria "a ballo" (ved. Es. musicale 1) e la seconda conformata al suo assetto originario di canzone in andamento binario (ved. Es. musicale 2).

Es. mus. 1. *Andand'a spasso*, Cantus, miss. 106 ss., Venezia, Gardane, 1549

Es. mus. 2. *Andand'a spasso*, Tenor, miss. 159 ss., Venezia, Gardane, 1549

Le due versioni tematiche non vanno tuttavia considerate sotto l'aspetto variantistico: esse mostrano in realtà una conoscenza approfondita della tradizione del testo da parte dell'anonimo compositore della frottola-caccia. Vale a dire che le fonti di riferimento sopravvissute tramandano ambedue le

---

[13] Vari casi del genere sono stati da me analizzati nel corso delle mie ricerche e costituiscono modelli esemplari; si vedano in particolare i saggi: Francesco Luisi, '*Ben venga Maggio.* Dalla Canzone a ballo alla *Commedia di Maggio*', in Piero Gargiulo (ed.), *La musica a Firenze al tempo di Lorenzo il Magnifico* (Firenze, 1993), 195-218; id., 'Il *Tentalora* ballo dei 'tempi passai': vecchie e nuove fonti', in Siegfried Gmeinwieser, David Hiley, Jörg Riedlbauer (ed.), *Musicologia Humana, Studies in honor of Warren and Ursula Kirkendale* (Firenze, 1994), 75-113; id., '*Cantasi a ballo.* Annotazioni formali su alcune laude savonaroliane in 'Una città e il suo profeta', in Gian Carlo Garfagnini (ed.), *Firenze di fronte al Savonarola* (Firenze, 2001), 426-49: 433; id., 'Presenze frottolistiche nelle laudi di Serafino Razzi', in Teresa Maria Gialdroni e Annunziato Pugliese (ed.), '*Faciam dolci canti*'. *Studi in onore di Agostino Ziino* (Lucca, 2003), 487-514; id.'Ancora sul *Ben venga Maggio.* Per un supponibile 'teatro di poesia in musica' a Siena nel primo Cinquecento', in Sabine Ehrmann-Herfort und Marcus Engelhardt (ed.),'*Vanitas fuga, aeternitas amor' Wolfgang Witzenmann zum 65. Geburtstag* (Analecta Musicologica 36, 2005), pp. 79-104 e da ultimo: id., 'El Marchexe de Salutio: filastrocca, canzone e danza a monte della novella di Boccaccio', in Rosy Moffa e Sabrina Saccomani (ed.), '*Musica se estendi ad omnia'. Studi in onore di Alberto Basso in occasione del suo 75° compleanno* (Lucca, 2007), 834-97.

soluzioni, sottolineando un percorso che parte dalla canzonetta per raggiungere un plausibile modello di danza: nel 1549, quando appare a stampa la frottola-caccia *Andand'a spasso*, la canzone *Uccellin, bell'uccellino* circola già sia come testo cantato, sia come aria 'a ballo' di matrice popolare. Quest'ultima circostanza è dimostrata da due fonti parallele, più o meno coeve e databili verosimilmente intorno alla metà del Cinquecento, in base alle quali da una parte si dimostra musicalmente l'esistenza di un vero e proprio ballo, intavolato per tastiera, intitolato *Occellino, bel occelino* e dall'altra lo si evoca in sede letteraria come ballo popolare assimilato a quelli 'tirai tutti dal canto figurao'. La versione musicale del ballo è riportata nel Ms Cl IV, 1227[14] della Biblioteca Nazionale Marciana di Venezia sotto il numero 14 ed è rigorosamente condotta in andamento ternario sottoposto al 'tempus imperfectum diminutum' seguito dal numero proporzionale 3, ascrivibile al moderno tempo senario 6/4 (ved. Es. musicale 3).

Es. mus. 3. I-Vn, Ms CL. IV, 1227, n.14, *Occelino, bel occelino*, intavolatura,
      linea superiore

La testimonianza letteraria è invece contenuta nelle Lettere di Andrea Calmo, un sagace e attento osservatore dei costumi del suo tempo che affida a fantasiose lettere i suoi ricordi nostalgici e trova modo di rimarcare la sua preferenza per i modi antichi anche a proposito del ballo: in una lettera indirizzata alla 'Signora Cavriola',[15] celebrata dallo scrittore con toni coloriti per le sue straordinarie doti di ballerina, si professa egli stesso in grado di ballare, purché si tratti di balli della sua giovinezza che, precisa, erano allora ricavati da canzoni in 'canto figurato', secondo un uso molto apprezzato dal 'volgo'. La testimonianza conferma la derivazione di molte arie da ballo derivanti da precedenti canzoni prescelte allo scopo per le loro peculiarità

---

[14] Cf. edizione moderna in Knud Jeppesen (ed.), *Balli antichi veneziani per cembalo*, (Copenhagen, 1962), preceduta dal saggio dello stesso studioso: 'Ein altvenetianisches Tanzbuch', in Heinrich Hüschen (ed.), *Festschrift Karl Gustav Fellerer zum sechzigsten Geburtstag am 7. Juli 1962 überreicht von Freunden und Schülern* (Regensburg, 1962), 245-63.

[15] Cf. Vittorio Rossi (ed.), *Le lettere di Messer Andrea Calmo* (Torino, 1888), in particolare Appendice III (*Balli e canzoni del secolo XVI*), pp. 414 e ss. La lettera *Alla signora Cavriola* è stata da me direttamente consultata sull'edizione *Delle lettere di M. Andrea Calmo*, Venezia, Fabio e Agostin Zoppini fratelli, 1584, *Residuo delle Lettere*, Libro IV, cc. 29v-31.

ritmiche, per la loro ispirazione di carattere popolare e la loro notorietà:

> "[...] E si ben non so far tanti tremoli, come haverè praticao, vederè che anche mi no sarò un goffo, anchora che 'l sia defferentia dalle cosse moderne alle antighe, pur al più del vulgo ghe pèiase questa Padoana de mazza porco, Zoioso, Anella, Fortuna, Torela mo, Vanni de Spagna, Saltarelo, *Oselino*, Descarga piere, la Conchiera, Bassadanza, Lassela andar la povera puta, Te parti cuor mio caro, el Toresan che canta in su la Torre, *tirai tutti dal canto fegurao*, che m'arecordo haver un per de calze paonazze, col mio zuppon de raso festechin, e scarpe bianche [...]."[16]

La *Canzone dell'uccellino*, a sua volta, doveva essere in voga in tempi precedenti alla sua assunzione nel 'canto figurato' e certamente doveva appartenere al repertorio di tradizione popolare.[17] Le fonti più antiche che la recepiscono anche musicalmente sono databili agli anni Venti del Cinquecento. Si ritrova in una nota frottola centonizzata – un modello compositivo che prelude agli esiti della futura villotta – che comincia "Vra diu d'amor". La composizione si trova nel Ms Q21 del Civico Museo Bibliografico Musicale di Bologna, n. 46,[18] e riporta nel Tenor alle misure 34 ss, l'intera citazione che si trascrive nel seguente Esempio

Es. mus. 4. I-Bc, Ms Q21, n.46, *Vra din d'amor*, Tenor, miss. 34 ss.

---

[16] Due dei balli ricordati da Calmo si riscontrano nella raccolta di balli della Marciana sopra citata: *Ocelino bel'ocelino* e *El torexam che canta*. Nella citazione i corsisi sono nostri.

[17] Giova ricordare che alla stessa canzone fa riferimento anche il noto testo centonizzato pubblicato con il titolo *Opera nuova nella quale si ritrova essere tutti li principii delle canzoni antiche e moderne poste in ottava rima, cosa piacevole et ridiculosa* (Bologna, Biblioteca Universitaria), ai versi 30-32: "Bello uselin satu volar in alto / come sai tu cantar bel oselino / falilon, falilela tortorino", e che viene evocata anche nella *Vacaria* di Ruzzante. Cf. Severino Ferrari, 'Documenti per servire all'istoria della poesia popolare cittadina in Italia nei secoli XVI e XVII: Un centone', in *Il Propugnatore*, 13 (1888), 301 e 304.

[18] Lo stesso brano è tramandato anche dal Ms Magl. XIX, 122-125, n. 31 della Biblioteca Nazionale di Firenze, dal Ms γ. L.11.8, cc. 55v-56, della Biblioteca Estense di Modena e nel *Libro Primo De la Croce*, cc. 20v-22 – ove è attribuito con le sigle F. P. (Francesco Patavino) – stampato a Roma da Giovanni Giacomo Pasoto e Valerio Dorico nel 1526. Cf. Knud Jeppesen, *La Frottola II. Zur Bibliographie der handschriftlichen musikalischen Überlieferung des weltlichen italienischen Lieds um 1500* (København, 1969), 104-5.

La stessa citazione, impiegata come refrain di coda della frottola *Da cholei ch'è so mio benel*, presente nella stessa fonte bolognese al n. 41, conferma, pur con invitabili varianti dovute al nuovo adattamento contrappuntistico, l'appartenenza del testo a una consolidata tradizione che ne rispetta i caratteri salienti, come si può vedere nell' Esempio musicale 5.

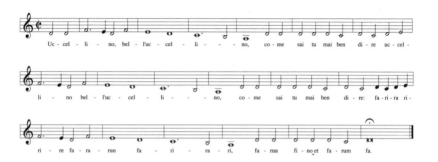

Es. mus. 5. I-Bc, Ms Q21, n.41, *Da cholei ch'è sol mio bene*, Cantus, Ripresa

Con altre varianti, che pure non annullano i punti cardine della citazione originale, si ritrova come ritornello della frottola *Mentre io vo per questi boschi*, presente nel Ms Cl IV, 1795-1798 della Biblioteca Marciana, al n. 58,[19] come appare dal seguente Esempio musicale 6.

Es. mus. 6. I-Vn, Ms CL. IV, 1795-98, n.58, Mentre io vo' per questi boschi, Cantus, refrain di coda

Come si è visto, dunque, la frottola-caccia del 1549 tiene conto della duplice tradizione che accompagna la canzone *Uccellino bell'uccellino*, ma, nel contesto generale dell'elaborazione musicale, la citazione non assume più la consueta posizione di refrain utilizzata nella frottola, né la funzione di

---

[19] Edizione moderna in Francesco Luisi, *Apografo miscellaneo marciano*, 126-7. Il brano è presente anche nel Ms R 142, c. 13*v* (solo parte di Tenor, con testo della seconda strofa 'Lieti fai') del Civico Museo Bibliografico Musicale di Bologna, attribuito a Marchetto Cara.

inserimento centonizzato, anch'esso già della frottola, che sarà ripreso dalla villotta sintagmatica. La novità sta ora nel porre la canzone come fulcro di una azione movimentata posta in musica che ritrae la concitazione della caccia, la narrazione, il richiamo, l'azione, l'onomatopea, l'interlocuzione tra i personaggi della divertente, ammiccante e licenziosa scenetta. Rinviando alla trascrizione completa posta in Appendice per una visione d'insieme, qui riportiamo il testo completo per un'analisi dell'assetto formale e stilistico della caccia (con le citazioni evidenziate dal nostro corsivo):

Andand' a spasso
sopra d'un monticello,
dov'er' un praticello
a la pianura,
là sù, per mia ventura,
veddi volar cantand' un bell'augello
sopra d'un arboscello.
Et di sotto havea teso la mia rete
e 'nvischiate le bacchette,
stando pur basso,
sol per prender quello.
"O vello, o vell', o vello:
vedil là come gli è bello!
Parmi verde talhor,
talhor par giallo:
o gli è un cuccho,
o un pappagallo".
"No, ch'el chucco vien d'aprile".
Su la più alta rama
cantava l'augel gentil.
Et tu con sottil arte
al fin quel prendi.
"Tendi la rete, tendi,
ch'el vola giù disteso".
Tirlirin, tirlirin, tirlirin.
"L'augel è preso
se ben ho inteso:
al cap' è un gardellino,
nel cantar un lugarino.
Gardellin, bel lugarino,
come sai tu ben cantare.

Ch'a la mia donna ti vorrò donare".
"Che di' tu, fiol de Dio?
Dammel a me, poi che l'augell' è mio!"
"Piglia, piglia, piglia
piglia e stringil pian pian,
che l'usellin, madonna,
ch'el non vi scampi fora di man".
"Ecco l'augell'hor eccol, eccol
gl'alza la cod'et tra' del becco,
tutta la notte, sera et mattina.
Occellino, bell'occellino
deh lassami dormire,
ché la notte se ne va".
"Cantiam prima el "fami fa'.
Dormi poi, figlia, et fa la nannina".

Si potrebbe sostenere che l'elemento peculiare di netto sapore villottistico è il ricorso al doppio senso e alle insinuazioni a sfondo sessuale, ma tali aspetti non sono affatto estranei alla tradizione della frottola, come non lo sono le assunzioni di sintagmi poetico-musicali. In realtà le villotte di Gardano non hanno ancora la caratterizzazione linguistica padana che realmente le distingue dalle frottole. Ne è la riprova la presenza, nella seconda edizione della *Bataglia taliana* pubblicata dallo stesso editore a Venezia nel 1552, di una villotta di Giordano Pasetto definita 'villotta alla padoana' in quattro parti che comincia *Audi bone persone*.[20] In questo caso siamo di fronte a una vera e propria composizione frottolesca 'alla villotta', ovvero centonizzata in vario metro, che ricorre a linguaggi padani, che usa espressioni da 'popolazzo', che evoca canzoni a ballo, che usa del triviale con ironia, che assume antichi motivi col solo pretesto di condurli sul binario del doppio senso. Ne discende che fuori da tale contesto ci troviamo per lo più di fronte alla frottola di memoria tempiana o alla frottola-caccia.

---

[20] Il testo è riportato interamente come esempio di villotta padovana in Francesco Luisi, *Scrittura e riscrittura*, 212-4.

DIE ENTSTEHUNG DER MUSIKALISCHEN GESCHICHTE. HISTORISIERUNG UND ÄSTHETISCHE PRAXIS AM BEISPIEL JOSQUINS

Laurenz Lütteken

HISTORISIERUNG DER MUSIK

Zu den Auffälligkeiten der Enzyklopädie *Die Musik in Geschichte und Gegenwart* gehört der Umstand, dass es wohl ein Lemma „Musikgeschichtsschreibung" gibt, nicht aber eines zur „Musikgeschichte".[1] Damit ist zwar einem Umstand Rechnung getragen, den schon Ranke und Droysen trennte, nämlich der Vorstellung, dass Geschichte nicht einfach da ist, wie Ranke glaubte, sondern, mit Droysen, ein Konstrukt erst ihres Interpreten.[2] Wenn auch Droysen selbst bezweifelte, dass dieses Modell für eine Geschichte der Kunst überhaupt tauglich sein könne,[3] so stellt sich dennoch die Frage, woraus sich unter diesen Prämissen eine ‚Geschichte der Musik' eigentlich zusammensetzt und wie jene ‚Tatsachen' beschaffen sind, die sie konstituiert.[4] Entscheidend sind dafür einerseits jene historiographischen Positionsbestimmungen, wie sie seit dem 19. Jahrhundert und, im Blick auf die Musik, besonders problematisch und umstritten vorgenommen werden.[5] Andererseits ist damit aber durchaus ein pragmatischer Aspekt verbunden, nämlich die auf den ersten Blick einigermaßen trivial anmutende Frage, ab wann sich eigentlich eine ‚Geschichte der Musik' konstituiert, ab wann also das Musikalisch–Vergangene überhaupt als ein Vergangenes wahrgenommen worden ist. Schon Herder nahm gerade das sperrige Verhältnis der Musik gegenüber der wahrnehmbaren Welt zum Anlass, gewissermaßen die Grenzen von Geschichte, deren, mit Thomas

---

[1] Dieser Befund trifft auch das *New Grove Dictionary of Music and Musicians*, sowohl in der Auflage von 1980 wie der von 2001. Auch dort gibt es einen Eintrag „Historiography", aber keinen „History".

[2] Vgl. dazu Otto Gerhard Oexle, „Von Fakten und Fiktionen. Zu einigen Grundsatzfragen der historischen Erkenntnis", in Johannes Laudage (Hg.), *Von Fakten und Fiktionen. Mittelalterliche Geschichtsdarstellungen und ihre kritische Aufarbeitung* (Köln, 2003), 1–42; auch Alexandre Escudier, „De Chladenius à Droysen. Théorie et méthodologie de l'histoire de langue allemande (1750-1860)", *Annales*, 58 (2003), 743–77.

[3] Dazu Carl Dahlhaus, *Grundlagen der Musikgeschichte* (Köln, 1977), 60ff. u. passim.

[4] Dazu grundlegend Hans-Joachim Hinrichsen, „Musikwissenschaft und musikalisches Kunstwerk. Zum schwierigen Gegenstand der Musikgeschichtsschreibung", in Verf. (Hg.), *Musikwissenschaft. Eine Positionsbestimmung*, Kassel 2007, 67–87.

[5] Merkwürdigerweise reichen selbst die anspruchsvollsten methodischen Selbstvergewisserungen kaum hinter das späte 18. Jahrhundert zurück (Dahlhaus, *Grundlagen*, 91ff.).

Mann zu sprechen, frühestes Morgengrauen in den Blick zu nehmen.[6] Dabei war ihm daran gelegen, jenseits dieser Grenzen gleichsam das Wesen der Musik und der Sprache zu ergründen. Andererseits ließe sich aber, sehr viel bescheidener, auch fragen, wo denn diese Grenzen überhaupt liegen, wann und wie die Musik in die Sphäre der Geschichtlichkeit eingetreten ist. Unabhängig also von dem Problem, wie jene ‚Tatsachen' beschaffen sein könnten, aus deren Reihung sich Musikgeschichte bildet, soll es hier um das Problem der bewussten Wahrnehmung von Vergangenem in der Musik gehen – und um die Konsequenzen, die sich aus diesem Umstand ergeben.

Wahrnehmung schafft zugleich Distanz, die Distanz des Gegenwärtigen zum Vergangenen. Diese Distanz erweist sich im Hinblick auf die Musik als besonders kompliziert, weil diese auf eine grundsätzliche Weise der Zeitlichkeit unterliegt und erst relativ spät zur materialisierten Form der Schriftlichkeit gefunden hat. Überdies ist das Verhältnis dieser Schriftlichkeit zur klingenden ‚Wirklichkeit' von Musik stets widersprüchlich, spannungsvoll und vielschichtig gewesen, so dass beides, Klang und Schrift, niemals eine wirklich störungsfreie Einheit im Sinne dessen bilden konnten, was in der Historiographie seit dem 19. Jahrhundert ‚Quelle' genannt wird.[7] Bewußtsein über eine historische Distanz schließt aber zugleich jene Faktoren weitgehend aus, die, um mit Maurice Halbwachs zu sprechen, als Bestandteil eines ‚kollektiven Gedächtnisses' gelten können.[8] Schon Aby Warburg hatte, bezogen auf Prozesse der Bildfindung, im Begriff der ‚Pathosformel' solche Prozesse der kulturellen Codierung folgenreich namhaft gemacht.[9] Sie prägen auch, allerdings viel zu selten und viel zu wenig systematisch reflektiert, den Umgang mit Musik. Ab einem gewissen Moment müssen derartige Codierungen überlagert worden sein von der bewussten, distanzierenden Wahrnehmung von Musik der Vergangenheit und damit von der willentlichen Auseinandersetzung mit ihr. Eine derartige Wahrnehmung bedarf zwar notwendig der schriftlichen Fixierung, doch beschränkt sich diese keineswegs auf das begriffliche Raisonnement über Musik, es existiert gleichfalls in der unbegrifflichen Musik selbst.

---

[6] Vgl. hier etwa Andreas Käuser, „Der anthropologische Musikdiskurs. Rousseau, Herder und die Folgen", *Musik und Ästhetik*, 4 (2000), 24–41.

[7] Vgl. hier Otto Gerhard Oexle, „Was ist eine historische Quelle?", *Die Musikforschung*, 57 (2004), 332–50.

[8] Maurice Halbwachs, „La mémoire collective chez les musiciens", *Revue philosophique*, 64/127 (1939), 136–65.

[9] Vgl. in diesem Zusammenhang auch Götz Pochat, *Der Symbolbegriff in der Ästhetik und Kunstwissenschaft* (Köln, 1982), 76ff.; zur Bedeutung des ‚Schemas' in der Historiographie Peter Burke, *Was ist Kulturgeschichte?*, aus dem Englischen übers. von Michael Bischoff (Frankfurt/M., 2005), 20ff.

Dieser Sachverhalt ist, zumal er eben bisher nicht systematisch erforscht worden ist, kompliziert. Seine Vielschichtigkeit legt den Verzicht auf lineare, punktuelle oder kausale Antworten nahe. Im Gegenteil, es ist wahrscheinlich, dass die ‚Entstehung' musikalischer Geschichte auf sehr verschiedenen Ebenen in sehr unterschiedlicher Form und, möglicherweise, nicht in einer homogenisierbaren Chronologie zu beobachten ist. Der Prozess bedurfte offenbar sehr verschiedener Voraussetzungen, und so ist, um ihn auch nur ansatzweise zu fassen, ein ganzes Bündel der unterschiedlichsten Faktoren geltend zu machen. In der folgenden Skizze sei daher der Blick auf einen dieser Faktoren gerichtet, nicht, um denkbare Antworten auf die Ausgangsfrage zu finden. Vielmehr sollen nur einige Koordinaten in einem weitgehend unvermessenen Gelände fixiert werden, innerhalb derer dann weitergehende Überlegungen möglich werden könnten.

ÜBERZEITLICHE GESCHICHTLICHKEIT

Bewusste Wahrnehmung von musikalischer Vergangenheit im Sinne einer Distanz bedeutet zugleich die willentliche Abgrenzung der eigenen Gegenwart. Derartige Abgrenzungen begegnen erstmals in einer differenzierten Form im 15. Jahrhundert. Verschiedene Indizien können hier geltend gemacht werden. Eines von ihnen ist die immer häufiger werdende Verbindung der kompositorischen Hervorbringung mit einem Namen, der allerdings auch im früheren 15. Jahrhundert weder der Regelfall ist noch aus einem konsistenten Motiv – etwa der Hervorhebung von Autorschaft – angefügt worden ist.[10] Gleichwohl musste die Verfügbarkeit von Namen, die im 14. Jahrhundert noch zu wenig spezifisch erfolgt ist,[11] musikalische Abgrenzungen erlauben, die nicht nur Zeitgenossen untereinander betraf, sondern auch die Gegenwart gegenüber der Vergangenheit. Die Namensnennungen, die Johannes Tinctoris in den 1470er Jahren und vor allem im *Liber de arte contrapuncti* aus welchen Motiven auch immer angebracht hat, lassen solche Abgrenzungsversuche erkennen. Die Erinnerung an eine Person der Vergangenheit, die sich auch als ‚Memoria' beschreiben lässt,[12] basiert auf der grundsätzlichen Möglichkeit,

---

[10] Dazu vom Verf., „Die Macht der Namen. Autorzuschreibungen am Beispiel des Codex Emmeram", *Archiv für Musikwissenschaft*, 62 (2005), 98–110; Michele Calella, *Musikalische Autorschaft. Der Komponist zwischen Mittelalter und Neuzeit* (Schweizer Beiträge zur Musikforschung; Kassel, in Vorb.).

[11] Einer der wichtigsten Autoren des 14. Jahrhunderts, Machaut, ist als Komponist in einer weitgehend literarisch determinierten Überlieferung greifbar, und selbst eine Handschrift gesteigerten ‚Autorenbewußtseins' wie der Squarcialupi-Codex stammt aus dem frühen 15. Jahrhundert und umschließt, aufschlussreich genug, weitgehend Repertoire der Vergangenheit.

[12] Otto Gerhard Oexle, „Memoria als Kultur", in ders. (Hg.), *Memoria als Kultur* (Veröffentlichungen des Max-Planck-Instituts für Geschichte, 121; Göttingen, 1995), 9–78.

diese Person tatsächlich zu identifizieren, was in der Musik nur das schriftlich fixierte ‚Werk' meinen kann. Guillaume Dufay hat auf seinem in Lille erhaltenen Grabstein diesen Aspekt der musikalischen Memoria akzentuiert, weil die Selbstrepräsentation als Musiker eines solchen Werkes bedarf, das über den Zeitpunkt des Todes seines Schöpfers Gegenwärtigkeit beanspruchen kann.

Doch musikalisch-kulturelles Gedächtnis in einem konkreten, auf das bewusste Detail gerichteten Aspekt offenbart sich auch in der Herausbildung eines differenzierten Gattungssystems. Die Gattung selbst stiftet einen musikalischen Denkzusammenhang, der kompositorische Bezüge erlaubt, und zwar sowohl zu den eigenen Zeitgenossen wie zu denen der Vergangenheit. Begreift man Komponieren als Denken in Musik, dann erschließt das Denken in verschiedenen, hinsichtlich des Anspruchsniveaus differenzierten Gattungen eine kompositorische Kontinuität, in der sich das handelnde Individuum positioniert. Die ‚Erfindung' der Cantus firmus-Messe im 15. Jahrhundert führt das deutlich vor Augen: Sie bedeutet nicht nur die Hypostasierung des Primats kompositorischer Interessen gegenüber anderen (wie denen der Liturgie), sondern zugleich die produktive Vergegenwärtigung eines Vergangenen (einer Chanson zum Beispiel) in einem neuen kompositorischen Zusammenhang.[13]

Mit diesem Phänomen hängt ein weiteres Indiz für Geschichtlichkeit zusammen, nämlich der kleine, in der zweiten Hälfte des 15. Jahrhunderts einsetzende und gegen 1500 zu einer gewissen Blüte gelangende Zusammenhang der Memorialkompositionen von Musikern für Musiker.[14] Gerade hierin wird die Form der erinnernden Vergegenwärtigung im vergänglichen Medium Musik zu einer besonderen Form der Memoria. Neben der genuin christlichen Gedächtniskultur stiftet Memoria ‚Adel', denn nur die Erinnerung an die Toten ermöglicht die Hervorhebung der eigenen Gegenwart.[15] Und Memoria lässt sich als ein übergreifendes soziales Phänomen beschreiben, in dem alle Lebensbereiche gleichsam ordnend integriert waren. Die einschlägigen Kompositionen partizipieren an beiden Aspekten, und gerade hierin wird auch so etwas fassbar wie Geschichtsbewusstsein. Eine besondere Rolle kommt dabei Josquin Desprez

---

[13] Vgl. zum Problem den Überblick bei Hermann Danuser, Art. „Gattung", in *MGG2*, *Sachteil* 3, (1995), 1042–69.

[14] Dazu vom Verf., „Memoria oder Monument? Entrückung und Vergegenwärtigung in der musikalischen Totenklage um 1500", in Andreas Dorschel (Hg.), *Resonanzen. Vom Erinnern in der Musik* (Studien zur Wertungsforschung, 47; Wien etc., 2007), 58-77.

[15] Otto Gerhard Oexle, „Memoria als Kultur", 37ff., vgl. auch ders., „Die Gegenwart der Lebenden und der Toten. Gedanken über Memoria", in Karl Schmid (Hg.), *Gedächtnis, das Gemeinschaft stiftet* (Schriftenreihe der Katholischen Akademie der Erzdiöze Freiburg; München und Zürich, 1985), 74–107; vgl. auch den Überblick bei dems., Art. „Memoria, Memorialüberlieferung", in *Lexikon des Mittelalters* 6, 1993, 510–3.

zu. Denn einerseits bezeichnen seine eigenen Memorialkompositionen einen besonderen Augenblick der bewussten geschichtlichen Reflexion, am deutlichsten wohl *Nymphes des bois/Requiem*, in dem das vom Betrauerten, von Ockeghem geschaffene Modell zu dessen Memoria vergegenwärtigt wird. Andererseits hat Josquins eigener Tod eine ganze Reihe ähnlich gelagerter Kompositionen ausgelöst,[16] mithin also über die Memoria eine bewusste Erinnerung des Verlusts in der kompositorischen Gegenwart.

Das hierin greifbare neue historische Bewusstsein ist breit kontextualisiert. Mit der Veränderung des Zeitbewusstseins im 14. Jahrhundert, also der Ersetzung der metaphysischen Kategorie Zeit durch eine physikalische im Umfeld einer sich erneuernden Aristoteles-Rezeption,[17] war zugleich auch eine Veränderung des historischen Bewusstseins verbunden. Diese Veränderung hat jedoch ein paradoxes Ergebnis gezeitigt: Mit der Wahrnehmung einer konkreten und konkret messbaren zeitlichen Situiertheit des Menschen ist die Auseinandersetzung mit der Vergangenheit zum Modus der Abgrenzung geworden, also zum Instrument der Hervorhebung der eigenen Gegenwart und ihrer Vorzüge, ihres ‚Adels'.[18] In diesem Sinne dient der Rekurs auf die dem Autor unmittelbar vorausgehende Vergangenheit bei Tinctoris vor allem dem Erweis, dass die eigene Gegenwart unvergleichlich sein müsse.

Solche Einschätzungen gründen in der Vorstellung, dass Geschichte nicht bloß, wie noch in scholastischer Deutung, in einem eschatologischen Sinne einfach existiere, sondern in einem komplexen Sinne ‚machbar' sei, wenn nur, mit dem Wort Macchiavellis, die „occasione" zum Handeln vom Schicksal bereitgehalten und vom Menschen genutzt würde.[19] Die Auseinandersetzung mit der Vergangenheit und die Hervorhebung der eigenen Gegenwart mussten indes einen Konflikt begründen, der nicht leicht lösbar war. Die immer differenziertere Hinwendung zur Vergangenheit, mündend in die schematische, schulbildend in der 1574 abgeschlossenen *Ecclesiastica historia secundum*

---

[16] Gemeint sind hier die anonymen *Absolve, quaesumus* bzw. das anonyme *Fletus date et lamentamini* sowie die *Musae Iovis*-Motetten von Benedictus Appenzeller und Nicolas Gombert und die Motetten von Hieronymus Vinders (*O mors inevitabilis*) und Philippe Verdelot (*Tribulatio et angustia*).

[17] Dazu immer noch grundlegend Anneliese Maier, „Die Subjektivierung der Zeit in der scholastischen Philosophie", *Philosophia naturalis*, 1 (1950), 361–98.

[18] Dazu Rudolf Wendorff, *Zeit und Kultur. Geschichte des Zeitbewußtseins in Europa* (3. Auflage, Opladen, 1985), 156ff.; auch Reinhart Koselleck, „Vergangene Zukunft der frühen Neuzeit", in ders., *Vergangene Zukunft. Zur Semantik geschichtlicher Zeiten* (Frankfurt/M., 1989, zuerst 1968), 17–37.

[19] Niccolò Macchiavelli, *Il principe. Der Fürst*, übers. und hrsg. von Philipp Rippel (Stuttgart, 1986, zuerst 1532), 42.

singulas centurias verwirklichte Teilung eines geschichtlichen Zusammenhangs in Jahrhunderte,[20] führte zu immer ausgeprägteren Bemühungen, die eigene Gegenwart systematischer zu ordnen und ihr, bei aller Dynamik, selbst einen historischen und damit auch historisierbaren Rang beizumessen. Die 1582 in der Kurie erfolgte Reform des Kalenders als Bemühen, Kalenderzeit und astronomische Zeit definitiv zur Deckung zu bringen, ist dafür nur das signifikanteste Beispiel.[21] Vor dem Hintergrund solcher Umwertungen bildete die Auseinandersetzung mit der Vergangenheit nicht mehr bloß ein Instrument zur Abgrenzung, sondern konnte, da immer differenzierter überblickbar, auch als etwas Eigenständiges bewert- und erfahrbar werden. Voraussetzung dafür war ein Umgang mit historischen Phänomenen, der durchaus vergleichbar war der Weise, in der sich humanistische Gelehrte die Antike aneigneten. Deren weite Entfernung wurde schon bei Petrarca dadurch überbrückt, dass man sie der Zeitlichkeit enthob und auf diese Weise unmittelbar vergegenwärtigen konnte.[22] Abgrenzung und Geschichtlichkeit korrespondieren also mit dem Willen, gerade das Vergangene immer gegenwärtig zu halten – was, im Blick auf die Musik, grundlegende Konflikte hervorrufen musste.

JOSQUIN ALS PARADIGMA

Das Nachleben Josquins im 16. Jahrhundert wurde in der Forschung gemeinhin als ein bloßes Rezeptionsphänomen beschrieben. An dieser Lesart haben sich in jüngerer Zeit jedoch Zweifel gebildet, vor allem deswegen, weil die zahlreichen gar nicht oder unterdessen zu einem großen Teil sogar negativ beantworteten Authentizitätsfragen Verwirrung hervorrufen mussten: Kann man von Rezeption auch dann sprechen, wenn die Konturen des rezipierten Gegenstands bis zur Unkenntlichkeit unscharf zu werden drohen?[23] Glareans beharrliches Festhalten an der herausragenden Position Josquins basiert, wie inzwischen nachgewiesen, auf einem Corpus an Werken, der nur zu einem Teil sicher auf den Komponisten zurückzuführen ist, zu einem weiteren Teil möglicherweise und in einem nicht unbeträchtlichen Maße sicher nicht.[24] So ist ein wichtiger Baustein für die Kanonisierung Josquins im Umfeld Luthers und

---

[20] Flacius Illyricus, *Ecclesiastica Historia [...] secundum singulas Centurias, perspicuo ordine complectens [...]* (Basel, 1560–1574); dazu Arndt Brendecke, *Die Jahrhundertwenden. Eine Geschichte ihrer Wahrnehmung und Wirkung* (Frankfurt/M.,1999).

[21] Dazu in diesem Kontext Wendorff, *Zeit und Kultur*, 185ff.

[22] Dazu immer noch Erwin Panofsky, „‚Renaissance' – Selbstbezeichnung oder Täuschung?", in ders., *Die Renaissancen der europäischen Kunst*, übersetzt von Horst Günther (Frankfurt/M., 1990, zuerst 1960), 15–54, hier v.a. 27ff.

[23] Vgl. hier den Forschungsüberblick bei Richard Sherr (Hg.), *The Josquin Companion* (Oxford, 2000).

[24] Zum Problem vgl. Calella, *Musikalische Autorschaft*.

der frühreformatorischen Musikauffassung die Motetten-Chanson *Nymphes nappés/Circumdederunt*, die man allerdings gerade nicht in ihrer komplizierten Wirklichkeit als anlassgebundenes Werk, sondern als Psalmvertonung, zum Teil sogar ohne Worte wahrgenommen hat, in jedem Falle ohne die werk- und gattungskonstitutiven Merkmale des französischen Textes.[25] Die Beispiele für derartige Widersprüche lassen sich vermehren. Was aber bedeutet es für das Bild eines Autors, wenn die Grenzen zwischen Authentizität und Fiktivität so fließend werden, dass Abgrenzungen in zunehmendem Maße fragwürdig erscheinen? Jessie Ann Owens hat 1997 daraus bereits den Schluß gezogen, dass es sich bei dem Komponisten in erster Linie um ein Bild des Komponisten handelt, dass also das, was sich mit Josquin verbindet, vor allem ein erst nach seinem Tod entstandenes projektives Konstrukt ist, dessen Relation zu einer wie immer definierten historischen Figur immer schwieriger zu bestimmen ist.[26] Rob Wegman schließlich hat im Versuch, positivistische Ansätze mit theoretischen Positionen der Postmoderne zu verbinden, die Wirklichkeit des Komponisten gewissermaßen dekonstruiert in die Erscheinungsformen der an ihn herangetragenen Wahrnehmungen.[27]

So plausibel diese Schlussfolgerung auf den ersten Blick erscheinen mag, gewissermaßen als ein in die Musik der frühen Neuzeit projizierter Idealtypus eines von Roland Barthes beschriebenen Lektüreverhaltens, so problematisch allerdings erweist sie sich bei näherem Hinsehen. In der dekonstruktivistischen Auflösung des Autors in ein von seiner Person und sogar, wenigstens partiell, von seinem Œuvre unabhängiges Bild werden nämlich zwei wesentliche Aspekte in den Hintergrund gedrängt, die für den gesamten Vorgang nicht unbedeutend sind: Zum einen der Sachverhalt, dass zwischen den autorisierten Werken Josquins und den ihm zugeschriebenen ein offenbar nicht willkürlicher Zusammenhang besteht, ein Zusammenhang, der sich nicht bloß in herkömmlichem Sinne als ,stilistische Nähe' beschreiben lässt; und zum anderen der keineswegs triviale Sachverhalt, dass diejenigen, die sich ausdrücklich auf Josquin berufen wollten, in der wie auch immer im Einzelfall begründeten Gewissheit gehandelt haben,

---

[25] Dazu Lawrence F. Bernstein, „ Chansons for Five and Six Voices", in Sherr, *Josquin Companion*, 393–422, hier 408.

[26] Jessie Ann Owens, ‚How Josquin became Josquin. Reflections on Historiography and Reception', in dies. u. Anthony M. Cummings (Hgg.), *Renaissance Cities and Courts. Studies in Honor of Lewis Lockwood* (Detroit Monographs in Musicology/Studies in Music, 18; Warren-Michigan, 1997), 271–80.

[27] Rob C. Wegman, „Who was Josquin?", in Sherr, *Josquin Companion*, 21–50, anschließend an andernorts formulierte Überlegungen (ders., ‚„And Josquin laughed...'. Josquin and the Composer's Anecdote in the Sixteenth Century", *The Journal of Musicology*, 17 (1999), 319–57). Vgl. auch Andrew Kirkman, "From Humanism to Enlightenment. Reinventing Josquin", *The Journal of Musicology*, 17 (1999), 441–58.

es hier in einem autoritativ gefestigten Sinne mit dem Komponisten selbst zu tun zu haben, und zwar eben auch bei jenen Werken, die heute gemeinhin, wie *De profundis*, als nicht authentisch gelten.

Im 16. Jahrhundert existierte folglich sehr wohl eine fest gefügte Vorstellung von dem, was man für Josquin halten durfte, und man hatte keinerlei Probleme, die unmittelbare Verbindung zwischen dieser Vorstellung und der konkreten historischen Person des Komponisten herzustellen. Es fällt demnach schwer, diese Person des Autors in der Fülle des Wahrgenommenen einfach aufzulösen. Ludwig Finscher hat daher dieses Deutungsmuster gerade nicht aufgegriffen, sondern, erstmals, für ein abweichendes, differenziertes Vorgehen plädiert.[28] Die ‚Rezeptionswege‘ erscheinen bei ihm nicht mehr als ein irgendwie, und sei es in der dekonstruktivistischen Verabschiedung vom Autor-Begriff, homogenisierbares Phänomen, sondern als eine komplizierte Koinzidenz höchst heteronomer und zum Teil widersprüchlicher Vorgänge. Friedrich Ohly hat zur Charakterisierung solcher Disparatheit den Begriff der ‚Gemengelage‘ verwendet,[29] um lineare und monokausale Erklärungsmodelle im Blick auf komplexe Denkfiguren jenseits dekonstruktivistischer Negation zu verabschieden. Und schon Helmuth Osthoff gebrauchte 1962, noch vor aller rezeptionsgeschichtlichen Forschung, im Blick auf Josquin die pointierte Formulierung vom „Spiegel der Nachwelt“, von der mittelbaren Entstehung eines Bildes also, in dem gleichwohl das ‚Original‘ auf bestimmte Weise zu erkennen bleibt.[30]

Die Besinnung auf diesen Gedanken, dass Josquin „im Spiegel der Nachwelt“ seine Identität zwar zum Teil verloren haben dürfte, ohne ihrer jedoch gänzlich verlustig zu gehen, verweist folglich auf eine andere Spur. Die fortwährende Auseinandersetzung mit dem Komponisten, und zwar nicht nur in der kompositorischen Wirklichkeit, sondern in einem differenzierten Schrifttum, ist vielleicht der erste spektakuläre Fall der Konstitution von Musikgeschichte, und zwar in jenem oben dargelegten Sinne der abgrenzenden Vergegenwärtigung. In ihm fließen die geltend gemachten Indizien der Geschichtsbildung gleichsam zusammen: der signifikante Name eines Autors, der willentlich mit komponierter Musik verbunden wird, seine Einbettung in ein differenziertes und für die Auseinandersetzung mit ihm prägendes Gattungssystem sowie

---

[28] Ludwig Finscher, Art. „Josquin Desprez“, in *MGG2. Personenteil* 9 (2003), 1210–82, hier 1269ff.

[29] Friedrich Ohly, *Zur Signaturenlehre der Frühen Neuzeit. Bemerkungen zur mittelalterlichen Vorgeschichte und zur Eigenart einer epochalen Denkform in Wissenschaft, Literatur und Kunst,* aus dem Nachlass hrsg. von Uwe Ruberg u. Dietmar Peil (Stuttgart und Leipzig, 1999), 3f.

[30] Helmuth Osthoff, *Josquin Desprez,* Bd. 1 (Tutzing, 1962), 79.

die in den Memorialkompositionen auf Josquin greifbaren Bemühungen, seinen ‚Adel' als denjenigen der Musik zu vergegenwärtigen. Josquin ist der ‚handelnde' Komponist des 16. Jahrhunderts schlechthin, wie der vielfach zitierte Bericht des Girolamo da Sestola von 1502 beweist.[31] Wenn sich aber in der Auseinandersetzung mit Josquin so etwas erkennen lässt wie eine bewusste musikalische Geschichtsbildung, dann dürfte es lohnen, dem Zusammenhang unter diesem Aspekt etwas detaillierter nachzugehen.

INDIVIDUALITÄT UND ZEITLICHKEIT

Betrachtet man die schriftlichen Auseinandersetzungen mit Josquin im 16. Jahrhundert, so fällt auf, dass der Komponist in ihnen stets als ein Individuum der Vergangenheit erscheint.[32] Das Motiv, sich seiner zu erinnern, ist folglich nicht das, was Glarean als „ostentatio ingenii" bezeichnet hat.[33] Im Zentrum steht vielmehr der Versuch, den dem Komponisten immer wieder attestierten Willen zur kompositorischen Verwirklichung unverwechselbarer ‚Individualität' zu verbinden mit der Einsicht, dass gerade dies dem Ergebnis seine Zeitlichkeit raube. Schon die ungewöhnliche Beisetzung Josquins im August 1521 vor dem Hochaltar der Kollegiatkirche Notre-Dame in Condé, mithin also an einem in seiner Repräsentativität selbst für den Propst nicht unbedingt selbstverständlichen Ort, lässt diesen Willen erkennen: im Gedenken an den Musiker, nicht an den Kleriker Josquin nicht etwa historische Distanz aufscheinen zu lassen, sondern eine gleichsam immerwährende, überzeitliche Vergegenwärtigung zu erreichen. So ist in dieser Geste bereits der Versuch erkennbar, den Widerspruch zwischen historischer Wahrnehmung und überzeitlicher Erinnerung an sie zu lösen. Und es prägt diese Tendenz nahezu alle schriftlichen Auseinandersetzungen mit Josquin, deutlich sichtbar auch in der Widmungsvorrede von Susatos Druck der großbesetzten Chansons von 1545.

Johannes Manlius beschrieb 1562 dieses Spannungsfeld unmittelbar. Einerseits habe der Komponist so lange probiert, bis seine Werke vollendet gewesen seien: „Quoties novam cantilenam composuerat, dedit eam cantoribus canendam, et interea ipse circumambulabat, attente audiens, an harmonia congrueret. Si non placeret, ingressus: Tacete, inquit, ego mutabo", also: wann immer er eine neue cantilena komponiert hatte, gab er sie den cantores zum Singen, wobei er zwischen ihnen herumschritt und aufmerksam hörte, ob die Harmonie

---

[31] Osthoff, *Josquin Desprez*, 211f.

[32] Vgl. die ausführlichen Darstellungen der Belege bei Osthoff, *Josquin Desprez*, 211ff.; Finscher, „Josquin Desprez", Sp. 1269ff.; Wegman, „‚And Josquin laughed'", passim.

[33] Glarean, *Dodekachordon* (Basel, 1547; Reprint Hildesheim und New York, 1969), 441.

zusammenstimmte. Wenn es ihm nicht gefiel, schritt er ein und sagte: Schweigt, ich werde es ändern.[34] Bereits in dieser Anekdote – und ihr Wahrheitsgehalt spielt in diesem Zusammenhang keine Rolle – zeigt sich der Komponist als derjenige, der seine Kompositionen mit aller Autorität für den einzigartigen Augenblick der ‚Aufführung' schafft – und dass sie erst deswegen überhaupt als überzeitlich erinnerbar gelten müssen. Besonders deutlich offenbart sich das auch in dem etwas früheren Versuch Glareans, den Komponisten zu einem zweiten Vergil zu machen.[35] Das entspricht nicht nur der Stiftung einer konkreten Autorität, sondern dem Versuch, den Komponisten im Augenblick der geschichtlichen Vergegenwärtigung aus dieser Geschichtlichkeit zu lösen und ihn mit einem überzeitlichen Vorbild der Antike zu versöhnen.

Derartige Bestrebungen sind gekettet an die besonderen Schwierigkeiten, die Musik überhaupt gegenwärtig zu machen, da, anders als in der Poesie oder in der Malerei, eine den Vorgang begünstigende materale Voraussetzung nur sehr bedingt gegeben war. Auch deswegen hat der Dichter Glarean auf die extensiven Notenbeispiele zurückgegriffen, da sie, im emphatischen Bekenntnis zum musikalischen Text, überhaupt erst die Voraussetzung für eine Memoria schaffen können.[36] Mit ihr ist eben auch eine besondere Eigenart der Wahrnehmung Josquins verbunden: die zunehmende Hinwendung zum Konkreten, zum konkreten Komponisten in konkreten Werken, zu dessen konkreter Lebenssituation, als deren Spiegel sich die Anekdoten erweisen, die offenbar in reicher Zahl über den Komponisten in Umlauf waren. Auch und gerade in solcher Konkretion wird der Komponist gewissermaßen der Zeitlichkeit enthoben, er erhält in einem übergreifenden Zusammenhang Gültigkeit.

Am weitesten in dieser Hinsicht allerdings ging wohl Martin Luther, der sich mehrfach zu Josquin geäußert hat. Die von Johannes Mathesius 1540 übermittelte Vorstellung, der Komponist sei „der noten meister", im Gegensatz zu seinen Kollegen, die von den Noten abhängig gewesen seien,[37] lässt gleichsam eine Inversion der materia-forma-Diskussion erkennen, aus der allein Josquin sich über die Geschichtlichkeit einer die Gesetze diktierenden materia zu erheben vermag. Aus diesem Grund schließlich wird die Zeitlichkeit des

[34] Johannes Manlius, *Locorum communium collectanea* (Basel, 1562), 542; zit. nach Osthoff, *Josquin Desprez*, 222.

[35] Glarean, *Dodekachordon*, 113.

[36] Zum Kontext auch Michele Calella, „Die Ideologie des Exemplum – Bemerkungen zu den Notenbeispielen des ‚Dodekachordon'", in Nicole Schwindt, *Heinrich Glarean oder: Die Rettung der Musik aus dem Geist der Antike?* (Trossinger Jahrbuch für Renaissancemusik, 5; Kassel, 2006), 199–212.

[37] Zit. nach Osthoff, *Josquin Desprez*, 88f.

Geschichte ,machenden' Komponisten in eine eschatologische Heilserwartung überführt: „Was lex ist, gett nicht von stad; was euangelium ist, das gett von stad. Sic Deus praedicavit euangelium etiam per musicam, ut videtur in Iosquin, des alles composition frolich, willich, milde heraus fleust, in nitt zwungen und gnedigt per [regulas], sicut des fincken gesang".[38] Die Annahme also, Josquin sei in der Lage, die Antinomie zwischen Lex und Evangelium zu exemplifizieren, setzt den Komponisten einer heilsgeschichtlichen Tatsache gleich. Indem die geschichtliche Musik des einen, handelnden Komponisten und seiner ,occasione' der göttlichen Offenbarung gleichkommt, verliert sie paradoxerweise ihre Geschichtlichkeit. Reinhart Koselleck hat darauf hingewiesen, dass im 16. Jahrhundert das Bewusstsein für zeitliche Prozesse erst an seinem Anfang steht, nämlich in der durchaus mühsamen Trennung eschatologischer Naherwartung und konkreter geschichtlicher Vorgänge, mit deren Hilfe das Individuum beginnt, sich in der Geschichtlichkeit gewissermaßen einzurichten.[39] Gerade an diesem Punkt wird Josquin jedoch die Geschichtlichkeit in der Überhöhung zur heilsgeschichtlichen Wirklichkeit wieder verweigert. Luther pointiert damit ein Deutungsmuster, das offenbar auf übergreifende Weise zentral war und in der Dichotomie von Lex und Evangelium aufgefangen werden sollte. Zahlreiche schriftliche Auseinandersetzungen mit dem Komponisten sind darauf zentriert, in der mit seinem Namen bezeichneten und von ihm geschaffenen Wirklichkeit das Überzeitliche und, im Sinne Luthers, das Eschatologische herauszupräparieren.

Johann Ott behauptete 1537, das Unnachahmliche des Komponisten gleiche einer Göttlichkeit („habet enim vere divinum et inimitabile quiddam").[40] Auch Giovanni Del Lago hat 1532 die Göttlichkeit hervorgehoben,[41] und Cosimo Bartoli betonte in seiner 1567 veröffentlichten Parallele zwischen Josquin und Michelangelo, dass beide den Liebhabern der Künste in der Gegenwart und in der Zukunft die Augen geöffnet hätten.[42] Hermann Finck hingegen wies 1556 darauf hin, Josquin, der Musiker der Vergangenheit, habe auch den

---

[38] Tischreden, hier zit. nach Matthias Herrmann, „,die Musica [...] ym dienst des, der sie geben und geschaffen hat [...]'. Über das altkirchlich-konservative Element in der Musik der Reformation", in Harald Marx u. Cecilie Hollberg (Hgg.), *Glaube und Macht. Sachsen im Europa der Reformationszeit. Aufsätze* (Dresden, 2004), 256–62, hier 259; zum gesamten Komplex auch die Analyse bei Martin Staehelin, „Luther über Josquin", in Wolfgang Hirschmann et al. (Hgg.), *Festschrift Martin Ruhnke* (Neuhausen–Stuttgart, 1986), 330–3.

[39] Koselleck, „Vergangene Zukunft der frühen Neuzeit", 25ff.

[40] Johann Ott (Hg.), *Novum et insigne Opus Musicum* (Nürnberg, 1537), Vorrede.

[41] Bonnie J. Blackburn u. Edward E. Lowinsky (Hgg.), *A Correspondance of Renaissance Musicians* (Oxford, 1991), 498.

[42] Cosimo Bartoli, *Ragionamenti accademici [..] sopra alcuni luoghi difficili di Dante* (Venedig, 1567), f. 35v.; zit. nach Osthoff, *Josquin Desprez*, 91.

Musikern der Zukunft den wahrhaftigen Weg gewiesen.[43] Diese Zeugnisse sind verbunden im Willen, dem verstorbenen Komponisten seinen Rang vor allem deswegen zu attestieren, weil er es mit seinen Werken vermocht habe, die Bedingungen der Zeitlichkeit regelrecht abzustreifen. Tilman Susato spricht in seiner Widmung der Chanson-Ausgabe von 1545 ausdrücklich von diesem Willen: Josquin nämlich eine „perpetuelle memoire" zu sichern.[44]

MUSIKTHEORIE ALS GESCHICHTSTHEORIE

Die schriftlichen Äußerungen über Josquin entstammen dem musikalischen Schrifttum im weitesten Sinne, also nicht nur der Musiktheorie, sondern auch Vorreden, Briefen und anderen Gattungen. Gleichwohl sind die Ausführungen im musiktheoretischen Zusammenhang von besonderem Interesse, weil hier übergreifende Kontexte existieren. Diese Kontexte sind durchaus, in einem komplizierten Sinne, historisch ausgerichtet. Das gründet zum einen in der Gattung selbst, denn musiktheoretisches Schrifttum umfasst spätestens seit dem Hochmittelalter eine Genealogie der musikalischen Erfindungen, ausgehend zumeist von der Jubal-Legende und mündend in Guido, im Falle Francos von Köln noch wirkmächtig ergänzt um die eigene Person. Damit erweist sich Musiktheorie immer auch als eine disziplinäre Geschichtstheorie, in der sich gleichwohl die Vergegenwärtigung der Vergangenheit vor allem aus dem Willen zur Legitimation heraus vollzieht. Mit den Namensnennungen im 15. Jahrhundert und insbesondere bei Tinctoris hingegen tritt eine neue Qualität deswegen hinzu, da dieser nicht nur über tote und lebende Komponisten schreibt, sondern sich auch sehr konkret mit deren Werken beschäftigt. Damit bricht nicht nur, wie oft bemerkt worden ist, die konkrete Gegenwart in das Musikschrifttum herein, sondern in nicht minderem Maße die konkrete Vergangenheit.

Musikalische Theorie wird damit um 1500 in einer eigenartigen Weise ‚historisch', und eines der bedeutendsten Dokumente dafür ist zweifellos Glarean. Er bezieht sich nachdrücklich auf die Vergangenheit, um aus ihr kompositorische Handlungsanweisungen für die Gegenwart zu gewinnen. Allein Josquin ragt für ihn aus dieser Vergangenheit als zeitlos gewordene Größe heraus. Das Konzept allerdings, das hinter dem *Dodekachordon* steht, basiert auf dem im Vorwort dargelegten Unterfangen, in der Berufung auf Boethius und Augustinus die rationalen Grundlagen der Musik mit ihrer

---

[43] Hermann Finck, *Practica Musica [...]* (Nürnberg, 1556). Reprint Hildesheim und New York, 1971, f. A ijr.

[44] Widmungsvorrede an Lazarus Tucher, in *Vingt & quatre chansons a cinq et a six parties [...]* (Antwerpen, 1545), Tenorstimmbuch, f. 1v.

affektiven Wirkmächtigkeit zu versöhnen – mit dem Ziel, die antike Hochblüte der Musik zu rekonstituieren.[45] Die Wendung in die Vergangenheit, die dem Autor als ‚ars perfecta' erscheint, wird getragen vom Versuch, die wahrscheinlich noch diffus wahrgenommene zeitliche Distanz erst zu vergegenwärtigen, dann zu überbrücken. Eine ähnliche Strategie verfolgt der Autor auch in seinen historischen Arbeiten. Die 1514 veröffentlichte *Helvetiae Descriptio* bedient sich der Geschichte vor allem, um die unvergleichliche Superiorität der Eidgenossenschaft gegenüber dem Reich zu sichern und zu verteidigen.[46]

In diesem Sinne konnte es auch, wie bei Adrian Petit Coclico, erstmals aber wohl schon bei Pietro Aron, interessant werden, die Schülerschaft als kompositorische Genealogie zu reklamieren. Auch hier wurde also die Geschichte bemüht, um sie, in der überzeitlichen Gültigkeit ihres Vertreters, in gewisser Hinsicht außer Kraft zu setzen. Wer sich in die Nachfolge Josquins stellte, bediente sich des historischen Bezugs vor allem, um den eigenen Standort zu festigen. Und hierin kann auch ein Schlüssel liegen für die kompositorische Auseinandersetzung mit dem Komponisten. Sie konnte in Zitaten, Gattungsanspielungen und Überbietungen münden, etwa bei Ludwig Senfl, aber auch in der schlichten genealogischen Indienstnahme wie beim in Regensburg wirkenden cantor Johannes Buechmaier, der 1559–60 in einem Codex eine unmittelbare Relation zwischen Josquin und seiner eigenen Person hergestellt hat – mit dem unverblümt in der Widmung zur Schau getragenen Ziel, sein eigenes Wirken auf diese Weise zu nobilitieren.[47]

KONFESSIONELLE UND GESCHICHTLICHE LEGITIMITÄT

Der Komponist wurde also zum Bestandteil eines musikgeschichtlichen Bildes, das zwar in der Vergangenheit wurzelt, aber deren überzeitliche Gültigkeit beschwört – eine Gültigkeit, der man erst langsam, zuerst wohl bei Sebald Heyden und Hermann Finck, mit Skepsis begegnet ist. Dieses Verfahren hat eine verblüffende Konsequenz gezeitigt. Je deutlicher die zeitliche Distanz zur Person Josquins hervortrat, umso nachdrücklicher musste auch die von ihm abgeleitete ‚ars perfecta' entrücken. Diese Entrückung bot dann aber selbst wieder Spielraum für eine ideengeschichtliche Inanspruchnahme eigener Art, und eine solche ereignete sich vor allem im deutschen Sprachraum. Das ist

---

[45] Dazu vom Verf. u. Beat Föllmi, Art. „Glarean", in *MGG2, Personenteil* 7, 1041–7, hier 1043f.

[46] Dazu Veronika Feller-Vest, „Glarean als Dichter und Historiker", in Rudolf Aschmann et al. (Hgg.), *Der Humanist Heinrich Loriti genannt Glarean. 1488–1563. Beiträge zu seinem Leben und Werk* (Glarus, 1983), 93–118, hier 106ff.

[47] Dazu James Haar, „Josquin as Interpreted by a Mid-Sixteenth-Century German Musician", in Stephan Hörner u. Bernhold Schmid (Hgg.), *Festschrift für Horst Leuchtmann zum 65. Geburtstag* (Tutzing, 1993), 179–205.

verwunderlich nur dann, wenn man die erheblichen Brüche und Zäsuren in der italienischen und in der französischen Musikgeschichte der 1520er und 1530er Jahre außer Acht lässt, Brüche, die es im deutschsprachigen Raum so nicht gab. Eine Ursache dafür mag auch in der massiven Hinwendung zu volkssprachlichen Gattungen liegen, die im deutschen Sprachgebiet nur zögerlich erfolgte und erst nach den deutschen Liedern Lassos 1567 wirklich anerkannt war. Die Wahrung der Gattungshierarchien mit der Motette und der Messe an der Spitze dürfte einer besonderen Wahrnehmung Josquins also zusätzlich den Boden bereitet haben.[48]

Die Entrückung Josquins in eine zunehmende Ferne bei gleichzeitiger Hervorhebung seiner geschichtlichen Unanfechtbarkeit führte nämlich zu divergierenden konfessionellen Inanspruchnahmen. Während Glarean an Josquin festhielt, um in seiner ‚ars perfecta' gewissermaßen eine musikalische Schicht greifen zu können, die noch vor den Verwerfungen durch die Reformation lag,[49] scheint Luther gleichzeitig die eschatologische Rolle Josquins vor allem deswegen festgeschrieben zu haben, um in seinen Werken – ähnlich wie Thomas Stoltzer – eine Vorahnung des Kommenden (vor allem hinsichtlich der Textbehandlung) festzustellen.[50] Josquin ließ sich folglich konfessionell ganz unterschiedlich funktionalisieren. Und während Glarean keine Gelegenheit versäumte, seinen ins Überzeitliche entrückten Komponisten durch Anekdoten, Werkanalysen und biographische Details in geradezu körperliche Wirklichkeit zurückzuholen,[51] so mühte sich Luther durch die Einbettung in die Dichotomie von Lex und Evangelium um etwas Ähnliches: den entrückten Komponisten wie einen heiligen Text kontemplativ erfahrbar zu machen. Beide Argumentationen sind hochrational, und beide sind in bestimmter Hinsicht mystisch. Während Glarean darum bemüht war, durch ein ‚Verständnis' der Werke auch der Person nahezukommen, gelang Luther im Januar 1537 eine regelrechte ‚unio mystica':

---

[48] Vgl. auch Honey Meconi, „ Josquin and Musical Reputation", in Barbara Haggh (Hg.), *Essays on Music and Culture in Honor of Herbert Kellman* (Épitome Musical, 12; Paris und Tours, 2001), 280–97.

[49] Dazu vom Verf., „Humanismus im Kloster. Bemerkungen zu einem der Dedikationsexemplare von Glareans ‚Dodekachordon'", in Axel Beer u. Verf. (Hgg.), *Festschrift Klaus Hortschansky zum 60. Geburtstag* (Tutzing, 1995), 43–57, hier 52ff.

[50] Dazu auch Ignace Bossuyt, *Die Kunst der Polyphonie. Die flämische Musik von Guillaume Dufay bis Orlando di Lasso*, aus dem Niederländischen übers. von Horst Leuchtmann (Mainz und Zürich, 1997), 93f.

[51] Dazu v.a. Klaus Hortschansky, „Musikwissenschaft und Bedeutungsforschung. Überlegungen zu einer Heuristik im Bereich der Musik der Renaissance", in ders. (Hg.), *Zeichen und Struktur in der Musik der Renaissance. Ein Symposium aus Anlaß der Jahrestagung der Gesellschaft für Musikforschung Münster (Westfalen) 1987. Bericht* (Musikwissenschaftliche Arbeiten, 28; Kassel, 1989), 65–86, hier 82ff.

er sei beim Gedenken an den vor über anderthalb Jahrzehnte zurückliegenden Tod des Komponisten in Tränen ausgebrochen.[52]

In dieser Funktionalisierung Josquins zeichnet sich hingegen auch eine Veränderung ab. Indem der Komponist sowohl für die Reformation wie für deren Gegner Gültigkeit besitzen konnte – Phänomene, die der Komponist selbst, wenn überhaupt, nur noch am Rande erlebt haben dürfte –, musste seine Entrückung ins Überzeitliche fragwürdig werden. Denn wenn am Ende der unterdessen aus der Tagesaktualität verschwindende Josquin Freunden und Feinden gleichermaßen zur Selbstverständigung dienen konnte, dann war er endgültig zu einer historischen Größe geworden. Hermann Finck stellte 1556 fest, dass die gewisse ‚Nacktheit‘ der Komposition („sed in compositione nudior") nicht mehr den Anforderungen der Gegenwart entspreche.[53] Er zog damit offenbar auch die Konsequenz aus einer für ihn nicht mehr bruchlos zu bewerkstelligenden Aneignung. Aus dem, was Josquin aus der Geschichte herausheben sollte, war damit endgültig Geschichte geworden.

KANONISIERUNG ALS HISTORISCHER PROZESS

Die schreibende und komponierende Auseinandersetzung mit Josquin unterlag offenbar selbst historischen Wandlungen, und die mit ihr verbundene Kanonisierung ist ein historischer Prozess, über den sich die Zeitgenossen des 16. Jahrhunderts durchaus klar geworden sind. Nicht einmal Luthers Begeisterung für den Komponisten hat langfristig wirken können, um 1600 war aus der angestrebten Zeitlosigkeit die absolute Geschichtlichkeit geworden. Allerdings rückt damit die Ausgangsfrage nach der ‚Entstehung‘ der Geschichte nochmals ins Zentrum. Nimmt man Osthoffs Gedanken vom Spiegelbild ernst, so stellt sich immer noch die Frage, was ein solches Spiegelbild am Ende eint. Warum konnte der Komponist in einem Prozess beginnender historischer Vergewisserungen ins Überzeitliche entrückt werden? Warum konnte er in ein eschatologisches Deutungsmuster eingepasst werden? Und warum konnte es möglich werden, ihn, und zwar nur ihn zu einer zentralen Figur innerhalb der konfessionellen Standortbestimmungen im Blick auf die Musik zu machen? Warum also griff man auf Josquin zurück, warum nicht auf Obrecht, Ockeghem oder Dufay?

In den zahlreichen Anekdoten und Auseinandersetzungen, die um den Perfektionsgrad der Kompositionen kreisen, wird deutlich, dass dieser Perfektionsgrad

[52] Dazu Osthoff, *Josquin Desprez*, 88.
[53] Finck, *Practica Musica*, f. Aijr.

für die Zeitgenossen eben nicht in einer weitgehenden Individualisierung bestand wie bei Ockeghem oder Obrecht, sondern in einer weitgehenden Normierung. Luthers berühmt gewordenes Wort, dass Josquin als Einziger die Materie der Musik wirklich zu formen gewusst hätte,[54] bezeugt vor allem, dass er – wie im Evangelium – ein ihr innewohnendes Gesetz aufgedeckt haben müsse. Immer wieder ist auch in der Bewunderung Glareans zu erkennen, dass der hohe Grad an Normierung als ein Befreiungsschlag im Blick auf eine widerspenstige Materie verstanden worden ist. Nur so erhält der Vergleich Bartolis zwischen dem Bildhauer Michelangelo und Josquin seinen tiefen Sinn. Der normierte Satz galt offenbar als Errungenschaft in einem Kontext, in dem solche Normierungen entweder nicht absehbar oder auch gar nicht vorgesehen waren. Das erklärt überdies, warum Josquin in der Wahrnehmung des 16. Jahrhunderts vor allem ein Motetten- und Messenkomponist gewesen ist: weil eben hier die Normierungen am weitesten reichen.

Diese Normierungen allerdings setzen alles frei, was in der Auseinandersetzung mit Josquin eine zentrale Rolle spielt: tatsächliche oder angemaßte Schüler-schaft, kompositorische Nachahmung, Entrückung in überzeitliche Gültigkeit. Erst allmählich ist, wie bei Finck, das Bewusstsein anzutreffen, dass solche Normierung im strengen Sinne keine Spielräume lassen kann, ‚nackt' erscheinen muss und, anders als angenommen, gerade keine historische Perspektive mehr in sich bergen kann. Kurzum: Josquins Kompositionen galten als vorbildlich, weil diese Vorbildhaftigkeit erkenn-, beschreib- und nachahmbar war. Und erst die Einsicht in diese Wirklichkeit hat die Distanz vergrößert. Die Kano-nisierung Josquins hat schließlich ihre eigene Dynamik entfaltet. Je nach-drücklicher der Komponist enthistorisiert worden ist und je weiter er sich gleichzeitig chronologisch vom jeweiligen Betrachter entfernt hat, desto historischer ist er damit schließlich geworden. In der im späten 15. Jahrhundert einsetzenden Historisierung von Musik ist Josquin ein wichtiger, vielleicht der zentrale Baustein. Die auf diese Weise ausgelösten Spiegelbilder werden zusammengehalten von einer großen normativen Kraft der Kompositionen selbst. Aus dem Versuch, das geschichtlich als distant empfundene Werk der Zeitlichkeit zu entziehen, ist im Laufe des 16. Jahrhunderts das immer stärker spürbare Bewusstsein hervorgegangen, es hier dennoch und vor allem mit Geschichte zu tun zu haben. Dieser Vorgang allerdings ist ein wichtiges Detail in der bewussten Geschichtsbildung im Blick auf die Musik. Es ist sicherlich nicht das einzige Indiz für die einsetzende historische Wahrnehmung, aber wenigstens ein sehr signifikantes.

---

[54] Dazu Staehelin, „Luther über Josquin".

Notations modales au seizième siècle

Nicolas Meeùs

Bien que la théorie des types tonals de Harold Powers[1] ait attiré l'attention, il y a plus d'un quart de siècle déjà, sur les particularités de la notation au seizième siècle, et bien que celles-ci aient fait déjà l'objet d'études approfondies,[2] les contraintes de la notation modale ne paraissent pas encore entièrement élucidées. Powers mentionne par exemple «le choix de l'une ou l'autre de deux combinaisons de clefs de plus en plus standardisées, dites 'chiavette' et 'chiavi naturali'»,[3] mais, en réalité, nous ne savons ni jusqu'à quel point ces combinaisons (qui ne sont jamais formellement décrites dans les textes théoriques de l'époque) étaient véritablement standardisées, ni pourquoi elle l'ont été, ni dans quelle mesure les compositeurs étaient libres de choisir l'une ou l'autre, ni quels ont été leurs critères de choix.[4]

La musicologie moderne dispose, grâce à Powers et à ses disciples, de statistiques relativement détaillées sur l'utilisation des types tonals. Mais la définition de ceux-ci reste trop sommaire : si la prise en compte de la finale et du système (régulier ou transposé) fait peu de difficulté, l'identification de la clef utilisée pour la voix de Superius («c_1», *ut* 1e ligne, représentant la clef de Superius des 'chiavi naturali', ou «g_2», *sol* 2e ligne, représentant celle des 'chiavette') ne suffit pas, parce qu'elle n'indique pas si les autres voix

---

[1] Harold Powers, « Tonal Types and Modal Categories in Renaissance Polyphony », *Journal of the American Musicological Society*, 34/3 (1981), 428-70.

[2] Notamment Anne Smith, « Über Modus und Transposition um 1600 », *Basler Jahrbuch für historische Musikpraxis* 6 (1982), 9-43; Andrew Parrott, « Transposition in Monteverdi's Vespers of 1610 : An 'Aberration' Defended », *Early Music*, 12 (1984), et Patrizio Barbieri, « 'Chiavette' and Modal Transposition in Italian Practice (c. 1500-1837) », *Recercare. Rivista per lo studio et la prattica della musica antica*, 3 (1991), 5-79.

[3] Powers, *Tonal types*, 436.

[4] Arthur Mendel, « Pitch in the 16th and Early 17th Centuries », *The Musical Quarterly*, 34 (1948), 132-3 : « Even the terms 'chiavette' and 'chiavi naturali seem to be no older than Paolucci [1765-1772], who is more than a hundred years too late to have any but a historian's authority in the matter »; Anne Smith, « Über Modus und Transposition », 28-39, recense les clefs recommandées pour chacun des modes par quinze théoriciens du seizième siècle : la diversité des combinaisons proposées est considérable, même si les deux combinaisons standardisées y apparaissent majoritaires. Selon Patrizio Barbieri, « Chiavette », 7, « the first writer expressly to mention the distinction between chiavi naturali and high clefs is Silvestro Ganassi, in his 1543 tutor » ; mais les combinaisons décrites (voir Barbieri, « Chiavette », 39-41) sont à trois voix et ne correspondent pas aux combinaisons standardisées dont il est question ici. Certains classements en 'chiavi naturali' et 'chiavette' se fondent exclusivement sur la clef du Cantus, ce qui est très insuffisant ; d'autres admettent dans ces catégories des variantes qui ne sont pas toujours assez clairement décrites (voir par exemple Jeffrey G. Kurtzman, « Tones, Modes, Clefs and Pitch in Roman Cyclic Magnificats of the 16th Century », *Early Music*, 22 (1994), 641-64.

respect les combinaisons standardisées, ni si certaines parties enfreignent la règle implicite de ne pas tracer de lignes supplémentaires au-dessus ou en dessous des portées. Il faudrait donc, pour une meilleure définition du type tonal, connaître plus précisément l'ambitus de chacune des voix, ainsi que l'utilisation des clefs pour chacune d'entre elles.

Rassembler des données statistiques à ce sujet constituera un travail collectif de longue haleine. Le texte qui suit vise seulement à attirer l'attention sur la nécessité de recueillir ces informations. Il sera divisé en deux parties : la première propose une réflexion théorique générale sur les contraintes de la notation; la seconde examinera comment et dans quelle mesure ces contraintes s'appliquent concrètement dans un recueil choisi arbitrairement pour les illustrer, les *Psalmi pœnitentiales* d'Alexandre Utendal, qui propose douze pièces, une pour chacun des douze modes.

1. CONSIDÉRATIONS THÉORIQUES

Il est difficile d'énoncer des règles générales sur les notations modales, parce que chaque œuvre et même chaque voix doit être considérée comme un cas particulier, pour lequel le compositeur jouit d'une relative liberté dans l'établissement des tessitures. Pour fixer les idées, cependant, nous partirons ici des quatre règles hypothétiques suivantes, pour en évaluer les conséquences possibles et déterminer ensuite dans quelle mesure elles sont respectées dans les oeuvres:

1. Les compositions sont écrites dans l'une des deux combinaisons standardisées, 'chiavi naturali' ou 'chiavette'. Nous verrons ultérieurement que, dans les *Psalmi pœnitentiales* d'Utendal, ces combinaisons ne sont pas respectées dans un cas sur quatre.

2. La notation se fait sans lignes supplémentaires. Sept pièces sur douze du recueil d'Utendal ne respectent pas cette contrainte.

3. Chacune des voix couvre son « octave modale » selon la convention habituelle de l'écriture *a voce piena* : dans les compositions de mode authente, le Tenor et le Cantus sont de tessiture authente et couvrent donc l'octave modale authente (quinte + quarte), alors que l'Altus et la basse sont de tessiture plagale (quarte + quinte); dans les modes plagaux, cette situation est inversée. Chez Utendal, bien que la tessiture de chaque voix soit presque

toujours plus large qu'une octave, elle ne comprend pas toujours l'octave modale, en particulier dans les voix de type plagal, qui n'ont souvent pas la quinte au-dessus de la « note nominale du mode »[5].

4. Chaque pièce peut être écrite en système régulier, sans armure et avec pour note nominale *do, ré, mi, fa, sol* ou *la*, ou en système transposé, avec une armure d'un bémol et avec pour note nominale *fa, sol, la, si♭, do* ou *ré*. Cette règle est la seule qui s'applique sans exception dans les *Psalmi pœnitentiales*.[6].

1.1 Combinaisons standardisées des clefs et disposition des voix

Les deux combinaisons standardisées induisent la même structure intervallique pour le chœur à quatre voix : les ambitus du Cantus et de l'Altus d'une part, du Tenor et du Bassus d'autre part, tels qu'ils sont définis par la clef et la portée à cinq lignes, sont distants l'un de l'autre d'une quinte, alors que la distance entre Altus et Tenor n'est que d'une tierce, comme le montre la Figure 1. Les clefs disponibles, de la clef de *sol* 1e ligne à celle de *fa* 4e ligne (colonne de gauche de la Figure 1), situent en effet toutes l'*ut*$_3$ « sur la ligne »; la distance entre elles est donc chaque fois d'une tierce. Chacune des deux combinaisons de clefs fait usage de clefs adjacentes pour la paire Altus – Tenor et de clefs non adjacentes pour les paires Superius – Altus et Tenor – Bassus. La distance entre Cantus et Tenor d'une part, entre Altus et Bassus d'autre part, n'est donc que d'une septième.[7]

---

[5] J'appelle « note nominale du mode » cette note qu'on pourrait appeler la « finale », si cela ne risquait de porter à confusion dans le cas de compositions polyphoniques dont les voix ne se terminent pas toutes sur la finale, ou encore la « tonique », si ce terme n'était pas aussi fortement associé à la tonalité classique. Dans chacune des voix de la polyphonie, quelle qu'en soit la note finale, la quinte et la quarte modales de la description dite « néo-classique » s'articulent autour de la « note nominale du mode ». Dans la description des types tonals proposée par Harold Powers, *Tonal types*, 437, c'est la fondamentale de l'accord final qui est considérée déterminante; si cette note correspond généralement avec la note nominale telle que je la décris ici, ce n'est pas toujours le cas, en particulier dans des sections autres que la dernière section de l'œuvre, ce qui pourrait engendrer une ambiguïté.

[6] Cette règle suppose un classement en douze modes. Elle s'adapte aisément au classement en huit modes : il suffit de considérer alors que les modes de *ré* et de *fa* peuvent comporter le *si♭* en version non transposée et que leur transposition éventuelle se fait alors à la quinte supérieure ou à la quarte inférieure. Les types tonals sont les mêmes, seulement leur attribution modale change.

[7] Patrizio Barbieri, « Chiavette », 6, indique l'existence de deux autres combinaisons de même structure : 'in contrabasso', utilisant une clef de *fa* 5e ligne, et 'soprano acutissimo', faisant usage de la clef de *sol* 1e ligne. Ces clefs sont en effet attestées au seizième siècle, mais leur usage paraît exceptionnel.

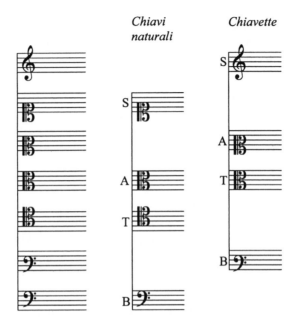

Figure 1. Distance entre les portées dans les combinaisons de clefs standardisées

Dans le cas d'une composition de mode authente, les deux paires de voix, Cantus-Altus d'une part et Tenor-Bassus d'autre part, se partagent la même « note nominale du mode », avec une distance d'une octave entre la note nominale de la paire aiguë et celle de la paire grave. Dans le cas d'une composition plagale, Altus et Tenor ont la même note nominale du mode, que le Cantus et le Bassus donnent respectivement à l'octave supérieure et à l'octave inférieure. Ou, pour dire ceci autrement : la note nominale d'une voix de type plagal est toujours la même que celle de la voix de type authente située au-dessus d'elle, et une octave plus haut que celle de la voix authente en dessous d'elle; à l'inverse, la note nominale d'une voix de type authente est à l'unisson celle de la voix plagale située sous elle, à l'octave grave de celle de la voix plagale au-dessus d'elle.

1.2 Position des notes nominales
Pour que l'ambitus d'une voix authente puisse couvrir sans ligne supplémentaire toute l'octave du mode, il faut que la note nominale ne soit pas écrite plus haut que la deuxième ligne de la portée, ce qui donne quatre possibilités pour la position de la finale authente : sous la portée, sur la première ligne, dans le premier interligne ou sur la deuxième ligne, comme le montre la Figure 2a. Cependant, une composition à quatre voix comporte toujours deux voix de type authente, distantes théoriquement d'une octave, mais notées à distance

d'une septième seulement dans les combinaisons standardisées des clefs. Une des quatre possibilités de noter l'octave modale authente s'en trouve éliminée, parce qu'elle demanderait une ligne supplémentaire dans l'autre voix de type authente. C'est ce que montre la Figure 2b, où on voit que la quatrième notation possible à la voix grave est éliminée parce qu'elle requiert une ligne supplémentaire à la voix aiguë. Ces contraintes sont indépendantes tant du choix du système de clefs (puisque les intervalles entre portées y sont semblables) que du type authente ou plagal de la composition dans son ensemble, puisqu'on y trouvera de toute manière une paire de voix authentes. On pourrait montrer par un raisonnement semblable qu'il n'existe que trois manières possibles de noter une paire de voix de type plagal.

Si l'on prend en compte les quatre voix ensemble, toujours dans l'hypothèse d'une notation d'octaves modales complètes, sans lignes supplémentaires et dans la relation intervallique des systèmes de clefs standardisés, on constate que le nombre des notations possibles se réduit encore. Dans la Figure 3 ci-dessous, les quatre notations théoriques possibles ont été attribuées chaque fois au Tenor : on voit qu'en modes authentes, deux possibilités s'éliminent en raison de dépassements à l'Altus et au Superius; en modes plagaux, une possibilité seulement doit être éliminée.

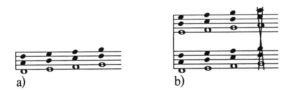

Figure 2. a) Notations possibles de l'octave modale authente dans la portée;
    b) Notations possibles de l'octave modale authente dans deux portées distantes
        d'une septième

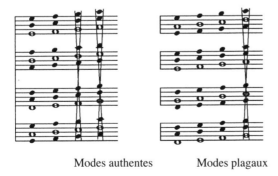

Modes authentes   Modes plagaux

Figure 3. Possibilités de noter les octaves modales à quatre voix

1.3. Choix des clefs et du système
Il reste, pour chaque mode, à choisir la combinaison de clefs qui permet de situer correctement les notes nominales.

1.3.1 Modes authentes
Comme on vient de le voir, il n'existe que deux positions possibles des notes dans les portées en mode authente, si les conditions théoriques sont respectées : l'une qui place la note nominale au ténor sous la première ligne, l'autre qui la place sur la première ligne. Les deux clefs possibles pour le Tenor sont la clef d'*ut* 4ᵉ ligne en 'chiavi naturali' et la clef d'*ut* 3ᵉ ligne en 'chiavette'. Avec la possibilité d'écrire en système régulier ou en système transposé, il en résulte huit notations théoriquement possibles, énumérées dans le Tableau 1 ci-dessous; le *mi* en système transposé n'est pas utilisé comme finale, de sorte que les possibilités réelles se réduisent à sept. Les notations qui placent la note nominale sur la ligne au Tenor sont les plus susceptibles de dépasser la portée vers le haut, en particulier à la voix d'Altus qui est la plus haute dans sa portée (voir la Figure 3). Par contre, les dépassement de la portée vers le bas sont moins probables, parce qu'ils affecteraient en premier lieu la note nominale elle-même, à la voix de Tenor. On constate que le mode ionien est le seul qui puisse s'écrire de deux manières. Les transpositions sont à la quinte inférieure pour le mixolydien et l'éolien, à la quarte supérieure pour l'ionien.

Clef du Tenor	Position de la note nominale au Tenor	Note nominale	Système	Mode
ut 4ᵉ ligne ('chiavi naturali')	Sous la portée	do_2	Régulier	Ionien
			Transposé	Mixolydien
	Sur la première ligne	$ré_2$	Régulier	Dorien
			Transposé	Éolien
ut 3ᵉ ligne ('chiavette')	Sous la portée	mi_2	Régulier	Phrygien
			Transposé	—
	Sur la première ligne	fa_2	Régulier	Lydien
			Transposé	Ionien

Tableau 1. Notations possibles en mode authente

1.3.2. Modes plagaux
L'écriture plus compacte des modes plagaux permet trois positions de la note nominale, qui se situera au Tenor sur la deuxième ligne, dans le deuxième interligne ou sur la troisième ligne. Avec les deux clefs et les deux systèmes, il en résulte douze notations théoriquement possibles, que le Tableau 2

ci-dessous passe en revue; le *si* n'est pas utilisé comme finale en système régulier. L'hypodorien est le seul pour lequel une seule notation est possible, en système transposé. L'hypoéolien ne peut s'écrire qu'en système régulier, l'hypophrygien ne peut s'écrire qu'en système transposé, mais l'un et l'autre peuvent l'être dans l'une ou l'autre combinaison de clefs. Les transpositions sont toujours à la quarte supérieure.

Clef du Tenor	Position de la note nominale au Tenor	Note nominale	Système	Mode
ut 4ᵉ ligne ('chiavi naturali')	Sur la deuxième ligne	fa_2	Régulier	Hypolydien
			Transposé	Hypoionien
	Dans le deuxième interligne	sol_2	Régulier	Hypomixolydien
			Transposé	Hypodorien
	Sur la troisième ligne	la_2	Régulier	Hypoéolien
			Transposé	Hypophrygien
ut 3ᵉ ligne ('chiavette')	Sur la deuxième ligne	la_2	Régulier	Hypoéolien
			Transposé	Hypophrygien
	Dans le deuxième interligne	$si_2/si\flat_2$	Régulier	—
			Transposé	Hypolydien
	Sur la troisième ligne	do_3	Régulier	Hypoionien
			Transposé	Hypomixolydien

Tableau 2. Notations possibles en mode plagal

1.4. Types tonals

À partir des deux tableaux précédents, on peut établir un tableau des types tonals possibles pour chaque mode (Tableau 3).[8] Les possibilités réelles sont évidemment plus nombreuses, mais seulement parce que certaines des conditions théoriques ne sont pas respectées : ou bien les octaves modales ne sont pas complètes, ou bien certaines voix utilisent des lignes supplémentaires. Conformément à l'usage de Harold Powers, les systèmes réguliers et transposé sont représentés par ♮ et ♭; les clefs d'*ut* 1ᵉ ligne ('chiavi naturali') et de *sol* 2ᵉ ligne ('chiavette') par les abréviations c_1 et g_2, respectivement; et les notes nominales sont données en notation alphabétique.

On notera dans ce tableau que le contraste entre les modes authente ou plagal peut toujours se faire par un changement de système, de régulier à transposé

---

[8] Une première version de ce tableau, avec une argumentation un peu différente, a été publiée dans Nicolas Meeùs, « Mode, ton, classes hexacordales, transposition », *Secondo convegno europeo di analisi musicale*, *Atti*, éd. par Rossana Dalmonte et Mario Baroni (Trento, 1992) 221-36.

ou de transposé à régulier. Le changement de système est obligé dans le cas des modes de *ré*, de *mi* et de *la*. Il est toujours possible d'écrire le mode plagal dans une autre combinaison de clefs que le mode authente, sauf pour les deux modes de *ré*, où les compositions authentes et plagales s'écrivent théoriquement toujours en 'chiavi naturali'. Mais il est notoire que ce ne sont pas là les notations favorites au seizième siècle.

Dorien :	♮–c_1–D	Hypodorien :	♭–c_1–G
Phrygien :	♮–g_2–E	**Hypophrygien :**	♭–c_1–A ou ♭–g_2–A
Lydien :	♮–g_2–F	**Hypolydien :**	♮–c_1–F ou ♭–g_2–B♭
Mixolydien :	♭–c_1–C	**Hypomixolydien :**	♮–c_1–G ou ♭–g_2–C
Éolien :	♭–c_1–D	**Hypoéolien :**	♮–c_1–A ou ♮–g_2–A
Ionien :	♮–c_1–C ou ♭–g_2–F	**Hypoionien :**	♮–g_2–C ou ♭–c_1–F

Tableau 3. Types tonals correspondant aux Tableaux 1 et 2

2. Notations modales dans les Psalmi pœnitentiales d'Alexandre Utendal

La seconde partie de cet article confronte les « notations théoriques » décrites jusqu'ici aux notations mises en œuvre par Alexandre Utendal dans les *Psalmi pœnitentiales*.[9] Les douze compositions modales d'Utendal sont composées chacune de deux à huit sections, mais celles-ci sont écrites toujours dans le même type tonal : le compositeur n'utilise donc qu'une seule notation pour chaque mode.[10] Dans les douze paragraphes ci-dessous, un exemple noté donnera pour chaque mode la position de la note nominale (♦) et la tessiture de chacune des voix pour chacune des sections de l'œuvre.

2.1 Dorien (Primus psalmus)
La notation théorique est en 'chiavi naturali', système régulier. Utendal choisit d'écrire en 'chiavette' et en système transposé, ce qui situe les notes un degré plus haut dans les portées et permet donc d'étendre les ambitus un degré plus

---

[9] Alexander Utendal, *Septem psalmi pœnitentiales, adiunctis ex prophetiarum scriptis orationibus eiusdem argumenti quinque, ad dodecachordi modos duodecim, hac quidem ætate doctiorum quorundam musicorum opera ab obscuritate vindicatos…*, Noribergae, Dietrich Gerlach, 1570. Fac-similé de la Bibliothèque royale de Copenhague, disponible à l'adresse http://www.kb.dk/da/nb/samling/ma/digmus/pre1700_indices/utendal_sept_poeni.html (dernière consultation le 5 mai 2007).

[10] Il faut souligner que ceci demeure vrai même dans les sections dont l'accord final n'est pas construit sur la note nominale du mode. Comme indiqué en note 5 ci-dessus, on pourrait objecter que ces sections ne sont pas dans le même type tonal que le reste de la pièce : c'est la raison pour laquelle il paraît nécessaire de fonder les types tonals sur les notes nominales, plutôt que sur l'accord final.

bas par rapport à la note nominale. La conséquence est que la partie d'Altus ne donne jamais la quinte modale au dessus de la note nominale. Par contre, les tessitures plagales s'étendent toujours plus bas que la quarte modale : le Bassus, en particulier, termine à l'octave sous la note nominale, avec une ligne supplémentaire sous la portée en clef de *fa* 3ᵉ ligne.

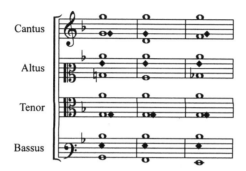

Figure 4. Dorien

2.2 Hypodorien (Secundus psalmus)

La notation théorique est en 'chiavi naturali', système transposé. C'est la notation choisie par Utendal : le contraste avec le mode authente s'établit donc par le changement de clefs, plutôt que par le changement de système. Les tessitures couvrent toujours l'octave modale, qu'elles dépassent assez peu. L'Altus (authente) descend à la quarte sous la finale, avec une ligne supplémentaire sous la portée, dans la deuxième section durant laquelle le Bassus se tait.

Figure 5. Hypodorien

2.3. Phrygien (Tertius psalmus)

La notation théorique est en 'chiavette' et système régulier. Utendal choisit plutôt une variante des 'chiavi naturali'. Sauf au Bassus, les notes sont écrites une tierce plus haut que dans la notation théorique, ce qui empêche de couvrir la quinte modale à l'Altus, mais permet à ces trois voix de descendre plus bas sous la note nominale; si Utendal avait choisi les 'chiavette', des lignes supplémentaires sous la portée auraient été nécessaires à de nombreuses reprises. Le Bassus est en clef de *fa* 3ᵉ ligne au lieu de 4ᵉ ligne, ce qui réduit la distance entre Tenor et Bassus à une tierce et diminue d'autant l'ambitus général du chœur; le Bassus (plagal) ne peut donc pas s'étendre plus loin que la quinte sous la finale; il peut monter par contre à la septième au-dessus de la note nominale, ce qu'il fait dans chacune des sections.

Figure 6. Phrygien

2.4 Hypophrygien (Quartus psalmus)

L'hypophrygien doit théoriquement s'écrire en système transposé, mais les deux combinaisons de clefs sont praticables. Utendal utilise la même variante des 'chiavi naturali' que dans le psaume précédent. Le contraste entre les deux modes se fait donc ici par la transposition. Comme dans le cas précédent, ce choix situe la note nominale plus haut dans l'ambitus des trois voix supérieure. Au Bassus au contraire la note nominale est au plus grave de l'ambitus; elle n'y est pas atteinte dans la dernière section, où le Bassus termine sur *la*₂, à l'octave supérieure de la note nominale théorique.

Figure 7. Hypophrygien

2.5 Lydien (Quintus psalmus)

La notation théorie est en 'chiavette', en système régulier. C'est celle que retient Utendal. Il faut noter que dans ce mode relativement difficile en raison du triton sur la finale, la notation en système régulier permet de baisser assez aisément le quatrième degré, ce dont Utendal se prive peu. Le Bassus descend plusieurs fois à l'octave sous la finale, ce qui requiert une ligne supplémentaire sous la portée.

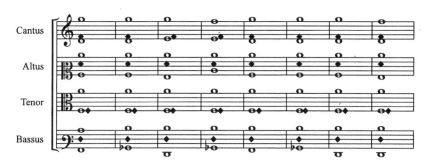

Figure 8. Lydien

2.6 Hypolydien (Sextus psalmus)

La notation retenue par Utendal, 'chiavi naturali' et système régulier, est l'une des deux notations théoriques possibles, contrastant avec le mode lydien par les clefs plutôt que par le système. L'autre notation théorique ('chiavette' et système transposé) aurait situé les notes un degré plus haut dans la portée; il aurait fallu alors des lignes supplémentaires au grave à l'Altus pour la première section et au Bassus pour les deux premières sections.

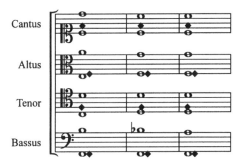

Figure 9. Hypolydien

2.7 Mixolydien (Septimus psalmus)

Utendal n'utilise pas la notation théorique en 'chiavi naturali' et système transposé, mais bien celle en 'chiavette' en système régulier, qui place les notes une tierce plus haut dans la portée. L'Altus ne peut donc pas faire entendre au complet la quinte du mode, au dessus de la note nominale, mais parcourt par contre toute l'octave sous cette note. Le Bassus, qui ne fait entendre la quinte modale que dans la dernière section, étire lui aussi considérablement la tessiture plagale sous la note nominale, jusqu'à la septième.

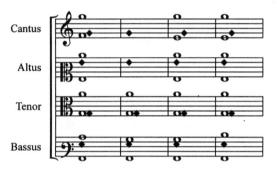

Figure 10. Mixolydien

2.8 Hypomixolydien (Oratio prima)

Deux notations théoriques sont possibles : 'chiavi naturali' en système régulier, ou 'chiavette' en système transposé. Utendal choisit la première, qui est la plus grave des deux et qui établit le contraste avec le mode précédent sur base des clefs plutôt que du système. Les octaves modales sont entendues à toutes les voix.

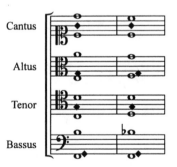

Figure 11. Hypomixolydien

2.9 Éolien (Oratio secunda)

Utendal préfère à la notation théorique, 'chiavi naturali' et système transposé, la notation en 'chiavette' en système régulier, qui place la note nominale une tierce plus haut dans la portée. Cette notation empêche le Cantus de couvrir toute l'octave modale. L'Altus ne peut donner la quinte modale et ne fait entendre la quarte au dessus de la note nominale qu'au prix d'une ligne supplémentaire dans la première section; par contre, il peut descendre de plus d'une octave sous la note nominale dans la deuxième section. Le Bassus ne peut pas non plus faire entendre la quinte modale au dessus de la note nominale, mais s'étend dans les deux sections jusqu'à l'octave en dessous.

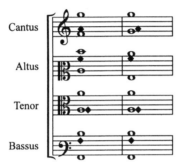

Figure 12. Éolien

2.10 Hypoéolien (Oratio tertia)

L'hypoéolien ne peut théoriquement être écrit qu'en système régulier, mais dans l'une ou l'autre des combinaisons de clefs. Utendal choisit une fois encore la notation la plus grave, en 'chiavi naturali', réduisant donc l'opposition avec le précédent à la combinaison des clefs. L'octave modale est entendue à toutes les voix, dans toutes les sections.

Figure 13. Hypoéolien

2.11 Ionien (Oratio quarta)

L'ionien est le seul mode authente qui autorise deux notations théoriques, en *chiavi naturali* et système régulier, ou en 'chiavette' et système transposé. Utendal choisit la première, la plus aiguë des deux. Les octaves modales sont entendues à toutes les voix dans toutes les sections.

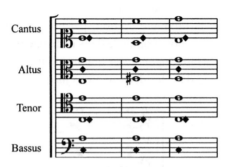

Figure 14. Ionien

2.12 Hypoionien (Oratio quinta et ultima)

Ici aussi deux notations théoriques sont possibles, en *chiavi naturali* et système transposé, ou en 'chiavette' et système régulier. Utendal choisit une version modifiée de la seconde, où le Bassus, comme dans les modes phrygiens, est à distance de tierce plutôt que de quinte du Tenor. Des deux notations théoriques, il retient donc celle qui place la note nominale au plus haut dans la portée, mais il compense cela par un choix anormal pour la clef du Bassus.

Figure 15 : Hypoionien

3. CONCLUSIONS

Un premier point qu'il faut souligner avec force, c'est que les notations retenues par Utendal sont toujours les plus économes en lignes supplémentaires au dessus ou en dessous de la portée. Pour chacun des douze modes, toute autre notation eut été moins favorable. Il faut en conclure que les choix sont dictés en premier lieu par les contraintes de notation, qui ne laissent pratiquement aucune marge de manœuvre. Patrizio Barbieri indique que certaines transpositions, chez Palestrina, pourraient se justifier par une volonté de respecter des notations modales traditionnelles;[11] mais cela ne paraît pas applicable au cas des *Psalmi pœnitentiales*.[12] Anne Smith suggère que la raison première des transpositions aurait été d'adapter la notation au diapason des instruments.[13] Ce n'est certainement pas le cas : au contraire, on pourrait montrer qu'il existe au seizième siècle et au début du dix-septième deux traditions parallèles mais distinctes du débat sur la transposition, l'une se préoccupant des contraintes de notation, l'autre des contraintes de diapason; mais ce point devra faire l'objet d'une autre étude.[14]

On peut encore faire les remarques suivantes à propos des choix faits par Utendal:
- Pour les modes authentes qui n'autorisent qu'une seule notation théorique, le compositeur en préfère une autre dans quatre cas sur cinq, chaque fois pour situer la note nominale plus haut dans la portée, donc pour pratiquer des tessitures relatives plus basses. Ceci se fait le plus souvent au détriment de la quinte modale à la voix d'Altus.
- Pour le mode ionien par contre, le seul mode authente qui autorise deux notations théoriques, Utendal choisit celle qui situe la note nominale une seconde plus bas que dans l'autre notation, ce qui autorise des tessitures plus aiguës relativement à la note finale.

---

[11] Barbieri, « Chiavette », 22.
[12] On peut noter en outre que les types tonals de Utendal ne correspondent pas, dans la plupart des cas, à ceux qu'utilise Lassus dans son cycle de 1584. Voir Harold Powers, *Tonal types*, 447, table 3.
[13] Smith, « Über Modus und Transposition », 13-14.
[14] Il est vrai sans doute qu'une notation anormalement aiguë ou anormalement grave pourrait inciter les instrumentistes à transposer; mais on ne peut y voir qu'une conséquence du choix notationnel, et pas sa raison d'être. Sur ce point, voir aussi Nicolas Meeùs, « Mode, ton, classes hexacordales, transposition », « Mode et système. Conceptions ancienne et moderne de la modalité », *Musurgia*, 4/3 (1997), 67-80, et « Le diapason, un problème conceptuel », *Observation, analyse, modèle : Peut-on parler d'art avec les outils de la science ?*, Actes du 2e Colloque international d'épistémologie musicale, éd. par Jean-Marc Chouvel et Fabien Levy (Paris, 2002), 59-76.

- Pour les modes plagaux qui autorisent deux notations, Utendal choisit presque toujours celle qui situe la note nominale au plus haut, autorisant donc un ambitus relatif plus grave.

- Le mode lydien est le seul mode authente pour lequel la notation théorique unique est acceptée, et le mode hypolydien est le seul où, des deux notations théoriques possibles, la plus aiguë est retenue. Il s'agit chaque fois de la notation en système régulier et on peut se demander si, dans ce cas précis, le critère de choix n'a pas été lié à la mobilité du *si* / *si♭*, qui serait devenu *mi* / *mi♭* en système transposé.[15]

- Chaque fois qu'une modification des combinaisons de clefs standardisées est effectuée (trois cas sur douze, en modes phrygien, hypophrygien et hypoionien), c'est pour remonter l'ambitus du Bassus et le rapprocher de celui du ténor. Dans deux cas sur trois, cette modification s'applique aux 'chiavi naturali' : il ne paraît donc pas justifié d'associer le resserrement de l'intervalle entre Tenor et Bassus aux 'chiavette', comme on l'a fait parfois.[16]

Il apparaît que lorsque les notations théoriques ne sont pas respectées, c'est souvent pour constituer des ambitus plus graves, relativement à la note nominale du mode. Ignace Bossuyt[17] a signalé la fonction rhétorique des dépassements de l'octave modale dans les *Psalmi pœnitentiales*. Tenant compte du texte mis en musique, il identifie l'hypobole dans les modes dorien, mixolydien et hypoéolien, pour lesquels les choix de notation décrits ci-dessus établissent en effet des tessitures graves, mais aussi dans le mode lydien, qu'Utendal note pourtant à son octave théorique. Bossuyt signale aussi l'hyperbole dans les modes hypodorien, hypophrygien, hypolydien et hypoéolien mais, de ceux-ci, l'hypolydien est le seul pour lequel Utendal choisit une notation qui favorise effectivement les tessitures aiguës. Il est possible que les choix d'Utendal aient été faits, dans certains cas, précisément pour rendre possible ces figures de rhétorique; mais dans d'autres cas les choix de notation paraissent plutôt s'y opposer. Bien entendu, les phénomènes relevés par Ignace Bossuyt concernent surtout des voix considérées séparément, alors que les choix de notation déterminent la composition dans son ensemble et affectent certaines voix plus que d'autres. De toute manière, le présent article ne pourra faire plus qu'attirer l'attention sur ces questions, qui requièrent une étude bien plus approfondie.

---

[15] Il faut rappeler cependant que les modes dorien et hypodorien, où le problème du degré mobile se pose de manière semblable, sont notés tous deux en système transposé, comme on l'a vu plus haut : la mobilité s'y situe sur *mi* / *mi♭*, plutôt que sur *si* / *si♭*.

[16] Voir Andrew Johnstone, « High clefs in composition and performance », *Early Music,* 34/1 (2006), 29-54.

[17] Ignace Bossuyt, « Die 'Psalmi Poenitentiales' (1570) des Alexander Utendal », *Archiv für Musikwissenschaft,* 38 (1981), 290.

NOTES FROM AN ERASABLE TABLET

John Milsom

How did sixteenth-century composers go about the task of writing down their extended polyphonic works? This question has been asked before, not least by Jessie Ann Owens in her important book on *Composers at Work: The Craft of Musical Composition 1450-1600*; and no one could disagree with her broad conclusion that there was probably 'no single "compositional process" for music of this period'. How a composer worked would have 'depended on factors such as his skill level, the kind of space he had available for writing, the number of voices, the conventions of genre, and demands of style', together with the specific musical ideas he wanted to explore in the individual piece.[1] Nevertheless, the surviving evidence leads Owens to a narrower conclusion that is both unexpected and startling: that 'composers of vocal polyphony neither needed nor used scores for composing. (…) Instead of scores, composers worked on short segments in quasi-score format and on longer segments in separate parts (for example, choirbook format)'.[2] She reaches this conclusion partly because of the absence of autograph scores that relate to composition, partly from her analysis of other autograph notations that clearly represent the work-in-progress. Cumulatively, the evidence strongly suggests that sixteenth-century composers did not habitually draft and preserve their polyphonic works in complete scores – which is to say, in a format that allowed them to survey a piece in its full length and breadth, much as we do when we read a score today.

It must be said, however, that in an earlier chapter of her book Owens addresses a subject that might call for some qualification of this view – or at least, of its universal applicability. Some sixteenth-century composers are known to have made use of erasable tablets (or 'cartelle') when devising new works, and very little is known about these mysterious tablets – about their use, their size, and (above all) about the quantity of music that would fit on to them. Owens herself suggests that 'cartelle' could have served a variety of purposes, including 'sketches, more extended drafts, even fair copies of entire compositions'.[3] She

---

[1] Jessie Ann Owens, *Composers at Work: The Craft of Musical Composition 1450-1600* (New York and Oxford, 1997), 193. I am grateful to Professor Owens for her generous sharing of ideas and materials over the course of many years, and to Margaret Bent and Bonnie J. Blackburn for making helpful comments on a draft version of the present study.

[2] Owens, *Composers at Work*, 313. In 'quasi-score' format, the voices are stacked one above the other, but usually not rigorously aligned; see Owens, *op. cit.*, 137.

[3] Owens, *Composers at Work*, 100-101, and Chapter 5 in general for a discussion of 'cartelle'.

also cites epistolary references to at least portions of complete pieces being retained by composers on 'cartelle' until the music was reckoned complete, or the tablets needed for another purpose.[4] This evidence could certainly challenge the view that sixteenth-century composers did not normally devise and scan their works in score or quasi-score. Indeed, it opens up the possibility that scores and quasi-scores of whole pieces might in fact have existed, albeit only while the work remained in erasable form, before being transferred to parchment or paper.

There are various reasons for believing the 'cartella', rather than paper, to have been a principal location for the act of composing large-scale works – whether in score, quasi-score, or another layout.[5] First, we are faced with the overwhelming evidence of the repertory itself: almost all sixteenth-century polyphonic works survive only in finished form, lacking any traces of the work-in-progress, and the absence of such traces might encourage us to believe in the widespread use of erasable surfaces. Second, the 'cartella' had two obvious advantages over paper: it lent itself to local erasure (and therefore to correction and revision of the work-in-progress); and it cost nothing to use, whereas paper was an expensive commodity to devote to something as ephemeral as a compositional draft. (Significantly, very few of the paper-based drafts discussed by Owens are written on single sheets used wholly for the act of composition. Instead, most of them make opportunistic use of available space in what are otherwise performers' books.) Third – and this is an issue not systematically explored by Owens – there is the evidence of the autograph partbooks or choirbooks into which sixteenth-century composers transferred their completed works. While a copy of a completed work may communicate little or nothing about the compositional process itself, nonetheless it may hint at the nature of the exemplar from which it was made. The present (necessarily brief) study sets out to look for evidence that might be gleaned from such autograph copies, specifically from the six sets of partbooks compiled by the composer Derrick Gerarde to preserve his own polyphonic works.

---

[4] See Bonnie J. Blackburn, Edward E. Lowinsky and Clement A. Miller (eds.), *A Correspondence of Renaissance Musicians* (Oxford, 1991), 120-3. The sixteenth-century writers of these letters refer to the size of 'cartelle', which were clearly not large enough to contain whole compositions.

[5] Margaret Bent (personal communication, and also frequently in her published writings) argues that composers might also have conceived whole works in their imaginations. The human mind should therefore be regarded as another principal location for the act of composing large-scale works.

Gerarde is an obscure figure, so a brief introduction to him may be helpful here.[6] The stylistic profile of his music, together with evidence gleaned from paper-study of his manuscripts, suggests that Derrick Gerarde was a Flemish-born composer active in the central decades of the sixteenth century, and was almost certainly alive in the 1560s. However, no documentary record of him has yet been found, and the most tangible traces we have of Gerarde are his autograph partbooks, all of which are now shelved among the Royal Appendix manuscripts in the British Library (hereafter 'RA'). Included in these partbooks are pieces by other Flemish composers that are not known to have appeared in print during the sixteenth century; this may imply some proximity to the composers concerned, the most celebrated of whom was Nicolas Gombert.[7] Gerarde seems also to have worked at some stage alongside a composer called 'Morel', who himself claimed to have served Henry Fitzalan, twelfth earl of Arundel (1512-80), in some unspecified capacity. Like Morel, Gerarde appears to have been resident in England for part of his life, and he certainly wrote at least two vocal works with English texts. The fact that his autograph partbooks subsequently passed into the ownership of either Arundel or his son-in-law John, Lord Lumley (c.1533-1609), implies that Gerarde, like Morel, had links with Arundel and/or Lumley; but it would be premature to conclude, as some have done in the past, that he was 'composer-in-residence' to one or other of those men.

As for his partbooks, the following two points can be made about them. First, the overwhelming majority of their contents are works by Gerarde himself, copied in his own hand. Only rarely do other copyists make an appearance, largely as assistants; they include Morel, and at least three other hands whose identities remain unknown. Second, many of Gerarde's autograph works show clear signs of having been revised or edited by the composer, sometimes by erasure or hatched cancellation, sometimes by the application of pastedown cancel slips or leaves on which replacement readings were then written. From

---

6   For further information about Gerarde, his partbooks and his musical circle, see Iain Fenlon and John Milsom, '"Ruled Paper Imprinted": Music Paper and Patents in Sixteenth-Century England', *Journal of the American Musicological Society*, 37 (1984), 139-63 at 146-7; John Milsom, 'The Nonsuch Music Library', in Chris Banks, Arthur Searle and Malcolm Turner (eds.), *Sundry Sorts of Music Books. Essays on The British Library Collections Presented to O.W. Neighbour on his 70th Birthday* (London, 1993), 146-82 at 162-4; and *idem*, 'Gerarde, Derrick', *New Grove II*.

7   The six partbook sets are: RA 17-22 (complete set of six partbooks; motets by Gerarde); RA 23-5 (three surviving partbooks; vocal works by Gerarde); RA 26-30 (complete set of five partbooks; vocal works by Gerarde); RA 31-5 (complete set of five partbooks; vocal works by Gerarde); RA 49-54 (complete set of six partbooks; vocal works by Gerarde and other composers); RA 57 (one partbook from an otherwise lost set; vocal works by Gerarde and other composers). For inventories of all six sets, see [Thomas Oliphant et al.], *Catalogue of the Manuscript Music in the British Museum* (London, 1842), 3-10.

this description, it will be clear that Gerarde's partbooks, though important witnesses to the process of revising completed pieces, might not be expected to tell us much if anything about the initial act of composing those works. By the time Gerarde came to copy a piece into his partbooks, the work in question seems always to have been fully formed and complete, bearing no obvious trace of how Gerarde had originally crafted it, whether on a 'cartella' or in some other way. Admittedly a few brief compositional drafts in quasi-score do exist within the partbooks, but these turn out to be the work of the unidentified hands, not of Gerarde himself.[8]

In 1995, the British Library lifted all the cancel leaves pasted into the partbooks to conceal rejected readings. The majority of these cancels are blank on their reverse sides, but two of them have music written on their own versos, and it is clear that Gerarde was here recycling paper he had previously used for another purpose. The two relevant pages, shown in Plates 1 and 2, have been cut from a large single sheet, on which Gerarde notated all six voices of his motet *Sic Deus dilexit mundum*. (He subsequently made normal partbook copies of this same work.) Plate 1 represents the upper left-hand quarter of the original sheet; it transmits segments of the top three voices, numbered '1-3' by Gerarde in the left-hand margin. Each voice occupies two staves; these would have extended on to the sheet's upper right-hand quarter, which is now missing. Plate 2 shows the lower right-hand quarter of the sheet, on which segments of the lower three voices are written; here, it is the lower left-hand quarter of the sheet (and therefore the openings of these three voices) that has gone astray. The total sheet would have measured a minimum of 30 cm in height and 40 cm in width. It has printed staves on both its sides (laid out in four blocks, each of five staves), and it was clearly manufactured with the aim of being folded twice, giving rise to a gathering of four leaves suitable for use in a partbook.[9] Gerarde, however, has used the sheet unfolded; and in order to give himself a total of twelve long staves, he has hand-ruled two additional staves, one at the top of the sheet, the other at the bottom, and linked the printed staves with

---

[8]   The quasi-scores analysed in Owens, *Composers at Work*, 137-41 (and illustrated as Plates 7.1 and 7.2) are the work of two different musicians, both of whom were apparently less experienced composers than Gerarde himself. The first of them, represented by Owens's Plate 7.1, elsewhere assisted Gerarde in the copying of the latter's *O souverain Pasteur* in RA 31-5; he wrote out the music of three of its voice-parts, the text-incipits in two partbooks, and the heading 'Priere devant le repas' in all five partbooks. The second unidentified hand, represented by Owens's Plate 7.2 (and Example 7.1), elsewhere copied the music of Gerarde's *Yf Phebus stormes* in RA 31-5, leaving insufficient space for the words to be added. Gerarde subsequently concealed these pages under pastedown cancel sheets, and made new copies of the piece, this time with text-underlay.

[9]   For further information about the printed staves on Sheet X, see Fenlon and Milsom, 'Ruled Paper Imprinted', 146-7 (Design 1j).

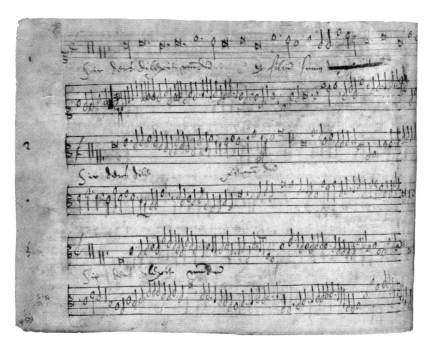

Plate 1. London, British Library, MS Royal Appendix 33, fo. 65*ʳ (inverted); by permission of The British Library

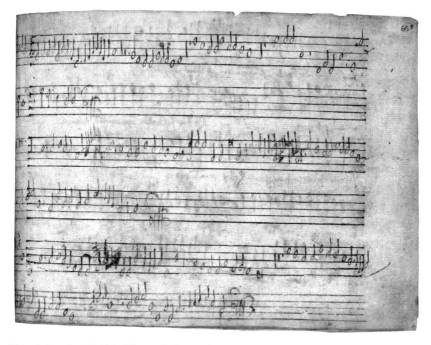

Plate 2. London, British Library, MS Royal Appendix 32, fo. 65*ʳ; by permission of The British Library

central manuscript extensions. By this means, all six voices of the motet can be accommodated on 'Sheet X' (as it is termed in the discussion below), two staves for each voice.

What was the purpose of Sheet X? It seems hardly possible that Gerarde could have used it for the act of composition itself, for the six voice-parts are fluently notated, largely without erasures, deletions, fluctuations of spacing or obvious changes of ink, all of which might be expected on a sheet used for active composition. Instead, each of the six voice-parts looks as if it has been copied in a single stint, without hesitancy or interruption. (The few significant changes made to Sheet X will be discussed below.) Nor does it seem likely that it was made as a test copy from which singers could try the piece out for correctness. Six people would have difficulty reading simultaneously from compact notation in this format, and in any case no text-underlay is provided beyond the first phrase. We can probably dismiss the idea that Sheet X was made for transmitting the piece to a recipient, since the words are absent, and there are places where the notated durations will not easily accommodate the words, suggesting that the piece is unfinished. And we should also take note of the fact that Sheet X is unique among Gerarde's known manuscripts. Nothing equivalent to it occurs elsewhere, not even among the other cancel leaves pasted into his partbooks. This lends it an air of abnormality.

The most likely explanation is that Sheet X was copied in exceptional circumstances directly from a 'cartella', presumably at a time when, for some reason, Gerarde needed to clear the tablet for another use, but did not have access to the partbooks into which he would normally transfer his finished works. If so, then these six voice-parts may look much as they did in the compositional draft – which is to say, as melodic lines that are musically complete but still untexted. It is even possible that Gerarde's numbering of the voice-parts as '1-6' (as opposed to the use of descriptive names such as 'Superius' and 'Tenor') hints at their vertical alignment on the 'cartella', in score or quasi-score. No significance need be read into the absence of the words, for Gerarde would have known perfectly well where each new text-phrase should begin, and could work out the details at a later stage – as indeed he did, when he transferred the piece into normal partbook format. Sheet X may therefore be what we might call a 'holding copy': it seems to preserve the piece in a state of limbo, fully drafted but awaiting polish and refinement.

If this hypothesis is correct, then it may help us to infer Gerarde's normal working practices. Because Sheet X has apparently been copied in a single stint, we can assume that Gerarde had visual access to the entire composition at the time when he transferred it to paper. This interpretation is overwhelmingly supported by his partbooks: Gerarde seems always to have been able to transcribe his voice-parts fluently, without changes of ink or unevenness of spacing that would hint at a more broken copying process. This is true of well over a hundred polyphonic compositions that Gerarde copied into his partbooks, many of which are written without concern for achieving visual neatness, and always apparently in a single stint. Whether or not a whole piece could be drafted on a single 'cartella', or needed more than one tablet, remains unknown. What does seem likely, however, is that the erasable copy lacked words – or rather, it did not need a complete set of words. On the contrary, it was probably Gerarde's normal practice to add full text-underlay only when he transferred the voice-parts from 'cartella' to partbook, adjusting the durations of notes as he did so. Again his partbooks reinforce that view: they contain many alterations to the text-underlay, showing how the raw melodic lines of the original conception lent themselves to multiple declamatory interpretations. As he drafted a work, Gerarde must have known broadly how words and music would fit together, but he left the finer details to be worked out later, and perhaps adjusted them over a lifetime.[10]

Sheet X gives us one further insight into Gerarde's compositional process. *Sic Deus dilexit mundum* falls into six sections, each of which has its own text-phrase, set to distinctive music. The sections are as follows:

I	Sic Deus dilexit mundum,
II	ut filium suum unigenitum daret:
III	ut omnis qui credit in ipsum,
IV	non pereat,
V	sed habeat vitam aeternam.
VI	Alleluia.

Section III, 'ut omnis qui credit in ipsum', is based on the *fuga* subject shown in Example 1. This is notated in two rhythmic forms, first in units (Ex. 1a), then rhythmicized and texted as in Gerarde's motet (Ex. 1b). [11] The subject will interlock with itself in two different ways (Ex. 2): in 'stretto *fuga*', in

---

[10] Several of the autograph drafts discussed by Owens are either untexted or underlaid with abbreviated words. The reason for compressing the text is obvious: words occupy more horizontal space than does music notation.

[11] 'Unit': a useful tool for the analysis of *fuga* (as indeed for other aspects of polyphony), in which the musical content of a passage is expressed wholly in notes of a single duration, presented as either beamed or unbeamed note-heads. See John Milsom, 'Absorbing Lassus', *Early Music*, 33 (2005), 305-20 at 308 ff.

which the second voice enters one unit after the first (Interlock A), or at the distance of two units (Interlock B).[12] Gerarde makes use of both interlocks, and we can probably legitimately imagine him composing this section by first sketching these two-voice interlocks, then building them into larger lattices and distributing them among the six voices, and finally adding accompanying lines that are melodically free. Sheet X reveals two places in Section III where Gerarde evidently changed his mind about the conduct of the accompanying free voices. Example 3 analyses the first of them, using three notational layers to reflect the likely compositional process. Example 3a shows the underlying lattice of *fuga*, expressed in units. Example 3b reconstructs (as far as is possible) Gerarde's original six-voice conception, as worked out on the 'cartella' and transferred to Copy X. Note in particular the long rests in Voice V. Finally, Example 3c shows the revised and final reading for the passage, overwritten on Sheet X; in the boxed section of the score, the *fuga* has been retained, but Voice VI and especially Voice V have been adjusted.[13] A slightly later passage in Section III is modified in a similar way (see Ex. 4). The principal change is again to Voice V, but this time the Superius (Voice I) has also been lightly revised. Presumably both changes were made almost immediately after Gerarde had transferred the piece from 'cartella' to Sheet X. The fact that he could make revisions to more than one voice-part at exactly the same moment in the piece may again hint that the copy on the 'cartella' – not yet erased at this point – was laid out in score or quasi-score.

Example 1. Derrick Gerarde, *Sic Deus dilexit mundum*, Section III, *fuga* subject: (a) expressed in units; (b) as rhythmicized and texted by Gerarde

---

[12] For a brief introduction to the concept of 'stretto fuga', see John Milsom, '"Imitatio", "Inter-textuality", and Early Music', in Suzannah Clark and Elizabeth Eva Leach (eds.), *Citation and Authority in Medieval and Renaissance Musical Culture: Learning from the Learned* (Wood-bridge, 2005), 141-51, at 146-51.

[13] The reconstruction in Example 3b inevitably relies upon guesswork because of erasures and overwriting on Sheet X. Voice III probably differed in some respects from the version in Example 3c.

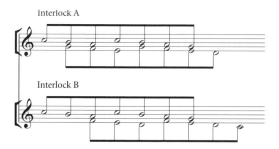

Example 2. Gerarde, *Sic Deus dilexit mundum*, Section III, alternative interlocks of *fuga* subject. Interlock A: at distance of one unit (stretto *fuga*); Interlock B: at distance of two units

Example 3. Gerarde, *Sic Deus dilexit mundum*, revisions made to Section III: (a) underlying *fuga*, with alternative interlocks of the subject; (b) reconstruction of original reading, partly transcribed from Sheet X (Voices IV, V and VI), otherwise using the partbook version in RA 31-5 (Voices I, II and III); (c) revised reading, as found on emended Sheet X (Voices IV, V and VI) and in RA 31-5 (all six voices). The passage revised by Gerarde is boxed

Example 4. Gerarde, *Sic Deus dilexit mundum*, revisions made to Section III: (a) underlying *fuga*; (b) reconstruction of initial draft, partly transcribed from Sheet X (Voices I, IV, V and VI), otherwise using the reading of RA [31-5] (Voices II and III); (c) revised reading, as found on emended Sheet X (Voices I, IV, V and VI) and in RA 31-5 (all six voices). The passage revised by Gerarde is boxed

At a later date, Gerarde made a much more significant change to this motet: he heavily revised his setting of the opening words, 'Sic Deus dilexit mundum', reducing its length from seventeen breves to ten. (His possible reason for doing so is discussed below.) The physical evidence of this revision is located not on Sheet X, but rather in the set of voice-parts that Gerarde subsequently copied into the partbooks RA 31-5. These voice-parts are a straightforward transcription of those on Sheet X, but edited in order that they can (and do) bear full text-underlay. Subsequently, Gerarde used a knife to scrape away Section I: he eliminated most of the musical notation and parts of the text-underlay, than entered replacement readings over the erasures. Plate 3 shows the adjusted state of the Superius part; note the uneven appearance of the notation on the top stave, where the revised reading has been entered over erasures. Gerarde's original setting of Section I would therefore have been lost, but for its chance survival on Sheet X. Example 5 shows both settings of Section I, the early version aligned above the revision in order to reveal connections and differences.[14] This is one of many such substantial changes that can be found among Gerarde's works. They fall into two categories: (1) alternative settings where the new music derives from that of the rejected reading (as is the case here); (2) newly composed passages that are musically unrelated to the rejected reading. In every case, Gerarde was always able to notate the replacement reading fluently and confidently, as if copying from another source, rather than composing straight into the partbooks. This is true of Section I of *Sic Deus dilexit mundum*: Gerarde erased very selectively, leaving the odd note or word that would still be valid in the replacement reading. Presumably, then, the replacement already existed when he made the erasure, allowing him to choose which notes to erase and which to leave. Most likely the replacement setting was again drafted on a 'cartella'.

Plate 3. London, British Library, MS Royal Appendix 31, fo. 37[v]; by permission of The British Library

---

[14] Voices I-III, which are missing from Sheet X, clearly began the motet with a trio identical to that sung by Voices IV-VI. Traces of erased notes in the partbook copy in RA 31-5 confirm this.

Example 5. Gerarde, *Sic Deus dilexit mundum*, revisions made to Section I: (a) reconstruction of first version, based on Sheet X (Voices IV, V and VI); (b) second version, transcribed from RA 31-5 (all six voices)

The story of *Sic Deus dilexit mundum* does not end here; two further stages in its genesis can be discerned. The first was the addition of a *secunda pars*, using the text 'Venite ad me, omnes qui laboratis', with a closing 'Alleluia' identical to the one at the end of *Sic Deus dilexit mundum*.[15] No space was left in RA 31-5 for the *secunda pars* to be placed beside its *prima pars*, and

---

[15] The two texts do not occur consecutively in the liturgy. 'Sic Deus dilexit mundum' (John 3:16) is an antiphon at Lauds on the second feria after Pentecost, whereas 'Venite ad me' (Matthew 11:28) is the Alleluia for Mass on the feast of All Saints. The two texts were also set as *prima* and *secunda partes* of a six-voice motet by Franciscus de Rivulo.

instead the two *partes* are separated by twelve other pieces – the only instance of such separation to be found anywhere in Gerarde's manuscripts. One of the partbooks, RA 35 (fo. 54ᵛ), explicitly states that *Venite ad me* is a *secunda pars*; but Gerarde may subsequently have changed his mind about the order of the two *partes*. This is implied by a later copy of the whole motet in RA 17-22, a partbook set containing neat versions of selected motets, prepared by Gerarde probably either for a prospective recipient or with publication in mind. Here, *Venite ad me* is placed first, *Sic Deus dilexit mundum* second (but without the indication of *secunda pars* that Gerarde was otherwise always careful to specify). The reversal of order may reflect confusion or a genuine change of mind. If intentional, it could explain Gerarde's decision to revise and abbreviate Section I of *Sic Deus dilexit mundum*: he may have eliminated an expansive setting appropriate for a *prima pars*, and replaced it with an abbreviated setting more suited to a *secunda pars*. But there is no doubt that Gerarde did in the end firmly decide that *Sic Deus dilexit mundum* should come first. In the alphabetical indexes to RA 17-22, copied in his own hand and bound at the end of four of the partbooks, *Venite ad me* is once again designated as *secunda pars*, notwithstanding the fact that it has been copied before its *prima pars*.

The last stage in the genesis of the motet is revealed by the copy in RA 17-22. In this late partbook set, *Sic Deus dilexit mundum* has been subjected to a further layer of refinement: more changes have been made to the text-underlay, the melodic lines are occasionally adjusted, and sharp signs inserted for notes that do not bear them in the earlier states of the work. Example 6 shows a sample of this final revision, and in the process returns to the passage first analysed in Example 3, focussing now on the series of changes made to Voice VI. Three states of its conception and refinement are placed in parallel score. Example 6a, taken from Sheet X, shows Gerarde's initial draft of the line, which was still untexted at this stage. Example 6b, transcribed from the early partbook version (RA 34, fo. 35ᵛ), shows how the words from text-phrase II ('unigenitum daret') were used up to the point where Voice VI first sings the *fuga* subject for Section III, at which point the words 'ut omnis qui credit in ipsum' logically make their first appearance. Example 6c, transcribed from the later partbook set (RA 20, fo. 22ᵛ), reveals that Gerarde subsequently moved the new text-phrase forward, so that the words 'ut omnis ...' are first sung to non-*fuga* music, and only subsequently to their proper *fuga* subject. Gerarde's reason for making this seemingly illogical change is in fact easily explained: Voice VI now enunciates the new words simultaneously with Voices I and II, who enter with the new *fuga* subject at exactly this place. (The relevant passage can be seen at the start of Example 3.) Changes such as this one presumably arose from Gerarde's experience of singing or hearing his motet. He would not have needed his 'cartella' to make them.

Example 6. Gerarde, *Sic Deus dilexit mundum*, revisions made to Voice VI at the junction between Sections II and III: (a) original reading (Sheet X, untexted); (b) intermediate version (RA 34, fo. 35ᵛ); (c) final version (RA 20, fo. 22ᵛ)

In summary, *Sic Deus dilexit mundum* probably evolved in the following stages, as suggested partly by the documentary evidence, partly by the music itself:

1. Gerarde divided his text into phrases, imagining melodic and polyphonic ideas that would suit them. Possibly he used his 'cartella' to calculate and sketch the main thematic ideas, especially when exploring alternative *fuga* interlocks (Ex. 2). Over a period of time, a draft of the entire motet emerged, probably in score or quasi-score. Local erasures and revisions were almost certainly made. Gerarde was broadly aware of how words and music would fit together, but he did not write the full text on the 'cartella' itself.

2. In a break with his normal practice, Gerarde transferred the voice-parts to Sheet X, rather than to partbooks. He did so diplomatically, without adding text-underlay. In the process, he made two small revisions to the polyphony (Exx. 3 and 4).

3. The contents of Sheet X were transferred into partbooks (RA 31-5). Gerarde added text-underlay as he copied, adjusting note-values as he did so.

4. At a later date, he composed a *secunda pars*, using the text 'Venite ad me, omnes qui laboratis'.

5. The opening section of *Sic Deus dilexit mundum* was rewritten in abbreviated form (Ex. 5); the revised setting was probably drafted on the 'cartella'. In order to accommodate this revision in the partbooks, the original music was selectively scraped away, and the new setting entered over the erasures. Either at this point or at an earlier or later stage, Gerarde also lightly edited other sections of the work.

6. Gerarde made a new copy of the complete motet in a new partbook set, RA 17-22. As he copied, he made further light revisions, including changes to the text-underlay (Ex. 6). This copy appears to be a final one; the only erasures on the page arise from the correction of copying errors, not from subsequent changes of mind.

In outline, this proposed chronology of events is remarkable mainly because it is so well documented, thanks to the survival of the motet in no fewer than three autograph copies, a situation that almost certainly cannot be matched by any other sixteenth-century musical work. It does, however, include a claim that will raise some readers' eyebrows: namely, that Gerarde drafted and was able to scrutinize a whole composition on his 'cartella', probably in score or quasi-score, giving him visual access to a lengthy and complex polyphonic work in a notational format that may not have been so very different from the scores we use today.[16] If this is correct, then Gerarde's working methods seem not to align with what Jessie Ann Owens has deduced about the practices of (for instance) Corteccia and Cipriano de Rore, whose surviving autograph notations

---

[16] Gerarde's reliance upon score or quasi-score is further suggested by the compositional drafts by his unidentified assistants, as cited in note 8 above. The musicians responsible for these drafts must have been close to Gerarde, perhaps as colleagues or pupils, and their use of quasi-score may therefore hint at Gerarde's own practice. That being said, the two composers responsible for these drafts adopted different layouts: the first of them, represented by Owens, *Composers at Work*, Plate 7.1, worked with the four voices arranged high to low in quasi-score, whereas the second, represented by Plate 7.2, ordered from low to high. Returning to Gerarde: it is just possible that some of the quasi-score drafts in an unrelated set of partbooks, RA 74-6, are in Gerarde's handwriting; see Peter Holman, *Four and Twenty Fiddlers: The Violin at the English Court, 1540-1690* (Oxford, 1993), 92-3 and Plate 2(a). The musical content of these pieces, however, is so remote in style and genre from the polyphonic works in Gerarde's own partbook sets that it is tempting to view the general resemblance of hands as coincidental.

show works being pieced together segment by segment in a modular fashion, without recourse to a cumulative score that would allow a whole work to be surveyed visually in a map-like way. Gerarde's conception too was probably modular, in the sense that each section of the motet would have been worked out separately. But the modules seem to have accumulated into a continuous draft on a 'cartella', which would have been erased only when the piece was complete and copied elsewhere.

Does it matter whether or not sixteenth-century composers drafted whole works in score or quasi-score? Arguably it does. The prevailing view emerging from recent scholarship is that modern scores project an anachronistic image of Renaissance polyphony, remote from the way it was experienced in its own day. This is certainly true if our concern is with sixteenth-century performers and audiences, who clearly did not often encounter scores of the pieces they sang and heard. But the situation may not be quite so straightforward with composers, particularly when they were actively involved in conceiving and assembling new works. Indeed, it now seems possible that a composer's-eye view of the work-in-progress might not always have been so very different from the one we obtain by reading a modern score. The words 'might' and 'may' are pertinent here. Jessie Ann Owens has brilliantly demonstrated that some composers could manage perfectly well without scores or quasi-scores. Derrick Gerarde, conversely, may regularly have used those formats, especially when composing extended *fuga*-based works, using his 'cartella' (as opposed to paper) to draft them in that layout; and other composers might well have done the same. If so, we should take comfort in the fact that, when we read such a work in score today, our visual experience of it may not differ radically from that of the composer at the moment of creation itself.

SELF-CITATION AND SELF-PROMOTION:
ZARLINO AND THE *MISERERE* TRADITION[1]*

Katelijne Schiltz

Through Patrick Macey's extensive research of Josquin des Prez's *Miserere mei Deus*, the historical context of this monumental motet, especially its connection with the Savonarolan reform movement and its repercussions at the Este court of Ferrara have received major attention.[2] Above all, Macey has shown how this piece generated a whole cluster of compositions throughout the sixteenth century, that bear musical, structural and/or textual references to Josquin's work.[3] One of the main elements of this intertextual web includes the use of Josquin's 'soggetto ostinato' – either literally or with slight variations – by composers such as Adrian Willaert, Cipriano de Rore, and Nicola Vicentino, who were all connected with the Este court at a certain point of their careers.[4] Macey's discoveries have brought to light a highly intriguing reception history, to which other scholars have also contributed.[5] In the present article, I wish to add yet another piece of evidence to the afterlife of this *Miserere* tradition. I will focus on two less-known motets by Gioseffo Zarlino, *Miserere mei Deus* and *Misereris omnium*, that were both published in the collection *Modulationes sex*

---

[1] It is a great pleasure to dedicate this article to Ignace Bossuyt. With vivid memories of his fascination with Josquin's *Miserere mei Deus* from the Leuven music history and analysis seminars, I wish to add a small contribution to its reception history. A shorter version of this text was presented at the Utrecht Colloquia in the Musicologies (January 2007) and at the Medieval and Renaissance Music Conference in Vienna (August 2007). I am grateful to Bonnie J. Blackburn, Cristle Collins Judd, and Frans Wiering for reading an earlier draft of this article and for their helpful comments.

[2] See his 'Savonarola and the Sixteenth-Century Motet', *Journal of the American Musicological Society*, 36 (1983), 422-52; *Josquin's Miserere mei Deus: Context, Structure and Influence* (Ph.D. dissertation, University of California, Berkeley, 1985); *Bonfire Songs: Savonarola's Musical Legacy* (Oxford, 1998); 'Josquin and Musical Rhetoric: *Miserere me, Deus* and Other Motets', in Richard Sherr (ed.), *The Josquin Companion* (Oxford, 2000), 485-530.

[3] Many of these pieces have been edited in *Savonarolan Laude, Motets, and Anthems*, ed. Patrick Macey (Recent Researches in the Music of the Renaissance, 116; Madison, 1999).

[4] Macey, *Josquin's Miserere mei Deus*, 157: 'Josquin's *soggetto* established itself as a kind of musical *topos* during the sixteenth century'.

[5] e.g. Bojan Bujic, '*Peccantem me quotidie*: Gallus's Homage to Josquin?', in Dragotin Cvetko and Danilo Pokorn (eds.), *Jacobus Gallus and His Time* (Ljubljana, 1985), 70-81; Ludwig Finscher, '*aus sunderem Lust zu den überschönen Worten*. Zur Psalmkomposition bei Josquin Desprez und seinen Zeitgenossen', in Hartmut Boockmann, Ludger Grenzmann, Bernd Moeller, and Martin Staehelin (eds.), *Literatur, Musik und Kunst im Übergang vom Mittelalter zur Neuzeit. Bericht über Kolloquien der Kommission zur Erforschung der Kultur des Spätmittelalters 1989-1992* (Göttingen, 1995), 246-61; Patrick Macey, 'Italian Connections for Lupus Hellinck and Claude Le Jeune', in Eugeen Schreurs and Bruno Bouckaert (eds.), *Giaches de Wert (1535-1596) and his Time. Migration of Musicians to and from the Low Countries* (Yearbook of the Alamire Foundation, 3; Leuven and Peer, 1999), 151-63.

vocum (Venice, 1566).[6] It will be shown not only how they inscribe themselves in the intertextual network that was initiated by Josquin, but also how they can be linked to the Ferrarese court in general and Duke Alfonso II in particular.

MISERERE MEI DEUS AND MISERERIS OMNIUM

Although Zarlino is mainly known for his theoretical writings, he also composed motets and a number of madrigals.[7] A first book of motets was published in 1549 under the title *Musici quinque vocum moduli* and has received attention in musicological literature because of its careful text underlay and the modal labels that were attached to the individual pieces.[8] In 1566, one year after Zarlino's appointment as chapel master of St Mark's in Venice, the collection *Modulationes sex vocum* was printed by Francesco Rampazetto.[9] It consists of thirteen pieces, all of which (except for *Exaudi Deus orationem - Scrutati sunt iniquitates*) contain a canon for two or three voices. Some of the canonic inscriptions are relatively straightforward technical instructions, others are conceived as enigmatic sentences. The book closes with a seven-part *Pater noster - Ave Maria*, which had already appeared in the collection of 1549.[10]

Miserere mei Deus and *Misereris omnium* share a number of musical and textual characteristics. First of all, both pieces have a common liturgical context, i.e. the beginning of the Tempus Quadragesimae: *Misereris omnium* is the Introit for the feast of Ash Wednesday, *Miserere mei Deus* the Gradual for the same day.[11] The text of the Introit's antiphon is taken from the Wisdom of

---

[6] For a modern edition of *Misereris omnium*, see Gioseffo Zarlino, *Drei Motetten und ein geist-liches Madrigal zu 4-6 Stimmen*, ed. Roman Flury (Das Chorwerk, 77; Wolfenbüttel, 1959), 19-24.

[7] For an overview of Zarlino's compositional oeuvre, see Roman Flury, *Gioseffo Zarlino als Komponist* (Winterthur, 1962).

[8] Mary S. Lewis, 'Zarlino's Theories of Text Underlay as Illustrated in His Motet Book of 1549', *Notes*, 42 (1985), 239-67 and Cristle Collins Judd, 'A Newly Recovered Eight-Mode Motet Cycle from the 1540s: Zarlino's Song of Songs Motets', in Anne-Emmanuelle Ceulemans and Bonnie J. Blackburn (eds.), *Music Theory and Analysis 1450-1650. Proceedings of the International Conference Louvain-la-Neuve, 23-25 September 1999* (Musicologica neolovaniensia, 9; Louvain-la-Neuve, 2001), 229-70. See now also *Gioseffo Zarlino: Motets from 1549 Part 1: Motets Based on the Song of Songs*, ed. Cristle Collins Judd (Recent Researches in the Music of the Renaissance, 145; Middleton, 2006) and *Gioseffo Zarlino: Motets from 1549 Part 2: Selected Motets from* Musici quinque vocum moduli *(Venice 1549)*, ed. Cristle Collins Judd (Recent Researches in the Music of the Renaissance, 149; Middleton, 2007).

[9] The only complete set of partbooks is kept at the Bavarian State Library (shelfmark 4 Mus.pr. 172#Beibd. 4).

[10] Cf. Cristle Collins Judd, '"How to Assign Note Values to Words": Gioseffo Zarlino's *Pater noster - Ave Maria* (1549 and 1566)', paper delivered at the Medieval and Renaissance Music Conference (Vienna, August 2007).

[11] Cf. *Graduale Triplex*, 62-3.

Solomon 11: 24 and 27,[12] which is followed by the psalm verse 'Miserere mei Deus, miserere mei: quoniam in te confidit anima mea' (Ps. 56: 2). The fact that the same psalm is also the source for the Gradual creates a strong connection between the two texts, which has major consequences for Zarlino's settings. Although the incipit of his *Miserere mei Deus* suggests that it uses the same text as Josquin's motet (Ps. 50), Zarlino's composition is based on another psalm (Ps. 56: 2-11),[13] whose text he divides – just like Josquin – into three parts (*Miserere mei Deus - Misit Deus misericordiam suam - Foderunt ante faciem meam*) of 60, 63, and 64 bars respectively. Nevertheless, as we will see, this identical textual opening serves as a kind of aural signal, which inspired Zarlino to make a clear musical reference to Josquin's masterpiece. Apart from their common liturgical origin, both *Misereris omnium* and *Miserere mei Deus* are written in the fourth mode, with final E and low cleffing.[14] According to Zarlino's *Istitutioni harmoniche* (Venice, 1558), this mode was indeed 'said by musical practitioners to be marvelously suited to lamentful words or subjects that contain sadness or supplicant lamentation'.[15] The two motets also use the same cantus firmus – albeit with some melodic differences – on the text *Ne reminiscaris Domine*, which is treated canonically.[16] In the case of *Miserere mei Deus*, Zarlino added the instruction 'Non quòd tres cantent: sed ter renovetur hic ordo, / Signa docent, quatuor prior incipe tempora linquens, / Scande sed ad Quartam, dein bis canta in Diapente' to describe the changing canonic relationship between Tenor and Sextus in the composition's three *partes* (see Plate 1).[17] The Tenor always starts at b. 17, but whereas in the *prima pars* the Sextus is the *dux* (b. 13), which is imitated a fourth below, in the two other parts this voice is the *comes* that duplicates the Tenor at the upper fifth after three (b. 20) and four breves (b. 21) respectively. The cryptic label 'Clavibus ingreditur, caetera cuncta patent' [He enters with the clefs, all the rest remains open] that is attached to the Tenor of *Misereris omnium* indicates a canon at the upper fifth between this voice and the Altus.

---

[12] 'Misereris omnium Domine, et nihil odisti eorum quae fecisti, dissimulans peccata, hominum propter paenitentiam, et parcens illis: quia tu es Dominus Deus noster'.

[13] Macey, *Josquin's Miserere mei Deus*, 175 mentions a similar case for Hubert Waelrant's *Miserere mei, Domine*, whose text is based on Matthew 15: 22-8.

[14] *Miserere mei Deus*: c2-c4-c4-f4-f4-f5; *Misereris omnium*: c2-c3-c3-f3-f4-f5.

[15] 'Questo medesimamente, secondo la loro opinione, si accommoda maravigliosamente a parole, o materie lamentevoli, che contengono tristezza, overo lamentatione supplichevole'.

[16] The antiphon *Ne reminiscaris Domine* (fourth mode) was usually recited before and after the seven Psalmi Poenitentiales (see also *Liber Usualis*, 1840): 'Ne reminiscaris Domine delicta nostra vel parentum nostrorum neque vindictam sumas de peccatis nostris' [Remember not, Lord, our offenses, nor the offenses of our forefathers, nor take Thou vengeance upon them]. The antiphon and the Psalms were sung during the so-called ceremony of the ashes on Ash Wednesday.

[17] [This shall not be sung by three, but this order shall be renewed three times. The signs teach you: you start by first dropping four pauses, but ascend a fourth. Then sing twice at the fifth].

Plate 1. Gioseffo Zarlino, *Miserere mei Deus*, canonic inscription of the Tenor
(by permission of the Bayerische Staatsbibliothek München, Musikabteilung,
4 Mus.pr. 172#Beibd. 4)

Zarlino even added a third layer to *Misereris omnium*. The Quintus shows a
short motif on the words 'Miserere mei Deus', which epitomize the central
theme of the motet as a whole. This voice's musical treatment unequivocally
refers to the *Miserere* tradition in general and Josquin's *Miserere mei Deus* in
particular. Its interpretation has to be deduced from the accompanying text:
'Canon. Qui canis haec, iteranda scias tibi saepius esse: / Semper & in reditu,
tempus te deserat unum. / Ad Quartam in primo reditu descendere debes: /
Ad Quintam veniens iterum, cane voce sub illa. / Deinde ascendendum toties
erit ordine eodem'.[18] The 'soggetto', which consists of three breves, is to be
sung nine times, starting alternately on *e'*, *b*, and *e*. Between these statements,
the number of rests systematically decreases (from nine until one), which
creates an effect of acceleration. However, contrary to a procedure Willaert
often used in his five- and six-part motets,[19] Zarlino does not diminish the note

---

[18] [Rule. You who sing this, should know that you must often repeat it: and each time you return
shall one rest desert you. On the first return you must descend a fourth, when you reach the
fifth, you should sing under that voice. Then you will have to ascend as often in the same or-
der]. Zarlino thus uses 'canon' here in its literal sense, i.e. as a rule (κανών) which indicates
how an unwritten part has to be deduced from a written one.

[19] On this collection and the presence of 'soggetti ostinati', see my 'Motets in their Place: Some
"Crucial" Findings on Willaert's Book of Five-Part Motets (Venice, 1539)', *Tijdschrift van de
Koninklijke Vereniging voor Nederlandse Muziekgeschiedenis*, 54 (2004), 99-118.

values of the 'soggetto' towards the end, but maintains its design throughout the motet (see the 'resolutio' in Plate 2). Interestingly enough, the ostinato's rhythmic layout is exactly twice the speed of Josquin's version (see Ex. 1a).[20] But whereas Josquin's 'soggetto' consists of a series of repeated notes with a semitone inflection at the end on the syllable '*Deus*', Zarlino writes a falling second on 'mei', which is then followed by a rising third on 'Deus' (see Ex. 1b). This melodic outline, oscillating between *mi-re-fa-mi*, is already anticipated at the very beginning of Zarlino's motet. It is sung – albeit in longer note values – by the Sextus (b. 1), Bassus (b. 3), and Cantus (b. 6), starting on *b*, *e*, and *e'* respectively. The contour of Zarlino's ostinato clearly follows Willaert's and Rore's treatment of the *Miserere*-cantus firmus in their settings of *Infelix ego*, Girolamo Savonarola's meditation on Psalm 50 (see Exx. 1c and 1d).[21] Structurally speaking, Zarlino's 'soggetto' most closely resembles the *prima pars* of Rore's motet: he too presents the ostinato (consisting of six breves) nine times in the Altus, alternating between *e'* and *b'*, but he maintains the numbers of rests between the statements (i.e. six).

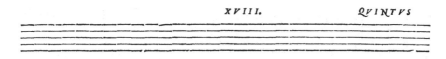

Plate 2. Gioseffo Zarlino, *Misereris omnium*, resolutio of the Quintus (by permission of the Bayerische Staatsbibliothek München, Musikabteilung, 4 Mus.pr. 172#Beibd. 4)

---

[20] However, in the *secunda pars* of Josquin's *Miserere mei Deus*, the ostinato appears in faster note-values.

[21] Savonarola wrote this text in his Florentine prison cell, shortly before he died. This meditation became one of his most-printed works.

Example 1. Comparison of the 'soggetto ostinato': (a) Josquin des Prez, *Miserere mei Deus*; (b) Gioseffo Zarlino, *Misereris omnium*; (c) Adrian Willaert, *Infelix ego*; (d) Cipriano de Rore, *Infelix ego*

At the point where, in the main text of *Misereris omnium*, the verses from the Wisdom of Solomon are followed by Psalm 56: 2 ('Miserere mei Deus, miserere mei: quoniam in te confidit anima mea'), Cantus, Sextus, and Bassus join with the words and the music of the ostinato by imitating its basic features, either literally or with melodic and/or rhythmic changes (bb. 41-58).[22] The words 'Miserere meus Deus' thus function as a signal, which is picked up by the other voices. A similar strategy emerges at the beginning of Zarlino's *Miserere mei Deus*. Here too, all voices – except for the two canonic parts – allude to the *Miserere* topos on the first words of Psalm 56: 2. The version in the Cantus (bb. 1-3) and Quintus (bb. 4-6) is even a literal quotation of the ostinato Willaert and Rore presented in their *Infelix ego*-settings (see above). Rhythmically speaking, apart from the last note, the layout of this motif is exactly the same as the ostinato of *Misereris omnium* (see Ex. 2).

Example 2. Gioseffo Zarlino, *Miserere mei Deus*, Cantus, bb. 1-3

---

[22] See for example the retrograde version in Bassus (*a-b flat-g-a*; bb. 46-8) and Cantus (*b-c'-a-b*; bb. 50-2).

THE 'EXEMPLA' IN *LE ISTITUTIONI HARMONICHE*

It is clear that the connections between *Miserere mei Deus* and *Misereris omnium* are not incidental, but carefully planned by Zarlino. This intention receives extra evidence from another source: the close relationship between the pieces is explicitly made in the revised edition of his *Istitutioni harmoniche* (Venice, 1573). Cristle Collins Judd has recently studied the sources and the role of Zarlino's 'exempla' in the two editions (1558 and 1573) of this treatise.[23] Elsewhere I have investigated the specific relationship between *Le istitutioni harmoniche* and the *Modulationes sex vocum*.[24] It is striking to see that Zarlino already mentions many motets from this collection in the edition of 1558, although the pieces were not published until 1566.[25] A similar case is the 'exempla' taken from Willaert's *Musica Nova*, which at the time of the treatise's appearance had not yet officially been published either.[26] Needless to say, this points to Zarlino's close involvement in the complicated publication history of Willaert's monumental collection, to which I will return later. To a present-day readership, Zarlino's method is rather surprising: why does one exemplify theoretical concepts with compositions that are not yet accessible for a broader public? Zarlino undoubtedly belonged to an elite circle of connoisseurs, a fact he stresses more than once via his choice of 'exempla'. However, his approach also underlines the fact that Zarlino was – as Judd puts it – a 'masterful manipulator of his printed persona'.[27] Indeed, in his dedication of the *Modulationes* to the 'Procuratori di San Marco', Philippus Iusbertus (who had been hired as a singer at St Mark's in 1562) explicitly links these pieces to Zarlino's treatise, in order to show that the chapel master was both an expert in the field of music theory and composition:

---

[23] See the comparative table in Cristle Collins Judd, *Reading Renaissance Music Theory: Hearing with the Eyes* (Cambridge, 2000), 202-5.

[24] Katelijne Schiltz, 'Musiktheorie und Kompositionspraxis: Über das Verhältnis zwischen Zarlinos *Istitutioni harmoniche* und den *Modulationes sex vocum*', in Ulrich Kaiser and Stefan Rohringer (eds.), *Musiktheorie – Begriff und Praxis: Kongreßbericht des 2. Kongresses der Deutschen Gesellschaft für Musiktheorie, 11.-13. Oktober 2002, München* (forthcoming).

[25] The first edition of *Le istitutioni harmoniche* can be consulted online via *Thesaurus Musicarum Italicarum*: <http://euromusicology.cs.uu.nl/>.

[26] The dedication by Francesco Dalla Viola dates from September 1558, but the title page carries the date 1559.

[27] Judd, *Reading Renaissance Music Theory*, 188.

'After that distinguished book to which he gave the title *On the Institutes of Harmony* in which he seems to discourse on the discipline of music with such learning and eloquence that no one yet (and let this be said with the indulgence of all) has treated this particular subject more clearly or fully, who is there that would not long for the second book of compositions? And all the more so, because he very frequently makes mention of these matters in the earlier book? Another motive is that all should understand that this same artist is able to discourse learnedly on the theoretical aspects of music and to produce the most lovely of all compositions'.[28]

In terms of 'exempla', there are some major differences between the two editions of *Le istitutioni harmoniche*, a fact that also affects the two motets under discussion. In the version of 1558, Zarlino only mentions *Miserere mei Deus*, which suggests that *Misereris omnium* was composed at a later date. Both motets are mentioned twice in the edition of 1573. In the fourth book of *Le istitutioni harmoniche*, which is dedicated to modal theory, Zarlino cites them side by side in his chapter on the hypophrygian mode.[29] After Josquin's *De profundis*, Willaert's *Peccata Domine*, *Rompi dell'empio cor*, and *Laura mia sacra*, he adds: 'I, too, have written many compositions in this mode, among them the motet *Miserere mei, Deus, miserere mei* for six voices, and also *Misereris omnium*'.[30] The third book of this treatise is devoted to counterpoint and compositional techniques, and contains a large chapter with 'Alcuni avertimenti intorno le Compositioni, che si fanno à più di Tre voci'. One of the possibilities Zarlino discusses is the canonic treatment of a cantus firmus: '[Composers] also took a cantus firmus tenor and added to it (as is still done today) two or three parts in consequence, writing further parts upon these'.[31] The first 'exempla' he mentions are Willaert's seven-voice motets *Verbum supernum* (on the chant *O salutaris hostia*) and *Praeter rerum seriem*,

---

[28] [Post illum librum cui titulum indidit De Institutionibus Harmonicis, in quo de musica disciplina ita docte pariter et diserte disputare videtur, ut nemo hactenus (quod pace omnium dictum esto) rem ipsam dilucidius, et copiosus tractaverit, quis est qui hunc alterum modulationum librum, non desiderat? idq; eo maxime, quod plurimum de iis in superiore libro illo meminerit? Huc accedit illud, quo intelligant omnes, eiusdem artificis esse, et de Theoricis musicae docte disserere, et modulationes quasque suavissimas efficere posse]. Translation quoted after Judd, *Reading Renaissance Music Theory*, 248.

[29] In the edition of 1558, the discussion on the fourth mode is to be found in chapter 21. Due to Zarlino's renumbering of the twelve modes in the edition of 1573, the hypophrygian mode became the sixth mode (chapter 23).

[30] [Composi ancora io molte cantilene, tra le quali si trova à sei voci il Motetto *Miserere mei Deus, miserere mei*: & anco *Misereris omnium Domine*].

[31] [Pigliavano anco un Tenore di canto fermo, sopra ilquale accommodavano (come fanno etiandio al d'hoggi) due, o Tre parti in Consequenza; & dapoi sopra di quelle fanno l'altre] (Book III, chapter 66).

which were to be published in his *Musica Nova*. Zarlino then cites three of his own compositions: apart from the seven-voice *Pater noster - Ave Maria*, he provides some details about his *Miserere mei Deus* and *Misereris omnium*, and focuses on their common affinities: 'Similar examples are the motets *Miserere mei Deus, miserere mei* on the antiphon *Ne reminiscaris Domine*, and *Misereris omnium Domine* on the same antiphon *Ne reminiscaris* and on another Tenor *Miserere mei Deus*; I composed both of them for six voices'.[32] Zarlino thus clearly stresses the double nature of *Misereris omnium*'s preexistent material, the cantus firmus being based on a Gregorian chant,[33] the ostinato referring to Josquin's *Miserere mei Deus* and the web of intertextual relationships it initiated.[34] These observations add a new twist to the interpretation of Zarlino's statements on the 'soggetto' in general, as he explains it in Book III, chapter 26 of his *Istitutioni harmoniche*. There, he compares the method of a composer to that of a poet:

> 'The poet's subject is [an incident of] history or a tale. Whether the story is of his own invention or borrowed from others, he adorns and polishes it with various embellishments as it pleases him. He omits nothing fit and suitable to delight the minds of his listeners, achieving thus something that is magnificent and marvelous. The musician has the same end, namely to serve and to please the minds of his listeners with harmonic accents, and he also has a subject upon which to construct his

[32] Ibid.: [Nella medesima maniera si ritrovano i motetti; *Miserere mei Deus, miserere mei*, sopra l'Antiphona, *Ne reminiscaris Domine*; sopra laquale etiandio & sopra un'altro Tenore, *Miserere mei Deus* si troverà composto il Motetto: *Misereris omnium Domine*: i quali composi à Sei: et la Oratione dominicale; *Pater noster*, con la Salutatione angelica *Ave Maria*: a Sette voci]. In the first edition of *Le istitutioni harmoniche*, Zarlino mentions Jachet de Mantua's *Descendi in ortum meum* for six voices. In the version of 1573, this 'exemplum' was substituted by his own *Misereris omnium*.

[33] In Book III, chapter 66 Zarlino gives some additional advice about the compositional process of such cantus firmi: 'Such consequents should be and usually are written before the other parts are composed, but in writing them one must always keep the unwritten parts in mind and consider how they will fit into the texture; otherwise he will have double the work when he finds later that something goes wrong in the consequent' [Tali Consequenze si sogliono, & si debbono veramente comporre, prima che si componghino le altre parti: ma bisogna haver sempre riguardo nel comporle, in qual maniera le parti, che si hanno da aggiungere, si possino accommodare nella cantilena: accioche non si habbia doppia fatica nel comporre tutto'l corpo della Compositione quando venisse alcuna cosa di sinistro in tali Consequenze].
It should be mentioned here that in the 1573-edition of *Le istitutioni harmoniche*, Zarlino treated canons more extensively (Book III, chapter 36), a fact that might be linked to the publication of the *Modulationes sex vocum*. See also Wolfgang Horn, *"Est modus in rebus..."*. *Gioseffo Zarlinos Musiktheorie und Kompositionslehre und das "Tonarten"-Problem in der Musikwissenschaft* (unpublished Habilitationsschrift, Hochschule für Musik und Theater Hannover, 1996), 170-85. I am grateful to Professor Horn for sharing the manuscript of his study with me.

[34] Interestingly enough, Zarlino does not mention Josquin's motet in his *Istitutioni harmoniche*.

composition, which he adorns with various movements and harmonies to bring maximum pleasure to the audience'.[35]

He then discusses the various possible origins of the musical subject:

'The 'soggetto' may be one of several kinds. It may be taken from a composition of another, fitted to his own and adorned by various parts, as he pleases to the best of his talent. Such a 'soggetto' may be of several kinds: it may be a tenor or other plain-chant part, or a part from a polyphonic composition ['canto figurato']. It may also consist of two or more voices, one of which may follow another in a fugue or consequence, or be organized in some other manner. Indeed, the types of such 'soggetti' are potentially infinite in number'.[36]

Through the double reference to the *Miserere*-motif – via the 'soggetto ostinato' of *Misereris omnium* on the one hand, and the opening of *Miserere mei Deus* on the other – Zarlino must have had a firm intention. After Willaert, Rore, Vicentino, and many others, he too wanted to be part of what had become a revered tradition by composing yet another variation on the *Miserere*-theme. In a recent publication on the genesis of Zarlino's *Si bona suscepimus*, Cristle Collins Judd observes a similar working method:

'Zarlino points to the possibility of composing out of a tradition or complex of works, thus giving the composer entry into a musical-discursive space through tangible connections to a group of other musical works. Such a framework of thought allows a compositional tradition's

---

[35] [[H]à nel suo Poema per soggetto la Historia, overo la Favola, la quale, o sia stata ritrovata da lui, overo se l'habbia pigliata da altrui: l'adorna, & polisse [...] con varij costumi [...]; cosi il Musico, oltra che è mosso dallo istesso fine, cioè di giovare, & di dilettare gli animi de gli ascoltanti con gli accenti harmonici, hà il Soggetto, sopra il quale è fondata la sua cantilena, laquale adorna con varie modulationi, & varie harmonie, di modo che porge grato piacere a gli ascoltanti.] English translation quoted after Guy A. Marco and Claude V. Palisca, *Gioseffo Zarlino: The Art of Counterpoint. Part Three of Le istitutioni harmoniche, 1558* (New York, 1983), 51.

[36] [Et tal Soggetto può essere in molti modi: prima può essere inventione propia, cioè, che il Compositore l'haverà ritrovato col suo ingegno; dipoi può essere, che l'habbia pigliato dalle altrui compositioni, accommodandolo alla sua cantilena, & adornandolo con varie parti, & varie modulationi, come più gli aggrada, secondo la grandezza del suo ingegno. Et tal Soggetto si può ritrovare di più sorte: percioche può essere un Tenore, overo altra parte di qualunque cantilena di Canto fermo, overo di Canto figurato; overo potranno esser due, o più parti, che l'una seguiti l'altra in Fuga, o Consequenza, overo a qualunque altro modo: essendo che li varij modi di tali Soggetti sono infiniti] (Ibid. 52).

accumulation of utterances to serve as a model for the creation of a musical work, to create a contrapuntal grammar of the *soggetto*'.[37]

One might even say that with *Misereris omnium*, Zarlino wanted to emulate Josquin's famous model by embedding the ostinato in a texture with two other layers (the main text and the canon), thus creating a polytextual motet in the true sense of the word.

ZARLINO AND THE COURT OF FERRARA

During the sixteenth century, composers recognized the expressive and contemplative power of Josquin's *Miserere mei Deus*.[38] The motet, written during Josquin's stay in Ferrara at the request of his patron Ercole I d'Este,[39] seems to have had a particular significance at the Estense court, which remained long after the composer's death. I have already mentioned the *Infelix ego*-settings by Willaert, Rore, and Vicentino, who also served one or more members of the Este-family for a certain period of their professional life. All of these motets are written for six voices and quote Josquin's ostinato – either literally or with slight changes – in one part. According to Patrick Macey, this means that 'we can thus begin to see the outlines of an interesting pattern of Este patronage'.[40] In the case of Zarlino's *Miserere mei Deus* and *Misereris omnium*, such a link with Ferrara has never been explored.[41] This is all the more surprising, since both motets appear in the manuscript Modena, Biblioteca Estense, Mus. Ms.

---

[37] Cristle Collins Judd, 'Learning to Compose in the 1540s: Gioseffo Zarlino's *Si bona suscepimus*', in Suzannah Clark and Elizabeth Eva Leach (eds.), *Citation and Authority in Medieval and Renaissance Musical Culture: Learning from the Learned* (Studies in Medieval and Renaissance Music, 4; Woodbridge, 2005), 184-205 at 205.

[38] See f.i. Lester D. Brothers, 'On Music and Meditation in the Renaissance: Contemplative Prayer and Josquin's *Miserere*', *The Journal of Musicological Research*, 12 (1992), 157-87. In his *Dum vastos Adriae*, a tribute to Josquin, Jachet de Mantua counted *Miserere omnium* among the composer's most famous works. See Albert Dunning, 'Josquini antiquos, Musae, memoremus amores. A Mantuan Motet from 1554 in Homage to Josquin', *Acta Musicologica*, 41 (1969), 108-16.

[39] On Josquin and Ferrara, see among others Lewis Lockwood, 'Josquin at Ferrara: New Documents and Letters', in Edward E. Lowinsky and Bonnie J. Blackburn (eds.), *Josquin des Prez. Proceedings of the International Josquin Festival-Conference Held at the Juilliard School at Lincoln Center in New York City, 21-25 June 1971* (London, New York, and Toronto, 1976), 103-37; Paul Merkley, 'Josquin Desprez in Ferrara', *The Journal of Musicology*, 18 (2001), 544-83.

[40] Macey, *Josquin's Miserere mei Deus*, 26.

[41] In his dissertation, Macey discusses Zarlino's *Misereris omnium* (he doesn't mention *Miserere mei Deus*), but sees no connection with the Este court: 'It seems more likely that they [Zarlino and Jacquet de Berchem] incorporated Josquin's *soggetto* as a generalized expression of penitence' (p. 178).

C313-314, which also contains Willaert's *Infelix ego*.[42] According to Jessie Ann Owens, these luxury partbooks were probably written in Ferrara about 1560.[43] If this hypothesis is correct, this means that *Misereris omnium* was composed about six years before its publication in the *Modulationes sex vocum*.[44] Since the partbooks were used at the ducal chapel, the pieces must have had a special significance for Duke Alfonso. One might even speculate that *Misereris omnium* was explicitly written to be included in the prestigious Este manuscript. But Willaert and Zarlino have even more in common as regards their relationship with the Este court. Archival research has pointed out that Zarlino was closely involved in the publication history of Willaert's *Musica Nova*. This monumental collection of motets and madrigals was dedicated to Alfonso d'Este, but it is known that the music circulated privately for some twenty years before it was printed in 1559 by Antonio Gardano. In 1554, Alfonso d'Este obtained the unique manuscript of Willaert's music from the singer Polissena Pecorina. A contract was made, but although this source is lost, a document from August 1572 (regarding a private agreement between Duke Alfonso and Pecorina's heirs) tells us that Zarlino was present as a witness of the transaction.[45] A few years later, in 1558, the publication of the *Musica Nova* was threatened by a conflict between Alfonso and the nobleman Antonio Zantani, who planned to print four of Willaert's madrigals prior to their publication in the *Musica Nova*. Alfonso, who wanted to be the sole owner of the music, took the matter very serious and engaged several persons to solve the problem. From a letter Zantani wrote to Girolamo Faleti (Alfonso's Venetian ambassador) we learn that both Gardano and Zarlino had been asked to defend Alfonso's case.[46]

---

[42] These manuscript partbooks also contain two other motets by Zarlino: *Si bona suscepimus* and *Ascendo ad patrem*, which were published in his *Musici quinque vocum moduli* and *Modulationes sex vocum* respectively.

[43] Jessie Ann Owens, *An Illuminated Manuscript of Motets by Cipriano de Rore (München, Bayerische Staatsbibliothek, Mus. Ms. B)* (Ph.D. dissertation, Princeton University, 1979), 67. She believes the manuscripts to be the work of Ernando Bustamante, who (together with his brother Domenico) was paid as a singer at the Este court from 1560 onwards: see also Anthony A. Newcomb, *The musica secreta of Ferrara in the 1580's* (Ph.D. dissertation, Princeton University, 1969), 228.

[44] The composition of *Miserere mei Deus* predates the manuscript, since it was already mentioned in the first edition of Zarlino's *Istitutioni harmoniche*.

[45] See document 75 in Jessie Ann Owens and Richard J. Agee, 'La stampa della "Musica Nova" di Willaert', *Rivista italiana di Musicologia*, 24 (1989), 218-305 at 294-8: 'Io pre Gioseffo Zarlino Clodensis fui presente et son testimonio di quanto di sopra è scritto' (p. 295).

[46] Owens and Agee, 'La stampa', 274 (document 45): 'Io non harei mai pensato che V. S. mi fese dispiacer né cosa che per lei mi dolese o dese fastidio che a peticion de certi mecanici come è il Gardana, Pre Isepo Zerlin, senza averme mai fato intender cosa alcuna […]'.

In the first part of his *Dimostrationi harmoniche* (Venice, 1571), Zarlino alludes to the publication history of Willaert's *Musica Nova* and Alfonso's efforts to protect Willaert's music. The setting of this treatise is the state visit Duke Alfonso II paid to Venice in April 1562. Zarlino reports that Alfonso also went to see Willaert, who 'did not leave his house because he suffered from gout'.[47] It is told how the Duke and the composer 'commemorated the courtesy his Lordship had shown [towards Willaert], and how dear his compositions were to him, and how through him a large part of compositions, which he had composed and which remained almost buried, had come to light'.[48] Needless to say, Zarlino refers to the many obstacles the publication of *Musica Nova* had to cope with, a fact that is also stressed in Francesco Dalla Viola's dedication of this print to Alfonso d'Este. Alfonso's visit to Venice has been described in various other documents.[49] The Duke was accompanied by about thirty singers and instrumentalists from the Ferrarese music chapel, under the direction of Francesco Dalla Viola, who had succeeded Cipriano de Rore as chapel master of Alfonso's court in 1559.[50] Music was sung at many occasions: in St Mark's, at the Palazzo Ducale, on the Canal Grande etc. One evening, Alfonso received the doge, the 'Signoria', and various ambassadors in his Venetian palazzo for a 'concerto maraviglioso di musica di varie sorti d'istromenti'.[51] Interestingly enough, Zarlino also contributed a piece for the festivities of Alfonso's Venetian visit: he composed the celebratory motet *Parcius Estenses proavos Ferraria - Clara sit innumeris*, which was to be published in the *Primo libro de gli eterni motetti* (Venice, 1567):[52]

---

[47] *Dimostrationi harmoniche*, 1: '[E]ssendo molestato dalle podagre, non si partiva di casa'.

[48] *Dimostrationi harmoniche*, 1-2: '[…] i quali commemoravano le cortesie, che questo Sig. eccellentissimo molte volte usato gl'havea; & quanto care gli erano le sue compositioni; & come per lui erano venute à luce una grandissima parte di quelle cose, ch'egli havea gia composto; le quali stavano quasi sepolte'.

[49] See for example Anon., *L'entrata che fece in Vinegia, l'Illustrissimo et Eccellentissimo S. Duca Alfonso II. Estense duca V. di Ferrara* (Venice, 1562) and C. Zio, *La solenníssima entrata dell'Illustrissimo, & Eccellentissimo Signor Duca di Ferrara ne la città di Venetia* (Bologna, 1562).

[50] The presence of Alfonso's musicians is also mentioned in Zarlino's *Dimostrationi harmoniche*, 1: 'This Lordship had taken with him the best musicians he had at his disposal. Among them was Francesco Viola, his chapel master and a dear friend of mine' (Havea questo Sig. seco menato i miglior Musici, ch'appresso di lui si ritrovavano; tra i quali […] era Francesco Viola suo Maestro di Cappella & mio singolare amico).

[51] Anon., *L'entrata che fece in Vinegia*, fol. 7r. Quoted after David Bryant, 'Alcune osservazioni preliminari sulle notizie musicali nelle relazioni degli ambasciatori stranieri a Venezia', in Francesco Degrada (ed.), *Andrea Gabrieli e il suo tempo. Atti del convegno internazionale (Venezia 16-18 settembre 1985)* (Florence, 1987), 181-92 at 190.

[52] David Bryant, 'Musica e musicisti', in Gaetano Cozzi and Paolo Prodi (eds.), *Storia di Venezia dalle origini alla caduta della Serenissima* (Rome, 1997), vi. 449-67 at 450 and 454.

Prima pars
Parcius Estenses proavos Ferraria iactet
  Et sileat priscos Itala terra Duces
Hic erit Alphonsus magno satus Hercule solus
  Qui referet populis aurea secla suis.

> [Let Ferrara be more sparing in her boasts of her Este
> forefathers, and the land of Italy be silent about her
> ancient dukes: this Alfonso, born of the great Ercole,
> shall alone be he that brings back the golden age to his
> peoples.

Secunda pars
Clara sit innumeris maiorum fama tropheis
  Maior hic aeterno faedere pacis erit
Obvia quid cessas Venetorum curia patrum
  En venit Eoo qualis ab orbe dies.

> Though his forebears' renown be illustrious for their
> countless trophies, he will be greater for the everlasting
> pact of peace; why do you tarry on your way to meet
> him, senate of the Venetians? Lo, he comes as gorgeous
> as the day comes from the east.][53]

It is not unthinkable that it was at this occasion that Duke Alfonso awarded
Zarlino with two golden medals. Indeed, as we can read in the inventory of
Zarlino's goods, which was drawn up shortly after his death in February 1590,
he kept 'doi medaglie d'oro del duca di Ferrara' in his house.[54] Thus although
Zarlino was never officially associated with the Este court, there is enough
evidence to assume that he had good connections with this family in general
and Duke Alfonso II in particular.[55]

---

[53] I am grateful to Leofranc Holford-Strevens for the translation of this text.

[54] Archivio di Stato di Venezia, Cancellaria inferiore, miscellanea notai diversi, b. 43, notaio G.N.
Doglioni (8 February 1590). Quoted after Isabella Palumbo-Fossati, 'La casa veneziana di
Gioseffo Zarlino nel testamento e nell'inventario dei beni del grande teorico musicale', *Nuova
Rivista Musicale Italiana*, 20 (1986), 633-49.

[55] It should also be mentioned here that Zarlino dedicated his treatise *Utilissimo trattato della
Patientia* (Venice, 1583) to 'Suor Leonora d'Este' (1515-1575). It is a moral text, in which he
advises her to bear her mother's death and to put her trust in God. Eleonora d'Este also inspired
Zarlino to write his *Sopplimenti musicali* (Venice, 1588), as we can read in Book VIII, chapter
3 (entitled 'Che gli Antichi sonavano in Consonanza; & se l'Organo nostro Istrumento sia
antico ò moderno').

With the composition of *Miserere mei Deus* and *Misereris omnium*, Zarlino was able to pursue several goals. First of all, he paid a double homage to the musical past by refering to a tradition that had started with Josquin's *Miserere mei Deus* and that was kept alive by the *Infelix ego*-settings of Willaert, Rore, and Vicentino. Through the publication of his musical diptych in the *Modulationes sex vocum* of 1566, it becomes clear once more that 'Zarlino masterfully and meticulously manipulated his public image through the medium of print'.[56] Around *Miserere mei Deus* and *Misereris omnium*, he has woven a web of self-citation on several levels. Not only do both pieces refer to each other through their liturgical (Ash Wednesday), thematic (penitential tone), and musical correspondences (quotation of the *Miserere*-motif, two-part canon on the same cantus firmus), but Zarlino also connects them twice in the revised edition of *Le istitutioni harmoniche*. Apart from their intrinsic qualities, *Miserere mei Deus* and *Misereris omnium* were part of Zarlino's 'hidden agenda', which consisted of strategically promoting his theoretical and musical achievements as being two unseparable pillars of his oeuvre.[57]

---

[56] Judd, *Reading Renaissance Music Theory*, 184.
[57] See also his statements about the 'musico perfetto' in Book I, chapter 11 of *Le istitutioni harmoniche*.

BEATI OMNES, QUI TIMENT DOMINUM À 5.
ODER: VON DEN SCHWIERIGKEITEN,
ORLANDO DI LASSOS MOTETTEN ZU EDIEREN

Bernhold Schmid

Kein Komponist des 16. Jahrhunderts war zu Lebzeiten weiter verbreitet als Orlando di Lasso. Aus den Jahren 1555 bis 1687 sind über 470 Einzel- und Sammeldrucke mit seinen ca. 1200 gedruckten Werken erhalten (wohingegen nur ca. 160 Sätze zeitgenössisch ausschließlich handschriftlich überliefert sind). Vor allem einzelne Chansons brachten es auf etwa 30 und mehr Drucke: So ist *Je l'ayme bien* 31 Mal gedruckt, davon allein im Jahr 1570 dreimal. Zu den 28 Drucken für *Susanne un jour* kommen noch 22 Ausgaben in Tabulatur. Und so manche Chanson wurde mehrfach kontrafaziert.[1] Auch die Motetten waren zum Teil außerordentlich weit verbreitet: So wurde das *Nürnberger Motettenbuch* 1562-4[2] in den dortigen Offizinen Montanus und Neuber, Ulrich Neuber bzw. Gerlach insgesamt achtmal aufgelegt; der Nachdruck bei Gardano (erstmals als 1562-10) liegt in fünf Auflagen vor; schließlich druckten auch Scotto (1566-14) und Rampazetto (1566-16) diese äußerst erfolgreiche Sammlung nach. Nimmt man zu diesen 15 Auflagen und Nachdrucken noch weitere Drucke, in die Motetten des Nürnberger Buchs aufgenommen wurden, etwa die bei Katharina Gerlach erschienenen *Fascicvli Aliqvot* (1582-8 und 1589-3) sowie Ausgaben bei le Roy & Ballard oder Haultin, so kommen wir auch hier auf bis zu 25 gedruckte Quellen.[3] Große Verbreitung erfuhren auch die im *Antwerpener Motettenbuch* (1556-1) bei Jean Laet erstgedruckten Sätze.[4]

---

[1] Vgl. dazu Horst Leuchtmann und Bernhold Schmid, *Orlando di Lasso. Seine Werke in zeitgenössischen Drucken 1555–1687* (Orlando di Lasso. Sämtliche Werke, Supplement, 1–3; Kassel, 2001), 1. 11–13.

[2] Die Drucksiglen nach Leuchtmann/Schmid, *Orlando di Lasso.*

[3] Zur Überlieferungsgeschichte der Nürnberger Motetten insgesamt siehe Orlando di Lasso, *Sämtliche Werke*, zweite, nach den Quellen revidierte Auflage der Ausgabe von F.X. Haberl und A. Sandberger, 3: *Motetten II*, hrsg. von Bernhold Schmid (Wiesbaden, 2004), S. LXXIII–LXXV. Ein ausführlich diskutiertes Stemma der Nürnberger Auflagen und der italienischen Nachdrucke des gesamten Werks in Orlando di Lasso, *Sämtliche Werke*, zweite, nach den Quellen revidierte Auflage [...], 5: *Motetten III*, hrsg. von Bernhold Schmid (Wiesbaden, 2006), S. XLIV–XLVI.

[4] Vgl. Lasso, *Sämtliche Werke*, 3, S. LXXI–LXXIII.

Trotz der oft großen Anzahl von Quellen gestaltet sich die Wahl der Leitquelle, der die Edition zu folgen hat, mitunter verhältnismäßig einfach.[5] So bei Drucken wie den Motettenbüchern aus Antwerpen oder Nürnberg, wo wir es jeweils mit recht sorgfältig erstellten Erstdrucken zu tun haben. Komplizierter wird die Situation, wenn bei einem als Leitquelle in Frage kommenden Druck ein Stimmbuch verloren ist, wie beim *Modvlorvm Orlandi de Lassvs. quaternis [...] vocibus modulatorum, Secvndvm Volvmen* 1565-11 (le Roy & Ballard). Dieser Druck könnte ein Erstdruck sein,[6] wiewohl im Titel ein Hinweis fehlt. Zumindest sind 21 der 25 enthaltenen Sätze dort erstbelegt; wenn man dann noch berücksichtigt, dass wir es mit einem vorzüglich ausgeführten Druckwerk zu tun haben, bietet sich 1565-11 als Leitquelle an. In solchen Fällen ist die fehlende Stimme am besten aus einem Druck zu ergänzen, der sich durch einen Vergleich der vorhandenen Stimmen als Nachdruck der ausgewählten Leitquelle entpuppt hat. Peter Bergquist hat entsprechende Abhängigkeiten für den zweiten Band der *Selectissimae Cantiones* 1568-4 (Theodor Gerlach) gegenüber 1565-11 (le Roy & Ballard) erkannt und für seine Ausgabe der Motetten aus 1565-11 den dort fehlenden Superius aus 1568-4 genommen;[7] die revidierte Neuausgabe der Motetten im Rahmen der Lasso-Gesamtausgabe verfährt für 1565-11 meist ebenso.

Wie jedoch ist zu verfahren, wenn sich beim Vergleichen des Notentexts der zwei genannten Quellen herausstellt, dass in einigen Fällen 1568-4 von 1565-11 deutlich abweicht? Bergquist hat eben diese Situation für zwei in beiden Drucken überlieferte Motetten festgestellt, nämlich für *Deus noster refugium* (1565-11,12; LV 223) und *Beati omnes, qui timent Dominum* mit secunda pars *Ecce sic benedicetur* (1565-11,15; LV 242).[8] Zwar ‚passt‘ im Fall des *Beati omnes* der Superius aus 1568-4 zu den vier von 1565-11 vorhandenen Stimmen, dennoch haben wir es mit klar unterscheidbaren Überlieferungssträngen zu tun. Es scheint deshalb nicht geraten, die in 1565-11 fehlende Stimme aus 1568-4 zu ergänzen.

---

[5] Bei den gedruckt überlieferten Sätzen spielen die handschriftlichen Quellen eine vergleichsweise geringe Rolle, da es sich oftmals um Abschriften nach Drucken handelt. Für die Edition
relevant sind selbstverständlich die wenigen vor der Drucklegung entstandenen Handschriften,
etwa München, Bayerische Staatsbibliothek, Mus.ms. 2744 aus den Jahren 1581-83, ein Codex
aus der Münchner Hofkapelle, der die in 1582-5 und in 1585-8 gedruckten Offertorien Lassos
enthält.

[6] Bergquist bezeichnet die in 1565-11 enthaltenen Sätze als „first editions"; vgl. Orlando di
Lasso, *The Complete Motets*, 4: *Motets for Six Voices from* Primus liber concentuum sacrorum
(Paris, 1564). Motets for Four to Ten Voices from Modulorum secundum volumen *(Paris,
1565)*, hrsg. von Peter Bergquist (Recent Researches in the Music of the Renaissance, 105;
Madison, 1996), S. xi.

[7] Ediert in Lasso, *Complete Motets*, 4. Zur Abhängigkeit der Quellen vgl. Bergquist in Lasso,
Complete Motets, 4, S. xv: „[...] are duplicated almost exactly [...]".

[8] Vgl. Bergquist in Lasso, *Complete Motets*, 4, S. xv.

Somit ist als erstes zu fragen, ob 1565-11 überhaupt als Leitquelle brauchbar ist. Und wenn ja, dann stellt sich als zweite Frage, welcher der sonstigen frühen Drucke zur Ergänzung des Superius herangezogen werden kann. Diesen Fragen sei im Folgenden für das *Beati omnes* nachgegangen. Ein gangbarer Lösungsweg ist nur aufgrund einer Kollationierung des gesamten Materials zu finden, bei der sich anhand unseres Stücks geradezu exemplarisch zeigen lässt, auf welche Schwierigkeiten der Herausgeber von Musik des 16. Jahrhunderts stoßen kann.

Zunächst ist jedoch eine nach Ländern und Verlegern geordnete Quellenliste für das *Beati omnes* aufzubauen:

Frankreich:	Le Roy & Ballard:	
	1565-11,15	Modvlorvm Orlandi de Lassvs. quaternis [...] vocibus modulatorum, Secvndvm Volvmen
	1573-11,1	Tertivs Liber Modvlorvm, Qvinis Vocibvs Constantivm, Orlando Lassvsio Avctore
	Haultin:	
	1576-14,12	Modvli. Quinque Vocum, Orlando Lassvsio Avctore
Italien:	Gardano:	
	1566-8,1	Orlandi Lassi Sacrae Cantiones [...] Liber Tertivs
	1569-4,1	Orlandi Lassi Sacrae Cantiones [...] Liber Tertivs
	1578-1,1	Orlandi Lassi Sacrae Cantiones [...] Liber Tertivs
	1587-1,1	Orlandi Lassi Sacrae Cantiones [...] Liber Tertivs
	1599-1,1	Orlandi Lassi Sacrae Cantiones [...] Liber Tertivs
	Tini:	
	1586-12,1	Orlandi Lassi Sacrae Cantiones [...] Liber Tertivs
Deutschland:	Theodor Gerlach:	
	1568-4,1	Selectissmae Cantiones [...] Qvinqve et Qvatvor Vocibvs (= 2. Teil)
	Katharina Gerlach:	
	1579-3,1	Altera Pars Selectissimarvm Cantionvm [...] Qvinqve et Qvatvor Vocibvs
	1587-3,1	Altera Pars Selectissimarvm Cantionvm [...] Qvinqve et Qvatvor Vocibvs
	Ulrich Neuber:	
	1569-15,8	Beati Omnes. Psalmvs CXXVIII [...] A Variis. [...] Mvsicae Artificibvs
	Nicolaus Heinrich:	
	1604-1,243	Magnum Opvs Mvsicvm

Tabelle 1. Die gedruckten Quellen zu Orlando di Lassos *Beati omnes*

Die Titelformulierungen deuten Abhängigkeiten an: Klar erkennbar sind die fünf Auflagen des *Liber Tertivs* bei Gardano, wobei allerdings die 1578-1 folgenden Drucke sowie Tinis 1586-12 inhaltlich verkürzt und umgestellt sind. Die minimalen Abweichungen beim Notentext sind als Flüchtigkeitsfehler einzustufen. Die beiden bei Katharina Gerlach erschienenen Auflagen der *Selectissimae Cantiones* 1579-3 und 1587-3 basieren auf 1568-4; allerdings wurden die späteren Auflagen erweitert und durch Leonhard Lechner gründlich revidiert, was auch im Fall des *Beati omnes* eine Rolle spielt. Heinrichs *Magnum Opvs Mvsicvm* (die von Lassos Söhnen veranstaltete ‚Gesamtausgabe' der Motetten ihres Vaters) greift auf Lechners Edition der *Selectissimae Cantiones* zurück.[9] Haultins 1576-14 fußt auf Le Roy & Ballards 1573-11. Der letztgenannte Druck aber ist keineswegs eine unmittelbare Auflage von 1565-11, wie schon seine Nummerierung als *Tertivs Liber* (gegenüber *Secvndvm Volvmen*) zeigt. Offen muss zunächst noch die Zuordnung des *Beati omnes*-Drucks 1569-15 bleiben; schon deshalb, weil dies der einzige Sammeldruck (bestehend aus insgesamt 17 *Beati omnes*-Vertonungen verschiedener Komponisten) ist,[10] während Lassos Motette ansonsten nur in Einzeldrucken (das heißt zusammen mit anderen Werken dieses Komponisten) überliefert ist. Erst ein genauer Vergleich des Notentexts lässt indes klare Aussagen über die Abhängigkeiten der Drucke untereinander zu und macht eindeutige Überlieferungsstränge erkennbar.

Der Einstieg hierzu ergibt sich über eine auffallende Textvariante der secunda pars im *Beati omnes*-Druck 1569-15, die auch Auswirkungen auf den Notentext hat:

---

[9] Das *Magnum Opvs Mvsicvm* greift auf die Auflage 1587-3 der *Selectissimae Cantiones* zurück, wie sich gelegentlich feststellen lässt; vgl. Lasso, *Sämtliche Werke*, 3, S. LXX und Lasso, *Sämtliche Werke*, 5, S. LXI (dort im kritischen Bericht unter ‚– D, T-U T. 62–63').

[10] Dieser im Jahr 1568 von Clemens Stephani zusammengestellte, 1569 bei Ulrich Neuber in Nürnberg erschienene Druck ist den Brüdern Graf Georg Ernst (1511–83) und Graf Poppo (1513–74) von Henneberg, deren Residenz in Schleusingen (Thüringer Wald) war, gewidmet. In der Widmungsvorrede führt Stephani aus, dass er die Hochzeit von Georg Ernst zum Anlass genommen hatte, verfügbare Motetten über den in der Hochzeitsliturgie eine Rolle spielenden Psalm „Beati omnes" zur Gratulation zusammenzustellen. Der Druck enthält neben Lassos Komposition Sätze von Nicolas Champion, Cristóbal de Morales, Jacob Meiland, Antonio Scandello, Wolfgang Figulus, Matthias Eckel, Wolfgang Ottho (Egranus), Joachim a Burck, Andreas Schwartz Francus, Nicolas Gombert, Thomas Stoltzer, Ludwig Senfl, Lupus Hellinck, Stephan Zirler, Loyset Piéton sowie eine anonym überlieferte Motette. (Für die obigen Angaben zum Anlass des Drucks danke ich Angelika Zippl ganz herzlich. Zum Inhalt des Drucks vgl. Leuchtmann/Schmid, *Orlando di Lasso*, 1. 249–53.)

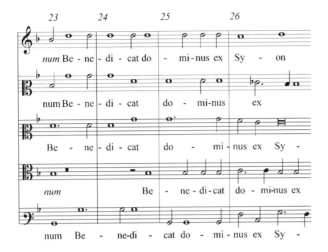

Beispiel 1. Orlando di Lasso, *Beati omnes*, secunda pars, T. 23–26 in der Fassung des
    Neuber-Drucks 1569-15

Der vertonte Text „Benedicat dominus ex Syon" weicht von der Fassung
der *Vulgata* ab; dort heißt es „Benedicat te Dominus ex Sion"; als Variante
gebräuchlich ist „Benedicat tibi Dominus ex Sion".[11] Betrachten wir dieselbe
Stelle nun in der Fassung des ältesten Drucks 1565-11, dessen Superius-
Stimmbuch verloren ist:

Beispiel 2. Orlando di Lasso, *Beati omnes*, secunda pars, T. 23–26 in der Fassung des
    Le Roy & Ballard-Drucks 1565-11

---

[11] Benutzt wurde folgende Ausgabe der Vulgata: *Biblia sacra iuxta vulgatam versionem*, hrsg.
von Bonifatius Fischer und Robertus Weber, 1–2, (Stuttgart, 1969). Band 1, 934 dieser Ausgabe enthält den Psalmtext; im kritischen Apparat wird „tibi" als Variante genannt, eine Fassung
ohne „te" oder „tibi" ist nicht aufgelistet.

Das in 1569-15 fehlende „tibi" ist jetzt ergänzt: um es unterzubringen, wurden Notenwerte aufgeteilt. Lediglich im Tenor fehlt „tibi" weiterhin; dort findet sich die aus 1569-15 bekannte Fassung. Der Version von 1565-11 folgt die französische Überlieferung, also 1573-11 und 1576-14; diese beiden Drucke enthalten jeweils den Superius, so dass die Stelle insgesamt folgendermaßen aussieht:

Beispiel 3. Orlando di Lasso, *Beati omnes*, secunda pars, T. 23–26 nach 1565-11 mit
ergänztem Superius aus 1573-11

Das folgende Notenbeispiel nach dem ältesten italienischen Druck 1566-8 bringt eine dritte Lösung, bei dem ebenfalls „tibi" – jetzt auch im Tenor – ergänzt wird, allerdings in anderer Weise als in 1565-11 und 1573-11:

Beispiel 4. Orlando di Lasso, *Beati omnes*, secunda pars, T. 23–26 in der Fassung des
Gardano-Drucks 1566-8

Diese Fassung findet sich in allen italienischen Drucken, darüber hinaus auch in der ersten Auflage der *Selectissimae Cantiones* bei Theodor Gerlach (1568-4). Die von Lechner redigierte Ausgabe 1579-3, außerdem die spätere Auflage 1587-3 und das *Magnum Opvs Mvsicvm* (1604-1) folgen der Version aus Beispiel 4 in den vier oberen Stimmen, oktavieren allerdings einige Noten des Basses nach unten:

Beispiel 5. Orlando di Lasso, *Beati omnes*, secunda pars, T. 23–26, Bass nach 1579-3

Zusammengefasst: für die fragliche Stelle haben wir es also mit vier Über-lieferungssträngen zu tun,

1) mit demjenigen des Neuber-Drucks 1569-15, der keine unmittelbare Nachfolge gefunden hat;

2) mit dem französischen Strang ab 1565-11;

3) mit dem italienischen Strang ab 1566-8, der Auswirkungen auf Deutschland hat (1568-4);

4) mit dem auf 1568-4 basierenden, durch Lechners redaktionellen Eingriff ab 1579-3 begründeten Strang.

Für das ganze Stück betrachtet ergeben sich allerdings keineswegs vier von einander unabhängige Traditionen. Vielmehr berühren sich die Überlieferungen in einigen Punkten, insbesondere die mit Lechner beginnende Überlieferung ist vielfach von anderen Drucken beeinflusst, wie später zu zeigen sein wird. Zunächst stellt sich die mit einiger Sicherheit zu beantwortende Frage, welche von den vier Überlieferungen des oben vorgestellten Abschnitts die älteste ist. Mutmaßlich handelt es sich um diejenige des Neuber-Drucks 1569-15 mit fehlendem „tibi"; trotz des fehlerhaften Texts könnte diese Fassung die von Lasso ursprünglich komponierte sein. Denn es ist sehr wohl denkbar, dass eine original hinsichtlich des Texts ‚falsche' (und als solche schon kursierende) Version später korrigiert worden ist. Hingegen ist der umgekehrte Weg, dass nämlich aus einer Version mit ‚richtigem' Text nachträglich eine in allen Stimmbüchern fehlerhafte Fassung entstanden wäre, kaum anzunehmen. Für die vorgetragene Argumentation spricht zudem, dass ja zwei Korrekturversuche vorliegen, von denen der eine gar noch in einem Stimmbuch die ‚falsche' Fassung übernimmt. Vielleicht hat Lasso ja selbst eine der beiden korrigierten Versionen veranlasst.

Es stellt sich die Frage nach derjenigen Quelle, der die Edition zu folgen hat. Zumindest auf den ersten Blick bietet sich 1569-15 als Leitquelle an (und nicht der älteste Druck 1565-11), da 1569-15 bei „Benedicat tibi Dominus ex Sion"

mutmaßlich die älteste Version überliefert. Eine Entscheidung ist allerdings
erst nach einer weiteren Prüfung des vorhandenen Quellenmaterials zu treffen.
Dabei erweist sich 1569-15 verschiedentlich als unzuverlässig: So fehlt in T. 69
der prima pars im Superius die erste Minima c^2; in T. 72 der prima pars steht im
Tenor als letzte Note ein a (statt b), das zum b im Bass und in der Quinta pars
dissoniert; und in der secunda pars findet sich im Tenor als zweite Note von T.
17 ein zumindest merkwürdig anmutendes d^1 (statt c^1). Des weiteren hat 1569-
15 diverse Abweichungen insbesondere bei der Textunterlegung, die sich weder
im von 1565-11 noch im von 1566-8 ausgehenden Überlieferungsstrang finden.
Stattdessen bieten alle anderen Quellen an den entsprechenden Stellen identische
Versionen. Die folgenden Beispiele demonstrieren die Varianten in 1569-15:

Beispiel 6a. Orlando di Lasso, *Beati omnes*, prima pars, T. 13–16, Quinta pars nach 1569-15

Beispiel 6b. Orlando di Lasso, *Beati omnes*, prima pars, T. 13–16, Quinta pars sonstige Überlieferung

Beispiel 7a. Orlando di Lasso, *Beati omnes*, prima pars, T. 24–26, Superius und Tenor nach 1569-15

Beispiel 7b. Orlando di Lasso, *Beati omnes*, prima pars, T. 24–26, Superius und Tenor sonstige Überlieferung

Beispiel 8a. Orlando di Lasso, *Beati omnes*, prima pars, T. 28–29, Contratenor nach 1569-15

Beispiel 8b. Orlando di Lasso, *Beati omnes*, prima pars, T. 28–29, Contratenor sonstige Überlieferung

Beispiel 9a. Orlando di Lasso, *Beati omnes*, secunda pars, T. 6–11, Contratenor nach 1569-15

Beispiel 9b. Orlando di Lasso, *Beati omnes*, secunda pars, T. 6–11, Contratenor sonstige Überlieferung

(Eine weitere Stelle sei nur erwähnt: die Unterlegung der T. 43–47 des Tenor in der I. pars lautet in 1569-15 nur „erit" statt „erit, et bene tibi erit".)

Die gezeigten, ausschließlich auf 1569-15 beschränkten Abweichungen (gegen die identische Version der übrigen Quellen), lassen den Schluss zu, dass 1569-15 wohl eigens redigiert worden sein muss, also zumindest an den Beispielstellen dann mutmaßlich doch von Lasso abweicht. Deshalb scheidet 1569-15 als Leitquelle aus, auch wenn die Passage mit fehlendem „tibi" in 1569-15 ursprünglich so auf Lasso zurückgehen könnte.

Als Leitquelle kommt also entweder doch der älteste Druck 1565-11 in Frage, zu dem dann freilich der Superius von einer anderen Quelle zu ergänzen ist, oder aber die älteste italienische Ausgabe, Gardanos 1566-8. Um dies zu klären, ist es sinnvoll, nochmal den Neuber-Druck 1569-15 heranzuziehen. Wie festgestellt wurde, ist bei eben diesem Druck aufgrund des Textfehlers bei „tibi" eine gewisse Nähe zu Lasso wahrscheinlich. Somit ist anzunehmen, dass 1569-15 (trotz verschiedener mutmaßlicher redaktioneller Eingriffe) auch an anderen Stellen Lassos Original nahe stehen dürfte. Es bietet sich deshalb an, denjenigen von beiden Drucken 1565-11 und 1566-8 als Leitquelle auszuwählen, der näher an 1569-15 steht, zu diesem Druck also charakteristische Gemeinsamkeiten aufweist. Dieses Kriterium erfüllt 1565-11, wie ein detaillierter Quellenvergleich erweist: in der Tat finden sich in 1569-15 und 1565-11 gemeinsame Eigenarten, während der 1566-8 folgende Strang an eben diesen Stellen abweicht:

Beispiel 10a. Orlando di Lasso, *Beati omnes*, prima pars, T. 34–35, Bass nach 1565-11 und 1569-15

Beispiel 10b. Orlando di Lasso, *Beati omnes*, prima pars, T. 34–35, Bass nach der 1566-8 folgenden Überlieferung

Beispiel 11a. Orlando di Lasso, *Beati omnes*, prima pars, T. 68–70, Contratenor nach 1565-11 und 1569-15

Beispiel 11b. Orlando di Lasso, *Beati omnes*, prima pars, T. 68–70, Contratenor nach der 1566-8 folgenden Überlieferung

Erwähnt sei ferner eine Eigenheit der Textunterlegung in der prima pars: in 1565-11 und 1569-15 lauten die T. 18–21 der Quinta pars „qui ambulant in viis eius", in 1566-8 ist zu lesen „Labores manuum tuarum". Im ersten Fall handelt es sich um eine markante Variante bei der Vorzeichensetzung, während die beiden anderen Beispiele sich hinsichtlich der Textunterlegung deutlich unterscheiden; die Stelle aus dem Tenor (Beispiel 11a/11b) weist zudem einen Eingriff in den Notentext auf.

1565-11 ist somit als Leitquelle 1566-8 vorzuziehen. Dies lässt sich über eine weitere Beobachtung stützen: Oben war anhand der Stelle „Benedicat tibi Dominus ex Sion" dargestellt worden, dass Leonhard Lechners Ausgabe der *Selectissimae Cantiones* (1579-3) einen eigenen Strang begründet, da er an dieser Stelle im Bass gegenüber der Vorgängerauflage 1568-4 redaktionell eingreift. 1568-4 ist, wie ebenfalls oben festgestellt, dem mit 1566-8 beginnenden Überlieferungsstrang zuzuordnen. Lechners Änderungen beziehen sich indes nicht nur auf den Bass bei „Benedicat tibi Dominus ex Sion". An den oben gezeigten Stellen, wo 1565-11 und 1569-15 gemeinsame Charakteristika gegenüber der mit 1566-8 beginnenden Tradition aufweisen, folgt Lechner nicht 1568-4 (und damit indirekt 1566-8); er greift stattdessen die Lesarten von 1565-11 und 1569-15 auf. Nun behauptet Lechner in der Vorrede zum ersten Band seiner Ausgabe (1579-2), er habe gegenüber der ersten Auflage der *Selectissimae Cantiones* „ex iustis & emendatis exemplis" korrigiert.[12] Wenn seine Formulierung den Schluss zulassen sollte, er habe Quellen aus Lassos Umkreis zur Korrektur der ersten Auflage der *Selectissimae Cantiones* heranzogen – er war schließlich Schüler Lassos –, dann sind die Gemeinsamkeiten seiner Ausgabe mit 1565-11 geeignet, den Vorrang dieses Drucks und seine Brauchbarkeit als Leitquelle zu bestätigen. Es könnte nun zwar der Verdacht aufkommen, Lechner habe sich an 1569-15 orientiert, da sich die Gemeinsamkeiten seiner Ausgabe 1579-3 mit 1565-11 ja auch in 1569-15 finden. Überlegungen dieser Art zerschlagen sich jedoch rasch: Wenn Lechner 1569-15 benützt hätte, dann wäre anzunehmen, dass einige der auf 1569-15 beschränkten Varianten auch in 1579-3 auftreten müssten, was definitiv nicht der Fall ist. Da nun 1565-11 sich als der zur Leitquelle geeignetste Druck erwiesen hat, ist noch zu klären, aus welcher Quelle der in 1565-11 fehlende Superius zu ergänzen ist. Es empfiehlt sich, den (wie 1565-11) bei Le Roy & Ballard verlegten Druck 1573-11 zu verwenden. Zwar ist 1573-11 (*Liber Tertivs*) keine unmittelbare Auflage von 1565-11 (*Secvndvm Volvmen*), des weiteren wurde 1573-11 verglichen mit 1565-11 einer Redaktion unterzogen.

---

[12] Die Vorrede Lechners ist abgedruckt bei Leuchtmann/Schmid, *Orlando di Lasso*, 2. 24.

Diese beschränkt sich aber auf geringfügige Details wie Klauselauszierungen,[13] während beide Drucke ansonsten demselben Überlieferungsstrang angehören.

Ergebnis des Quellenvergleichs ist also zum einen, dass 1565-11 ergänzt durch den Superius aus 1573-11 als Leitquelle 1566-8 vorzuziehen ist. Zum anderen lässt sich ein einigermaßen gesichertes Stemma für die Überlieferung von *Beati omnes, qui timent Dominum* aufbauen; ‚x' bezeichnet eine nicht erhaltene, aber hypothetisch angenommene gemeinsame Vorlage:

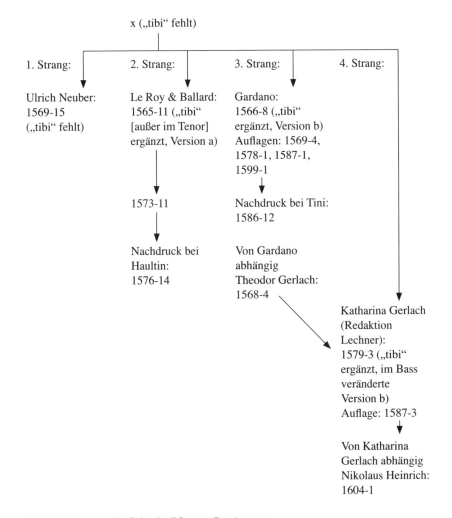

Tabelle 2. Stemma für Orlando di Lassos *Beati omnes*

---

[13] Vgl. z.B. prima pars, Contratenor T. 70, wo die in 1565-11 fehlende Klauselauszierung durch Fusae in 1573-11 ergänzt wurde. (Eventuell wäre für eine Edition des *Beati omnes* nach 1565-11 und 1573-11 die Auszierung im Superius in der secunda pars T. 6 zu eliminieren.)

Nicht präzise zu entscheiden ist freilich, ob Lechner für seine Ausgabe 1579-3 (außer auf die Vorgängerauflage 1568-4) direkt auf 1565-11 oder (wie durch Pfeil im Stemma angegeben) auf eine mit 1565-11 gemeinsame Vorlage zurückgegriffen hat. (Ebenso besteht zumindest theoretisch die Möglichkeit, dass Gardanos Fassung 1566-8 auf dem le Roy & Ballard-Druck 1565-11 beruht. Gardano hätte dann erkannt, dass die ihm vorliegende Version 1565-11 im Tenor fehlerhaft ist und im Zug der Korrektur des Tenors dann auch die übrigen Stimmen an dieser Stelle umgestaltet und alle weiteren Varianten gegenüber 1565-11 eingebaut.)

Das Resultat der obigen Diskussion der gedruckten Quellen zur Motette *Beati omnes, qui timent Dominum* ist deren Edition nach 1565-11 und 1573-11 in Band VII der revidierten Neuausgabe von Orlando di Lassos *Sämtlichen Werken*.

ÜBER ‚NATIONALSTILE' IN DER MOTETTE DES 16. JAHRHUNDERTS

Thomas Schmidt-Beste

„Der Stil der Kirchen und Höfe ist und bleibt bis zum Ende des 16. Jahrhunderts ein internationaler Stil."[1] Dieses Diktum Ludwig Finschers aus einem Aufsatz über „Die Entstehung nationaler Stile in der europäischen Musikgeschichte" (1984) könnte die Suche nach ‚nationalen' Elementen in der Musik des 16. Jahrhunderts von vornherein als vergebliche Liebesmühe erscheinen lassen. Der imitativ-polyphone Stil der Komponisten, die seit der berühmten, von Raphael Georg Kiesewetter und François-Joseph Fétis beantworteten Preisfrage „Welke verdiensten hebben zich de Nederlanders vooral in de 14e, 15e en 16e eeuw in het vak der toonkunst verworven?" aus dem Jahr 1826[2] als ‚Niederländer' figurieren[3] (heute politisch korrekter, aber mit denselben Konnotationen: ‚Franko-Flamen'[4]), ist allemal in der geistlichen Musik das „übernationale musikalische Idiom des Zeitalters", um erneut Finscher zu zitieren.[5] Wenig versprechend scheint somit die Suche nach ‚nationalen Charakteristika' in einer Musik, die in ganz Europa im Wortsinne ‚dieselbe Sprache' – Latein – spricht und die von Personen komponiert wurde, deren Mobilität und Internationalität immer wieder staunen lässt. Der bekannte Topos von Johannes Tinctoris bis zu Vincenzo Giustiniani, dass die Franzosen singen, die Deutschen brüllen, die Spanier heulen oder jammern, die Engländer jubilieren und die Italiener alternativ meckern, blöken oder klagen, ist zwar hinlänglich bekannt;[6] aber erstens handelt es sich eben um einen – zunehmend abgenutzten – Topos, einen schon damals offenbar zumindest teilweise satirisch eingesetzten Stereotyp mit unklarem Realitätsbezug, und zweitens bezieht sich dieser Topos eben auf die Art des Singens, und nicht auf die hier interessierende Art des Komponierens.

---

[1] Ludwig Finscher, „Die Entstehung nationaler Stile in der europäischen Musikgeschichte", in *Europäische Musik zwischen Nationalismus und Exotik* (Forum Musicologicum, 4; Winterthur, 1984), 33–56, hier 41.

[2] Publiziert Amsterdam 1829.

[3] Vgl. Jozef Robijns, Art. „Niederländische Musik", in *MGG* 9 (1961), 1461–1507.

[4] Vgl. Klaus Hortschansky, Art. „Frankoflämische Musik", *MGG2. Sachteil* 3 (1995), 673–88; auch Ignace Bossuyt, *Die Kunst der Polyphonie. Die flämische Musik von Guillaume Dufay bis Orlando di Lasso* (Zürich und Mainz, 1997) [Original: *De Vlaamse polyfonie* (Leuven, 1994)].

[5] Ludwig Finscher, „Die nationalen Komponenten in der Musik in der ersten Hälfte des 16. Jahrhunderts", in Franz Giegling (Hg.), *Bericht über den Neunten Internationalen Kongress Salzburg 1964* (Kassel, 1964), i. 37–45, hier 39.

[6] Vgl. Finscher, „Die Entstehung nationaler Stile", 36–40.

Die einzige *musikalische* Charakterisierung, die vermeintlich ‚nationale' Kategorien bemüht, liegt dagegen schon einige Jahrhunderte zurück: Die Notationstheorie des italienischen Trecento – bei Marchettus von Padua und anderen – differenziert bekanntlich zwischen einem „modus gallicus" oder „aer gallicus" im Gegensatz zum „modus" oder „aer ytalicus". Wie in den letzten Jahren von Oliver Huck schärfer als bisher herausgearbeitet, betrifft diese Unterscheidung grundlegende Mensurprinzipien: Grob gesagt, verstanden die Theoretiker unter „modus gallicus" die Disposition rhythmischer Werte in einem dreizeitigen Grundmuster, unter „modus ytalicus" die in einem zweizeitigen.[7] Und in der Tat verwenden französische Kompositionen bis weit ins 15. Jahrhundert hinein vorrangig die dreizeitige ‚prolatio maior', was auch in der Textdeklamation in einer Präferenz für alternierende lang–kurz–lang–kurz–lang–Rhythmen resultiert; die italienische Musik der Zeit gibt sich kosmopolitischer, indem sie neben der häufigeren Zweizeitigkeit durchaus auch den „modus gallicus" einsetzt – die Musik also gleichsam durch die Verwendung einer ‚Fremdsprache' anreichert.[8] Der Frage, welches ‚Nationalbewusstsein' sich in dieser Unterscheidung von ‚französisch' und ‚italienisch' manifestiert und inwieweit hier Prinzipien der jeweiligen volkssprachlichen Dichtung ihren Niederschlag finden, kann in diesem Kontext allerdings nicht nachgegangen werden – zumal diese spezifische Differenzierung sich im 16. Jahrhundert durch die allgemeine Durchsetzung der zweizeitigen Mensuren in Luft aufgelöst hat und auch im Schrifttum nicht mehr thematisiert wird.

Das ‚Nationale' scheint demnach in den Augen der Zeitgenossen – allemal was die geistliche Musik betrifft – keine vorrangige Rolle zu spielen. Gleichwohl stieß Finschers Skepsis gegenüber Nationalstilen im 16. Jahrhundert, wenn man die im Kongressbericht abgedruckte Diskussion als Anhaltspunkt nimmt, schon 1964 auf fast einhellige, im Tonfall meist vehemente Ablehnung;[9] die Vertreter der jeweiligen ‚nationalen' Musikwissenschaften fühlten sich offenbar bemüßigt, für das ihrige Territorium sehr wohl eine ‚eigene' Musik oder einen ‚eigenen' Kompositionsstil in Anspruch zu nehmen. Was aber dabei

---

[7] Vgl. Oliver Huck, „‚Modus cantandi' und Prolatio. ‚Aere ytalico' und ‚aere gallico' im Codex Rossi 215", *Die Musikforschung*, 54 (2001), 115–30; Thorsten Burkard und Oliver Huck, „Voces applicatae verbis. Ein musikologischer und poetologischer Traktat aus dem 14. Jahrhundert (I-Vnm Lat. Cl. XII.97 [4125]). Einleitung, Edition, Übersetzung und Kommentar", *Acta musicologica*, 74 (2002), 1–34.

[8] Vgl. Thomas Schmidt-Beste, „Aer ytalicus – aer gallicus? Text setting and musical rhythm in sacred compositions of Antonio Zacara da Teramo and his contemporaries", in Francesco Zimei (Hg.), *Antonio Zacara da Teramo e il suo tempo* (Documenti di storia musicale abruzzese, 2; Lucca, 2004), 279–99.

[9] „Symposium ‚Die Nationalen Komponenten in der Musik der ersten Hälfte des 16. Jahrhunderts'", in Franz Giegling (Hg.), *Bericht über den Neunten Internationalen Kongress Salzburg 1964* (Kassel, 1966), ii. 81–7.

alle Disputanten mit Finscher einte, war das Bemühen, die jeweils postulierten ‚Nationalstile' auch und vor allem der geistlichen Musik im Rahmen einer als selbstverständlich vorausgesetzten Stildichotomie zu verorten: derjenigen zwischen dem ‚franko-flämischen' – damals noch ‚niederländischen' – und dem ‚italienischen' Stil. Jeder schien zu wissen, worum es sich dabei handelte und setzte dieses Wissen auch beim Leser bzw. Zuhörer voraus. Da sich vor allem in diesem Spannungsfeld ein großer Teil gerade der geistlichen Musik des 16. Jahrhunderts anzusiedeln scheint und da sich meiner Meinung nach gerade hier das Prekäre einer ‚nationalen' Definition besonders deutlich zeigt, wird sich auch der folgende Beitrag hierauf konzentrieren.

Zunächst einmal gilt es, die unausgesprochenen Assoziationen, die sich mit der Dichotomie ‚franko-flämisch' gegen ‚italienisch' verbinden, in aller Kürze zu artikulieren. Johan Huizinga bringt den Stereotyp in seinem zwar bereits 1924 zum ersten Mal in deutscher Sprache publizierten, aber für das Geschichtsbild auch des ausgehenden 20. Jahrhunderts nach wie vor prägenden ‚Klassiker' *Herbst des Mittelalters* auf den Punkt:

> „Betrachtet man das italienische Quattrocento in seinem erhebenden Gegensatz zum spätmittelalterlichen Leben anderswo, dann empfindet man dieses Jahrhundert als ein Zeitalter des Ebenmaßes, der Heiterkeit und der Freiheit, rein und klangvoll […]. Überschaut man dagegen mit einem Blick die französisch-burgundische Welt des fünfzehnten Jahrhunderts, dann ist der Haupteindruck: düstere Grundstimmung, barbarische Pracht, bizarre und überladene Formen, eine fadenscheinig gewordene Phantasie".[10]

Huizinga meint hier zwar nicht die Musik, ja er meint nicht einmal das 16. Jahrhundert. Dennoch ist die Behauptung wohl nicht übertrieben, dass genau diese Vorstellung bis heute der Scheidung von ‚franko–flämischer' und ‚italienischer' Musik auch im 16. Jahrhundert zugrunde liegt: das Komplexe, Dichte, Mathematische, Polyphon–Verschlungene, Scholastische, Gotische, Nordische, ‚Dunkle' gegen das Schlichte, Lockere, Verständliche, Homophon–Deklamatorische, Humanistische, Südliche, ‚Helle' – letztlich eben auch:

---

[10] Johan Huizinga, *Herbst des Mittelalters* (München, 1924); original: *Herfsttij der middeleeuwen* (Haarlem, 1919, 5. Ausgabe 1941); hier zitiert nach der 11. Ausgabe (Stuttgart, 1975), 462–3.

Mittelalter gegen Renaissance.[11] Diese Dichotomie als ein durch ein bestimmtes Geschichtsbild geprägtes Vorurteil zu entlarven ist einfach, löst aber das Problem nicht: Abgesehen von der Hartnäckigkeit, mit der sie sich wie alle wohletablierten historischen Stereotype hält, scheint sie ja doch auch auf tatsächlich divergierende Kompositionsstile Bezug zu nehmen. Ein neues Erklärungsmodell für diese Stildivergenz müsste also anstelle des alten zumindest plausibel gemacht werden. Es zeigt sich allerdings, dass dabei geographische und kulturelle Aspekte durchaus eine Rolle spielen können, aber nicht in einem Sinn, der landläufig als ‚national' verstanden wird.

Zunächst gilt es, zwischen zwei Dingen zu unterscheiden: der geographischen Herkunft des Komponisten und dem Ort, an dem oder für den seine Kompositionen entstehen. Angesichts der geradezu chamäleonartigen Wandlungsfähigkeit der franko-flämischen Komponisten, die im 16. Jahrhundert ganz Europa bevölkerten, ist der erste dieser beiden Gesichtspunkte als primäres Definitionskriterium für einen ‚nationalen' Stil wohl hinlänglich diskreditiert und daher vergleichsweise rasch abzuhandeln. Als Beispiel hierfür kann Adrian Willaert dienen. Aus Brügge oder Roeselaere, jedenfalls aus Westflandern, stammend und damit auch flämischer Muttersprachler, verbrachte er offenbar zunächst einige Jahre in Frankreich und wurde dort zu einem der Protagonisten der dreistimmigen Chansontradition, bevor er ab etwa 1514 in Italien zu einer der prägenden Figuren des Madrigals wurde, später auch noch Villanellen publizierte, sich also sogar in einer neapolitanischen – wohlgemerkt nicht ‚italienischen' – Gattung betätigte. Und in der geistlichen Musik ist die stilistische Vielfalt nicht geringer: Wenn man Willaerts Motettenoeuvre durchgeht, fällt der Blick zunächst auf eine Reihe von vierstimmigen Kompositionen vermutlich aus seiner römischen Zeit, überliefert in den frühen, um 1520 entstandenen italienischen Handschriften, vor allem dem an der päpstlichen Kurie entstandenen Medici–Kodex (Florenz, Biblioteca Medicea–Laurenziana, Ms. Acquisti e doni 666) und dem Rusconi–Kodex (Bologna, Civico Museo Bibliografico Musicale, Ms. Q19), beide kopiert im Jahr 1518. Hier ist in der relativ offenen, gelegentlich mit Geringstimmigkeit und Homophonie operierenden Textur noch der Einfluss Josquins und seiner Generation zu spüren, wenn auch schon hier nicht in der beim älteren Meister zu konstatierenden

---

[11] Vgl. Laurenz Lütteken, „Italien, Deutschland und die Entstehung der musikalischen ‚Renaissance' im 19. Jahrhundert", in Bodo Guthmüller (Hg.), *Deutschland und Italien in ihren wechselseitigen Beziehungen während der Renaissance* (Wolfenbütteler Abhandlungen zur Renaissanceforschung, 19; Wiesbaden, 2000), 195–209, besonders 205; vgl. auch Annette Kreutziger-Herr, *Ein Traum vom Mittelalter. Die Wiederentdeckung mittelalterlicher Musik in der Neuzeit* (Köln etc., 2003), 163–7 („Deutsches, Nordisches Mittelalter").

Klarheit der Textpräsentation.[12] Ab 1527 schreibt Willaert in Venedig dann spezifisch venezianische Musik: Auffallend, da vom übrigen Oeuvre deutlich abgegrenzt, sind in dieser Zeit vor allem die doppelchörigen achtstimmigen Psalmen,[13] die bereits Willaerts Schüler Gioseffo Zarlino als Höhepunkt der Gattung hervorhob.[14] Diese Werke unterscheiden sich nun aber von den entsprechenden Psalmen und anderen liturgischen Vertonungen italienischer Komponisten womöglich in ihrer kompositorischen Qualität, keineswegs jedoch stilistisch: Die leicht durch polyphone Elemente aufgelockerte Bibelrezitation ist ganz ähnlich nicht nur bei Jacquet de Mantua, sondern auch bei Gaspare de Albertis oder Ruffino d'Assisi zu finden, wie überhaupt der vier- oder achtstimmige homophone Deklamationsstil auf der Basis des Falsobordone die liturgische Mehrstimmigkeit (Psalmen, Magnificat, Passionen, Lamentationen) der Zeit prägt.[15] Wohlgemerkt aber handelt es sich bei diesem Rezitations- oder Deklamationsstil, wie noch weiter auszuführen sein wird, nicht primär um einen spezifisch italienischen, sondern um einen spezifisch liturgischen Stil, dessen in der Tat besonders klare Art der Textpräsentation auf die entsprechenden Choralgattungen rekurriert. Die gleichzeitig komponierten freien, d.h. nicht unmittelbar liturgisch gebundenen Motetten Willaerts nämlich entsprechen keineswegs dem Stereotyp ‚italienischer' Musik: Es handelt sich um vorwiegend fünfstimmige und durchimitierte Kompositionen in ‚franko-flämischem' Kontrapunkt. Typisch hierfür sind etwa Willaerts Vertonungen in den *Cantiones quinque vocum selectissimae ... Liber primus* (Straßburg, 1539). Augenfällig ist in diesen Stücken nicht nur durchweg der ‚normale' imitatorische Beginn, sondern noch mehr die große Dichte und Melismatik des darauf folgenden Kontrapunktes, in schärfstmöglichem Kontrast zu den Psalmen für die venezianische Liturgie, obwohl ja auch diese Stücke in und vermutlich für Venedig komponiert wurden. Dies ist, wenn man denn die stereotype Dichotomie bemühen will, quintessentiell ‚niederländische' Musik. Noch in der *Musica Nova* von 1559 publiziert Willaert archaisierende

---

[12] Vgl. vor allem die Motetten aus dem römischen Medici–Kodex von 1518; vgl. *The Medici Codex of 1518. A Choirbook of Motets Dedicated to Lorenzo de' Medici, Duke of Urbino* [Edition, Faksimile und Kommentar], hrsg. von Edward E. Lowinsky (Monuments of Renaissance Music, 3–5; Chicago und London, 1968). Vgl. Ludwig Finscher, „Von Josquin zu Willaert – ein Paradigmenwechsel?", in Hanns-Werner Heister (Hg.), *Musik/Revolution. Festschrift für Georg Knepler zum 90. Geburtstag* (Hamburg, 1997), i. 145–173, hier 159ff.

[13] Vgl. Adrian Willaert, *Opera Omnia*, hrsg. von Heinrich Zenck und Walter Gerstenberg, viii [*Psalmi vesperales*] (Corpus Mensurabilis Musicae, 3; o.O., 1972).

[14] Vgl. Gioseffo Zarlino, *Istitutioni harmoniche* (2. Ausgabe, Venedig, 1573, repr. Ridgewood, 1966), 329–30 (über die Psalmvertonungen); ferner ebda. 422, über die richtige Textvertonung und Textunterlegung: „Ma perche in questa materia so potrà havere infiniti essempi, essaminando le dotte compositioni di Adriano & di quelli, che sono stati veramenti & sono suoi discepoli: & osservatori delle buone Regole [...]".

[15] Vgl. Thomas Schmidt-Beste, *Textdeklamation in der Motette des 15. Jahrhunderts* (Epitome Musical; Turnhout, 2003), 327ff. („Rezitatorische Gattungen").

Tenormotetten mit kanonischen Cantus Firmi, wie z.B. das sechsstimmige *Veni sancte spiritus* oder das siebenstimmige *Verbum supernum prodiens/O salutaris hostia*.[16] Auch diese Werke unterscheiden sich in der Art ihrer Textbehandlung und kontrapunktischen Dichte kaum von den zeitgleich entstandenen Motetten anderer Komponisten, und zwar – das ist entscheidend – unabhängig davon, ob diese in Italien (etwa durch Jacquet de Mantua oder Maistre Jhan) oder eben in Flandern und Frankreich (etwa bei Nicolas Gombert, Clemens non Papa oder Thomas Crecquillon) komponiert wurden.[17]

Gerade in der Motette scheint sich in den 1530er Jahren im Gegenteil eine Art ‚gesamteuropäischer Einheitsstil' auszubilden, mit phrasenweise geordneter und motivisch strukturierter Durchimitation, überlappenden Phrasen, vergleichsweise kurzen, der Liturgie oder der Bibel entnommenen Prosatexten, deren Deklamation dem grammatischen Akzent des Lateinischen folgt, sowie durchgängiger Vollstimmigkeit, d.h. dem Verzicht auf Abstufungen der Textur, wie wir dies von Josquin und seinen Zeitgenossen kennen. Zu betonen ist dabei erneut, dass die in Italien komponierten Motetten sich auch in den vermeintlich ‚italientypischen' Aspekten – ‚Korrektheit' der Textdeklamation und Textverständlichkeit durch Homophonie und Klarheit der Textur – keineswegs von den in Flandern entstandenen Kompositionen abheben. Man mag diesen Stil als ‚franko–flämisch' oder ‚niederländisch' bezeichnen, da die Franko-Flamen nun einmal die Protagonisten der Musik des 16. Jahrhunderts und damit auch dieses Musikstils waren. Es ist aber durchaus unklar, ob das entsprechende Satzmodell in den Jahrzehnten nach 1500 eher nördlich oder eher südlich der Alpen seinen Ausgang nahm – und somit ist eine ‚nationale' Verortung desselben gerade in diesem Fall hinfällig. Abgesehen einmal davon sind die kontrapunktisch–polyphonen Motetten Costanzo Festas und Giovanni Pierluigi da Palestrinas – von Italienern für Italiener komponiert – denen Willaerts ebenfalls ganz ähnlich.

Überhaupt scheint, soweit man sehen kann, die ‚franko–flämische' vielstimmige Durchimitation in ihrer Dichte und Komplexität des Satzes um die Jahrhundertmitte herum am intensivsten und konsequentesten nicht in Flandern, sondern an den habsburgischen Hofkapellen in Wien und Prag kultiviert; es scheint fast, also ob die zugegebenermaßen fast alle gezielt

---

[16] Vgl. Finscher, „Von Josquin zu Willaert", 155: „Der vorherrschende Eindruck dieses Stils ist Dichte der Struktur bis zur Undurchhörbarkeit, Klangfülle, Kontrastarmut, gleichmäßig hohe Intensität. [...] dieser Stil [kann] insgesamt wie in fast jedem seiner Details als extreme Reaktion auf Josquin, als anti-josquinisch verstanden werden [...]".

[17] Vgl. Thomas Schmidt-Beste, „Motivic structure and text setting in the motets of Clemens and Crecquillon", in Eric Jas (Hg.), *Beyond Contemporary Fame: Reassessing the Art of Clemens non Papa and Thomas Crecquillon* (Epitome musical; Turnhout, 2005), 255–82.

aus den habsburgischen Niederlanden importierten Musiker – Arnold von
Bruck, Jacobus Vaet, Pieter Maessens – noch ‚niederländischer' komponieren
wollten oder sollten als ihre in der Heimat gebliebenen Kollegen, was sich
auch in der hier besonders lange anhaltenden Pflege von kanonischen cantus–
firmus–Künsten niederschlägt. Die bei Willaert zu beobachtende Flexibilität
nicht nur in der Übernahme, sondern auch in der eigenständigen Prägung
von ‚fremdnationalen' Stilen ließe sich anhand vieler weiterer Komponisten
exemplifizieren – berühmte Beispiele wären Josquin Desprez, Jacques Arcadelt,
Orlando di Lasso, Cipriano de Rore. Kaum erinnert werden muss auch an den
vielbesprochenen ‚Mailänder Motettenstil', in dem ebenfalls zwei Italienfahrer
– Loyset Compère und Gaspar van Weerbeke – gemeinsam mit einem
Einheimischen – Franchino Gaffori – ein autochthones, aus der Lauda hervor
gegangenes Modell mit aus der Heimat mitgebrachten Erfahrungen in liedhafter
Deklamation zu einem zwar kurzlebigen, aber extrem charakteristischen Stil
verschmolzen.[18]

Noch schärfer lässt sich die Unabhängigkeit von Kompositionsstil und Herkunft
des Komponisten aber an der umgekehrten Situation nachweisen – also der
Präsenz vermeintlich ‚italienischer' Stilelemente in der Musik nördlich der
Alpen. Willaerts venezianische Psalmen oder der ‚Mailänder Motettenstil'
verkörpern ja das gewohnte Muster der assimilationsfähigen franko–flämischen
Italienfahrer, sind also noch Teil des traditionellen Interpretationsschemas.[19]
Das direkte Gegenstück zu Figuren wie Willaert, Josquin oder Lasso fehlt
zwar, da italienische Komponisten kaum den Weg in die Niederlande oder nach
Nordfrankreich fanden; aber es gibt sehr wohl Franko–Flamen, die in Flandern
‚italienisch' komponieren und Italiener, die in Italien ‚franko–flämisch' schrieben.
Costanzo Festa etwa, wohl der erste bedeutende einheimische Musiker Italiens
im 16. Jahrhundert, vertritt zwar in seinen liturgischen Kompositionen für die
päpstliche Kapelle erwartungsgemäß durchweg den klaren, rezitatorischen,
homophon–deklamatorischen Stil, in seinen Prosamotetten die ebenfalls stark
deklamatorische und durch Texturwechsel aufgelockerte post–Josquinsche
Textur. Andererseits ist er auch der Komponist von nicht weniger als siebzehn
Tenormotetten, einer erstens quintessentiell ‚niederländischen' und zweitens in
den 1530er Jahren auch nördlich der Alpen eigentlich schon längst obsoleten
Form. Sogar doppelte und kanonische Cantus firmi fehlen nicht – so etwa in

---

[18] Vgl. Ludwig Finscher, *Loyset Compère (c. 1450-1518). Life and Works* (Musicological Studies
  and Documents, 12; o.O., 1964); Ders., Art. „Motetti missales", in *MGG2. Sachteil* 6 (1997),
  549–52.
[19] Vgl. Wulf Arlt, *Italien als produktive Erfahrung franko-flämischer Musiker im 15. Jahrhundert*
  (Vorträge der Aeneas-Silvius-Stiftung an der Universität Basel, 26; Basel, 1993).

der sechsstimmigen Vertonung von *Exaltabo te Domine*,[20] mit „Benedictus domine deus" im ersten und „Cum iocunditate" im zweiten Tenor.

Dies ist in jeder Hinsicht ‚franko–flämische' Musik, noch dazu in ihrer konservativeren Ausprägung. Was könnte einen Komponisten, der Italien nie verließ, zu Werken in diesem Stil veranlasst haben? Die Antwort liegt wiederum eben nicht in seiner Herkunft, sondern in seiner Wirkungsstätte begründet – der päpstlichen Kapelle in Rom. Die generelle Tendenz zur Retrospektivität im Repertoire dieser Institution führt in den Jahrzehnten um 1500 zu einem regelrechten Boom der Tenormotette, die in einer der ältesten Handschriften des Fondo – dem Kodex Biblioteca Apostolica Vaticana, Cappella Sistina 15 (CS 15) von ca. 1495–1500 – zuerst dokumentiert ist und bis in die 1540er Jahre fortlebt.[21] Gewiss geht auch diese Tradition in CS 15 von Werken ‚niederländischer' Komponisten aus: von Johannes Regis, Loyset Compère, Gaspar van Weerbeke, Josquin Desprez und anderen. In den ersten Jahrzehnten des 16. Jahrhunderts wird aber aus einer allgemein–niederländischen dann eine spezifisch lokal–römische Tradition: schon in CS 15 sind außer den ältesten vertretenen Komponisten – Regis und Busnoys – alle übrigen direkt oder indirekt mit der päpstlichen Kapelle assoziiert. Josquins ‚altmodischste' Motette, *Illibata dei virgo nutrix*, entstammt wahrscheinlich diesem Kontext, und Compère und Weerbeke, die mit dem ‚Mailänder Motettenstil' immerhin direkt zuvor das exakte stilistische Gegenteil (und eine extrem ‚italienische' Schreibart) vertreten hatten, kehren hier gleichfalls zur archaischen Tenormotette zurück – und das wiederum wohl kaum aufgrund ihrer Herkunft, sondern eben aufgrund der lokalen Stilvorgaben.[22] Festa tat somit, indem er die Tradition der Tenormotette fortschrieb, aus heutiger ‚nationaler' Sicht etwas sehr Merkwürdiges – aus damaliger Lokalperspektive aber etwas ganz Naheliegendes. Immerhin publizierte selbst Palestrina noch 1570 und 1582 zwei *L'homme-armé*–Messen, quintessentiell ‚franko–flämische' Werke also, die James Haar wohl zu Recht der retrospektiven Traditionspflege der Cappella Sistina zugeordnet hat.[23]

---

[20] Vgl. Costanzo Festa, *Opera Omnia*, hrsg. von Albert Seay, iv (o.O., 1977), 1–14.

[21] Vgl. Richard Sherr, „*Illibata Dei Virgo Nutrix* and Josquin's Roman Style", *Journal of the American Musicological Society*, 41 (1988), 434–64; Repr. in ders., *Music and Musicians in Renaissance Rome and Other Courts* (Variorum Collected Studies Series, 641; Aldershot, 1999).

[22] Ebda., 443–51.

[23] James Haar, „Palestrina as historicist: The two L'homme armé Masses", *Journal of the Royal Musical Association*, 121 (1996), 191–205.

Und nicht genug damit, dass es mitten in Italien einen Ort gab, an dem Tenor-motetten und Cantus–firmus–Messen noch Jahrzehnte nach ihren gesamt-europäischen Verfallsdatum von Italienern komponiert und gesungen wurden; auf der anderen Seite der Alpen finden sich Stücke von Franko–Flamen, die auf den ersten Blick umstandslos einem ‚italienischen' Satzmodell zuzuordnen wären. Das beginnt schon damit, dass die schlichte liturgische Mehrstimmig-keit ebenfalls dem psalmodisch–rezitatorischen Typus zuzuordnen wäre: Schon Gilles Binchois vertonte in den 1430er Jahren seinen 113. Psalm *In exitu Israel de Aegypto* in voll deklamatorischem, dem Prosaakzent des Lateinischen durchweg verpflichteten Fauxbourdon.[24] Und der entsprechende homophone Rezitationstypus fand ebenso umstandslos in Psalm– oder sonstige Prosamotetten des Nordens seinen Eingang, wie er dies im Süden tat. Bei Jacob Obrechts vierstimmigem *Inter praeclarissimas virtutes* etwa handelt es sich zwar um eine Tenormotette; die Außenstimmen, die einen Prosatext erheblicher Länge vertonen, sind gleichwohl in homophoner Deklamatorik reinsten Wassers abgefasst (vgl. Beispiel 1).[25]

Über weite Strecken deklamatorisch sind auch Obrechts *Laudemus nunc Dominum* und *O preciosissime sanguis* sowie (wiewohl im Rahmen eines stärker polyphon aufgelockerten Satzes) – *Beata es Maria* und *Factor orbis*. Dies aber hat – genauso wie gleich gestaltete Passagen aus dieser und einer Reihe anderer Motetten – nichts mit ‚italienischen' Einflüssen im Werk des Komponisten zu tun, auch wenn dies bisweilen angenommen wird,[26] und ist im Übrigen auch keine Ausnahme; die Komposition zitiert vielmehr eine Tradition der liturgischen oder zumindest liturgienahen Prosadeklamation, die im Norden ebenso verbreitet war wie im Süden. Die Liste entsprechender Beispiele ließe sich beliebig fortsetzen, etwa mit den Psalm- und Bibelmotetten Pierre de La Rues oder Jean Moutons. Als Extremfall wäre schließlich noch Ninot le Petit zu nennen: Falls es sich bei diesem Komponisten nicht, wie lange angenommen, um den päpstlichen Musiker Johannes Baltazar alias ‚Lepetit', sondern nach Louise Litterick um den Sänger und Priester Jean Lepetit aus

---

[24] Edition in Gilles Binchois, *The Sacred Music*, hrsg. von Philip Kaye (Oxford und New York, 1992), 203–17; vgl. Schmidt-Beste, *Textdeklamation*, S. 331–4.

[25] Edition in Jacob Obrecht, *Collected Works*, xv [*Motets 1*], hrsg. von Chris Maas (New Obrecht Edition; Utrecht, 1995), 55–68; Beispiel 1: 55–6.

[26] Vgl. Albert Dunning, *Die Staatsmotette 1480–1555* (Utrecht, 1970), 17: „Der fast durchwegs syllabische, oft – im dritten Teil fast zur Gänze – gleichrhythmische, mit Tonrepetitionen stark durchsetzte, melodisch weitgehend vom Wortakzent geprägte, harmonisch wenig differenzier-te Satz weicht von dem komplizierten Bild der überwiegenden Mehrzahl der Obrechtschen Motetten ab. Vielleicht wollte sich Obrecht mit diesem vorwiegend vertikal orientierten, der Frottola angenäherten Werk dem italienischen Klangbild anpassen".

Beispiel 1. Jacob Obrecht, *Inter praeclarissimas virtutes*, T. 1–32

dem ostfranzösischen Langres handelt,[27] würden dessen kompromisslos deklamatorische Prosamotetten das traditionelle Bild des ‚franko–flämischen‘ Stils vollends zum Einsturz bringen.[28]

All das bedeutet nichts anderes, als dass wir uns von der Idee ‚nationaler‘ Stile in der geistlichen Musik verabschieden müssen, sowohl im Sinne der biographischen Herkunft als auch im Sinne eines geographisch einheitlichen Stiles, zumindest soweit er Regionen betrifft – etwa Sprach- oder Kulturräume – die sich auch nur im weitesten Sinne unter dem modernen Begriff der ‚Nation‘ zusammenfassen ließen. Allenfalls lassen sich Regionalstile in einem geographisch engeren Sinne definieren, und auch in diesen – wie etwa dem Mailänder Motettenstil oder der römischen Tenormotette – sind Satztechnik, Text und Deklamation durch einen institutionellen oder liturgischen Usus definiert, der unbedingt lokales, nicht aber nationales Selbstbewusstsein erkennen lässt, genauso wie die erwähnte Villanella eben primär eine neapolitanische und keine italienische Gattung ist. Selbst das immer wieder gern genannte Beispiel des ‚typisch englischen‘ Stils um 1500[29] ist in diesem Sinne zu relativieren: Das Zusammenfallen von Herkunft der Komponisten und spezifischer kompositorischer Ausprägung erklärt sich hier wohl primär daraus, dass der Personalaustausch zwischen England und dem Kontinent in dieser Zeit vergleichsweise gering war; ein hypothetischer franko–flämischer Komponist, den es um 1500 nach England verschlagen hätte, hätte wohl ebenfalls im Stil des Eton Choirbook komponiert.

Nur ein einziger Hoffnungsschimmer verbleibt in der Suche nach ‚nationalen‘ Elementen in der geistlichen Musik des 16. Jahrhunderts: Es könnten sich in der Vertonung auch lateinischer Texte Spuren der Muttersprache des Komponisten finden lassen. Diese Suche teilt zwar die bisher als Einheit behandelten Franko-Flamen in mindestens zwei Lager auf – die französischen und die flämisch-holländischen Muttersprachler – was die Postulation eines ‚franko–flämischen‘ Stils als ‚Nationalstil‘ noch einmal zusätzlich in Frage stellt; gleichwohl bestünde hier zumindest die Chance, einen analytisch fixierbaren Unterschied zwischen den Kompositionen verschiedener Musikergruppen herausarbeiten

---

[27] Vgl. Louise Litterick, „Who wrote Ninot's Chansons?“, in Richard Sherr (Hg.), *Papal Musicians in Late Medieval and Renaissance Rome* (Oxford und Washington, 1998), 240–69.

[28] Siehe vor allem seine Motetten *O bone Jesu* und *Psallite Noe Iudaei credite*; vgl. Ninot Le Petit, *Opera Omnia*, hrsg. von Barton Hudson (Corpus Mensurabilis Musicae, 87; o.O., 1979), 66–83 und 84–95.

[29] So bereits Finscher, „Die nationalen Komponenten“, 45: „Demgegenüber ist die geistliche Musik der Provinz, wie sie sich im Eton Choirbook spiegelt, als einzige im europäischen Raum dieser Zeit anscheinend unberührt von niederländischen–italienischen Vorbildern und prägt einen ganz eigenen, in seiner Isoliertheit mit vollem Recht national zu nennenden Stil aus [...]“.

zu können, der sich in irgendeiner Form als ‚national' definieren ließe. Dieses Problemfeld hier auch nur zu umreißen, würde den Rahmen dieses Aufsatzes sprengen; es sei allerdings darauf hingewiesen, dass dieser Ansatz zwar Möglichkeiten, aber in ebenso großem Maße in dieser Frage auch Fallstricke bietet. Zentral ist in diesem Kontext die in den letzten Jahren wieder stärker in den Vordergrund rückende Diskussion um die ‚französische' Endbetonung des Lateinischen. Einerseits aber wird diese in den Werken tatsächlich frankophoner Komponisten oft überbewertet und alles, was irgendwie nicht den Betonungsregeln der klassischen Prosodie entspricht, umstandslos als ‚französisch' eingestuft[30] – so etwa in Josquins berühmtem *Ave Maria ... virgo serena*, dessen fünfte Strophe im Tripla–Rhythmus in der Tat zahlreiche ‚falsche' Betonungen aufweist. Diese sind aber auf die Divergenz zwischen Versrhythmus und Prosodie zurückzuführen und eben nicht auf ‚französische' Betonung – „Ave verá virgínitás/Immaculáta cástitas/Cuiús purificatio" etc. Andererseits erscheinen aber auch in den Prosavertonungen etwa von Jean Mouton und Pierre de La Rue zahlreiche Passagen, deren deklamatorische Orientierung auf eine proparoxytonisch–oxytonische Kadenz hin in der Tat nur über eine muttersprachliche Beeinflussung erklärlich scheint.[31]

Auch hier spielt aber der Wirkungsort neben der Herkunft eine wichtige Rolle: Die in Italien und Deutschland wirkenden frankophonen Komponisten legen den Manierismus der Endbetonung meist rasch ab – was eben beweist, dass es sich um einen Manierismus handelt und nicht um eine gleichsam unterbewusste Handlung, zumal er bei Verdelot und Arcadelt ganz abwesend ist und auch Mouton, La Rue und andere ‚franko–flämische' Komponisten in ihren Motetten über weite Strecken den ‚korrekten' grammatischen Pänultima-Akzent des Lateinischen berücksichtigen. Andererseits zeigt sich an der Vertonung des 29. Psalms – *Exaltabo te* – durch den in Mechelen und Antwerpen tätigen Flamen

---

[30] Den Ausgangspunkt nimmt diese Diskussion in den Diskussionsbeiträgen Arthur Mendels zum Workshop „The Performance and Interpretation of Josquin's Motets", in Edward E. Lowinsky und Bonnie J. Blackburn (Hgg.), *Josquin des Prez. Proceedings of the International Josquin Festival-Conference ... New York City, 21–25 June 1971* (London, 1976), 645–62, hier 660–2; vgl. danach auch Louisa Spottswood, „The Influence of Old French on Latin Text-Setting in Early Measured Polyphony", in Bryan Gillingham und Paul Merkley (Hgg.), *Beyond the Moon: Festschrift Luther Dittmer* (Musicological Studies, 53; Ottawa, 1990), 163–82; Rebecca Stewart, „Jean Mouton: Man and Musician. Motets Attributed to Both Josquin and Mouton", in Willem Elders und Frits de Haen (Hgg.), *Proceedings of the International Josquin Symposium Utrecht 1986* (Utrecht, 1991), 155–70, besonders 156–7; zuletzt David Fallows, „French and Italian accentuation in Josquin's motets", in Nicoletta Guidobaldi (Hg.), *Regards croisés. Musiques, musiciens, artistes et voyageurs entre France et Italie au xve siècle* (Tours und Paris, 2002), 105–18. Für den gegensätzlichen Standpunkt vgl. Schmidt-Beste, *Textdeklamation*, 35–40 et passim.

[31] Vgl. ebda., 430–47.

Beispiel 2. Noel Bauldeweyn, *Exaltabo te*, T. 13–34

Noel Bauldeweyn, dass durchaus auch Komponisten, deren Muttersprache nicht Französisch war, im entsprechenden Kontext entsprechend textierten (Beispiel 2): „benedicám tibí" – „et laudabó" – „nomén tuúm" – „in saéculó".[32]

Selbst in zweifelsfrei italienischen Lauda–Vertonungen finden sich ähnliche Muster.[33] Es zeigt sich, dass es lohnen würde, in diese Richtung weitere Untersuchungen anzustellen; pauschale Urteile über eine vermeintliche ‚französische Endbetonung' und eine auf dieser Basis unternommene Verortung bestimmter Werke und Stile verbietet sich jedoch bis auf Weiteres.

Letztlich zeigt sich hier wie auch im Vorhergehenden, dass das Kriterium des ‚Nationalen' in der geistlichen Musik des 16. Jahrhunderts schlicht und ergreifend zu grob ist, um wertvolle Aufschlüsse – oder auch nur handliche Etiketten – zur Verfügung zu stellen. Was diese Musik so interessant macht, ist im Gegenteil gerade das immer unterschiedliche Wechselspiel zwischen je nach Textvorlage und Texttyp unterschiedlichen Traditionen, regionalem Usus, liturgischen Vorgaben, sprachlicher Prägung von Komponist oder Wirkungsort und – was man nicht vergessen sollte – schlichter persönlicher Vorliebe.

---

[32] Ausgabe in *Sixteenth-Century Motet*, hrsg. von Richard Sherr, v (New York und London, 1992), 210–23; Beispiel 2: 211.

[33] Vgl. Schmidt-Beste, *Textdeklamation*, 67–72.

AN UNKNOWN ORGAN MANUSCRIPT WITH MAINLY MAGNIFICAT-SETTINGS BY LASSUS (1626)

Eugeen Schreurs

INTRODUCTION

Very few organ manuscripts from the Low Countries from before 1650 have been preserved.[1] Among the rare exceptions of such manuscripts intended for church use are 'Liège, Université, Bibliothèque, 153 (olim 888) (*Liège Organ book*)' (*Liber fratrum cruciferorum leodiensium*), compiled for the Crutched Friars of Liege, and 'London, British Library, Add.29486' (1618), of unknown destination, containing preludes in all eight modes and alternatim Mass and Magnificat settings.[2] We know from numerous archival accounts that the organ was frequently used in church services, either alone or as accompanist of a vocal ensemble — often described in the archives as 'het singen in het orgel' [literally 'singing in the organ'], sometimes alternating with plainchant.[3]

Improvisation may well have played an important role, and may in part explain the lack of sources on the one hand, and the abundant quantity of instruments on the other. The fact that such organ books were often produced by the organist himself, and therefore did not belong to the church fabric or a chapter or a monastic community, also helps to explain the dearth of surviving sources. For such manuscripts did not form part of the music library (see e.g. the numerous music inventories of the seventeenth and eighteenth centuries).[4] These organ manuscripts were usually kept near the organ and sometimes taken home. When a new organist took up his post it may be assumed that organ books with older music could enjoy less attention. In addition, such organ manuscripts rarely had any (visual) artistic value, as they lacked illuminations, unlike the

---

[1] I wish to thank Peter Strauven for his critical comments and for providing examples. I am indebted to Peter Van Dessel for the English translation and Stratton Bull for advices. For keyboard manuscripts (harpsichord/virginals) see Godelieve Spiessens, *Zuid-Nederlandse Klavecimbelmuziek. Harpsichord Music of the Southern Low Countries* (Monumenta Flandriae Musica, 4), p. x.

[2] See in this connection John Caldwell, art. 'Sources of keyboard music to 1660, §2(iv): The Netherlands', *Grove Music Online* (accessed 05 May 2007). Most of the manuscripts mentioned show English influence.

[3] Guido Persoons, *De Orgels en de Organisten van de Onze Lieve Vrouwkerk te Antwerpen van 1500 tot 1650* (Brussel, 1981), ex. 116. Kristine K. Forney, 'Music, Ritual and Patronage at the Church of Our Lady, Antwerp', *Early Music History*, 7 (1987), 21ff.

[4] For an overview of music inventories from the Southern Netherlands see Bruno Bouckaert, 'Muziek en repertoire te Gent. De 18de-eeuwse muziekinventaris van de Ekkergemse Sint-Martinuskerk als stille getuige van een veelzijdige muziekbibliotheek', *Musica Antiqua*, 16/2 (1999), 75-6.

choirbooks belonging to the corpus of Petrus Alamire and his collaborators.[5] Finally, the religious strife of the sixteenth century will not have contributed to the preservation of older manuscripts. However, it should be noted that the organ's part in the liturgical services increased with time. Illustrative in this respect is the list of feast days on which the organ could be heard in the collegiate church of Our Lady in Tongeren.[6]

Festa que continentur in libro organi et in organisando consueta	
Andree	Petri et Pauli
Nicolai	Visitationis B.M.
Conceptionis B.M.	Marie Magdalene
Stephani	Jacobi
Joannis	Laurentij
Innocentium	Assumptionis B.M.
Circumcisionis Dni.	Bartholomei
Epiphanie	Nativitatis B.M.
Vincentij	Exultationis S. Crucis
Conversionis S. Pauli	Lamberti
Purificationis B.M.	Mathei
Annuntiationis B.M.	Materni
Vigilie Pasche	Mauritij
Pasche cum 3. ferijs	Michaelis
Octave Pasche	SS. Omnium
Philippi et Jacobi	Martini
Inventionis S. Crucis	Catharine
Dedicationis ecclesie	Cecilie
Ascentionis Domini	Simonis et Jude
Pentecostes cum 3. fer.	In ultima commemoratione
Trinitatis	B.M.V. ante quadragesimam

Nota in omnibus precedentibus festis duplicibus in primis et secundis vesperis organum Hm. pulsatur
Omnibus Dominicis in secundis vesperis Hm. org. pulsatur

Figure 1. List of feasts on which the organ was played in Tongeren according to a fragmentary mid-seventeenth century obituary[7]

---

[5] See e.g. the collection of codexes of the Illustrious Confraternity of Our Lady of 's-Hertogenbosch in Véronique Roelvink, *Gegeven den sangeren. Meerstemmige muziek te 's-Hertogenbosch in de zestiende eeuw* ('s-Hertogenbosch, 2002). See also Herbert Kellman, *The Treasury of Petrus Alamire. Music and Art in Flemish Court Manuscripts. 1500-1535* (Gent and Amsterdam, 1999), 80-3.

[6] The Tongeren *Liber ordinarius* of the fifteentth, early seventeenth and late eighteenth century also show that the role of the organ increased, so that in time the instrument could be heard daily, and even more than once a day. See Eugeen Schreurs, *Het muziekleven in de Onze-Lieve-Vrouwekerk van Tongeren (circa 1400-1797). Een archivalisch georiënteerd onderzoek naar het muziekleven van een middelgrote kapittelkerk in het prinsbisdom Luik binnen haar stedelijke context* (D.Phil. thesis, Katholieke Universiteit Leuven, 1990), 39-40.

[7] Tongeren, Stadsarchief, Kapittel, 14, fol. 83. See also Schreurs, *Het muziekleven*, 37.

History of the Berx manuscript

Within the framework of the localisation activities of Resonant, Centre for Flemish Musical Heritage, founded in 2002, this manuscript was submitted to staffers of the centre. A Leuven musicology student, Kris Gabriels, informed Steven Marien, recently graduated and then working for the Alamire Foundation, of the existence of a paper organ manuscript, which had been found in an attic. The manuscript belonged to Mr. Carlo Berx of Alken who had received it from an uncle, who had managed to recuperate the twenty-six leaves from a book-binding found in the attic of a castle in the vicinity of Tongeren. In view of the task of Resonant, I undertook the further valorisation of the manuscript.

It indeed appeared to be a rather unique find, for — as already said in the introduction — such manuscripts are quite exceptional. So right away we also examined the possibility of its valorisation. Since Carlo Berx was an active member of the choir *Kleine Cantorij*, founded by Luc Ponet in Tongeren, also an organist, and since the cultural heritage festival 'Artuatuca' and the 'Basilica concerts' ('Festival of Flanders) were interested in organizing a concert around this manuscript, 'Resonant' decided to realize a transcription, making the manuscript available to contemporary performers. The Leuven musicologists Peter Strauven and Jan Moeyaert have transcribed most of the music into a modern critical edition. This will be made available online, together with an introduction and critical commentary, in the course of the year 2008-2009.[8] At the same time the manuscript itself will be made available in digital format on the same website, which will ensure its (digital) conservation. Within the context of the preservation and on the basis of the transcriptions, the whole has been restored by Steven Marien in its original sequence and returned to the owners in an acid-free wrapper.

A selection of pieces was performed by Luc Ponet at two concerts in Tongeren. The first concert (1 July 2005), with the 'Capilla Flamenca' and 'Oltremontano', was also the opening concert of the Festival of Flanders Limburg. The second concert with the 'Kleine Cantorij' concluded the symposium 'Tongerse muziekhandschriften en het leven van de kanunniken' organized on 8 July by the 'Heritage Cell Tongeren', 'Artuatuca', and 'Basilica concerts'. At the symposium a number of music manuscripts were presented, as well as the initial findings concerning the Berx manuscript, and a small exhibition was organized around music manuscripts in the Tongeren municipal archive.

---

[8] See www.resonant.be.

Plate 1. Sample of a page from the Berx manuscript with a canzona by Trofeo and the mention of the presumable owner/copyist Adolphus Rusen (fol. 1v)

Description of the Berx manuscript

As already said, the twenty-six paper folios (seven of them bifolios; height 30.8 cm – width 19.5 cm) were recuperated from an otherwise unidentified binding where they served as filling. The leaves are quite undamaged, and preserved at almost full size, but show some traces of moisture and fire. There is no original foliation. In the context of its study and edition the leaves were numbered in pencil. On the basis of content, paper and handwriting the manuscript can be divided into three parts. The difference in lining also indicates this: thus the height of the staves is 1.47 cm in part 1, 1.3 cm in part 2, and 1.4 cm in part 3. Most of the folios have been provided with six continuous staves of ten lines (see Pl.1). Only in part 3 are some folios without staves (see below). Mensural (bar)lines appear in parts 1 and 2 after each semibrevis. The scribe of part 3 was clearly less consistent, drawing mensural lines after the semibrevis or, less frequently, after the brevis. I will discuss these three parts in the presumably original sequence.

Part 1: Two canzonas
This part consists of just two loose sheets, of which the watermark (a crossbeam) suggests a provenance from the Strasbourg region.[9] They contain two incomplete four-part canzonas. The headings 'primi toni' and 'secondi toni' on the recto side of the folios — the six staves on this side are otherwise completely blank — suggest that several canzonas were notated per modus. The first canzona is by Ruggier Trofeo, probably a pupil of Rovigo, born in Mantua around 1550, court organist in Mantua, then organist of San Marco in Milan, and finally in the service of the Savoy family in Turin, where he died in 1614. The second canzona is by Francesco Rovigo, born in 1541/42, pupil of Claudio Merulo (1533-1604), court organist in Mantua and Graz (1582), and again in Mantua in 1590, where he died in 1597.[10] Around 1583 the two organists jointly published a first edition, now lost, of *Canzoni da suonare di Francesco Rovigo et Ruggier Trofeo*, with canzonas for 4 and 8 voices. Only the 'partitura' survived, while the presumably attendant partbooks meant for

---

[9] C.M. Briquet, *Les filigranes. Dictionnaire historique des marques du papier dès leur apparition vers 1282 jusqu'en 1600. A Facsimile of the 1907 edition with Supplementary Material contributed by a Number of Scholars,* ed. Allan Stevenson, (Amsterdam, 1968), i, nr. 988, iii, nr. 988. With thanks to Chris Coppens, head of the Tabularium, K.U.Leuven Central Library, for this information.

[10] For the biographical data see Thomas W. Bridges, 'Rovigo, Francesco', *Grove Music Online* (accessed 12 April 2007) and Pierre M. Tagmann and Michael Fink, 'Rovigo, Francesco', *Grove Music Online* (accessed 10 April 2007). For the edition of the canzonas see *Francesco Rovigo and Ruggier Trofeo. Canzoni da suonare à quattro, & à otto (Milan, [1613?]),* in James Ladewig (ed.), *Italian Instrumental Music of the Sixteenth and Early Seventeenth Centuries,* 22 (New York and London, 1988).

Example 1. Transcription of part of the canzona by Rovigo with indication of the missing notes

instrumental ensemble were lost. The work was re-issued around 1613 in Milan by the printer Filippo Lomazzo under the title *Partitura delle canzoni da suonare a quattro & à otto*.[11] It is not clear which edition served as the source for our manuscript; but the latter certainly has less authority than the print, because of its incomplete state (see Ex.1).

The canzonas, like the Magnificats, have clearly been arranged by mode and the scribe has adapted the order of the works presumably in accordance with his own needs. But this could also be due to the fact that the manuscript was based on the lost 1583 edition. Be that as it may, here the *Canzona Ottava* of Trofeo is the opening piece. The second canzona, by Rovigo, corresponds to the *Canzona Seconda* in the Milan print. It strongly seems that the page with the Trofeo work is also the opening page of the manuscript's canzona part. The scribe has adapted the title: *Aliquot canzon in modum* [mistake; struck through] *fugae per 8 tonos distributae*.[12] The copyist of the two canzonas was the regular canon Adolphus Rusen of Neuss, who according to the inscription was 'organista' as well. A check of the Staatsarchiv in Düsseldorf revealed that an Adolf Kusen (sic) from Cologne was indeed a 'Regulier Canonick' in the Augustinian monastery (Oberkloster) of Neuss.[13]

From a musical viewpoint the manuscript differs little from the Milan print. There are also copies of these canzonas in the so-called Turin keyboard tabulatures, a set of sixteen manuscripts notated in German organ tabulature probably compiled in southern Germany, possibly Augsburg.[14] Of the Trofeo canzona 47 of the 102 bars have been preserved. The melodic deviations (e.g. in bar 9 in the Altus where a note of the middle part is missing, or in bar 16 [Bassus]) are minimal. In bar 33 a *c* has erroneously slipped into the Bassus, thus creating a 6/4 chord. Of the Rovigo canzona 46 of the 84 bars survive. Here a number of notes have been omitted in the middle parts: for instance in the Altus in bars 20, 23, 32, and 36, thus affecting the polyphonic structure.

---

[11] The only surviving copy is now in the Biblioteca Municipale 'A. Panizza' in Reggio Emilia.

[12] For the use of the term 'fuga' see Paul Walker: 'Fugue, §4(ii): 17th century: Theory: terminology, structure', *Grove Music Online* (accessed 6 May 2007).

[13] Düsseldorf, Staatsarchiv, inventory 121-68, Neuss Oberkloster, 221-4. The monastery, which since 1430 belonged to the Windesheimer congregation, was (temporarily?) suppressed in 1623, presumably with the intention to merge it with the monastery in Bonn.

[14] These manuscripts are now in Turin, Biblioteca Nazionale Universitaria, MS F1, fols. 74v-100r; they contain canzonas 1 to 7 and 9 to 17; 3 of the 19 canzonas are thus missing.

Part 2: Fifteen Magnificats

Part 2 consists of eighteen paper folios whose watermark has not yet been identified. At the end of this Magnificat section of the manuscript, on fol. 20, we read that Nicolaus a Rivo completed this work in 1626: 'finis coronat opus. Anno 1626'. I could find no further information on this a Rivo as yet. The whole is written in a professional hand, albeit less carefully than part 1. Often the part-writing has been reduced, which could indicate that the manuscript was meant for private use. This is the most substantial section of the manuscript with fifteen Magnificat settings of Lassus of which two are incomplete. Judging from the reference to the numbering in Roman numerals, the settings were copied from the posthumous print published by Lassus' son Rudolphus: *Iubilus. B. Virginis. Hoc est Centum Magnificat... IV. V. VI. VII. VIII. Et X. vocibus composita, nunc vero Rudolphi de Lasso melopaei et organiste labore, et impensa proelo data*, München, Nicolaus Heinrich, 1619. There is a complete exemplar consisting of six partbooks in the Bayerische Staatsbibliothek in Munich.[15]

In the Berx organ manuscript, in accordance with the then current alternatim practice, only the even verses have been entered. The copyist follows a modal order and therefore based himself on the 1619 edition, not on earlier prints of Lassus' Magnificats. The whole is incomplete because, for instance, the Magnificats in the first tone are entirely lacking and there is only one setting in the second tone — although this is not a wholly conclusive argument — but primarily because two settings are incomplete: no. 9 (in the numbering of the Berx manuscript) has been entered up to verse 6, and no. 10 only starts from the end of the second verse. But the end of the Magnificat section does seem to be confirmed by the copyist's words 'finis coronat opus'.

The compiler of the manuscript opted exclusively for alternatim settings, indeed the most usual method applied by Lassus within this genre meant for vesper services.[16] The odd verses were presumably sung in plainchant (see also below, conclusion). For the even verses the copyist wrote the text of (mainly) the upper voice beneath the organ part. In my opinion there are three possible ways to perform these pieces, which I list in descending order of probability:

---

[15] David Crook, *Orlando Di Lasso's Imitation Magnificats for Counter-Reformation Munich* (Princeton, 1994), 14-6.
[16] Crook, *Orlando*, 5.

(1) Odd verses plainchant – even verses solo organ, whereby the organist/compiler would of course fill out the at times harmonically rather meagre, often two-part passages. In any event the harmonic scheme is limited mainly to Superius and Bassus (or bottom voice), which have been notated just about complete. The middle parts have been notated less consistently.

(2) Odd verses plainchant – even verses one singer (Superius) with organ accompaniment. In this case the organist played a kind of 'basso seguente' whereby mostly (but not always) the top and bottom voices served as a framework for the 'keyboard reduction', but with a number of inconsistently inserted embellishments. In this connection, reference may be made to the aforementioned practice of 'cantare in organis' as employed in the cathedral at Antwerp and by several confraternities in the Low Countries.[17] But the question is whether monasteries like that in Neuss had singers with sufficient vocal capabilities and whether the soloist involved also sang from this manuscript. Another question arises concerning the text (mostly of the upper voice) that appears beneath the score: is it intended for a solo upper voice, or was it written out solely to aid the organist in following the prosody and meaning of the text? What then with the works (e.g. the duets) transmitted without words?

(3) Odd verses plainchant – even verses vocal ensemble with organ accompaniment.[18] This could explain the reference to the Roman numbering in the Lassus print, which enabled the singers to easily locate the right Magnificat. But it is clear that the copyist may have repeated these Roman numbers simply as a kind of source indication. This hypothesis of a possible performance practice is actually invalidated by the fact that such monasteries generally did not have a choir of four to ten (professional) singers able to perform such repertory, unless they brought in singers from outside for special feast days.

---

[17] See Persoons, *De Orgels*, 116; Forney, *Music, Ritual and Patronage*, 21ff; Schreurs, *Het muziekleven*, 33ff. For an intabulation of Lassus' Magnificat 8 in the manuscript Basel, Universitätsbibliothek, Ms. F.IX.44, fol. 252v-256, see *Orlando di Lasso. Magnificat 1-24*, ed. James Erb (Orlando di Lasso. Neue Reihe, 13; Kassel-London, 1980), p. lxxxix, 291-9. This is a version *colla parte*, without diminutions.

[18] Here reference may be made to the practice of also performing instrumental ensemble-canzonas with organ accompaniment, also those of Rovigo en Trofeo. See Ladewig (ed.), *Italian Instrumental Music*, p. xi-xii.

Example 2. Magnificat *Aurora lucis rutilat*, verse 4

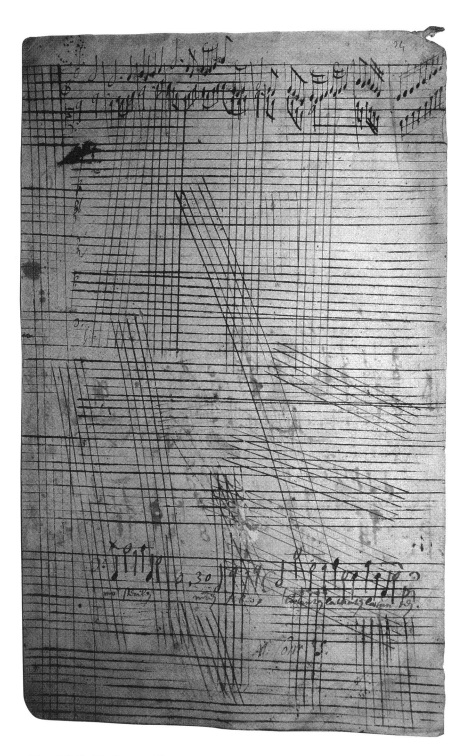

Plate 2. Folio 24v from part 3

The works a Rivo selected are in four to ten parts, but in general he confines his arrangements mostly to three or four parts, sometimes to just two (cf. Ex. 2, Magnificat *Aurora lucis rutilat,* verse 4 'Quia fecit'; see e.g. bars 37-8 where he reduces even eight-part writing once to a single voice). Some embellishment in the form of ornamentation (runs, diminutions on cadences) has sometimes been added, but certainly not systematically (ibid., bar 36 ascending runs the Bassus; bar 39, sixteenths in the Superius; bar 65, supplementary descending run in the Superius). Sometimes a rhythm is adapted (ibid., bar 49, fourth note in the Superius instead of a half). 'Musica ficta' in some instances differs from or confirms that in the new Lassus edition (ibid., bar 55, bar 59, *f* sharp in the Superius). As usual, almost half of Lassus' Magnificats are parodies of motets, chansons or madrigals, either his own (e.g. *Aurora lucis rutilat; Margot laborez les vignes*) or by his contemporaries (e.g. Anselmo De Reulx: *S'io credessi per morte;* Giovanni Maria Nanino : *Erano capei d'oro*).[19]

Part 3: Mass parts and fragments/sketches

The third part of the manuscript (six folios) is the most puzzling. It contains mostly Mass parts, improvisatory sketches, 'probae penne', and short preluding pieces. They are often unfinished and rather sloppily notated, with regularly entire blanks, without even staves. This section is not dated, but the watermark (a double eagle) points again to a provenance in the Strasbourg area.[20] Many of the settings appear to be of a rather amateuristic level, and are probably the work of a still unknown third organist.

---

[19] Crook, *Orlando*, 16ff. counts 40 parody settings among a total of 101 Magnificats.
[20] C.M. Briquet 1907/1968, i, nr. 997, iii, nr. 997.

Conclusion

Within the framework of a regular monastery music usually played an important role, albeit a lesser one than in secular collegiate churches.[21] How this manuscript came to the Tongeren area is not clear; it was possibly just recuperated paper from a bookbinder. In view of the format, the modal arrangement, the dating and the ownership marking (cf. part 1: Rusen; part 2: a Rivo), it would seem justified to regard at least parts 1 and 2 as a whole, intended for the regular monastery in Neuss, even though different hands are involved. Part 3 may be a later and more sketchy addition.

Given the relatively limited number of sources with organ music from this period and region, and in view of the information the manuscript offers with regard to alternatim practice and application of 'musica ficta', this manuscript is an acquisition/addition worthy of further study and inclusion in the corpus of keyboard manuscripts from the first half of the seventeenth century. It also reveals that the influence of North-Italian organ music was considerable even in Middle and Northern Europe.

---

[21] Schreurs, *Het muziekleven*, 342-6.

Appendix. Composition of the Berx Organ Manuscript

[Folio] (in pencil)	Title	Composer	Model parody setting
Part I	Copyist: Adolpho Rusen		
1r	Blank staves		
1v	Canzon	Ruggiero Trofeo	
2r	Blank staves		
2v	Canzon	Francesco Rovigo	
Part II	Copyist: Nicolaus a Rivo		
3-4	Magnificat	Lassus	Las, je n'iray plus (Lassus)
4v-6	Id	Id	
6-6v	Id	Id	
6v-8	Id	Id	S' Io credessi (de Reulx)
8-9	Id	Id	
9-11	Id	Id	
11-11v	Id	Id	[incomplete: deest vers 8-12]
12-13	Id	Id	[incomplete: deest verse 4-12] [Omnis homo primum bonum vinum ponit (Lassus]
13-13v	Id	Id	
13v-15	Id	Id	Beau le cristal (Lassus)
15-16	Id	Id	Margot laborez les vignes (Lassus)
16v-17v	Id	Id	Erano capei d'oro (Nanino)
18-18v	Id	Id	
18v-19	Id	Id	
19-20	Id	Id	Aurora lucis rutilat (Lassus)
20v			
Part III	Copyist	?	
21	Incomplete	Anon	
21	Osanna	Anon	
21v	Textless	Anon	
22	Christe	Anon	
22	Kyrie	Anon	
22	Ultimum Kyrie	Anon	
22v	Entirely blank		
23	Textless (partly scetches)	Anon	
23v	Textless	Anon	
23v	Only superius	Anon	
24	Duo (incomplete)	Anon	
24	*Probae penne*; sketches of Bassus part	Anon	
24v	Proemium Kyrie	Anon	
24v	Kyrie eleyson Aliud	Anon	
25	Kyrie Totum duplex vel Secundum Kyrie	Anon	
25	Christe	Anon	
25	Aliud Christe	Anon	
25v	Entirely blank		
26	Textless	Anon	
26v	Entirely blank		

[1]   Sigla: - IIMS: *Italian Instrumental Music of the Sixteenth and Early Seventeenth Centuries.*
        - SWNR: Lasso, *Sämtliche Werke, neue Reihe*
[2]   Transposed fifth down.
[3]   Transposed fifth down.
[4]   Transposed fifth down.

Modus	Number of parts	Annotation in original	=Edition[1]	Modern edition Ladewig/Erb
		Primi toni		
1	4	Canzon in modum fugae	IIMS, 8	1988
		Secundi toni		
2	4	Canzon di Francesco Rovigo	IIMS, 2	1988
2	5	[Magnificat 2 Toni à 5] [XXXIII]	SWNR, 57	15, p. 46
3	4	[Magnificat Tertij toni a 4] [IX]	SWNR, 27	14, p. 21
3	4	Magn: X à 4	SWNR, 19	13, p. 265
3	4	S'io Credessi Magnif. XI à 4 hoc vero in ordine 3. tertij toni	SWNR, 88	16, p. 221
4	4	Magnificat 1. 4 toni a 4 XIII.	SWNR, 20	13, p. 261
4	5	Magnific. 2 4 toni à 5 XL	SWNR, 76	17, p. 48
4	8	Aliud magnif. 4. toni 8 vocu(m) [XCIV]	SWNR, 63	15, p. 138
5	6	[Magnificat Quinti toni à 6] [LXXIX]	SWNR, 66	15, p. 181
6	4	Sexti toni à 4. XVII	SWNR, 22	13, p. 272
6[2]	4	Aliud 6 toni à 4 XVIII	SWNR, 89	16, p. 230
7[3]	4	Incipiunt septimi toni Magnificat à 4. Margot laborez les vignes XXII.	SWNR, 83	16, p. 154
7[4]	5	Aliud à 5 LIII Erano capei d'oro	SWNR, 97	17, p. 64
8	4	Magnif: Octavi toni à 4 XXIII	SWNR, 32	14, p. 69
8	4	Aliud à 4 XXIV	SWNR, 24	13, p. 283
8	10	Aliud 10 vocum [C]	SWNR, 101	17, p. 124
		Finis coronat opus. Anno 1626. f. Nicolaus a Rivo		
		[No modus given]		

La musique et l'éducation des jeunes filles d'après *La montagne des pucelles* / *Den Maeghden-Bergh* de Magdaleine Valéry (Leyde, 1599)

Henri Vanhulst

Au seizième siècle, de nombreux manuels de conversation bilingues paraissent dans les Pays-Bas méridionaux. Ils présentent le même texte, qui est généralement conçu sous la forme d'un dialogue, en néerlandais et en français, les deux versions étant imprimées l'une en regard de l'autre. Les objectifs de ces ouvrages ne sont manifestement pas toujours les mêmes : alors que certains auteurs abordent les sujets les plus variés et donnent un vocabulaire de base utile aux situations les plus courantes de la vie quotidienne, d'autres poursuivent un but plus ambitieux et ne s'adressent nullement aux débutants. Certains proposent même des vocabulaires tellement spécialisés que l'on peut s'interroger sur l'utilité de leur ouvrage dans le contexte de l'apprentissage d'une langue. Cette tendance est illustrée notamment par le chapitre sur l'imprimerie et la calligraphie que Plantin publie à Anvers en 1567 : il n'est nullement conçu pour les « jeunes enfans », comme le dit pourtant la page de titre.[1] Les musicologues connaissent plus particulièrement les *Seer gemeyne Tsamencoutingen / Collocutions bien familieres* de J(e)an Berthout que René Lenaerts a exploité jadis dans son étude sur la chanson polyphonique en langue néerlandaise[2] et dont nous avons récemment essayé de circonscrire la portée, car il nous semble que les passages relatifs aux pratiques musicales ont donné lieu à des interprétations erronées et à des conclusions hâtives.[3]

Un autre manuel de conversation bilingue dans lequel il est question de musique, est imprimé dans les Provinces-Unies, où l'emploi du français se développe après la division des anciens Pays-Bas non seulement à cause des réfugiés venus des régions francophones mais aussi parce qu'il s'agit de la langue du commerce international et que les classes aisées locales y voient un signe de distinction sociale.[4] L'ouvrage sort en 1599 des presses de Jan Paedts

---

[1] Stanley Morison et Ray Nash, *An Account of Calligraphy and Printing in the Sixteenth Century from Dialogues Attributed to Christopher Plantin, Printed and Published by Him at Antwerp, 1567* (Anvers, 1964).

[2] René Lenaerts, *Het Nederlands polifonies lied in de 16de eeuw* (Malines et Amsterdam, 1933), 154-9.

[3] Henri Vanhulst, « La musique dans les manuels de conversation bilingues de la Renaissance. Les *Seer gemeyne Tsamencoutingen / Collocutions bien familieres* de Jean Berthout », *Revue belge de Musicologie / Belgisch Tijdschrift voor Muziekwetenschap*, 59 (2005), 93-124.

[4] B. van Selm, *« Een menighte treffelijcke Boecken ». Nederlandse boekhandelcatalogi in het begin van de zeventiende eeuw* (Utrecht, 1987), 235-6.

Jacobsz. à Leyde, qui avait imprimé dès 1585 une adaptation quadrilingue des célèbres *Colloques ou dialogues / Colloquien oft tsamensprekinghen* du maître d'école anversois Noël de/van Berlaimont.[5] La page de titre, qui est à nouveau bilingue, révèle que l'auteur du manuel est une femme qui tient une école française pour jeunes filles à Leyde. Cette dernière information y figure même uniquement en français :

> LA MONTAIGNE ‖ DES PVCELLES, EN NEVF ‖ DIALOGVES, SVR LES NOMS DES ‖ neuf Muses, contenant diverses belles & ver- ‖ tueuses Doctrines, à l'instruction ‖ de la jeunesse. ‖ Den Maeghden-Bergh/ in ‖ negen t'samen-spraken/ op de namen vande ‖ neghen Musen/ inhoudende verscheyden schoone ‖ ende deuchdelicke leeringhen/ tot onder= ‖ wijsinge vande jonckheyt. ‖ *Par Magdaleine Valery, Maistresse d'Escole Françoise* ‖ *de jeunes filles en la Ville de Leyden.* ‖ [gravure] ‖ TOT LEYDEN. ‖ By Jan Paedts Jacobsz. ‖ Anno 1599.[6]

Les renseignements disponibles au sujet Magdaleine Valéry sont rares. À l'instar de Bert van Selm,[7] nous suggérons de la rattacher à la famille d'Adriaen Valerius, l'auteur du fameux *Neder-landtsche Gedenck-Clanck* de 1626. Nous savons, en effet, que ce dernier est probablement le fils d'un soldat français, François Valéry, qui s'est établi à Middelburg en 1569, où il exercera quelque vingt ans plus tard la fonction de notaire.[8] Si Adriaen va opter pour la forme latinisée de son nom, d'autres membres de la famille ne l'imitent pas, car lors du baptême de son fils Franchois — notons que le prénom est français ! —, qui a lieu à Vere le 8 février 1604, le témoin du côté paternel s'appelle Magdalena Valéry.[9] Le lien de parenté avec Adriaen n'est pas précisé dans l'acte, mais il pourrait s'agir de sa sœur ou d'une cousine.[10] Serait-elle l'auteur de l'ouvrage ? L'hypothèse semble assez plausible, mais demande des investigations plus poussées. Le texte lui-même ne donne que peu de renseignements d'ordre biographique et rien ne prouve, en outre, que ces derniers ne relèvent pas de la

---

[5]   San Marino (Cal.), Huntington Library, Rare Books 15140.

[6]   L'ouvrage de format in-8° contient 48 feuillets non chiffrés. L'unique exemplaire est conservé à Wolfenbüttel, Herzog-August-Bibliothek, P 2138.8° Helmst. La page de titre porte les ajouts manuscrits : « G. G. T. J. G. S. 1666 ». van Selm, *Een menigte*, 241, reproduit la page titre qui est ornée d'une gravure qui représente la Maistresse assise sous un dais et entourée de ses neuf élèves.

[7]   van Selm, *Een menighte*, 314 n. 281.

[8]   Adriaen Valerius, *Nederlandtsche Gedenck-clanck*, éd. par P. J. Meertens, N. B. Tenhaeff et A. Komter-Kuipers (Amsterdam, 1942), p. xiv.

[9]   *Ibid.*, p. xv.

[10]   *Ibid.*, p. xvii, donne un arbre généalogique incomplet de la famille Valerius, qui ne mentionne aucune femme du nom de Magdalena/Madeleine.

fabulation. En tout cas, la Maîtresse, qui est sans doute Magdaleine même,[11] se dit âgée d'environ 26 ans (f. B$_5$v et E$_7$v) et précise qu'elle a fréquenté des écoles à Anvers, Bruges et Middelburg (f. B$_6$v), la ville de François Valéry. Elle a vécu à Hoorn (f. A$_2$r) « avec toute [sa] famille » (f. A$_2$v) et y a déjà eu une activité d'enseignante (f. F$_7$v). Elle réside depuis peu de temps à Leyde quand elle y publie son ouvrage.[12] C'est parce qu'il existe depuis 1575 dans cette ville une université destinée à « la jeunesse masculine », qu'elle va y ouvrir une école pour jeunes filles, répondant ainsi au désir de « mainte famille vertueuse » (f. A$_2$r). Comme elle le fait « pour complaire à [son] trescher pere » (f. A$_2$v), il n'est pas impossible que Magdaleine soit la fille d'un homme exerçant une profession telle que celle de notaire.

La publication de *La montaigne des pucelles / Den Maegden-Bergh* est la première étape dans la réalisation du projet (« pour commencement et premices de mes devoirs », f. A$_2$v). L'ouvrage commence par une dédicace (f. A$_2$r-v) datée du 31 mai 1599 qui est uniquement donnée en français. S'adressant aux édiles de Leyde, l'auteur note la présence dans la ville de « Brabansons, Flamens, Walons et autres gens illec refugez » à côté de « bourgeois natifs » (f. A$_2$r). Son initiative s'adresse « aux filles de ces pays » (f. A$_2$r) — notons le pluriel ! — qu'elle qualifiera ultérieurement de manière plus précise de « filles de gens de bien » (f. B$_6$r), c'est-à-dire celles dont les parents sont disposés à payer un minimum de cent florins pour couvrir « les despences de bouche » (f. C$_3$r) des internes. Elle veut « instruire […] en la langue Françoise et autres arts honnestes » et l'auteur se range résolument parmi les « bonnes, doctes, et vertueuses instructrices et maistresses » dont « la jeunesse feminine [a] autant besoing » (f. A$_2$r) que les jeunes hommes. Quant au choix du français, Valéry n'en donne aucune justification et considère manifestement l'apprentissage de la langue comme l'une des matières obligatoires du programme (f. E$_8$v). Elle fait d'ailleurs allusion à Peeter Heyns, fondateur en 1555 d'une école bilingue pour jeunes filles à Anvers, où les frais du pensionnat revenaient à une moyenne de cinquante florins dans les années 1580.[13] À l'opposé de Valéry, Heyns est resté célèbre grâce notamment à son *Cort onderwys van de acht deelen der Françoischer talen, tot voorderinge ende profijt der Duytscher ionc-heyt* de 1571 et à trois pièces de théâtre qu'il a écrites en français pour ses élèves. Heyns avait quitté sa ville natale en 1585 et avait fini par se fixer à Haarlem, où il ouvre

---

[11] Le titre du sixième dialogue précise que la Maîtresse se prénomme Magdaleine (f. C5r).

[12] Selon van Selm, *Een menighte*, 240, Valéry a écrit son ouvrage à Hoorn ou à Leyde et elle l'a publié à compte d'auteur. Étant donné que la dédicace a certainement été rédigée à Leyde, c'est dans cette ville que Valéry a achevé son manuel. Elle l'avait sans doute commencé à Hoorn, qu'elle n'a quitté que quelques semaines plus tôt.

[13] Maurits Sabbe, *Peeter Heyns en de Nimfen ...uit den Lauwerboom... Bijdrage tot de Geschiedenis van het Schoolwezen in de 16e Eeuw* (Anvers et La Haye, s. d.), 27.

une école française dans les années 1590.[14] Étant donné que Magdelaine Valéry fait état de son décès (f. D$_6$r), qui est intervenu en février 1598, elle présente de manière implicite sa propre école dans le prolongement de l'initiative de Heyns, d'autant qu'elle insiste sur la rareté de tels établissements (f. E$_7$r-v).

La rédaction de *La montaigne des pucelles / Den Maegden-Bergh* répond à un objectif publicitaire (« pour recommander mon Escole », f. A$_2$v). L'allusion aux neuf Muses dans le titre se retrouve dans le nombre de dialogues dont chacun met en scène une jeune fille originaire d'une ville différente des provinces du Nord. Ces élèves potentielles ont des noms qui rappellent très vaguement celui d'une Muse — Emerence renvoie à Erato, Melosine à Melpomène etc. Elles viennent chercher des informations sur le projet éducatif et sur des aspects pratiques tels que la situation de l'école ou le montant des coûts. Leurs conversations avec la Maistresse permettent à l'auteur de montrer ses connaissances humanistes, de prouver la rectitude de sa foi, d'exposer les matières qu'elle compte enseigner et de convaincre les jeunes filles — et le cas échéant le parent qui les accompagne[4] — de la nécessité de savoir lire, écrire et compter. Valéry en profite pour étaler sa propre culture et affirmer ses qualités morales : les allusions aux philosophes grecs et à la mythologie alternent avec de rares conseils de savoir-vivre et, surtout, avec de nombreux renvois à la Bible et, en particulier, aux psaumes. Si Valéry ne cesse de parler de vertu, elle s'emploie à donner aux jeunes filles une formation qui en fera non seulement de bonnes mères de famille (f. A$_2$r), mais aussi des femmes capables d'exercer une activité professionnelle dans le commerce, car elle enseigne également des principes de comptabilité.[15] En somme, *La montaigne des pucelles / Den Maegden-Bergh* n'est certainement pas un manuel pour débutant(e)s : les thèmes abordés sont très éloignés de la vie quotidienne et les phrases souvent longues ne sont nullement dans le style du langage courant. L'interminable poème liminaire de François Hierosme, intitulé *Epigramme de la Montaigne des pucelles* (f. A$_3$r – A$_4$v), détonne tout autant dans un ouvrage de ce genre, parce qu'il n'est d'aucune utilité pour les élèves. Le poète, dont nous ignorons tout, a certainement lu très attentivement le manuel Magdaleine Valéry car il en paraphrase plusieurs thèmes dans des vers d'une navrante médiocrité.

---

[14] Ad. Meskens, « Heyns, Peter », *Nationaal biografisch woordenboek*, vol. 15 (Bruxelles, 1996), col. 338-40.
[15] Rappelons qu'à la Renaissance les femmes représentent environ un tiers de la population active dans des villes comme Leyde ou Haarlem. Voir Gaia Servadio, *Renaissance Woman* (Londres et New York, 2005), 216.

Les passages relatifs à la musique, que nous éditons dans l'Annexe, démontrent l'inspiration calviniste du projet de Valéry. Ils sont non seulement peu nombreux, mais restreignent les pratiques vocale et instrumentale à l'exécution de psaumes et autres chants de caractère spirituel. La musique ne fait pas partie de la formation : elle est confinée dans le domaine des distractions et se pratique le soir. Cela n'empêche pourtant pas Emerence, l'une des futures élèves, d'entendre chanter en s'approchant du pensionnat, mais Valéry s'est probablement permis cette contradiction, parce qu'elle voulait dès le début du dialogue présenter le principal centre d'intérêt de la jeune fille. Tout comme dans l'école anversoise de Heyns,[16] les élèves peuvent apprendre la musique avec un professeur particulier et quelques-unes semblent manifestement attirées par cette possibilité.

Dans le troisième dialogue, Emerence dit qu'elle a déjà appris à jouer de l'épinette en exécutant des danses. La Maistresse s'offusque d'un tel répertoire, mais son interlocutrice réplique que la pratique reste la même, quelle que soit la nature des œuvres. S'appuyant sur l'inévitable référence à David, la Maistresse reconnaît qu'à l'origine, la musique faisait déjà partie des cérémonies religieuses et qu'elle continue à inciter l'homme à louer Dieu. Elle estime néanmoins que ses élèves doivent renoncer à toute musique profane — « danseries » et « chansonnettes legeres » — et Emerence se plie volontiers à cette exigence. Le passage permet à l'auteur de citer quatre instruments : le luth, la harpe, l'orgue et l'épinette — « Clavesimble » dans la version néerlandaise.[17]

Comme Emerence intervient dans le quatrième dialogue pour convaincre Tonette de devenir sa condisciple, elle évoque combien la Maistresse est bien disposée à l'égard de la musique. Elle mentionne l'épinette et le cistre — « Clavesimble » et « Cytere » — et utilise à ce propos le terme « snaerspel », qui est plus adéquat que l'expression « jeux Musical » de la version française. Il est encore question de l'épinette — « Clavesimble » — dans le cinquième dialogue : le père de la future élève annonce qu'il fera envoyer un tel instrument, afin que sa fille ait l'occasion de s'exercer. La réplique de la Maistresse met en évidence la fonction quasi moralisatrice de la musique, puisqu'elle « faict […] oublier beaucoup de fantasies qui autrement troublent l'homme »…

---

[16] Sabbe, *Peeter Heyns*, 30.
[17] P. A. F. van Veen et Nicoline van der Sijs, *Etymologisch Woordenboek. De herkomst van onze Woorden* (Utrecht et Anvers, 1997), 829, situent la première mention du mot *spinet* en 1599.

Il n'est peut-être pas inutile de rappeler que Sebastiaan Vreedman, l'auteur de deux livres de musique de cistre parus à Louvain chez Phalèse en 1568 et 1569,[18] vit à Leyde à partir de 1586, où il est dix ans plus tard actif en tant que facteur de cistres.[19] Certes, Vreedman, qui se dit Malinois mais appartient très probablement à une famille de Leeuwarden,[20] propose un répertoire qui ne correspond guère à la conception rigoriste de la musique telle que Magdaleine Valéry l'expose à plusieurs reprises. Le second livre de Vreedman est même entièrement fait de danses, tandis que le premier, qui est axé sur le domaine vocal, contient davantage de pièces de caractère profane que de chansons spirituelles et autres chants du même genre. On y trouve néanmoins un nombre assez élevé d'incipit littéraires néerlandais. En outre, l'éditeur a imprimé deux versions du recueil qui ne diffèrent sans doute que par la langue utilisée pour la page de titre et le texte liminaire[21]. Le choix du néerlandais dans ce cas-ci est d'autant plus significatif qu'il est exceptionnel de la part de Phalèse qui se sert habituellement du latin ou du français. Le lien entre le cistre et les provinces septentrionales des anciens Pays-Bas est d'ailleurs confirmé par les origines de Fredericus Viaera — un Frison — qui est l'auteur du seul autre recueil que Phalèse ait publié pour cet instrument.[22]

Faute de sources dans le domaine de la musique de clavier, il est impossible de faire un rapprochement à ce propos. Pauline, la dernière jeune fille à se présenter à la Maistresse et qui affirme chanter la plupart des psaumes, fait néanmoins quelque peu penser à Suzanne van Soldt dont le nom, suivi de l'année 1599, figure sur la page de titre d'un manuscrit qui est la seule source de musique de clavier que l'on puisse rattacher aux anciens Pays-Bas pour tout le seizième siècle.[23] Née à Londres en 1586, elle est la fille d'un commerçant anversois qui a émigré en Angleterre avant 1577, et il n'est pas exclu qu'elle ait suivi d'autres membres de sa famille que l'on retrouve dans les années 1600 à Amsterdam et Haarlem. Le manuscrit, qui a été copié en partie dans les anciens Pays-Bas, présente la version pour clavier de treize psaumes et deux chansons spirituelles, soit près de la moitié du contenu de la source. Il a manifestement

---

[18] RISM-B/I 1568[24] et 1569[37]. Henri Vanhulst, *Catalogue des Éditions de musique publiées à Louvain par Pierre Phalèse et ses fils (1545-1578)* (Bruxelles, 1990), 134-6 et 150-2, détaille le contenu des deux livres.

[19] Alfons Annegarn, *Floris en Cornelis Schuyt. Muziek in Leiden van de vijftiende tot het begin van de zeventiende eeuw* (Utrecht, 1973), 49.

[20] Rudolf Rasch, « De familie Vredeman, ofwel Leeuwarden-Mechelen-Leeuwarden », *Revue belge de Musicologie / Belgisch Tijdschrift voor Muziekwetenschap*, 59 (2005), 125-42.

[21] La version néerlandaise n'est connue que par une mention dans les archives de Plantin. Voir Vanhulst, *Catalogue*, 137.

[22] RISM-B/I 1564[21].

[23] GB-Lb, Add. 29485. Voir Alan Curtis (éd.), *Nederlandse klaviermuziek uit de 16e en 17e eeuw* (Amsterdam, 1961), p. x-xii, xxvi-xxxii, xlv-xlvii et 1-36.

servi à aider Suzanne à apprendre à jouer d'un instrument à clavier et la jeune fille a donc été initiée à la musique, du moins en partie, par le répertoire que pratiquait Pauline.

Grâce aux recherches de van Selm, nous savons que l'auteur a soumis quelques exemplaires de son ouvrage aux autorités de la ville de Leyde. Le jeudi 8 juillet 1599 « Magdalena Valerij » reçoit la permission d'ouvrir son école qui fonctionnera comme pensionnat et pourra aussi accueillir des élèves externes, à condition d'y enseigner tant le français que le néerlandais.[24] Quant à *La montaigne des pucelles / Den Maegden-Bergh*, le titre est cité, uniquement en français, dans la rubrique « School-goedt in Frans ende Duyts » du *Catalogus vant gheene tot Amsterdam by groote menichten vercocht sal worden, uyt de Winckel van Saligher Cornelis Claesz. Boeck-vercooper, op den 10 Mey, 1610*.[25] Si la mention dans le catalogue de vente après décès d'un des libraires les plus importants d'Amsterdam suggère que l'ouvrage de Valéry a pu s'employer comme manuel de conversation, une annonce parue dans l'*Oprechte Haerlemse Courant* du 28 mai 1669 démontre en outre que l'expression « Maeghden-Bergh » est restée associée pendant des décennies à la notion d'école pour jeunes filles. C'est en effet le nom que Catharina Colleth, qui vient de s'établir à Haarlem, choisit pour la « Fransse Gereformeerde School […] voor jonge Dochterkens » qu'elle compte y ouvrir.[26]

ANNEXE

Critères d'édition
- Dans les deux versions du texte, nous faisons la distinction entre *i* et *j* et entre *u* et *v*, nous résolvons les abréviations, nous supprimons les trémas et les traits d'union qui ne correspondent pas à l'usage actuel et nous ajoutons une ponctuation adéquate.
- Dans la version française, nous ajoutons l'accent aigu à la voyelle *e* dans une syllabe accentuée et l'accent grave dans les prépositions et adverbes.
- Dans la version néerlandaise, nous remplaçons la barre oblique par la virgule.

---

[24] van Selm, *Een menighte*, 314 n. 281. Le document est conservé au Regionaal Archief Leiden, Gerechtsdagboek E (Stadsarchief Leiden 1575-1816, inv. nr. 49), f. 64r-v.
[25] Voir van Selm, *Een menighte*, 226 et 237, pour une reproduction de la page de titre du catalogue et de la page mentionnant le manuel de Valéry.
[26] Les annonces parues dans l'*Oprechte Haerlemse Courant* sont disponibles sur internet (http://home.wxs.nl/~jhelwig/ohc/ohc.htm ; voir le numéro 6690528,3).

De derde t'samensprekinghe: Erato   *Le troisiesme Dialogue : Erato*

f. B₂v

[Emerentia] — Waer hoore ick so zoetelick singhen? Ist hier niet daer my mijn ouders hebben belast te gaen? Het denckt my jae, naer het teecken dat ic hier sie uytsteken, te weten der Maegden-Berch. Ick sal aende deure cloppen.
[…]

[Emerence] — Où est que j'oys si harmonieusement chanter ? N'est ce pas ici où mes parens mont commandé d'aller ? Me semble que si, selon l'enseigne que je y vois propendre, à sçavoir le mont des pucelles. Je toucheray à l'huys.
[…]

f. B₄r

[…]
E[merentia] — Wat verheuginghe heeftmen alsmen den tijdt tot den avont heeft ghebracht?
M[eesteresse] — Indien eenighe dochter lust heeft om te leeren de conste van Musijcke, oft op de Clavesimble te spelen eenighe Lofsanck, Psalm oft eerlicke Liedeken, dat wort haer gheleert.
E. — Dat soude my rechts ghelijcken, want ick hebbe alreede eenighe danspelen gheleert.
M. — De danserijen comt toe de wereltsche dochters

[…]
E[merence] — Quelle recreation a on ayant employé le jour jusques au soir ?
M[aistresse] — S'il y a quelque Fille qui a envie d'apprendre l'art de Musique, ou de jouer à l'espinette quelque Canticque, Pseaume ou honneste Chanson, on la lui apprend.

E. — Cela me duyroit proprement, car j'ay desjà apprinse à jouer quelques danses.

M. — Les danseries competent aux filles mondaines

f. B₄v

ende lichtveerdige, ende niet die God vreesen.
E. — Die soodanighe lichte liedekens gheleert heeft, can oock wel Goddelicke Liedekens vaten.
M. — Seer wel, want de Musijcke wort op de selve grepen ghespeelt, naer dat die vanden meester geleert wort. Ende men hoort daghelicx inden Tempel hoe soetelick de Psalmen Davids op den Orgel gaen.

et legeres, et non à celles qui craignent Dieu.
E. — Qui a apprinses telles chansonnettes legeres, sçaura aussi bien comprendre chansons divines.
M. — Fort bien, car la Musicque se joue sur les mesmes touches, selon qu'elle s'apprend du Maistre. Et on oit journellement comment harmonieusement les Pseaumes de David se jouent aux orgues.

E. — Ick achte dat de oude die de conste van singen ende spelen van instrumenten, geen lichtveerdicheyt daer meer en hebben willen inbrenghen.

E. — J'estime que les anciens inventeurs de l'art de Musicque et des Instruments n'ont par iceux voulus induire aucune legereté.

M. — Neen, waerlick, want het is seker
dat den sanck ende Musicael spel, inden
ouden Testamente, is een deel gheweest
vande Goddelicke Ceremonien, die met de
comste Jesu Christi te niete ghedaen zijn.
Ende daeromme vermaent den Psalmist
David in vele Psalmen datmen God sal
loven met ghesanck, met Luyten, Harpen,
Orghelen ende allerley instrumenten van
ghenoechte.
Leest daerop den Cviij[en],

M. — Non pourvray, car il est certain
que le chant et jeu Musical a esté au vieil
Testament une partie des Ceremonies
divines, lesquelles sont abolies par
la venue de Jesus Christ. Et par ce,
admoneste David le Psalmiste, qu'on loue
Dieu par chants, par Luts, Harpes, Orgues
et toutes sortes d'instrumens.

Lisez sur ce le 108,

f. B₅r

f. B5r

Cxliiij, Cxlvij, Cxlix ende Cl Psalmen.
E. — Ick verheughe my, Meester[e]sse, dat
ghy de musicke lief hebt ende prijst.
M. — Ick houde selfs dat de voyselicke
ende instrumentale Musijcke seer groote
cracht heeft om de herten te roeren om
God te loven.
E. — Ick begeere dan by u te blijven
woonende, indien ick mijne verheuginghe
daer in houden mach.
[…]

144, 147, 149 et 150 Pseaumes.
E. — Je me delecte, ma Maistresse,
qu'aimez la Musique et la louez.
M. — Je tiens mesme que la Musique, tant
vocale qu'instrumentale, a tresgrande force
pour esmouvoir les cœurs à louer Dieu.

E. — Je desire donc bien demourer chez
vous, si j'y puis prendre ma delectation.
[…]

De vierde t'samensprekinghe, Thalia

Le quatriesme Dialogue. Thalia

f. B₆v
[…]
E[merentia] — Sy [de Meesteresse] is
de joncheyt seer goetgonstich om haer
selven te laten vermaken met eenighe
eerlicke exercicien van snaerspel, als van
Clavesimble ofte Cytere, of Musijck-
sanck, naer dat een yeder ghesint ist.

[…]
E[merence] — Elle [la Maistresse]
est aussi fort favorable à la jeunesse
pour la laisser recréer de quelque
honneste exercice de jeux Musical, tant
de l'espinette que du Cystre, ou de la
Musique vocale, selon l'affection de
chacun.

T[onijnken] — Dat is recht dat ick wel
begheere.
[…]

T[onette]. — Voylà droictement ce que
j'appete.
[…]

De vijfde t'samensprekinghe. Melpomene | Le cincquiesme Dialogue. Melpomene

f. C₃v

[...]

P[hillips] — Wat exercitie van spel hebt ghy onder uwe discipelen om haer te vermaken? Want mijn dochter singt gheerne gheestelicke liedekens.
M[eesteresse] — Daer in moet ickse prijsen, ende sal goede mede hulpe hebben van andere dochters daer inne oock lust hebbende.

P[hilipe] — Quel exercice de jeu avez-vous entre voz disciples pour se recréer ? Car ma fille chante voulontiers chansons spirituelles.
Maist[resse] — En ce faut il que je la prise et aura bonne correspondence d'autres filles qui y prennent aussi delectation.

f. C₄r

P. — Ick sal een Clavesimble hier bestellen om haer daer mede te oeffenen.
M. — Dat spel is musicael ende vermakelick. Het doet oock vele fantasien vergeten die anderssins de mensche beswaren.
P. — Het is een waerachtighe sake.
[...]

P. — J'envoieray icy une espinette pour soy exercer d'icelle.
Ma. — Ce jeu là est Musical et fort recreatif. Il faict aussi oublier beaucoup de fantasies qui autrement troublent l'homme.

P. — C'est une chose veritable.
[...]

De achtste t'samensprekinghe. Polimma. | Le huictiesme Dialogue. Polimma.

f. F₂r

M[eesteresse] — [...] Ghy cont wel, dencke ick, de Psalmen Davids lesen.

P[aulina] — Ja ick, Meester[e]sse, ick can den meestendeel daer van niet alleene lesen, maer oock wel singhen, want mijne ouders daerinne my seer ghestiert hebben.
[...]

M[aistresse] — [...] Vous sçavez bien, comme je pense, lire les Pseaumes de David.
P[auline] — Ouy, ma Maistresse, je sçay non seulement lire, mais aussi chanter la plus part d'iceux, car mes parens m'y ont fort instigez.
[...]

JOHANNES TINCTORIS
AND THE ART OF LISTENING

Rob C. Wegman

If there is one day in the life of Johannes Tinctoris about which I would love to know more, it is that fateful day, some time around 1480, when he was visiting Bruges and found himself listening to two blind viol players. Tinctoris, at the time, was in his mid-forties, and he had served for almost ten years as the chief musician at the royal court of Naples. During that decade he had published an impressive series of music treatises – treatises that had won him a reputation as the pre-eminent authority on music of his age. Yet for all its intellectual depth and scope, this formidable body of theoretical reflection seems to have left him somehow unprepared for what he was to hear that day in Bruges. All we know about the occasion comes from Tinctoris himself. A few years after the event he published one last treatise, *De inventione et usu musicae* (c.1481-83), and it is here that the memory surfaces, in the midst of a long discussion of musical instruments. Without warning, he interrupts his matter-of-fact description of bowed string instruments to share with us a little story from his personal life. Here is what he writes[1]:

'(**1**) Neque preterire in animum venit: quod exiguo tempore lapso: duos fratres Orbos natione Flamingos: viros quidem non minus litteris eruditos quam in cantibus expertos: quorum uni Carolus: alteri Johannes nomina sunt. Brugis audiverim: illum supremam partem et hunc tenorem plurium cantilenarum: tam perite: tamque venuste hujusmodi viola consonantes: ut in ulla nunquam melodia: me profecto magis oblectaverim.

[(**1**) Nor should I pass over the fact that a little while ago, I heard in Bruges two blind brothers – men of Flemish birth who, in truth, are no less learned in literary studies than they are versed in music, of whom one is called Carolus and the other Johannes – making concord on this kind of viol (the former playing the top part, and the latter the tenor of many songs) so skillfully, and so gracefully, that I truly have never found greater delight in any harmonious sound.

(**2**) Et quia rebecum (si sonitor artifex et expertus fuerit) modulos illis quam simillimos emittat: quibuslibet *affectus spiritus mei (occulta quadam familiaritate)* ad leticiam quam simillime *excitantur*.

(**2**) And since the rebec can produce tunes as similar as possible to those [of the viol], if the player be a craftsman and experienced, *the affections of my spirit (through some hidden kinship) are aroused*, by any [tunes] whatsoever, to joyous delight in as similar as possible a way.

---

[1]   After Karl Weinmann (ed.), *Johannes Tinctoris (1445–1511) und sein unbekannter Traktat 'De inventione et usu musicae'* (Regensburg, 1917), 45-6.

(3) Hec itaque duo instrumenta mea sunt. mea inquam: hoc est quibus inter cetera: animus meus ad *affectum pietatis* assurgit: quaeque ad contemplationem gaudiorum supernorum: *ardentissime* cor meum *inflammant*.

(3) These two instruments are mine, therefore. 'Mine', I say, that is by which, among other things, my mind rises up to *a feeling of devotion*, and which *most ardently* set my heart *aflame* to a contemplation of the joys on high.

(4) Quo mallem ea potius ad res sacras: et secreta animi solamina semper reservari: quam ad res prophanas et publica festa interdum applicari'.

(4) Therefore I would prefer to have them reserved always for sacred matters and the private solace of the mind, rather than have them used sometimes for profane matters and public feasts].

The two blind musicians, Johannes and Carolus, have been identified as the brothers Jean and Charles Fernandes. Unfortunately no other contemporary has written about their manner of playing, yet it is clear from documents that they were internationally famous, not only as musicians but as humanist scholars as well. They were in fact prolific writers, and if their collected works were to be printed today, they would probably run into several volumes.[2] Tinctoris's account of the Fernandes brothers and their viol playing is of course well known, and has already invited much scholarly commentary.[3] And yet, although its surface meaning seems clear enough, there is a lot going on beneath the surface of the text – and one of my aims in this paper is to bring out some of those deeper undercurrents of thought.

Take, for example, the words printed in italics: 'the affections of my spirit (through some hidden kinship) are aroused', 'a feeling of devotion', 'most ardently', 'aflame'. In his article 'Reading and Reminiscence: Tinctoris on the Beauty of Music', Christopher Page has pointed out that these are in fact direct borrowings from an old but extremely influential text, the *Confessions* of St Augustine (*Conf.* X. xxxiii). One is reminded of that well-known chapter in Umberto Eco's *Name of the Rose* in which Adso of Melk recounts how he spent a night of passionate love-making with a beautiful peasant girl, but is unable to describe the experience except by drawing on the language of the *Song of Songs*. For Tinctoris, too, it seems, the performance at Bruges left him

---

[2]   The lives of Jean and Charles Fernandes will be the subject of a forthcoming article provisionally entitled 'The Blind Brothers of Bruges'.

[3]   See f.i. Anthony Baines, 'Fifteenth-Century Instruments in Tinctoris's De Inventione et Usu Musicae', *Galpin Society Journal*, 3 (1950), 19-26, at 24-5; Ian Woodfield, *The Early History of the Viol* (Cambridge, 1984), 78-9; Christopher Page, 'Reading and Reminiscence: Tinctoris on the Beauty of Music', *Journal of the American Musicological Society*, 49 (1996), 1-31, at 11-7. For the date of the treatise, see Ronald Woodley, 'The Printing and Scope of Tinctoris's Fragmentary Treatise "De inventione et vsv mvsice"', *Early Music History*, 5 (1985), 239-68.

groping for words that could adequately convey its powerful effect on him, and St Augustine's language found its way into his narrative almost unbidden – or so it would seem. And yet, when we turn to the Church Father's own words, it turns out, paradoxically, that the two texts are completely at odds. St Augustine is talking about the pleasures of the ear, in a longer section devoted to the bodily senses and their perils. His attitude is one of profound ambivalence. Our Church Father admits that music has a powerful effect on him. Indeed it has sometimes moved him to tears. One chant in particular made a deep impression on the Church Father, shortly after his conversion in Milan, the Ambrosian hymn *Deus Creator omnium*. As St Augustine recalls elsewhere in his *Confessions*: 'How I wept during your hymns and songs! I was deeply moved by the music of the sweet chants of your Church. The sounds flowed into my ears and the truth was distilled in my heart. This caused the feelings to overflow. Tears ran, and it was good for me to have that experience'. And yet, the Church Father is also worried, deeply worried, that he is merely indulging in pleasurable sensations, that the sounds of plainchant might charm the ears, but distract from the words on which he feels he ought to focus. For that reason he has sometimes felt that one should do away with singing in church altogether, and just read the words aloud:[4]

'Voluptates aurium tenacius me implicaverant et subjugaverant; sed resolvisti, et liberasti me. Nunc in sonis quos animant eloquia tua, cum suavi et artificiosa voce cantantur, fateor, aliquantulum acquiesco; non quidem ut haeream, sed ut surgam cum volo. Attamen cum ipsis sententiis quibus vivunt, ut admittantur ad me, quaerunt in corde meo nonnullius dignitatis locum, et vix eis praebeo congruentem.

[The pleasures of the ear had a more tenacious hold on me, and had subjugated me; but you set me free and liberated me. As things now stand, I confess that I have some sense of restful contentment in sounds whose soul is your words, when they are sung by a pleasant and well-trained voice. Not that I am riveted by them, for I can rise up and go when I wish. Nevertheless, on being combined with the words which give them life, they demand in my heart some position of honour, and I have difficulty in finding what is appropriate to offer them.

---

[4] St Augustine of Hippo, *Confessions*, X. *xxxiii*, trans. Henry Chadwick (Oxford and New York, 1991), 207-9.

Aliquando enim plus mihi videor honoris eis tribuere quam decet, dum ipsis sanctis dictis religiosius et *ardentius* sentio moveri animos nostros *in flammam pietatis*, cum ita cantantur, quam si non ita cantarentur; et omnes *affectus spiritus nostri* pro sui diversitate habere proprios modos in voce atque cantu, quorum nescio qua *occulta familiaritate excitentur.* Sed delectatio carnis meae, cui mentem enervandam non oportet dari, saepe me fallit, dum rationem sensus non ita comitatur ut patienter sit posterior; sed tantum quia propter illam meruit admitti, etiam praecurrere ac ducere conatur. Ita in his pecco non sentiens, sed postea sentio.

Sometimes I seem to myself to give them more honour than is fitting. *I feel that when the sacred words are chanted well, our souls are moved and are kindled to a flame of piety, more religiously and with a warmer devotion than if they are not so sung. All the diverse emotions of our spirit have their corresponding modes in voice and chant, and are stirred through a mysterious inner kinship.* But my physical delight, which has to be checked from enervating the mind, often deceives me when sense perception is unaccompanied by reason, and not patiently content to be in a subordinate place. It tries to be first and to be in the leading role, though it deserves to be allowed only as secondary to reason. So in these matters I sin unawares, and only afterward become aware of it.

Aliquando autem hanc ipsam fallaciam immoderatius cavens, erro nimia severitate: sed valde interdum, ut melos omne cantilenarum suavium quibus Davidicum Psalterium frequentatur, ab auribus meis removeri velim, atque ipsius Ecclesiae; tutiusque mihi videtur quod de Alexandrino episcopo Athanasio saepe mihi dictum commemini, qui tam modico flexu vocis faciebat sonare lectorem psalmi, ut pronuntianti vicinior esset quam canenti. Verumtamen, cum reminiscor lacrymas meas, quas fudi ad cantus Ecclesiae tuae in primordiis recuperatae fidei meae, et nunc ipso quod moveor, non cantu, sed rebus quae cantantur, cum liquida voce et convenientissima modulatione cantantur, magnam instituti hujus utilitatem rursus agnosco.

Sometimes, however, by taking excessive safeguards against being led astray, I err on the side of too much severity. I have sometimes gone so far as to wish to banish all the melodies and sweet chants commonly used for David's psalter from my ears and remember being often told of bishop Athanasius of Alexandria. He used to make the Reader of the psalm chant with so flexible a speech-rhythm that he was nearer to reciting than to singing. Nevertheless, when I remember the tears which I poured out at the time when I was first recovering my faith, and that now I am moved not by the chant but by the words being sung, when they are sung with a clear voice and entirely appropriate modulation, then again I recognize the great utility of music in worship.

Ita fluctuo inter periculum voluptatis et experimentum salubritatis; magisque adducor, non quidem irretractabilem sententiam proferens, cantandi consuetudinem

Thus I fluctuate between the danger of pleasure and the experience of the beneficent effect, and I am more led to put forward the opinion (not as an irrevocable view) that the custom of singing in Church is to be approved, so that through the

approbare in Ecclesia; ut per
oblectamenta aurium infirmior
*animus in affectum pietatis
assurgat*. Tamen, cum mihi accidit
ut me amplius cantus, quam res
quae canitur, moveat; poenaliter me
peccare confiteor, et tunc mallem
non audire cantantem.

delights of the ear the weaker *mind may rise up
towards the devotion of worship*. Yet when it
happens to me that the music moves me more
than the subject of the song, I confess myself to
commit a sin deserving punishment, and then I
would prefer not to have heard the singer.

Ecce ubi sum: flete mecum, et pro
me flete, qui aliquid boni vobiscum
intus agitis unde facta procedunt.
Nam qui non agitis, non vos haec
movent. Tu autem, Domine Deus
meus, exaudi; respice, et vide, et
miserere, et sana me, in cujus oculis
mihi quaestio factus sum, et ipse est
languor meus'.

See my condition! Weep with me and weep
for me, you who have within yourselves a
concern for the good, the springs from which
good actions proceed. Those who do not
share this concern will not be moved by these
considerations. But you 'Lord my God, hear,
look and see' [Ps. 12: 4] and 'have mercy and
heal me' [Ps. 79: 15]. In your eyes I have become
a problem to myself, and that is my sickness].

For St Augustine, it seems, musical sounds are the equivalent of mind-altering drugs. Once you abandon yourself to those sounds, once you relinquish control, you do not know *what* they will end up doing to you. They may move you to tears, but they may also rouse you to violent anger, or cause suicidal despair, or provoke lascivious desire. Like Ulysses before the Sirens, you may find yourself powerless to resist them.

How is it that music can exert such extraordinary power over humans? St Augustine does not claim to have the definitive answer, but his neo-platonist background leads him to suggest one possibility: that there is a mysterious inner kinship between music and the human soul. It is as if music provides direct, sounding counterparts to particular states of mind. Take, for example, the innate human capacity for anger. According to St Augustine's explanation, anger cannot but be provoked by musical sounds that represent anger. That is how the mysterious inner kinship works. Just tune in to a heavy metal station, and before you know it you are chopping the veggies with all the frenzy of a deranged psychopath. Here is how St Augustine himself puts it, in one of the sentences to which Tinctoris later alluded: 'All the diverse *emotions of our spirit* have their corresponding modes in voice and chant, and are stirred through *a mysterious inner kinship* [between them]'. If music is so powerful and so potentially dangerous, then perhaps it would be better not to use it at all. But in the end St Augustine is not so sure. The extraordinary power of music may still be useful in church. For example, he knows from personal experience that scriptural words move him much more deeply *with* musical tunes than without them. That is what he meant when he said: 'The sounds flowed into my ears and *the truth was distilled into my heart*' – literally, the truth was refined, purified to its essence ('eliquabatur') by music. To quote another of the sentences to which Tinctoris would later allude: 'I feel that when the sacred words are chanted well, our souls are moved, and kindled *to a flame of piety*, more religiously and *with a warmer devotion*, than if they are not so sung'. So that is why St Augustine ends up recommending the use of music in church. Because he has personally experienced this effect, he concludes (perhaps not unreasonably) that others are bound to experience the same thing. Still, it is a cautious recommendation, one that he might well retract on further reflection. For St Augustine dreads music as much as he loves it. For him, there are only two beacons of certainty in the treacherous waters of musical delight: the words of the plainchant, on the one hand, and his own determination to resist the seductive powers of music, on the other. So it is not surprising that St Augustine, like most church fathers, strongly condemned music without words, or with the wrong words. In particular, he tirelessly inveighed against instrumental music. Not only did instrumental sounds smack of the theater and its immoral entertainments, but they lacked words, and thus seemed to exist merely for the arousal of sensuous pleasure. Such music was far too dangerous to be accorded even a limited place in the life of devout Christians.

How ironic it seems, then, that Tinctoris invokes his words precisely when he is writing about instrumental music. It is the theorist's experience listening to two viols, and viols performing secular tunes at that, which he implicitly likens to St Augustine's experience of psalm singing in church. Tinctoris completely ignores the critical distinction: that one involves scriptural words, and is therefore permissible, and the other has no words at all, and is therefore reprehensible. There is no way St Augustine could have approved of the way his words were being used here. Nor could he have had much respect for a man who admitted, without any moral scruples, that he had allowed himself to be carried away by the sound of two fiddles. By modern standards, obviously, Tinctoris has completely misread St Augustine. But that is precisely why his text is so interesting. A misreading of this magnitude tells us that Tinctoris was at great pains to bring across a point of his own – a point in which he believed so firmly that either it colored his understanding of St Augustine, or else led him to be knowingly oblivious to what the Church Father had meant to say. But what was that point? Why did he insert this extraordinary passage into an otherwise matter-of-fact discussion of musical instruments? What is the take-home message here?

The obvious place to start looking for an answer is the last sentence, labeled number four in the quotation above. Here, after all, is where we might expect Tinctoris to sum up his conclusions. At first sight it looks like a general recommendation, that the viol and rebec should always be reserved for sacred settings – presumably in church, perhaps during Elevation – rather than for profane matters and public feasts. But is that, in fact, the take-home message? If Tinctoris seriously expected the recommendation to be implemented, to be made binding for all those who played and heard the viol and rebec, then he should offer compelling arguments, founded in truth and reason, as he always did elsewhere. Otherwise, why issue a general recommendation in the first place? A story from his personal life, though undeniably disarming, was not going to convince many readers. Then again, it does not look as if Tinctoris really expected anyone to follow his recommendation. Apart from anything else, he seems to be consciously abdicating his scholarly authority here, by using the word 'mallem', which means 'I would prefer' or 'I would rather'. What he is saying, in so many words, is: 'if it were up to me'. He expresses a personal preference. The rest of us are presumably still free to disagree. This is confirmed by the preceding sentence, sentence number three: 'These two instruments are mine, therefore'. In other words, other people's favorite instruments might well be different ones altogether. And he goes on: '*mine*, I say, that is by which... *my* mind rises up to a feeling of devotion, and which most ardently set *my* heart aflame to a contemplation of the joys on high'. I, me, mine – this is really about himself and how these instruments affect him personally. If you or I are not moved by the viol in exactly the same way, it does not mean that there is anything wrong with us. All it means is that we are not Tinctoris.

This, in turn, is confirmed by the sentence before it, sentence number two. This is the place where Tinctoris invokes St Augustine's 'mysterious inner kinship'. Now, there is a small but very significant alteration as these words are lifted from the *Confessions* to Tinctoris's treatise. Indeed I would go so far as to speak of another misreading – this one more serious than the first. St Augustine speaks in general terms, terms that apply to all of us. He says: 'All the diverse emotions of *our* spirit have their corresponding modes in voice and chant, and are stirred through a mysterious inner kinship'. Every human being, according to the Church Father, has a range of emotions, each of which corresponds directly to a particular mode of singing, causing us to be moved to different emotions by different kinds of music. And although he does not say it in so many words, the implication is that we are all moved in the same way by the same sorts of music. It is not as if a sad tune will cause you to be sad, whereas someone else will become angry, and yet another joyful. If music were that erratic and unpredictable in its effects, then St Augustine would not have allowed it to be used under any circumstances. Tinctoris, however, is not interested in generalities. He changes the 'our' of St Augustine's 'our spirit' into 'me' and 'my spirit'. The consequence is that the hidden kinship with viols and rebecs has become unique to him alone. What he is saying, in effect, is this: I feel a special bond with these instruments, and that is why I call them mine. The implication, once again, is that Tinctoris is not really talking about the instruments so much as about himself. It is true that the viol and rebec are needed to awaken a peculiar sensibility within him. But since none of us may share that sensibility, the instruments function really like a mirror, in which he perceives the reflection of his own individuality. That, it seems, is why he abdicates his authority as theorist here, and simply shares a story from his personal life. It is as if he is saying: listen, I am about to tell you something that may strike you as absurd, but believe me, it does make sense if you hear what I experienced.

So the take-home message is really that there is no take-home message. Tinctoris does not presume to state objective facts about the musicianship of the blind brothers, the songs they played, or even their instruments. On the contrary, he makes it quite clear that everything he writes about them is mediated by his personal experience. If it had not been for that experience, he probably would not have written about the occasion in the first place. It does not matter if none of us, on that occasion in Bruges, would have responded the way he did. Even if the whole world disagreed with Tinctoris about the viol, it would not diminish the value of the experience to him personally. Its value is not contingent on the agreement of others. In fact, its value would not be contingent even on the agreement of St Augustine. Tinctoris's reasoning is exactly the opposite of the Church Father's. The latter endorsed church music because his personal experience led him to conclude that it could be beneficial for everybody. Tinctoris, by contrast, emphasizes that *his* personal experience cannot serve as the basis for any general pronouncement, because it is utterly subjective. This is a massive conceptual discrepancy. But I do not think that Tinctoris was particularly troubled by it. For when we look more closely, it is apparent that he does not actually treat the Church Father as an authority to back up his account, in the way he quotes Aristotle or Boethius on particular theoretical issues. Rather, his relationship to St Augustine is like that of a humanist who wants to speak like Cicero, and who knows his writings inside out, but who nevertheless wants to say his own thing. That, I think, is why Tinctoris does not bother to spell out that he is borrowing from the *Confessions*: it would not have added anything to the point he is making here. As far as he is concerned, the only authority he needs to speak about his experience in Bruges is the experience itself.

Compare this with a text written some eight years previously, in *Liber de natura et proprietate tonorum*, a treatise completed in 1476. In this passage, unlike the later one, Tinctoris does invoke St Augustine as an authority in the traditional sense, to lend support to a theoretical point he is making. Interestingly, the point in question is closely related to the issues raised by the Bruges story. Tinctoris claims that different people respond to music in different ways:[5]

'Nempe unius et eiusdem toni carmen possibile erit et planctivum et remissum et rigidum et medium esse, tum ex parte compositorum et pronunciatorum, tum instrumentorum et sonitorum. Quis enim huius artis peritus ignorat alios planctive, alios remisse, alios regide, alios medie componere, pronunciare et sonare, quamvis eorum compositio, pronunciatio et sonitus eodem tono ducantur?

[To be sure, it will be possible for a song in one and the same mode to be mournful, gentle, stern, or moderate, not only with respect to composers and performers, but to instruments and players as well. For what person skilled in this art does not know how to compose, perform, or play some [songs] mournfully, some gently, some sternly, and some moderately, even though they are all composed, performed and played in the same mode?

Vocum etiam et instrumentorum genera quaedam planctiva, quaedam remissa, quaedam rigida et quaedam media naturaliter aut artificialiter sunt aut efficiunt. Unde et secundum ea differentias harmoniarum, cum de fistulis et organis, tum de cytharis et aliis instrumentis loquens ipse philosophus assignat.

Certain types of voices and instruments, by nature or by design, are mournful, certain gentle, certain harsh, and certain moderate, or have those effects. That is why that philosopher [Aristotle] assigns differences of harmonies accordingly, speaking now of pipes and organs, then of lyres and other instruments.

Quarumquidem harmoniarum aliae aliis aetatibus et moribus conveniunt, decent et expediunt, nec earum apud omnes eadem est delectatio aut simile iudicium. Remissus enim animus harmoniis remissis delectatur, e converso rigidae rigido sunt acceptae'.

Of these harmonies certain ones are agreeable, fitting, and useful for different ages and customs, and there is not the same delight or a similar judgment to all [people]. A gentle soul is delighted by gentle harmonies, and conversely stern ones are agreeable to a stern soul].

---

[5]   Johannes Tinctoris, *Liber de natura et proprietate tonorum* (1476). After Johannes Tinctoris, *Opera theoretica*, ed. Albert Seay, i (Corpus Scriptorum de Musica, 22; n.p., 1975-78), 68-69.

In other words, music is not going to move you unless it precisely matches your peculiar temperament, your psychological make-up. If you are not a particularly cheerful person, say, then cheerful melodies will leave you relatively indifferent. Which is to say that music really serves as a kind of mirror in which you recognize your own individuality, your peculiar sensibility. In the end, the only reason why you happen to like some kinds of music more than others may be that they agree better with you personally. Your preference may be as subjective as Tinctoris's preference for viol music.

Tinctoris presents this observation as a general truth-claim, and so he needs to demonstrate it if readers are going to agree with him. To that purpose, he turns to St Augustine. This time, interestingly, he does treat the Church Father like a proper authority. He quotes a sentence from the *Confessions* in its entirety, not just isolated words and phrases, and he makes sure to properly credit the quotation, not just weave the words inconspicuously into his own narrative. Tinctoris continues:

'Quod Augustinus sentire videtur in libro Confessionum dicens: *Omnes affectus species nostri pro sua diversitate habent proprios modos in voce atque cantu quorum occulta familiaritate excitantur*'.	[St Augustine is seen to believe this in a book of his Confessions, when he says: 'All the diverse emotions of our spirit have their corresponding modes in voice and chant, and are stirred through a mysterious inner kinship'].

By quoting this sentence he commits the very same misreading that we find some eight years later in the Bruges story. Tinctoris claims that every individual has a mysterious inner kinship with the music he or she happens to prefer, just as he himself was to feel such a kinship with the sounds of the viol and rebec. Needless to repeat, St Augustine had never implied anything of the kind. For him, the mysterious inner kinship was between the entire range of emotions, in all of us, and the different sorts of music that could elicit these emotions, in all of us. In other words, for him responses to music were universally shared, not peculiar to individuals.

To appreciate the significance of Tinctoris's text, let us now broaden our perspective a little, and consider late-medieval thinking about music listening in general. Let us begin with a text from the writings of the cardinal and theologian Nicholas of Cusa. Not that he was an expert on music, but for our purposes he does not need to be. For what his text illustrates is what any man of education, including Tinctoris himself, would have taken as accepted in the mid-fifteenth century. The specific question that concerns Nicholas of Cusa may seem a little academic at first: how do humans and animals hear polyphony? And this is how he answers it. Senseless animals, Nicholas says, find pleasure in consonant sound, just like us. Yet they are unable to understand *why* it is pleasurable, because they lack the faculty of reason. They are wholly at the mercy of mere aural sensations. Humans, on the other hand, do have the capacity to understand, since they can determine the mathematical ratios of consonances – and it is those ratios that ultimately account for the pleasure. You only need to do the math: a 3:2 ratio here, a 2:1 ratio there, and then comes the proverbial 'Aha Erlebnis': Ah! So *that* is why we like those fifths and octaves so much.[6]

'Quando enim audimus concinentes voces: sensu attingimus. Sed differentias & concordantias: ratione & disciplina mensuramus. Quam vim: in brutis non reperimus. Non enim habent vim numerandi & proportionandi. Et ideo incapaces sunt disciplinae musicae: licet sensu voces nobiscum attingant & moveantur concordantia vocum ad delectationem.

[When we hear voices singing together we arrive at this through the sense. But we measure differences and consonances through reason and study. We do not find this power in beasts, for they do not have the power of numbering and of making proportions. And for that reason they are incapable of the science of music, although they hear sounds through the sense as we do, and are moved to delight by the consonance of sounds.

Anima igitur nostra: rationalis merito dicitur, quia est vis ratiocinativa seu numerativa, in se complicans cuncta, sine quibus perfecta discretio fieri nequit.

Therefore our soul is deservedly called rational, because it is the power of calculating or numbering, enfolding all in itself, without which perfect distinction cannot be made.

Quando enim sensu auditus movetur ad motum delectationis ob dulcem harmonicam concordantiam, & intra se invenit rationem concordantiae in numerali proportione fundari: disciplinam ratiocinandi de musicis concordantiis per numerum invenit'.

For when one is moved by the sense of hearing to delight, on account of a sweet harmonious consonance, and discovers within oneself that the reason of consonance is founded in numerical proportion, one discovers the art of calculating musical consonances through number.]

None of this, of course, is unusual for its time. Nicholas of Cusa is simply repeating what he had learned by reading Boethius as a student – *De musica* was a standard text in the medieval liberal arts curriculum. Yet there are a number of corollaries that are worth drawing out.

---

[6] Nicholas of Cusa, *De ludo globi, II* (1462-63). Text and trans. after Nicholas of Cusa, *De Ludo Globi: The Game of Spheres*, trans. Pauline Moffitt Watts (New York, 1986), 104-5. Cf. Heinrich Hüschen, 'Nikolaus von Kues und sein Musikdenken', in Friedrich Wilhelm Riedel and Hubert Unverricht (eds.), *Symbolae Historiae Musicae: Hellmut Federhofer zum 60. Geburtstag* (Mainz, 1971), 47-67.

First of all, the teachings rehearsed by Nicholas of Cusa seem to answer the dilemma felt by St Augustine, who so desperately clung to *words* to keep the musical experience from becoming sinful. He need not have worried. For as Nicholas of Cusa confirms, even when there are no words, one can still find worthwhile things to appreciate in music. Those things are the consonances, and their underlying mathematical ratios. The great thing about these ratios is that they can be empirically demonstrated, on the measuring tool known as the monochord – which is basically a single string stretched along a ruler. So the appreciation of consonance is really an appreciation of objectively demonstrable truth, of 'certain' knowledge. More than that, the truth in question stems directly from the mind of the divine creator, just as surely as the Word of God does. After all, did not the Book of Wisdom say that God has 'ordered all things in measure and number and weight'? Surely the truth of that was borne out beautifully by consonances. Not that you needed to be a mathematician to arrive at this kind of appreciation. Even music theorists were not going to remind themselves of numerical proportions at every turn. The crucial ability in question here, the ability that animals were thought not to have, was that of making abstractions. Imagine, for example, that you hear the following sounds, produced, respectively, on an organ, on two clarinets, by your kitchen blender, and two singers:

Example 1.

According to Nicholas of Cusa, an animal would register four completely different sonorities, all of them vaguely pleasurable. But, or so his argument implies, a human would say: they are really the same sound, for I hear a fifth in every case. This idea of 'a fifth' is obviously an abstraction. It reflects a decision to focus only on intervallic relationships, and to disregard issues of sonority, orchestration, loudness, pitch, acoustic environment, or social setting. Needless to add, the fifth as such does not exist except as an idea: it resides somewhere in the same realm as, say, $e = mc^2$, or the number fifteen. There is a further corollary as well. If I am able to abstract the idea of 'the fifth' from a bewildering variety of sounds; and if it can be shown that this idea reflects objective mathematical truth – then it means that on the highest level, on the level of the rational soul, musical experience is not 'subjective' but 'objective'. For the mathematical truth I respond to on that level is just as true for you as it is for me, or anybody else – it is universal.

This is useful to know for a variety of reasons. First of all, it means that I can listen to polyphony without any guilt or self-consciousness. I do not need to learn how to listen, or to acquire an art of listening. So long as I am enjoying consonances for what they are, which seems easy enough, I can actually claim to be engaging in musical appreciation of the highest order. True, composers and professional musicians may be able to hear a lot more than that. They may be able to tell, for example, how a motet is put together, what structure it has, what rhythmic proportions are being used. But all that pertains merely to human handiwork. Styles and techniques may come and go, musical tastes may change over time, or vary between countries or individuals. All of that is historically contingent and subjective, and it divides specialists from lay folk – which is probably why Nicholas of Cusa has no interest in talking about it. After all, how could any of this compare to music's power to unite *all* listeners, learned as well as unlearned, in a shared appreciation of objective and divinely-inspired truth? This is perhaps one reason why late-medieval eyewitness descriptions of music seldom give us the kind of information that we would most like to have: what piece was heard, who was the composer, how was it performed, and what sort of appreciation did listeners have of its technical, compositional qualities? Instead, writers seem to be going on and on about the 'wondrous sweetness' of the consonant sounds, in language that is bound to strike the modern reader as conventional and commonplace. And yet, from their own point of view, these writers were really focusing on what was all-important – and they left out details that would have been of interest only to a handful of specialists. It was simply not their job to write like experts for experts. It may also explain another feature of late-medieval eyewitness descriptions of musical events: the tendency for writers to assume, quite unselfconsciously, that if *they* found delight in a musical performance, then everybody else must have as well. This follows logically from the fact that true musical experience was known to be objective. In this period, paradoxically, the most private musical experiences, deep within the rational soul, were also the most public ones, since the truths found most deeply within are precisely the truths most valid for everybody else. If there was anyone who did not find delight, then there had to be something seriously wrong with him – though this was almost impossible to conceive.

This attitude of serene confidence in the goodness and truth of consonant sound, and its universal appreciation by all humans, is what characterizes late-medieval musical culture. Take, for example, the following document, in which the author, a humanist writing at the Papal Curia in the late 1430s, speaks of 'divine hymns and psalms…sung with different and diverse voices', that is, sung in polyphony. He does not tell us what we would most like to know: whether these were the hymns by Dufay, which had in fact been written in

Rome in the 1430s. Instead he waxes lyrical over what he calls the 'incredible sweetness and harmony' of the music. So overwhelmed is he by the memory alone of such musical splendor, that he cannot imagine how anyone could possibly remain unmoved when hearing it in real life. This is how he puts it:[7]

'Sunt archiepiscopi, epiescopi, patriarchae, protonotarii aliique paene infiniti ordines, omnes maxima dignitate et auctoritate ad Dei cultum instituti et inventi, qui cum in unum vel ad sacrificium vel ad quamvis rem divinam obeundam conierunt et, sedente pontifice maximo in augusta illa pontificum sede collocato, cuncti ex ordine assederunt ac divini illi hymni ac psalmi disparibus variisque vocibus decantantur, quis est tam inhumanus, tam barbarus, tam agrestis, quis rursus tam immanis, tam Deo hostis, tam expers religionis, qui haec aspiciens audiensque non moveatur, cuius non mentem atque animum aliqua religione occupet et stupore perstringat et dulcedine quadam deliniat? Cuius non oculi mirifice aspectu ipso pascantur oblectenturque? Cuius non aures incredibili cantus suavitate et harmonia mulceantur? Quo quidem spectaculo quod in terris pulchrius, quod maius, quod divinius, quod admiratione, quod memoria ac literis dignius reperitur, ut non homines modo, qui intersunt et quibus hoc natura datum est, sed ipsius etiam parietes templi et exultare quodammodo et gestire laetitia videatur?'.

[Archbishops, bishops, patriarchs, protonotaries, and other orders almost beyond limit have all been instituted and invented, with the greatest dignity and authority, for the worship of God. When they have convened as one body to attend either the sacrifice or any other divine service, and [when] they have all sat down in order, the Pope being seated in that venerable throne of the Popes, and *[when] those divine hymns and psalms are sung with different and diverse voices, [then] who is so uncultured, so uncivilized, so boorish, who again is so savage, so inimical to God, so lacking in reverence, that he, seeing and hearing these things, is unmoved, whose mind and soul are not seized with some feeling of reverence, and overcome by stupefaction, and captivated by a certain sweetness, whose eyes are not marvelously nourished and delighted by the very sight, whose ears are not charmed by the incredible sweetness and harmony of the song?* Indeed, what could be found in this world that is more beautiful, that is greater, that is more divine, that is more worthy of wonder, of remembrance and the historical record, than this sight – so that not just humans, who take part [in all this] and to whom this is given by nature, but the very walls of the temple seem to be elated in some way, and to exult with happiness?]

This is the kind of certainty and conviction that Tinctoris could no longer bring himself to express when he wrote about the Fernandes brothers. Somewhere

---

[7] Lapo da Castiglionchio the Younger, *De Curiae Commodis*. Text and trans. after Christopher S. Celenza, *Renaissance Humanism and the Papal Curia: Lapo da Castiglionchio the Younger's De Curiae Commodis* (Papers and Monographs of the American Academy in Rome, 31; Ann Arbor, 2000), 130-33. Cf. Giovanni Zanovello, 'Les humanistes florentins et la polyphonie liturgique'', in Perrine Galand-Hallyn and Fernand Hallyn (eds.), *Poétiques de la Renaissance: Le modèle italien, le monde franco-bourguignon et leur héritage en France au XVIe siècle* (Travaux d'Humanisme et Renaissance, 348; Geneva, 2001), 625-38 and 667-73, at 629 and 669-70, and Rob C. Wegman, 'Musical Understanding in the Fifteenth Century', *Early Music*, 30 (2002), 46-66.

along the line things must have changed for him. Evidently he had stopped believing in a premise that had been taken as self-evident all his life. But what was the truth he abandoned? And why did he lose faith in it?

The document from the Papal Curia that I just quoted, and countless documents like it, tells us one important thing about late-medieval musical culture: there was no art of listening. You did not need to learn how to listen if you wanted to properly appreciate polyphony. The hard thing rather was *not* to appreciate it. To remain totally unmoved by polyphony, it was necessary for the hearer to be uncultured, uncivilized, boorish, savage, inimical to God, and lacking in reverence. Now, where were you going to find such a rare individual? By contrast, nothing could be easier than to appreciate polyphony, to let your ears be charmed by the incredible sweetness and harmony of the sound. Even animals can do that, as Nicholas of Cusa assured us. True, animals lack the ability to make abstractions, to conceptualize the idea of the fifth, let alone to comprehend its mathematical basis. But even the lowliest choirboy can be taught what a fifth is, and can recognize one without a moment's hesitation. Still, there is something missing in all of this. Remember the four sonorities in Example 1. Technically these are all fifths. But that is an observation that seems worth making only if you are prepared to completely disregard everything else: sonority, orchestration, loudness, pitch, acoustic environment, or social setting. The question is: why would you disregard all of that? How would that enrich rather than impoverish our musical understanding? Take the first sonority, for example, a fifth sounded near the bottom end of a grand organ. By no stretch of the imagination could this sonority be called sweet and agreeable. Musically it would probably be more useful as noise. Which is to say that the concept of the fifth, and its mathematical basis, does not begin to tell us how and why a given sonority can be heard as musically interesting.

It is this realisation that lies at the basis of Tinctoris's most important treatise on music, the *Liber de arte contrapuncti*, completed in 1477. In it, he spends two entire books to discuss a question that all conventional counterpoint treatises dispensed with in a couple of sentences: what is a consonance, and what is a dissonance? For Tinctoris, there are two answers to that question. First, there is consonance and dissonance as they are defined by reason and tradition – which is the easy answer that counterpoint manuals normally gave. But second, and more important, there is our subjective impression as to how sweet and agreeable a given sonority is. For example, reason and tradition tell us that the sonority played near the bottom end of the grand organ is a consonance, a fifth. But our musical sensibility tells us that it lacks sweetness, or to put it more neutrally, that it approximates noise. From the point of view of theory this represents a troubling discrepancy – this is not supposed to happen, not if we insist that a consonance is intrinsically pleasing to the ear. But Tinctoris does not seek to deny it or explain it away. On the contrary: he makes it clear at every turn that what you 'know' in theory does not always have to agree with what you 'hear' in practice.

A good example is his discussion of the sixth, in the first book of the *Liber de arte contrapuncti*. Tinctoris begins by observing that tradition is not unanimous as to whether it is a consonance or not. This, he explains, is because it really depends on how you listen to it. If you hear a sixth by itself, that is, alone, it sounds rather harsh and unpleasant – at least to his ears. To quote from his discussion:[8]

'Diapente cum semitonio est concordantia ex mixtura duarum vocum diapente ac semitonio ab invicem distantium constituta, sicut mi, E la mi gravis, et fa, C sol fa ut, ut hic:	[The fifth with semitone is a consonance, made by the combination of two pitches at a distance from each other of a fifth and a semitone, just as *mi* E *la mi* grave and *fa* C *sol fa ut*, as here:

Diapente autem cum tono concordantia est ex mixtura duarum vocum diapente ac tono ab invicem distantium effecta, sicut fa, F fa ut gravis, et sol, D la sol re, ut hic:	The fifth with whole tone is also a consonance, made by the combination of two pitches at a distance from each other of a fifth and a whole tone, just as *fa* F *fa ut* grave and *sol* D *la sol re*, as here:

Porro omnis sexta, sive perfecta sive imperfecta, sive superior sive inferior fuerit, apud antiquos discordantia reputabatur, et ut vera fatear, aurium mearum iudicio per se audita, hoc est sola, plus habet asperitatis quam dulcedinis'.	On the other hand, every sixth, be it perfect or imperfect, above or below, was considered by the ancients as a discord, and, *to confess the truth, heard by itself, that is, alone, by the judgment of my ears, it has more asperity than sweetness*].

[8]   Johannes Tinctoris, *Liber de arte contrapuncti (1477)*, I. vii. 2, 4, 6. After Johannes Tinctoris, *Opera theoretica*, 2, 11-89, at 32-3. Trans. after Johannes Tinctoris, *The Art of Counterpoint*, trans. Albert Seay (Musicological Studies and Documents, v; n.p., 1961), 34. See also Klaus-Jürgen Sachs, 'Boethius and the Judgement of the Ears: A Hidden Challenge in Medieval and Renaissance Music', in Charles Burnett, Michael Fend, and Penelope Gouk (eds.), *The Second Sense: Studies in Hearing and Musical Judgement from Antiquity to the Seventeenth Century* (London, 1991), 169-98; Rob C. Wegman, 'Sense and Sensibility in Late-Medieval Music: Reflections on Aesthetics and "Authenticity"', *Early Music*, 23 (1995), 298-312; Rob C. Wegman, 'Johannes Tinctoris and the "New Art"', *Music & Letters*, 84 (2003), 171-88.

Then again, who is going to listen to a sixth by itself? All you would hear is a sonority so abstract, so divorced from any musical context or purpose, that every judgment about it would be meaningless in any case. What really matters is what you do with it musically. Depending on how you use the sixth, it might well exhibit the most wondrous, the most captivating, the most exquisite sweetness. But the composer does have to learn how to use it, and the listener must learn how to appreciate what the composer is doing. The Art of Composition and the Art of Listening are really two sides of the same coin – which is why Tinctoris teaches them both in his counterpoint treatise.

The upshot is that Tinctoris is not interested in consonance as defined by reason and tradition. What matters to him is sweetness as perceived by those who have learned to appreciate it. Sweetness is a subjective quality – that is why he said, a moment ago, 'according to the judgement of *my* ears', admitting scope for disagreement. Unless you have trained your ears, unless you have acquired the Art of Listening, you may never become a very discriminating connoisseur of sweetness, even though you might be able to tell consonance from dissonance. As I have argued in my essay 'Sense and Sensibility in Late-Medieval Music', Tinctoris regarded sweetness as a quality contingent on a whole range of subtle musical conditions, including scoring, spacing, orchestration, voice-leading, intervallic superimpositions, even tempo. Indeed at one point he says that something may sound horrible when performed slowly, but wondrously sweet if you speed it up a bit. Then again, if you perform a piece too fast, as modern performers routinely do, you lose all sweetness.

Perhaps this gives us a clue to that extraordinary experience Tinctoris had in Bruges. He tells us that the Fernandes brothers played the tenors and top voices of many songs. So we may assume that these were well-composed, and that the composers had taken care of proper consonance handling. But consonances, by themselves, did not warrant a truly out-of-this-world experience. The sweetness that Tinctoris heard, and that moved him to the core of his being, was contingent on something else, some other quality. It could have been a combination of many things: tempo, phrasing, dynamics, intonation, what not. But all Tinctoris will say about it is that the sound of the viol was decisive. This is what carried the consonances from mere pitch relationships, defined in abstract terms, to a level of almost otherworldly sweetness. Not that Tinctoris ever understood why the viol moved him so much. All he could offer by way of explanation was St Augustine's notion of a mysterious inner kinship – which does not actually explain anything. But then, if sweetness is subjective, what *is* there to be understood about it? Why does a stretch of counterpoint sound better when you speed it up a bit? Or when you play it on viols rather than flutes? Or when you sing it at the top of your range rather than near the bottom? Or when you sing it soft or loud, with vibrato or without? All you can say is that experience teaches you this.

So Tinctoris cannot prove anything about the viol. He cannot tell us how to listen to it. All he can do is share his own experience, for whatever it may be worth. I see his decision to share that experience as an act of generosity. It was an invitation for readers to see if they could change their minds about the viol (if they wished to), if they could hear some beauty in its sound that they might never have suspected otherwise. If they did not hear it, that was alright, too: we can take or leave Tinctoris's account, it does not oblige us to anything. Still, if we wish to pick up a take-home message, then it is not hard to discern one. That message could be summarized as follows. To all of us it may be given to have a mysterious inner kinship with certain kinds of music, and if we do, the resulting experience may well be one of ecstasy. That experience is necessarily subjective, however, since other people need not have the same inner kinship, with the same kind of music, as we do. For that reason we will not be open to the kind of experience he had at Bruges if we insist that the only worthwhile musical truth is objective, and valid irrespective of who is listening, or how. It is certainly possible to listen to music objectively, and to write about it in terms of objective truth. Throughout the late Middle Ages it had in fact been assumed that this was the only worthwhile way to listen to music. But Tinctoris was the first theorist, so far as I know, to acknowledge a fundamentally different way of listening that was essentially subjective. In this as in so many other respects, he emerges as one of the most profound and original musical thinkers of his age.

CONTRIBUTORS

Pieter Bergé is Professor of Music Analysis, History and Theory (1750-1900) at the University of Leuven. His main research topics are Arnold Schoenberg, German opera during the Weimar Republic, Formenlehre, instrumental music from 1770-1830, and 'analysis-and-performance'-issues. He published two monographs on Schoenberg's operas (*Moses und Aron*, *Von heute auf morgen*), and numerous articles on Haydn, Beethoven, Schubert, Brahms, Krenek, Busoni, Schnebel and others. He is the current president of the Dutch-Flemish Society for Music Theory and co-editor of the series *Analysis in Context. Leuven Studies in Musicology*.

Peter Bergquist is Professor Emeritus of Music History, Theory, and Bassoon at the School of Music and Dance, University of Oregon. His research interests have included Schenkerian analysis, Renaissance music theory, and Gustav Mahler, but his main focus for many years has been the music of Orlando di Lasso. His papers on that subject have appeared in journals, *Festschriften*, and conference proceedings. He is general editor of Orlando di Lasso, *The Complete Motets*, twenty-one volumes and supplement (A-R Editions, 1995-2007), of which he edited thirteen volumes himself, and the editor of four volumes in Lasso's *Sämtliche Werke, neue Reihe* (Bärenreiter, 1956-96). In 1983 and 1990 A-R Editions issued two other volumes of Lasso's music that he edited. He also edited *Orlando di Lasso Studies* (Cambridge, 1999), which includes essays by eleven Lasso scholars, including Ignace Bossuyt. Bergquist's undergraduate studies as a bassoon major were conducted at the Eastman School of Music and Mannes College of Music, and he received his M.A. and Ph.D. in musicology from Columbia University.

Stanley Boorman studied at King's College, London University, with Thurston Dart and Ian Bent among others. He has taught at Nottingham and Cambridge in England, and at the University of Wisconsin in the USA. He is currently a Professor of Music at New York University. His research has focussed on printed and manuscript sources of the Renaissance, with particular interest in the structure and content of the source. This has led to the belief that sophisticated study of an edition or manuscript tells us more than we expect about the history of the music contained, its transmission and reception, and about details of performing practice. He has recently published a bibliographical study and catalogue of the volumes produced by Ottaviano Petrucci, with an essay exploring their technical aspects to derive information about patronage, market and performance. A collection of his papers on musical bibliography has been published as *Studies in the Printing, Publishing and Performance of Music in the 16th Century*, and a study of the structural patterns of early printed music, with analysis of the reasons for anomalies, has recently appeared in *Studies in Bibliography*.

David J. Burn studied musicology at Merton College, Oxford, completing a doctorate on the mass-propers of Heinrich Isaac in 2002, under the supervision of Reinhard Strohm. From 2002-03, he was a Guest Researcher at Kyoto City University of Arts. From 2003-07, David Burn was a Junior Research Fellow at St. John's College, Oxford, during which he carried out further research on sixteenth-century mass-proper repertories. He was appointed to a lectureship at the University of Leuven in 2007. Published articles, on various aspects of renaissance music, have appeared in the *Revue de musicologie*, the *Journal of Musicology*, the *Archiv für Musikwissenschaft*, and *The Journal of Music Theory*. Current projects include the completion of a book on Heinrich Isaac's mass-propers and an edition of the mass-propers of Francisco Corteccia.

Mark Delaere is Professor and Head of Musicology at the University of Leuven. His research covers mainly music from the 20th and 21st centuries, with a special focus on the interaction of analysis, history, theory and aesthetics of music. Book publications include *Funktionelle Atonalität. Analytische Strategien für die frei-atonale Musik der Wiener Schule* (1993), *New Music, Aesthetics and Ideology* (1995), and *Pierrot lunaire. A collection of musicological and literary studies* (2004). He wrote several entries for the new editions of *The New Grove* and *Die Musik in Geschichte und Gegenwart*, and contributed chapters to books and articles to periodicals on the music of e.g. Schoenberg, Goeyvaerts, Messiaen, Hindemith, Bach and Brahms. His current research is on tempo relationships in contemporary music (Carter, Ferneyhough, Stockhausen, Andriessen). He is General editor of the book series *Analysis in Context. Leuven Studies in Musicology*.

Willem Elders is retired Professor of Music History before 1600 at Utrecht University. Among his publications on Renaissance music, the following books may be mentioned: *Studien zur Symbolik in der Musik der alten Niederländer* (Bilthoven, 1968); *Composers of the Low Countries* (Oxford, 1991); *Symbolic Scores: Studies in the Music of the Renaissance* (Leiden and New York, 1994). From 1968 to 1988 Elders was the editor of the *Tijdschrift van de Koninklijke Vereniging voor Nederlandse Muziekgeschiedenis*. In 1984, he organised together with the Westdeutsche Rundfunk in Cologne an international Josquin symposium, and a second Josquin symposium in 1986 at Utrecht University.

He is presently chairman of the Editorial Board of the *New Josquin Edition*, to which he himself so far has contributed six volumes. Elders was awarded the Dent Medal by the International Musicological Society in 1969, and the medal of the Koninklijke Vereniging voor Nederlandse Muziekgeschiedenis in 1989.

Iain Fenlon is Professor of Historical Musicology in the Faculty of Music, and a Fellow of King's College at Cambridge University. He has held visiting appointments at Wellesley College, Massachusetts (1978-9), Harvard University (1984-5), the British School in Rome (1985), the Centre de Musique Ancienne, Geneva (1988-9), the École Normale Supériéure, Paris (1998-9), and the University of Bologna (2000-2001). In 1984 he was awarded the Dent Medal of the Royal Musical Association. Iain Fenlon is the founding editor of *Early Music History* (1981-). His principal area of research is music from 1450 to 1650, particularly in Italy. An early monograph on music on sixteenth-century Mantua explores how the Gonzaga family patronised the reform of liturgical music and the secular arts of spectacle. With James Haar he has written a study of the emergence of the Italian madrigal, which establishes the importance of its Florentine origins, and his 1994 Panizzi lectures on early Italian music print culture are published by The British Library. *Giaches de Wert: Letters and Documents* (Paris, 1999) provides editions with commentary of the composer's letters, including an important cache of autographs discovered in the late 1990s. Most of his writings, some of which are gathered together in *Music and Culture in Late Renaissance Italy* (Oxford, 2000), explore how the history of music is related to the history of society. His most recent book, *The Ceremonial City: History, Memory and Myth in Renaissance Venice*, has been published by Yale University Press in November 2007.

Sean Gallagher is Associate Professor of Music at Harvard University. His research focuses on music in France, Italy, and the Low Countries in the fifteenth century. He is co-editor of *Western Plainchant in the First Millennium* (Ashgate, 2003) and of *The Century of Bach and Mozart: Perspectives on Historiography, Composition, Theory and Performance* (Harvard University Press, forthcoming 2008), and is currently completing a book on Johannes Regis. In Fall 2007 he was visiting professor at Villa I Tatti in Florence. His contribution to this volume is part of a larger research project on fifteenth-century Italian chansonniers.

Barbara Haggh is Professor of Music at the University of Maryland, College Park, Chair of the International Musicological Society Study Group 'Cantus Planus', and Vice President of the International Musicological Society. She has published articles on music in Ghent, Brussels, Cambrai, and at the Sainte Chapelle in Paris, as well as on the manuscript 'F', the music theory treatises ascribed to Aurelian and Ciconia, 'historiae' and other chant by composers from Cambrai, and the responsory *Gaude, Maria virgo*.

John Irving is Professor of Music History and Performance Practice at the University of Bristol. His main interests are the instrumental music of Mozart, especially the piano and chamber music on which he has published three books (two more are in preparation) and numerous articles, book chapters and reviews, and music in Elizabethan England. He is also active in the field of performance, specialising in the fortepiano repertoire of the classical period. He is a frequent speaker at musicology conferences in the United Kingdom and internationally and is a Council Member of the Royal Musical Association. In addition to his work on Mozart, he is fascinated by the history and development of the piano. He is General editor of a new series of monographs on William Byrd, and editor of several volumes of the series *Musica Britannica* and *Corpus of Early Keyboard Music*.

Eric Jas is Lecturer in the Department of Musicology at Utrecht University. His main field of research is Franco-Flemish music of the fifteenth and sixteenth centuries. Among his publications are two volumes of the *New Obrecht Edition* and the proceedings of the Utrecht conference *Beyond Contemporary Fame. Reassessing the Art of Clemens non Papa and Thomas Crecquillon* (Turnhout, 2005). He is a member of the editorial board of the *New Josquin Edition* and the General editor of the *Tijdschrift van de Koninklijke Vereniging voor Nederlandse Muziekgeschiedenis*.

Mary S. Lewis is Professor of Music at the University of Pittsburgh. She is the author of the three-volume study and catalogue, *Antonio Gardano, Venetian Music Printer 1538-1569* (New York, 1988-2005). The Music Library Association has awarded her Gardano study its Vincent Duckles Award for best bibliography or reference work of 2005. Prof. Lewis has published numerous articles and reviews on music printing and sixteenth-century music, and edited two volumes of motets for Garland's motet series. She has held Fellowships from the Guggenheim Foundation, the National Endowment for the Humanities, the Bibliographical Society of America, and the American Philosophical Society, among others. She holds the Ph.D. from Brandeis University and an MA from Columbia University. Her future projects include studies on a major sixteenth-century Venetian manuscript and on aspects of Giovanelli's *Novus Thesaurus Musicus*.

Francesco Luisi e' Professore Ordinario di *Storia della musica medievale e rinascimentale* e *Storia delle teorie musicali* e direttore dell'Istituto di Musicologia presso l'Università degli studi di Parma. Si occupa principalmente di storia della musica dall'Umanesimo al Barocco e pubblica saggi, studi storici ed edizioni critiche riguardanti specialmente la polifonia dal Quattrocento al Settecento. Ha al suo attivo oltre 300 titoli, fra cui ca. 70 saggi, 10 edizioni critiche, due monografie monumentali (*La musica vocale nel Rinascimento* e *Laudario giustinianeo*), curatele di edizioni anastatiche e di volumi miscellanei, edizioni pratiche, recensioni, voci per enciclopedie musicologiche (*MGG* e *Dizionario enciclopedico universale della musica e dei musicisti*), presentazioni discografiche, corrispondenze, note di programma ecc. E' responsabile scientifico della nuova Edizione Nazionale delle opere di Pierluigi da Palestrina e cura l'edizione integrale del Corpus delle Frottole di Ottaviano Petrucci.

Laurenz Lütteken, Studium der Musikwissenschaft, Germanistik und Kunstgeschichte an den Universitäten Münster und Heidelberg. 1991 Promotion mit einer Arbeit über Guillaume Dufay. Nach Tätigkeit als freier Journalist und längeren Stipendiatenzeiten in Rom und Wolfenbüttel sowie Assistentenzeit an der Universität Münster Habilitation ebd. 1995 (mit einer Studie zum späteren 18. Jahrhundert), anschließend Ernennung zum Hochschuldozenten. 1995-96 Lehrtätigkeit an den Universitäten Heidelberg und Erlangen-Nürnberg. 1996 Berufung auf den Lehrstuhl für Musikwissenschaft an der Universität Marburg, 2000 Ablehnung eines Rufes nach Leipzig, seit 2001 Ordinarius für Musikwissenschaft an der Universität Zürich.

Nicolas Meeùs est Docteur en musicologie de l'Université catholique de Louvain et Habilité à Diriger des Recherches de l'Université Paris-Sorbonne. Il a dirigé le Musée Instrumental de Bruxelles et enseigné au Conservatoire royal de Bruxelles et à l'Université de Louvain à Louvain-la-Neuve. Il est actuellement Professeur à l'Université Paris-Sorbonne, directeur adjoint de l'École doctorale «Concepts et Langages» et directeur du Centre de recherche «Patrimoines et Langages Musicaux» (http://www.crlm.paris4.sorbonne.fr). Ses recherches portent sur la théorie musicale et son histoire, depuis la théorie modale médiévale jusqu'à la théorie schenkérienne, ainsi que sur la sémiotique et l'analyse musicales. Il a réalisé la traduction française de *Der freie Satz* (*L'Écriture libre*) de Heinrich Schenker.

John Milsom is a consultant musicologist who has held academic posts in England and America. He has published widely on sixteenth-century topics, with particular emphasis on the social history of Tudor music, and on the works and musical thought of Josquin Desprez. Many of his recent writings focus on the analysis of compositional method in sixteenth-century polyphony, with specific reference to the principles and practice of fuga. He has a keen interest in polyphonic works that underwent substantial revision, giving rise to two or more different versions, and his contribution to the present volume hints at a much larger project-in-progress. He has also created (and continues to expand) the online Christ Church Library Music Catalogue, a major research project that addresses the contents and provenance history of the eighteenth-century music collections at Christ Church, Oxford.

Katelijne Schiltz studied musicology at the University of Leuven and Early Vocal Music at the Conservatory of Tilburg. She wrote a dissertation on the motets of Adrian Willaert, which was published as a book (*'Vulgari orecchie / purgate orecchie'. De relatie tussen publiek en muziek in het Venetiaanse motetoeuvre van Adriaan Willaert*) in 2003. Together with Bonnie J. Blackburn, she is the editor of *Canons and Canonic Techniques, 14th-16th Centuries: Theory, Practice, and Reception History* (2007). She has published numerous articles on music in Cinquecento Venice, canons and theological aspects of music. She is a member of the editorial board of the *Dutch Journal of Music Theory*, the *Yearbook of the Alamire Foundation* and *Analysis in Context. Leuven Studies in Musicology*. She is currently preparing a monograph on (riddle)canons in the Middle Ages and the Renaissance and an edition of Gioseffo Zarlino's *Modulationes sex vocum* (Venice, 1566).

Bernhold Schmid studierte ab 1976 Musikwissenschaft, Neuere Deutsche Literatur und Mittelalterliche Geschichte an der Ludwig-Maximilians-Universität München und promovierte 1985 mit einer Dissertation über den Gloria-Tropus *Spiritus et alme*. 1984-1985 war er Assistent am Institut für Musikwissenschaft München, seit 1985 ist er Mitarbeiter der Musikhistorischen Kommission der Bayerischen Akademie der Wissenschaften, wo er seit 1996 ausschließlich für die Orlando di Lasso-Gesamtausgabe zuständig ist. Er publizierte Arbeiten zu Themen aus der Musikgeschichte des Mittelalters (Tropen, Musiktheorie, zentraleuropäische Musik des 15. Jahrhunderts) und der Renaissance (insbesondere zu Orlando di Lasso und seinem Umkreis), außerdem zur Musik der Zeit um 1900 (u.a. zu Richard Strauss bzw. Arnold Schönberg und deren Verhältnis zu Thomas Mann). Schmid ist stellvertretender Vorsitzender der Gesellschaft für Bayerische Musikgeschichte. Für die gemeinsam mit Horst Leuchtmann herausgegebene Arbeit *Orlando di Lasso. Seine Werke in zeitgenössischen Drucken 1555-1687* erhielt er 2003 den Vincent H. Duckles Award der amerikanischen Music Library Association.

Thomas Schmidt-Beste is Professor and Head of Music at Bangor University. He studied at the universities of Heidelberg and Chapel Hill (USA) and received his doctorate in Heidelberg in 1995 with a thesis on Felix Mendelssohn's aesthetics. After working in Heidelberg for the 'Cappella Sistina' research project (from 1995 to 2002), he received his Habilitation in 2001 and was appointed to a Heisenberg Senior Research scholarship. In 2004 and 2005 he was a visiting professor in Frankfurt, before being appointed at Bangor in 2005. His main areas of research are the sacred music of the fifteenth and sixteenth centuries and German instrumental music of the late eighteenth and nineteenth centuries. Recent publications include *Textdeklamation in der Motette des 15. Jahrhunderts* (Turnhout, 2003), *Die Sonate* (Kassel, 2006), and a critical edition of Mendelssohn's 'Scottish' Symphony in the *Leipziger Ausgabe der Werke von Felix Mendelssohn Bartholdy* (Wiesbaden/Leipzig, 2005).

Eugeen Schreurs is both music scholar and performer. He studied viola da gamba (W. Kuijken) at the Brussels Conservatoire and musicology at the University of Leuven. As instrumentalist he was co-founder and member of the 'Capilla Flamenca', with which he made several recordings. He obtained his Ph.D. in 1991 with a study of musical life in Tongeren (ca. 1400-1797), applying the so-called 'urban musicology' method. As co-founder and coordinator of the 'Alamire Foundation, international centre of the Music in the Low Countries' (1990-2002) he laid, together with B. Bouckaert, the groundwork for similar studies of other cities (i.e. Antwerp, Brussels, Diest, Ghent, Lier, Maastricht). He is co-founder and (was) editor in chief of the *Facsimile Editions* of Alamire Publishers, of the *Yearbook of the Alamire Foundation*, and of the series *Monumenta Flandriae Musica*. He teaches at the Antwerp Conservatoire. In 2002 he co-founded 'Resonant, Centrum voor Vlaams muzikaal erfgoed'. This centre for Flemish musical heritage is directed by him ever since.

Henri Vanhulst est professeur ordinaire à l'Université Libre de Bruxelles, où il enseigne depuis 1979. Il est membre du comité directeur de la Société Internationale de Musicologie, secrétaire de la Société belge de Musicologie et coéditeur de la *Revue belge de Musicologie*. Ses recherches concernent la musique vocale et instrumentale de la Renaissance, l'histoire de l'édition musicale, l'étude des sources tant imprimées que manuscrites, la circulation des partitions en Europe, l'histoire de l'enseignement de la musique et la vie musicale à Bruxelles. Il est l'auteur du *Catalogue des Éditions musicales de Pierre Phalèse et ses fils (1545-1578)* (Bruxelles, 1990) et de *The Catalogus librorum musicorum of Jan Evertsen van Doorn (Utrecht 1639)* (Utrecht, 1996). Il a édité en fac-similé neuf recueils instrumentaux de la Renaissance, est l'auteur d'une trentaine d'articles et a présenté des communications lors d'environ cinquante colloques internationaux dont les actes ont été publiés. Il a également collaboré au *New Grove Dictionary of Music* et à la nouvelle version de *Die Musik in Geschichte und Gegenwart*.

Rob C. Wegman is a Dutch musicologist specializing in the history of fourteenth- to sixteenth-century music. He has written two monographs, *Born for the Muses: The Life and Masses of Jacob Obrecht* (Oxford, 1994) and *The Crisis of Music in Early Modern Europe, 1470-1530* (New York, 2005), and a range of articles exploring such varied angles as musical aesthetics, sociology, archival studies, textual criticism, palaeography, and music theory. His contribution to the present volume is one in a series of articles addressing the concept of musical subjectivity in the early modern period.

Index of Names